Secrets of Gatehouse

By
Lilly Adam

ISBN: 9798680205839
Independently Published

Dedicated to my wonderful readers; I hope you enjoy reading this book as much as I enjoyed writing it.

"Hope" is the thing with feathers -
That perches in the soul -
And sings the tune without the
  words -
And never stops - at all –
By Emily Dickinson

Also written by Lilly Adam:

May of Ashley Green
Stella
Poppy Woods
The Whipple Girl
Rose
Whitechapel Lass
Daisy Grey
Beneath the Apple Blossom Tree
Faye

CHAPTER ONE
February 1840

If there was one lesson in life which Claire Shepherd had drummed into her children's heads, it was to always be honest, never to tell a lie and never to steal, no matter how tempting it might appear, but as with any of life's lessons, they were all too easily ignored.

"When I grow up I'm going to be a princess and live in a huge palace; I will have my very own bed, and have servants who..."

"Be quiet, Martha, you can't be a princess unless you marry a prince, and there ain't no bloody way that's going to happen!"

Claire's hand seemed to stretch out from the other side of the kitchen as she slapped Frank across his face, leaving a bright red print of her fingers behind.

"I'll have none of that bad language Frank Shepherd, not in this house and not in front of your sister!"

Frank stared defiantly at his mother, refusing to rub his sore face or allow her or Martha to witness his humiliation.

"I'm not a boy to be struck, *mother*, I'm fourteen and almost a man!"

"You're not a man!" laughed Martha, "you don't even have any whiskers like Pa...Just because..."

"Hush yourself, Martha, and go to your chores,"

interrupted Claire, crossly. "Be you fourteen or forty, young man, I *will not* have swearing under my roof. Now if you've finished your porridge, you'd best get out to the stable and help your pa fix last night's storm damage."

Pouring out the last tepid cup of tea, Claire sank onto the settle. It wasn't quite eight o'clock and she already felt weary and not looking forward to the long day ahead. Her swollen belly contracted, feeling like a solid bolder; it wasn't her time yet but experience had taught her that this was simply her body preparing itself. Her fifth baby, she mused, where did the years go? It only seemed like yesterday that she'd been a young girl, only a few years older than Martha, in fact, and had married her childhood sweetheart, Silas Shepherd. She'd been the happiest sixteen year old in Bagley village on that memorable warm spring day back in 1824 and although another year had passed before she'd conceived her first child and there had been worrying times when she'd thought it would never happen, Claire and Silas always reminisced on those peaceful days when they could selfishly indulge in each other's company and temporarily forget about their arduous farm work and daily chores. Now, life was so much harder and constantly demanding; Claire incessantly worried about the future of her children. Frank had changed during the last year, he was no longer a boy but his transformation into manhood had made him arrogant and defiant. Silas had tried to assure Claire that he was simply establishing his unique personality and that his horrid moods and change of character would soon calm down. Claire wished she could believe this. Then there was Martha, strong-willed and with her head in the clouds for most of the time, dreaming of another life and impossibilities. At thirteen years old her plain girlish looks were fading away; she was becoming quite the beauty, and quite a worry, especially to Silas, who took to warning off any young man, who dared to make eyes at her, with one of his steely-eyed glares. Easing herself up from the settle, Claire peered out of the window, wondering what had happened to Jane and Amy; they'd taken longer than it normally took to collect the eggs and would be late for school again if they didn't hurry up; they were most likely annoying their pa with silly chatter and knowing Silas, he would simply put up with it only to complain to her later about *her* children, not his...always hers when they were misbehaving.

Claire set about cleaning the kitchen and making a start on the washing and baking, life was tough being a farmer's wife, especially on a tenant farm, with the likes of Reginald Brunswick breathing down their necks. In their walking out years, she and Silas had dreamt of one day owning a small piece of land and a farmhouse and expanding over the years. But with four children and another one due in two months, their dreams had long been buried and it became a subject forgotten and never spoken about anymore. Claire winced from the pain of her sore and chapped hands, they resembled those of a fifty-year-old woman not one of thirty-two, she pondered, sadly. She was feeling old and unattractive and with such a heavy workload, these days, she never seemed to find five minutes to herself anymore, considering it a bonus if she managed to pull the hairbrush through her lank and lifeless hair, of a morning. Without fail, every day Silas told her how beautiful she was and how she'd not aged a day since they'd wed, but his words came from his mouth, not his heart and although she appreciated his efforts to please her, they were quite meaningless. Now she viewed Martha with a touch of envy, she was growing from a plain girl into an attractive woman and she was more mature than most of the other girls of her age who lived in Bagley village. Her only downfall was her tendency to have her head in the clouds most of the time. She lived in a dream world, refusing to acknowledge the true way in which poor, country folk lived. Claire worried more for Martha's future, then she did for her other children's, knowing that if she didn't soon wake up to reality and grow out of her overactive imagination she was sure to be disappointed with life.

The sound of the privy door repeatedly slamming in the wind forced Claire to go outside and secure it; she wrapped her thick, shawl around her shoulders, the strong wind was making it feel much colder and the mass of accumulating dark clouds overhead looked threatening. There was no sign of any of the children, which only added to Claire's annoyance. The sound of Silas hammering the loosened stable panels echoed across the barren fields. It was a sombre time of year, thought Claire, void of colour and warmth; she had counted eleven consecutive days now since she'd last seen a glimpse of the sun; she longed for the spring which would bring life and colour to the land again, and the arrival of her baby, easing her heavy load. She was already praying that this would be her last baby, her body was exhausted and crying out for a respite from the strains of being with child. Three stillborn babies were buried in the nearby cemetery, two boys and girl, and she'd lost count of how many miscarriages she'd endured, but it was near to half a dozen. Five healthy children were more than enough to thank the Lord for, and raising them with such a meagre income was proving more of an impossible task with each passing year.

Jane and Amy burst noisily in through the kitchen door, each carrying a pitiful amount of eggs in their baskets, their noisy giggles and chitchat disturbed Claire's thoughts,
"Squire Brunswick is doing his rounds Ma!" announced Jane. "I heard him tell Pa that the storm has left Bagley village in need of lots of repairs *and* I heard him ask Frank if he wanted to earn a few shillings too."
"Jane Shepherd! I hope you haven't been making a nuisance of yourself, listening in on the grownup's conversations!"
"She spoke to '*Squinty Eye*' too, Ma," added Amy, eager to get her elder sister into trouble.
"I had to Ma, he started talking to me first and he said that I might be able to work at his house for a few hours when I'm finished with school in the summer."
Trying with all her might to remain calm, Claire took the eggs and counted slowly to ten in her head.
"What do you think Ma; I could make some money to help you and Pa..."
Having only reached to number six, Claire couldn't hold her tongue for a minute longer,
"How many times have I told you that the Squire Brunswick's brother is an untrustworthy man...I'm surprised at you, Jane. You are to stay well away from him, *do you understand*, my girl...and that goes for you too Amy."
"But why is he so bad, Ma? Martha said, that just

because he's got a disfigured face and can't walk properly doesn't mean he's not a good man. I'll be ten in the summer and old enough to start earning a wage!"

"You've got chores to do here, my girl and with the arrival of the new baby in the springtime, I will be needing even more help and you won't be any good to me if you're working for *that man*. Now do as you're told and I don't want to hear another word mentioned about *Bruce Brunswick*. Have you girls seen Martha?" she added in her next cross breath.

Jane and Amy shook their heads, not daring to disclose how their big sister was in the dairy having a full grown-up conversation with *Squinty Eye*.

"Come on Amy, we'll be late for school! Fetch our bonnets and lunch tins...I'll race you there; winner gets the other's pudding tonight!"

"Ah that's not fair, you're much faster than me!" protested Amy.

"I'll give you a head start, *come on!*"

"Bye Ma, have a good day!" they shouted in unison as they raced out of the kitchen, allowing a cold blast of air to blow in.

Claire's second attempt to wash up the breakfasts dishes had once more been thwarted. She sat back down again, her entire body feeling tense and deeply troubled; Bruce Brunswick was nothing but bad news and the day which Claire had dreaded seemed to have arrived all too quickly. He was the black sheep of the Brunswick family and had been outcast for most of his life. Even his mother refused to entertain him in her twilight years. Whatever he'd done to his family and how his scared and disfigured face and physical disability had come about was unknown to most folk who were still alive; there had been many rumours, all as disturbing as each other. Reginald Brunswick had been the Squire of Brunswick Estate for eighteen years since he was forty years old and since the death of his father. He was a strict but firm Squire and providing nobody caused him to be provoked, he was generally fair. He was also the local magistrate, often criticized for his severity towards his tenants when it came to handing out their punishments. Since his mother had passed away, seven years ago, Reginald had allowed his one and only brother back on to the Brunswick Estate, but not to reside in the Manor House, where his wife and three, now grown-up children lived, but had allocated him the gatehouse. It seemed to suit Bruce Brunswick, it was a larger than average house which was situated on the other side of a slight hill which kept it out of sight from the Manor House, giving Bruce Brunswick the privacy he wished for.

Caught up in her usual daydreams, Martha had been milking the cows when Bruce Brunswick had crept into the dairy; he'd stood watching her for a while before gaining her attention by purposely coughing. His unsightly appearance had never bothered Martha, her imagination could stretch further than most girls of her age who would run and cower by his presence. She conjured up the image of Bruce Brunswick being a fearless pirate who had single-handedly fought off a colossal fire breathing sea creature which had melted the skin upon his face. He was banished by his family because they were all jealous of his heroism and didn't want him to gain the fame and respect from the folk of Bagley village and beyond.

"Mr Brunswick, can I help you? I think Pa is fixing the barn...did you want to speak to him?" Martha knew she was talking too much and too fast; she felt shy that she looked so unkempt in her stained work dress and equally soiled apron. She'd left the house in such a mood too that she'd not even brushed or tied her thick brunette hair back and sensed that the wind had not done it any favours.

"No, I'm just waiting for the Squire; he's conversing with your father, my dear."

"Oh..."

Bruce smiled, though only one side of his face moved.

"How old are you Miss Shepherd, if you don't mind me asking?"

Martha didn't mind at all, she was proud of her

grown-up age, "I'm thirteen!" she expressed proudly.

"*Quite the young lady!* Are you planning on going into service, Miss Shepherd?"

Nobody had ever addressed her as *Miss Shepherd*, before, it was always plain Martha as though she were no older than her childish sisters. This heroic swashbuckling pirate was making her feel like a young woman of the world and she liked it immensely.

"I have to help my parents, Mr Brunswick, Ma is going to have another baby soon and she needs me here."

Bruce took a step closer to Martha and removed a strand of straw which was entangled in her hair. She felt embarrassed and could feel the heat coming to the surface of her cheeks. He calmly dropped the straw onto the ground and continued talking.

"I suppose that all the girls in Bagley village have marriage on their minds now, after the great Royal wedding of the year, last week! What about you, Miss Shepherd?"

"I'm too young for marriage, Mr Brunswick, but when the time comes, mine won't be all that different from Queen Victoria and Prince Albert's wedding; I intend to marry a wealthy, handsome Prince and spend my days in a grand palace, or maybe even a castle, locked away from the eyes of the world and I will never have to milk a cow again or do any chores. I will wear the finest silk gowns, in the latest fashions from Paris and my diamond jewellery, will sparkle like hanging stars on a clear night..."

Bruce couldn't contain himself for a second longer and burst out laughing; Martha could only stare in shock, as she considered how much more grotesque laughing made him appear, especially as he seemed to have no control of his body and dribbled liberally. Silas Shepherd and the Squire had been drawn into the dairy by the sound of Bruce's obnoxious voice; Silas clenched his teeth together in annoyance as he viewed the proximity of Bruce Brunswick to his vulnerable daughter.

"*Martha!* Go inside and help your ma, this instant!"

"But I'm in the middle of milking, Pa," she protested.

Silas said nothing, but the anger written so clearly across his face as he stared at Martha, together with the Squire and his loathsome brother's eyes boring into her, caused Martha to flee from the dairy in a flood of tears.

"*I did nothing wrong, Pa!*" she cried out as she ran past him.

Reginald Brunswick was already beginning to think that it was a mistake in allowing his brother to accompany him.

"Now are you sure you can manage all the repairs by yourself, Mr Shepherd?"

"Yes thank you Sir; Frank is as strong as any young man these days, between us we'll have things put right before the end of the week!" "Very good, very good...we'll be on our way then...I dare say there'll be plenty of other tenants in need of some assistance. Good day, Mr Shepherd, give our kindest regards to your family."

CHAPTER TWO

By lunchtime, it was clear to Claire that Martha
had upset Silas; he'd finished the repair jobs to
the stable and barn and considered himself
fortunate that the storm damage hadn't been
worse. He'd consumed his lunch, avoiding any
eye contact with his daughter. Frank had failed
to show up, and nobody knew of his
whereabouts. After spending the entire morning
cleaning the kitchen and baking, Claire looked
around at the repeated mess and the clumps of
mud which had carelessly been brought in again
from the fields.

"Where's Frank?" Silas demanded. "He was
supposed to be giving me a hand with the
repairs."

"And Martha was supposed to be giving me
some help with the housework, but instead it's
taken her the best part of the morning to milk six
cows!" added Claire.

"You're too soft on them, Claire, most parents
would have taken the belt to them by now,
taught them to respect and obey their
parents...they'll turn out to be far better
future men and women for it, you mark my
words, woman!"

"*No!* I *will not* physically punish my children,
Silas; you know how I feel about that, they are
not beasts to be struck, God gave us tongues and

the ability to talk for a reason."

"Alright my love, calm yourself now. I'll talk to Frank when he shows up. But you need to teach your daughter to know her place...I didn't like what I saw today; no daughter of mine should behave in such a flirtatious manner...talking to that bloody *Bruce Brunswick*, as though he was one of the family."

"Language, Silas...It's no wonder that I had to punish Frank for swearing earlier today!"

"Punish?" quizzed Silas.

"Ma slapped him across the face!" declared Martha, speaking for the first time throughout lunch.

"I see; so it's fine when you see fit to use your hand, but I'm forbidden?"

"Martha, go upstairs and make the beds before your sisters return from school!" ordered Claire, crossly.

"But I haven't finished my lunch!"

"Do as you're told!" screamed Claire, causing Martha to dramatically burst into tears and flee from the kitchen.

Burying her face in the palms of her hands, Claire was overwhelmed with the entire discord which seemed to be spreading so fast in her once tranquil home.

"What's happening to us, Silas...where have we gone wrong? I don't think I can cope anymore!" Silas, who'd been ready for a heated discussion, was suddenly filled with sympathy for his poor wife. Leaving his chair at the head of the kitchen table, he pulled Claire up and allowed her to sob in his arms. She was half his size, a petite woman, who he always felt the urgent need to protect. Sometimes, it became easy to overlook the burdens which she had to cope with and he wanted, more than anything in the world, to be able to make her life easier and lift the miseries of life, which she handled so bravely.

"Oh, my poor *Claire;* it's been a long and difficult winter; life will take on a new light when the spring and our new baby arrive."

"What are we going to do with that girl? She's such a dreamer, Silas, and Frank has become so hostile lately...What's happening to my beautiful family? And by the way, Silas, Martha is *no flirt,* she has no idea of the ways of the world, she only sees the good in folk. Most girls of her age would have run from the likes of *Squinty Eye,* trying to converse with them. Do you honestly think that Martha would flirt with *him,* of all people?"

"That might be the case, but she *was* being overly familiar with him, and she needs to be spoken to about how to conduct herself in the company of men before someone gets the wrong idea."

"And you need to speak to young Frank about showing some respect...he's getting quite out of hand...he's a young man Silas, not a boy. Remember when you were his age?"

Claire poured the remainder of the lukewarm

tea from the pot,
"Drink up Silas, it's a shame to waste good tea."
"I remember when it was just you and me, under
this roof...happy carefree days, and we never
had a crossword for each other. But no matter
what life throws at us my beautiful wife, know
that *you* are my world!"
"Oh Silas, my darling, we both have so much
more to cope with now compared to those
honeymoon days...they are simply memories
now, gone, but forever cherished."

 Frank planted his feet down heavily with every
step, his hands were pushed deep into the
pockets of his patched and stained
working trousers, and he was soaked to the skin.
His brown, collar-length hair continuously
dripped and his face was already so wet that it
made no difference to him anymore. Like a
raging fire inside of him, his anger steered his
every step towards the nearby town of Epsom.
After spending the morning working for the
Tyler family on their farm and being paid
sixpence for clearing a field of its rocks and
stones, ready for ploughing, he felt proud of his
wealth, but he wasn't going to hand it over to his
ma...it was all his. He had been treated how a
working man should be treated by the Tyler
family, not like a boy and in that short period
he'd also fallen in love with Sarah Tyler, the
family's eldest of two daughters. Four years

previously, he'd been in the same class at school as Sarah; she'd been a freckled, plain-faced skinny girl in those days, who barely said a word to anyone apart from her only best friend. Today had been quite the eye-opener for Frank and when she'd brought out a mug of hot tea and a bun for him, and asked if he'd remembered her from their school days, he was taken by complete shock. Although her freckles remained, they now only seemed to complement her pretty face and her clear blue eyes. She was no longer that scrawny looking girl but had grown into a shapely young woman and on that miserable day, when his ma had struck him, his sister had laughed, mockingly at him and his pa had talked down to him, Sarah immediately became the glowing lantern in his dreary life. She had chatted to him for the briefest of moments, only weather and family talk but in those poignant minutes, she'd made Frank feel important and touched his heart with her softness. He couldn't even remember the colour of the dress she'd been wearing; he was too conscious of how scruffy and filthy his appearance was and had felt embarrassed by it. He'd wanted to ask her if she'd care to take a Sunday afternoon stroll, should the weather improve by then, but by the time he'd rehearsed the words in his head, Sarah had said a quick goodbye, stating that she had to hurry back before she became soaked. Even her voice was attractive, Frank had mused as he'd watched her disappear across the muddy field towards the farmhouse.

He wasn't a dreamer like his sister, but now, Frank was seriously considering his future life with Sarah as his wife, even if his entire family would ridicule his feelings, once again telling him that he was too young to harbour such thoughts.

The busy market town of Epsom was quieter than usual, the storms and heavy downpours had kept many folk in their homes, but it turned out to be to Frank's advantage. It took more than a winter's storm to keep the old woman on the penny rag stall away from the market, and from the moment Frank viewed her lack of customers, he knew she'd be desperate to take his money. She proudly displayed to him all the clothes which she considered to be the perfect fit for him. She was without a single tooth in her mouth but smiled broadly at him, happy to have a customer at last.

"I got these expensive wears from a very respectable and wealthy family over in Great Bookham; sadly they lost their son in a tragic riding accident, but he must have been of a similar shape and size to you. That was back in thirty-six; but yesterday, the housekeeper there gave me first pickings; she told me how the lad's mother had finally agreed to empty her boy's wardrobe."

Frank couldn't be sure that the old woman's story was wholly true, but he expressed his sadness in the same breath as he explained how he only had four pennies to spend and that his pa would thrash him with the horsewhip if he failed to return home without a smart jacket. "You don't strike me as the disobedient type, you seem like a very sensible young man to me!" she expressed, causing Frank's ego to swell simply by her referral to him as a young man, not a lad or a boy.

Eager to make a few pennies on such a dark and wretched day, a deal was quickly made and Frank happily parted with his four pennies in exchange for an impressive brown twill jacket, a pair of cord trousers in a slightly darker shade and a new pair of good, sturdy boots made from fine quality leather; a tweed cap was added as part of the bargain. With a couple of pennies left, Frank, decided to make the peace with his ma and purchased a remnant of pretty lilac material and a poke of tea leaves.

The smile on his ma's face when Frank handed her the small gift, made him glad that he'd spent his last hard-earned money on the items. The fact that he'd done a day's work on the Tyler farm, however, wasn't such good news to his ma.

"Your pa needed you here Frank, there was too much work for one man to handle on his own.

You should have asked his permission first. Your poor pa will work himself into an early grave; then we will all be destined for the workhouse! *Is that what you want for your family Frank?*"

As Claire's words travelled into Frank's ears, his mind was set on only one thought; he couldn't wait for Sarah Tyler to see him in his smart new attire and felt quite confident that she wouldn't be able to refuse his invitation to walk out with him on the next clement Sunday.

He proudly showed off his clothes to his ma but sensed she considered them to be an unnecessary purchase.

"You're going to look smarter than your pa, Frank. You best not tell him that you spent all your money on them; they look far more expensive than what you paid too."

"I told you, Ma, they used to belong to the son of a richer folk's family, who died!"

"Well, you just leave the talking to me son, your pa is not in the best of moods right now and he's not had a chance to rest his bones since the storms. It won't bode well for him to witness you strutting around like a fancy cockerel whilst he's had to do all the work by himself!"

Grabbing his new clothes from off the table, once again feeling humiliated, Frank wished to leave the presence of his nagging mother. She was cross, he could tell and nothing he did these days seemed to meet with her approval.

"Why does everyone treat me like a stupid boy in this house? Mr Tyler and his family view me as a young man; they showed me nothing but respect and trusted my judgement and ability!"

"For pity's sake, Frank, you worked on the field picking out rocks for a day...that doesn't make you a man...and what does Mr Tyler care about your wellbeing? So long as his field is ready for ploughing...you just remember where your loyalties lay my lad and remember your duties, first and foremost to your own family. Mr Tyler only has two daughters...do you honestly think he'd have taken you on if that wasn't the case?"

"Alright, *mother*, you've said your piece, now if you don't bloody mind, I'm going to my room, and I don't want any supper, so leave me alone!"

Just as Frank marched out of the kitchen, through the small door which led up the two flights of stairs to his room in the attic, Silas came through the back entrance with Martha, Jane and Amy.

"What are all the raised voices for?" demanded Silas as he searched Claire's downcast face.

Jane took a sharp intake of breath as she noticed the piece of pretty fabric on the table.

"Are we to have new dresses, Ma?" she cried, excitedly.

"Martha and Jane, help with the supper, your ma isn't feeling well" instructed Silas.

"Is she going to have the baby?" enquired Amy in a small voice.

"No my sweetheart, it's not my time yet," confirmed Claire, reassuringly as she rested on the settle, her eyes watery.

That night, Silas forbade anyone in the family to even attempt to enter Frank's bedroom. He didn't come down for supper and the following morning he left home before sunrise, leaving the essential field preparation work before ploughing could begin, for his father to deal with. Heading straight to the Tyler's farm to offer his services for another day, Frank had decided that he would now concentrate on earning as much money as was possible so that by the time he reached the age of sixteen, he'd be in a good financial position to ask Sarah to become his wife. He prayed that Sarah had been thinking as much about him as he had of her since their brief meeting. It was his biggest worry and he had to know. With his head down, Frank increased his speed, his stomach felt empty and he hoped that Mrs Tyler might offer him some breakfast when he arrived. He also prayed that the rain would hold off for the day. He'd just reached the crossroads halfway between his home and the Tyler's farm when he became aware of distant voices. He lifted his head and in the semi-darkness of sunrise, he was quite convinced that Sarah Tyler and her sister were walking towards him.
"Morning, Frank! Pa didn't mention that you

were coming to work again" voiced Sarah, now only a couple of yards away.

Frank's sombre mood was instantly lightened; what could be better than Sarah being the first person of the day to set his eyes upon. She was wearing a thick shawl, tightly wrapped around her shoulders; the brim of her dark green bonnet partly shaded her pretty face but Frank made sure to take notice of the colour of her dress on this day; it was dark grey, a typical working dress, but even that seemed to take on a special beauty on Sarah's shapely body.

"Morning, Sarah; you're out early."

"I could say the same for you, Frank Shepherd!"

"I'm going to see if your pa needs me today."

Sarah's twelve-year-old sister, let out a sigh, "Come on Sarah, or I'll be late!"

Sarah ignored her. "What about your place then, isn't there enough work to be done there, your farm is larger than ours, you know?"

Frank licked his dry lips, "I thought I could start early, work 'till lunch and then spend the afternoon helping my pa."

"Let's go Sarah!" pestered Lydia Tyler.

"Shush yourself *Lydi* or I'll make you walk by yourself."

"Well I suppose you could go and ask Pa, by all means, I'm sure he'd be glad of the help...I must be on my way though, Lydia starts her new job on the Brunswick Estate today; she's a bit nervous, that's why she's being so bad-mannered."

Frank smiled; he knew what an annoying responsibility it was being the eldest in the family.

"She's going to work at Brunswick Manor?"

"No...*They* only take on *townies* from Croydon, and such places," asserted Sarah, sounding like the voice of experience. "Lydia is going to work at the gatehouse, aren't you Lydi?"

"Yes, if I don't get the sack before I even start; please, Sarah, can we go?"

"Would you like me to walk with you? You won't have to return on your own then?" offered Frank, feeling quite shocked that Mr Tyler would allow his daughter to work for that creepy *Squinty Eye*, especially Lydia, who was renowned as being somewhat of a simple-minded girl and a real worry to her parents.

"I'd like that very much Frank Shepherd!" declared Sarah.

Frank couldn't help thinking how his day was already proving to be a success, even before sunrise.

CHAPTER THREE

During the following few weeks, the farming community of Bagley village was kept busy with the gruelling task of preparing the land ready to sow the year's crops. Frank was working flat out from sunrise to sunset; mornings were spent on the Tyler's farm and in the afternoon he assisted his pa. His heart was overflowing with love for Sarah which spurred him on to work harder than he'd ever worked before, during his short life. She had agreed to walk out with him of a Sunday afternoon and this magical day was the focal point of every painstaking minute which Frank spent on the land. His back now permanently ached, and his hands were covered with painful blisters, but he had already put aside three shillings and sixpence, carefully hidden inside one of his socks and pushed to the back of his drawer. He had also given his ma the occasional penny to prevent her from thinking that he'd saved any of his earnings, Frank had committed one of the sins which his mother had warned him about since as long as he could remember.

Once a week, he would jump on the back of a wagon which was heading in the direction of Epsom and mingle amongst the Saturday shoppers in the thriving market town. It was a day when many folk took the afternoon off to shop for provisions and those special treats after a hard-working week. The weather had changed since the middle of March and although the winds remained strong, often leaving a trail of destruction behind them, the sun seemed to brighten each blustery day and the rain tended to conveniently fall during the night. He was sharp-eyed and stealthy and Frank already prided himself on what an expert he'd become at lifting the varied items from off the market stalls and high street shops without parting with a single farthing and without the slightest suspicion from the shop keepers and costermongers. Cheeses, pies, cakes, reels of thread, buttons and ribbons, items of cutlery and even a small decorative milk jug were among many of the items which he'd stolen. Plagued by guilt, to begin with, and the fear of being caught, it took little time before Frank came to realise that he was quite the expert thief. Knowing that his parents would be devastated and ashamed of him if his actions came to light and that Sarah and her family would never speak to him again, every time he committed the criminal act, he told himself that it would be the last, but he'd come up with what he considered to be, a brilliant idea and hoped with all his heart that it would prove successful.

He lay back on his small attic bed, relishing in its comfort upon his aching body. Now he knew how a man felt at the end of a working day and would never again take his pa's complaints in vain. The advantages of being the only male sibling were that he had his own private space. It was only a modest-sized attic, but it was a place where he could block out work and family from his thoughts and plan his future, a future with Sarah at his side. Convincing himself that she harboured genuine feelings for him, Frank became even more determined to work harder, he wanted to offer her a secure and wholesome life, not a life of toil from dusk to dawn like his ma had married into. Sarah would want for nothing and they would live in the town and endure a clean life, always smartly dressed and without a pound of mud clinging to the soles of their footwear at the end of each day. Frank smiled to himself, maybe he was similar to his sister Martha, he mused, she lived in a dream world and everyone was always reprimanding her because of it. With him, though, it wouldn't simply be a fantasy; his dreams *would* one day become reality. The pleasant aroma of his ma's vegetable stew wafted up through the small cottage, reaching Frank's nostrils, his stomach immediately rumbled. He was in his family's good books once again and took great pride in receiving their daily praise and compliments. His ma insisted on rubbing duck fat into his chapped hands every evening, and would now bring two bowls of hot water with added dried geranium and lavender for her men to soak their tired feet in.

Sunday afternoons were the highlight of Frank's week and it was now common knowledge, mostly spread by Martha, in the close community of Bagley village that Frank Shepherd and Sarah Tyler were sweethearts. It was a pleasantly warm April afternoon as they strolled through the copse which backed onto the Brunswick Estate. Sarah coyly linked her arm in Frank's and every so often would break away to pick bluebells as they walked. The peaceful silence of the copse was suddenly broken by the horrifying, piercing scream of a young girl which froze the sweethearts in their tracks.

"That's coming from bloody *Squinty Eye's* house!" declared Frank as he hurried through the thick overgrowth to reach the boundary wall. Sarah followed in his footsteps.

"Where's your Lydia?"

"She didn't come home this Sunday!" replied Sarah, with the look of fear upon her face.

The screaming continued, sending a cold shiver through both Frank and Sarah.

"*He's a bloody monster!*" yelled Frank in a panic. "Does that sound like your sister?"

"I can't tell...I've never heard *anyone* screaming like that before; she's the quiet one in our family."

Frank knew that he had to take action. He was unable to reach the top of the lofty wall and it would take too long to walk around the vast acres of land to gain access through the front gate, which might not even be open, especially with it being a Sunday. He clambered up a nearby tree and made a hazardous leap onto the wall. As he lost his balance, he quickly glanced at Sarah's concerned face before he fell, with a thud onto the ground of the Brunswick Estate. At that very moment, the distressed screaming abruptly ceased. Suddenly surrounded by silence, Frank pulled himself up, brushing his smart new clothes with the flat of his hand as he picked up his dislodged cap. The loud blast of gunfire shook him to his core and as he looked towards the gatehouse, a dishevelled looking Bruce Brunswick was marching across the land, brandishing his pistol. Frank froze, terrified of this bulky hideous looking man, who couldn't even walk in a straight line.

"What are you doing on my land you insolent, peasant boy?"

A long thread of saliva dangled from his obscure mouth as he panted noisily, like an out of breath hound. His only visible eye resembled a lump of hot coal, as it burnt through Frank; it was the first time that Frank had ever seen Bruce without his hat on. The entire right side of his misshapen head was bald, the skin was heavily wrinkled and the top of his ear appeared to be moulded to the side of his head. Bruce Brunswick aimed his pistol directly at Frank as he hurried up the slight incline of the grassy bank. All of a sudden Frank felt immature and vulnerable as every inch of his body trembled. He wanted to run but feared that Bruce wouldn't hesitate to fire the pistol into his back. He didn't want to die...

"*Answer me*...are you spying on me, you damned *village runt*?"

"What have you done to Lydia Tyler? Her sister is on the other side of the wall...we heard her screaming!" shouted Frank, trying to hide the quiver in his voice.

Bruce stamped his foot down hard like a spoilt child,

"Why don't you foul people stay out of my life...always prying...*it angers me, can't you see?*" Frank could only assume that Bruce was drunk; on the few occasions where he'd met him, in church or whilst he'd been out with the Squire, Bruce had always appeared calm, well mannered and politely spoken. Today, however, Frank was seeing him in a different light.

"I'm not prying Mr Brunswick, I was out walking with Lydia's sister and we heard screaming, coming from over the wall..."

"Up to no good I can imagine!"

Bruce suddenly swung around on the spot and yelled at the top of his brusque voice, "*Lydia! Lydia!*"

The fresh, bright red bloodstains upon the back of his shirt immediately caught Frank's eye, increasing his fear.

A few very long minutes passed before Lydia came hurrying towards them, she was smiling, as though there was nothing unusual about the scene before her eyes; there wasn't even a hint of fear or nerves upon the simple girl's happy looking face.

"Did you call for me Sir?" she questioned, timidly, bobbing her head, courteously to Bruce Brunswick.

"*There*! Feast your eyes upon your sweetheart's sister...As you can see for yourself, there is nothing whatsoever wrong with her."

Lydia stopped directly behind Bruce as she caught her breath.

"Hello Frank, why isn't Sarah with you?"

"Hello, Lydia...are you alright? We heard screaming..."

"*Look at her, you stupid boy*...clearly she is alright!" exclaimed Bruce, sharply.

"Sarah is over there, Lydia, no need to worry," expressed Frank as he gestured towards the high wall. "Who was making all that noise then Lydia?"

Bruce was quick to intervene, "You've got the answer to what you came snooping for, now get off my land...*Now!*"

Frank felt his entire body jolt by the harshness of Bruce's amplified voice. There was definitely something going on in the gatehouse and he didn't feel it was right to walk away and leave Sarah's half-witted sister with such a deranged brute.

"Can I take Lydia with me to visit her family...It is *Sunday* after all?"

Once again, Bruce stamped his foot down in a show of anger and Lydia ran towards Frank.

"It's alright Frank, *honestly*, Mr Brunswick has asked me to stay here today because Molly is ill, so she's going home...I've been learning how to do her job."

Frank didn't get the chance to ask any more questions, he took his eyes off Lydia for a split second and in that instant, he knew that Bruce was about to fire his pistol. He lowered the barrel and Frank's spontaneous reaction was to cover his manhood with his hands; the click of the trigger filled Frank's ears as Bruce shot at his lower leg, forcing Frank to fall to the ground in agony. Bruce let out a loud and jovial laugh, "I would never shoot a man in such a vital area...I might be mean, but not *that* mean! I trust you've learned a valuable lesson today, *lad*?" He yanked Lydia's arm roughly, practically dragging her along behind him as he continued to laugh.

"If you're not off my land in five minutes, I might well be out doing some more rabbit hunting! And don't be getting any smart ideas to trouble my brother and his family...they're not at home!"

On hearing the shots, Sarah had thrown caution to the wind, hitched up her long skirt and

petticoats and climbed the tree. Her distressing sounds took Frank's attention away from the large hole in his new cord trousers and the blood which was gushing from his lower leg. Her pretty head was all he could see, just visible as she peered over the wall looking horrified.
"Oh, my dear Lord! What happened...are you able to walk? Shall I go and fetch your pa?"
Frank couldn't find it in him to reply to her barrage of questions, he was in shock and his entire body was shaking; he'd never been shot before and never imagined it could be so painful. Knowing he'd not be able to scale the wall, he silently prayed that the gates to the Estate would be open, providing he could make the distance; he had to get out of Brunswick's territory.
"Meet me at the gates, Sarah; I can't get back over the wall."

Thankfully the gate had been left open, most likely because Squire Brunswick and his family had gone out and were expected back later that day. Sarah bandaged Frank's bleeding leg with a strip of cotton torn from her petticoat and helped him back home.
Silas and Claire were devastated and couldn't believe what had happened to their beloved Frank. Consumed with anger, Silas marched back and forth in the kitchen, much to the annoyance of Claire who was attending to her

son's wounded leg. Feeling out of place amidst the family crisis, Sarah made herself useful, assisting Martha to make a pot of tea.

"I'm going to take this up with the Squire at first light...how dare that ignorant brother of his fire a shot at a young boy...it's surely a crime for the magistrate to deal with!"

"*Silas*, please sit down before you make yourself dizzy! Thank God it's not as bad as it looks; it's no more than a deep graze and should heal up quickly with rest and a clean dressing every day. I think that our Frank was in the wrong too; he *was* trespassing after all!"

"That doesn't warrant shooting at the poor boy, though does it? Only a lunatic would take such drastic actions!" expressed Silas angrily.

"*I'm not a boy!*" objected Frank, feeling embarrassed in front of Sarah. "I'm a working man!"

"Well you won't be a working man for the next few weeks, that's for sure!" declared Claire. Martha giggled, she'd had more than enough of Frank lately, thinking that he could act like another father towards her just because he was earning and presenting their ma with copious gifts every week.

"*Be quiet Martha!*" he scolded.

She placed the teapot down onto the table clandestinely making a mocking face at her brother.

"I don't understand what you were doing there

in the first place, Frank," questioned Claire as they all sat around the kitchen table, now joined by Jane and Amy, both aghast that their big brother had been shot, but pleased that they'd have some intriguing news to tell their classmates the following day.

"It was my fault really," said Sarah, in a small voice. "There was the most disturbing screaming coming from the gatehouse...I panicked and thought it was my sister."

"Are you sure that your sister is perfectly safe with that man?" asked Silas, "I wouldn't trust him within a few yards of any of my girls." Claire issued Silas with one of her looks, warning him to be careful of what he said in front of the Tyler girl.

"It's because she's not like most girls her age, she's more like a young child, but she's a very capable kitchen maid. Ma said that nobody else would employ her around here and she doesn't want her to go into service away from Bagley village," explained Sarah.

There were lots that Claire and Silas wanted to say, but knew it would be inappropriate in front of Sarah.

"Bruce Brunswick had bloodstains on the back of his shirt!" stressed Frank, who was sat on the settle, with his legs stretched out in front of him.

"And we definitely heard somebody screaming, Mrs Shepherd," added Sarah.

"Your sister said that someone called Molly was

leaving because she was ill...could she have been making all that noise, do you think?"

"A poor girl making all that noise needs a doctor, in my opinion," stated Claire.

"Well, I believe we certainly should be grateful to The Almighty for bringing Frank home to us...It could have been far worse, who knows what that man is capable of. I will certainly be speaking to Reginald Brunswick as soon as possible."

"Quite right too, Silas, but who is this Molly girl...I don't recall anyone from the village with a daughter by that name?" quizzed Claire, looking quite baffled.

"I think she came from a town...Croydon I think or maybe even London...well that's what Lydia told me; she sometimes gets names and places a bit muddled though."

"Let's wait until the morrow; everything can appear much clearer in the light of a new day," declared Claire as darkness quickly descended upon the unforgettable Sunday.

"Silas will see you safely back to your home in the wagon, won't you Silas?"

"Of course I will, it's been a distressing day for us all!"

"Thank you, Mr Shepherd."

CHAPTER FOUR

It was during the early hours of the following morning when Claire woke up shivering from the cold with her nightgown soaking; her waters had broken and even though it was a couple of weeks earlier than she'd expected, the sense of relief that her baby would soon be in the world infused her with the strength she needed to tackle the forthcoming pains of childbirth. Quietly leaving the bedroom, she took a spare blanket out of her storage trunk and crept down the small staircase. She welcomed the warmth from the wood burner in the kitchen which hadn't yet completely gone out as she added a few stove-lengths to the burner and went about boiling the water. A cup of extra sweet tea would aid her through the imminent toil and pains of her labour. The gripping contractions had already begun, although still bearable and quite mild. It was far too early to wake anyone, especially dear old Mrs Thatcher, Bagley village's one and only midwife. She prayed that she'd hold out until daybreak, as her mind suddenly became plagued by the nightmare times when there had been deathly silence after her labour and the sweet cry of new life had failed to sound out through the small cottage. Strangely, they seemed to be her only memories at present with the birth of Amy, her last living child failing to find the tiniest of places in her mind. She sipped the hot tea in between her pains, which were now coming strong and frequently. It was still pitch black outside, the world was asleep and she was alone and nervous. No longer caring whether her baby was a boy or a girl Claire's only concern was that it was alive and crying. Little over another hour had passed by and Claire now knew that the arrival of her baby would not hold out until dawn; overcome by the most wretched of pains, Claire's petite body was taken over by the unstoppable urge to push her baby into the world. There was no time for worrying anymore; hard work and prayers were now in vital need. Awoken by the throbbing pain in his leg, Frank was sat up in his bed, mulling over how he was going to keep up with his weekly savings now that he'd be unemployable to work the land for a couple of weeks; no farmer would want a lame farmhand, he mused, becoming increasingly angry with the Squire's demented brother. He really couldn't believe how Sarah's pa could allow his daughter to work for such an unstable man. Then there was the devious plan which he'd been constantly thinking about lately; why work like a beast until your back was broken and your hands blistered when there were rich pickings to be taken from the likes of the wealthy folk who looked down upon the land workers as ignorant peasants. He was quick and nimble and light on his feet when the need arose. Would his wounded leg be too much of a handicap though, he pondered...maybe in a week or two it would be much improved and he could set his plan into motion. His thoughts had miraculously taken his mind off the pain; he felt a rush of excitement flow through him as he imagined his future with Sarah. The unwavering need to know if she felt the same way about him became suddenly paramount; Frank wasn't a fool and he knew that girls often walked out with a boy simply for the status of 'walking out' with someone and the minute a more desirable or richer man appeared on the scene, lads like him became yesterday's leftovers. He had to know the truth...did Sarah genuinely love him? Did she lie in bed dreaming of a future with him as he did of her? A sudden loud crashing sound from downstairs broke into his reverie, it sounded as though it was coming from the kitchen and the immediate thought that *'Squinty Eye'* had broken in, still in a rage that he'd been trespassing, was foremost in Frank's prediction. Taking his treasured cricket bat with him, he hobbled downstairs, trying to be as quiet as possible. The sound of his pa snoring came from his parent's bedroom. Frank pushed the door to his sister's room slightly; the girls were sleeping soundly in their large shared bed. His ears were suddenly filled with the most distressing sound...It was his ma and she was definitely in some kind of trouble. The pain in his leg seemed to immediately vanish as he lifted the willow bat high above his head and hastened down the last small flight of stairs to the door leading into the kitchen.

If it was bloody Squinty Eye, he would surely be armed, thought Frank as he prepared to burst in, take the intruder by surprise and swing for him with as much power as he could muster. His ma was silent, leaving Frank fearing the worst. He pulled back the door and was taken by complete shock at the sight which befell his eyes. In the dim candlelight, his ma was sat on the rug, with a tiny baby cradled in her arms. He held his breath as he prayed to hear any sound emanating from his newborn sibling, hoping with all his heart not to bear witness to the misery of his mother in mourning again. The kitchen drawer was upturned onto the floor, its contents sprawled across the room; a pair of scissors was discarded to one side. His mother's gentle voice spoke in whispers; she appeared calm, which was hopefully a positive sign, thought Frank as he stood motionless and shy in case his mother would not wish his male presence in such a female-oriented situation.

A tiny cry suddenly filled his ears and he released his breath, together with a sigh of relief.

"Are you alright Ma?"

"You have another sister, Frank; she's beautiful!

"The break in her voice made Frank want to

hurry to her side, but he felt too awkward and shy.

"I'll go and fetch Pa!"

The baby's cries grew louder as he hopped back up the stairs using the walls as support.

He went into his sister's room first and shook Martha,

"*Get up Martha!* Ma needs you, she's just had the baby...go and make tea and boil water."

Frank still had no idea as to why boiled water was always insisted upon by the midwife when his ma had given birth, his logic told him that it was surely an unsafe requirement, but always feeling too bashful to ask, it would probably remain a mystery until he became a father himself.

"*Oh, Frank!*" complained Martha in a sleepy voice, "The beautiful maids were just about to throw the most fragrant of rose petals at my feet in the handsome prince's white marble palace!"

"*Oh shut up Martha, you're such a foolish, bloody girl!*"

"Just be quiet, *Frank Shepherd*, you're not my pa, you know and I've got a good mind to tell Ma that you swore again!"

Turning his back on his annoying sister, Frank wasn't bothered to argue with her, it would wait until daytime, he decided. Desperate to reach the solitude of his room again and to rest his painful leg, Frank quickly woke his pa.

The Shepherd's cramped kitchen became a hub of excitement as the early morning sun rose above the distant fields of Bagley village. Martha, Jane and Amy were all in awe of their new baby sister, all delighted that their ma had produced another girl. Relieved that his wife and baby were both healthy, Silas kept the disappointment of not been blessed with a son completely to himself. As much as he cherished all of his daughters, they were not a lot of use on the farm and in years to come, he wouldn't be able to manage the heavy workload by himself. He sat drinking his tea, watching as the females all surrounded the baby like a flock of clucking hens. Claire looked extra beautiful he considered, tired, but calm and serene, with a sense of relief radiating from her.

"What shall we name your new sister then?" questioned Silas.

An immediate barrage of names became incomprehensible as they flew loudly out of the sister's mouths, leaving Claire laughing at their enthusiasm.

"Let's name her Victoria, after our lovely queen!" suggested Martha.

"I think there are becoming too many 'Victoria's', these days," objected Silas.

"How about Grace, that's a good, strong and meaningful name," stressed Claire.

The name immediately received the approval from Amy, Jane and Silas, although Martha emphasised how she preferred the names Alexandria and Alberta, causing her younger sister to giggle.

"I think Grace is the perfect name for her!" declared Silas as he peered down at the tiny pink-faced baby sleeping in his wife's arms."

After the early morning's excitement, both Jane and Amy were reluctant to attend school and pleaded with their ma to allow them to stay at home for the day to help out.

"You girls *must* go to school," insisted Claire, "besides, don't you want to tell your friends about baby Grace?"

Quickly persuaded, they were both already looking forward to announcing their news in the classroom.

"I think we should all have boiled eggs for breakfast today because only Ma can make tasty porridge!" voiced Jane.

Frank had arrived back down into the kitchen, glad to witness a relatively normal scene, with the addition of his newest sister.

"How's your leg today, son?" asked Silas, as he viewed Frank's pale complexion.

If truth be told, it was hurting far more than it had done on the previous day but insisting on keeping up his brave and manly bravado, Frank answered his father in a relaxed voice,

"It's fine, thanks Pa; it was only a slight graze, after all!"

"You're very brave, Frank; I'm proud of you, I doubt very much that I'd have made light of it if that idiot, Brunswick had taken a shot at me!" Frank grinned smugly, as he sat down on the settle with his leg resting upon the seat.

"Shall I make the porridge, then Ma?" offered Martha.

"Your ma needs to retire to her bed with baby Grace, she's had a difficult night and needs her rest!" expressed Silas.

Claire couldn't have agreed more, feeling exhausted and in need of sleep, she gladly allowed Silas to aid her and the newborn up the stairs to bed, with Martha following behind carrying another cup of tea and a thick chive of bread spread with Claire's very own plum jam.

"Hurry up, Amy, put your boots on; let's go and collect the eggs before they all come back down; Martha's porridge looks and tastes more like Pa's seed grain; come on, Hurry!"

Amy couldn't stop giggling as she squeezed her feet into Jane's old boots that she'd already outgrown.

"How do you know what seed grain tastes like? We might have to harvest your belly; maybe you have a field of wheat growing in it!"

"Oh be quiet and stop being so silly, little miss big feet! Of course, I haven't tasted the seed grain, that's not what I meant! Those boots were fit for me 'till I was eight, you know; why do you have such huge clod hoppers?"

"They're to narrow for my feet and they're too long...I look like a clown," exclaimed Amy as she struggled to push her chubby feet into Jane's cast-offs.

"Bring those bread crumbs with you for the chooks, Amy!"

They hurried out of the kitchen into the cold April air. It was a bright, sunny day and the heavy dew sparkled in the thick tufts of grass which had suddenly begun to randomly sprout on the yard. The early morning chorus of jubilant birdsong was a heavenly reminder of springtime.

" Someone's left the barn door open, Jane!" alerted Amy.

"Our one-legged brother, I expect," tutted Jane.

"Don't be so horrid to Frank, he was shot...He could have been killed you know!" Amy burst out into a flood of tears at the very thought of what she'd said. "Oh God, that would have been awful!" she continued, sniffing in between her heartbroken sobs.

Jane gave her the briefest of cuddles, before proceeding to tickle her sister's sides, immediately shifting Amy's downcast mood.

"Now stop being a little misery, we have a new sister, remember and Frank is going to be fine! You go and fetch the eggs while I close the barn door."

Amy obediently skipped towards the chicken

coup, her tummy was rumbling and she hoped that the hens had laid a decent quantity of eggs so that she'd get a whole one to herself. A broad smile covered her face; there were at least eight eggs. She gathered them eagerly but gently, expecting Jane to return at any moment.

With her basket full, she threw the pocket full of crumbs to the squawking hens and hurried to see what was taking Jane so long,

"*Amy! Amy!* Quickly come and see what I've found!" cried Jane.

Amy dumped the basket onto the ground and ran to her sister's aid.

Jane was stood next to the remaining bales of last year's harvest hay; a baby was lying still and lifeless in between two of the golden bales.

Amy stood motionless, staring down, sadly at the purple-tinged baby.

"*Somebody has left their dead baby in our barn!*" stated Jane.

"How do you know it's dead...It might just be sleeping!"

"But no sound or movement is coming from it...and it's not pink like *our* new baby!"

"What shall we do?" asked Amy in a sad voice.

"Let's take it to Ma and Pa!"

"You carry it, then, Jane, you're older than me," stated Amy, warily, not even wanting to touch the lifeless infant.

With a serious expression, beyond her years, Jane carefully lifted the small bundle into her arms.

"Do you think it's a girl or a boy?" questioned Amy.

"Looks like a boy to me," guessed Jane, "girls are much prettier!"

"Don't forget the eggs, Amy!"

Silas was aghast at the sight which befell his eyes. Jane stood holding the baby, while Amy blurted out everything she felt relevant to the situation, most of which went ignored. After his initial shock, Silas was quick to take the baby from Jane's hold and wrap it in Claire's warm shawl which had been hanging up above the stove. Frank, Martha, Jane and Amy all watched silently as their pa frantically massaged the baby's back and chest. They'd watched him do the same to the newborn lambs when they'd arrived into the world without any sign of life and most of the time, his actions had proved successful and the small lamb would miraculously bleat and stagger to its anxious mother.

Silence engulfed the entire kitchen; everyone seemed to be holding their breath as they willed the limp baby to make a sound. A sudden splutter followed by a tiny gurgling cough was quickly preceded by the much-awaited sound of the baby's crying. Relief and cries of delight transformed the silent kitchen into a room of jubilation as the baby's complexion soon

transformed into a healthy rose-pink hue.
"It looks pretty enough to be a girl now,"
whispered Jane into Amy's ear.
Becoming increasingly noisy the baby's cries
soon overtook the entire cottage, filling every
corner and waking Claire, who immediately
presumed the cries were coming from little
Grace.
Thrown into a state of confusion, as she viewed
her sleeping baby, Claire wondered if the lack of
sleep and the stress of childbirth, not to mention
the trauma of the '*what ifs*' which had plagued
her thoughts, concerning Frank's unfortunate
ordeal, had caused her mind to play tricks on
her. But it was no use, she had to leave the
warmth and comfort of her bed and follow the
disturbing sound.
"That sounds like a typical *noisy boy*!" voiced
Amy. "A girl wouldn't be so impolite and make
that racket!"
They giggled in unison, unheard above the noisy
infant.
Silas made a declaration to his concerned
children that the baby was most likely hungry
and at that very instant the kitchen door opened
and dressed in her nightgown, her chestnut
brown hair loosely hanging down over her
shoulders, Claire viewed the strange scene in
disbelief.
In all the excitement, the fact that Claire was in
need of a hearty breakfast had been overlooked.

No eggs were on the boil, the bread had not been toasted and the kettle had yet to be filled from the outside pump.

"Somebody left this poor newborn for dead in our barn...can you believe it!" Claire recognised her husband's distraught voice and the paleness of his face if none of her children had. She gently took the screaming baby from Silas, sat down, unbuttoned her nightgown and put the baby to her breast. A much-welcomed tranquillity once again resumed as the baby suckled hungrily. Silas issued orders for Frank and Martha to organise breakfast as Amy and Jane informed their ma of how they'd discovered the baby and how their pa had miraculously brought it back to life. All the while, Silas and Claire shared furtive glanced to one another, both with the same thoughts on their minds, but not wanting to say too much in front of the children.

The thin coverlet which the infant had been wrapped in felt damp, upon Claire's lap, she clandestinely lifted it; there was no napkin covering the baby boy, and a grubby length of string had been used to tie off the umbilical cord.

"Do you know if it's a boy or a girl Ma?" asked Amy in a small voice.

"He's a poor little boy, my darling!"

"Why is he poor?"

"He's been abandoned, that's why my darling, and doesn't have the love and care of his mother!"

"We could keep him; then Grace will have someone to play with while we're at school!" suggested Amy, innocently.

The spontaneous suggestion which had sprung from their young, not quite seven-year-old, certainly left Silas and Claire with a dilemma on their minds.

CHAPTER FIVE

Until Silas and Claire were decided about what to do regarding the delicate situation they faced, they considered it best to keep Jane and Amy away from school. Silas instructed that the family should not mention a word to anyone about both babies or even that their mother had given birth.

Martha was in her element dreaming up exotic anecdotes of how and why the baby had come to be abandoned on their farm but already Frank's disturbed mind kept thinking about the screaming which he and Sarah had heard coming from the Brunswick Estate. Who *was* Molly and where was she now, he mused over and over in his mind, annoyed that the increasing pain in his leg was preventing him from going out in search of some answers.

Claire and Silas had spent the morning in private, going over the matter until Claire's eyes couldn't stay open for another minute. She had rattled her brain until she'd given herself a headache but couldn't think of a single soul in Bagley village who could be the baby's mother or would be concealing an out of marriage pregnancy. They had temporarily given the abandoned baby a name; he was now referred to as baby George, a name which Claire might have given to Grace if she had been born a boy.

Baby George now shared Claire and Silas's bedroom along with baby Grace; he slept in an empty drawer alongside Grace's wooden crib, which had been skillfully made by Silas for Frank, fourteen years ago and since passed down to sleep all of the Shepherd babies. Martha managed to organise the cooking duties between herself, Jane and Amy and as the younger girls prepared a selection of root vegetables for the evening's supper, Martha set about kneading the huge lump of dough, as she daydreamed of what life might be like if she'd been born into a wealthy aristocratic family. Silas was deeply troubled, not just by the abandoned baby, but also by the atrocious behaviour of Bruce Brunswick. He had yet to take the matter up with the Squire but because of the new situation, he wanted to keep himself to himself until a resolution had been reached. He also knew that it would put a huge strain on Claire, having to feed and tend to the demanding needs of two babies of the same age. Silas didn't know why the sudden thought had occurred to him, but after a long and drawn out morning, in the few minutes of solitude which he miraculously found himself in, a notion sprung to his mind that just maybe, the distressed mother had left a letter with her son which Jane and Amy had overlooked. After hurrying to the barn, and searching in between every bale of hay and behind all the sacks of seed and the entire ploughing paraphernalia, Silas left the barn downcast with all hopes of an answer out of his hands. He tended to the few livestock which he kept, mucked out the stables and groomed his two prize mares. The weather was changing again and a heavy downpour looked imminent. The heavy task of ploughing the fields and sowing the seeds would have to be done within the following few days, he reminded himself; it couldn't be at a worse time too and Silas knew that he'd receive very little help from his family this year.

By late afternoon, a strong easterly wind had arrived along with cold driving rain. Claire was looking more like her usual self, with the colour returning to her cheeks after her day's bed rest. Martha and Jane took it in turns to attend to her needs and keep the cups of hot tea and snacks at hand throughout the day, while Amy's visits up to her parent's room were to coo over the newborns and quiz her ma about baby George; Silas had compared her to a mischievous lamb who kept leaving the flock as he ordered her to leave her poor ma to rest.

As she fed both babies, Claire's strong feelings of sorrow for the poor abandoned baby were equal to the strong bond of love which she felt for her new daughter; she nursed and attended them indiscriminately and already suspected that baby George would remain in her life for a while to come.

The pleasant aroma of the simmering stew which Martha had cooked caused everyone's empty stomachs to rumble and their mouths to water. While Jane and Amy laid the table and arranged a tray for their ma, Silas re-dressed Frank's extremely sore looking leg.

"I don't like the look of that wound, son!" he uttered as he bathed it in cold tea.

"It's fine Pa! Please don't fuss, I'm not a boy!" As much as Silas respected his boy's urgent need to prove himself a man, he was not blind to the pain which was etched on his face as the festering leg was bathed.

"Even fully grown men are allowed to admit to pain, Frank," he replied sternly. "That leg is going to be cleaned at least six times a day...you won't thank me in years to come when you're walking around with a wooden one, God forbid."

The thought had never occurred to Frank, but his pa's forthright words did put fear into him; Sarah would never marry him if he became a cripple he thought, alarmingly.

"You're right Pa; it *is* giving me a lot of pain." Silas studied his son, his heart full of love for his first child, who was in such a desperate hurry to grow up.

"It doesn't make you any less of a man to admit that you're in pain, son!" He patted him on his shoulder; a man to man gesture.

The unexpected rapping on the door caused everyone to wonder who would be calling at supper time and during such atrocious weather. "Let *me* answer that!" insisted Silas, as Martha hurried to the door.

Looking as though she'd swam through a raging river to arrive at the cottage, Lydia Tyler, stood soaked to the skin. Unfamiliar to Silas, he stared aghast at the dripping young girl.

"Oh Good heavens!" exclaimed Martha as she rushed to greet her.

"This is Lydia Tyler, Pa, the sister of Frank's sweetheart!"

"Come in Lydia; come in and warm yourself," invited Silas, shocked as to why this girl was out and about in such a wretched evening.

"Is Sarah alright?" called out Frank from the settle.

Lydia stepped timidly over the threshold, glad to be out of the wind and rain. She was shivering uncontrollably and within a few seconds had left a puddle on the floor.

"I haven't seen Sarah, since *that day*," she replied to Frank. "I've come from the gatehouse, but I got lost. I've been trying to find your cottage for ages; everything looks so different in the dark though."

"You must take off your outer garments, Lydia, and I'll hang them near the stove to dry. My pa will take you back to old Squinty Eye's place, won't you Pa?"

If the circumstances hadn't been so worrying, Silas would have laughed out loud at how his daughter mimicked her mother in her absence. "What brings you out on such an evening, Lydia?" enquired Silas.

With a confused expression on her face, Lydia answered, "Well it wasn't evening when I left. Mr Brunswick needed an important letter delivered...He did ask cook, but she promised me a surprise if I delivered it!"

"Hmm...How very noble of her," muttered Silas under his breath.

"You must stay and taste my special supper which I've spent all afternoon cooking!" insisted Martha as she peeled off Lydia's dripping shawl and flimsy bonnet.

"It *does* smell nice in here!"

"We helped too, didn't we Jane?" called out Amy, annoyed that after it had taken her over an hour to scrape and dice the carrots and turnips, Martha was claiming all the credit.

"So, er, where *is* this important letter, young Lydia?" inquired Silas.

"Oh yes, silly me, I tucked it in my bloomers for safekeeping...and it hasn't got a single drop of rain on it!"

As Silas felt his cheeks turning red, Jane and Amy were unable to hold their giggles as Lydia simply pulled up her soaking skirt and petticoat revealing her long bloomers which held the letter. She passed it quickly to Silas before hurrying to the table where Martha had already set an extra place.

As he glanced at the envelope, Silas could tell by the fine quality of the stationery that the letter was of some importance. He sensed a bad feeling about it and decided that its contents could wait until after he and his family had eaten.

Thankfully, by the time that Silas ventured out to take Lydia back to the gatehouse, the rain had ceased and the wind died down a little.

"Are you happy working for Mr Brunswick?" probed Silas.

"It's alright I suppose...I don't really see him very often as I'm always in the kitchen. He's quite scary though, but my pa says that he's harmless."

Silas bit his tongue, not wanting to express his true feelings about Bruce Brunswick to the simple and trusting girl at his side.

The cook and another young maid were standing by the gated entrance to the Brunswick Estate, clearly angry by Lydia's tardiness.

"Two hours, we've been in and out of the house looking for you, *you stupid girl!* I'm froze to me marrow! And don't think that I bothered to save you any supper, because I didn't; young Viola had your share!"

Lydia had never witnessed Mrs Bunting so angry before, even when she'd burnt an entire batch of bread rolls, and broken dishes, Mrs

Bunting had not given her such a dressing down.

"Did you deliver the Master's letter? Please tell me that you at least did *one thing* right for a change!"

"Yes, Mrs Bunting, of course I did," replied Lydia, on the verge of breaking down into a flood of tears, her confidence wavering as Viola sided with Mrs Bunting, with a look of triumph across her smug face. How she loathed that stuck up little maid who thought she was better than anyone in Bagley village, just because she came from the town, mused Lydia crossly. Furtively glancing over her shoulder, Lydia checked to make sure that the lovely Mr Shepherd had left, she would hate for him to view the awful welcome she was receiving from her superiors.

"Come along, girl, get inside! Haven't me and poor Viola spent enough time out in the cold and rain, waiting for your return! It's no wonder that your poor ma and pa sent you packing. And don't think that I won't be tempted to tell Mr Brunswick how long you took to deliver his important letter, you half-wit!"

As usual, Lydia spoke without thinking, "Mr Brunswick asked you to take the letter anyway; I heard him with my own ears!"

Mrs Bunting stood still in her tracks, resting her clenched fists upon her ample hips, her mouth pursed so tightly that it resembled a hen's behind.

"Are you a witness to this insulate little fool's rudeness, young Viola?"

Viola stretched her neck a little before adding her comment, "I doubt these farming families even bother to teach their hoards of children any manners, Mrs Bunting!"

"Well I think it's about time somebody did!" declared Mrs Bunting as she turned her back and hurried inside.

The speed in which Viola grabbed hold of Lydia's bedraggled damp hair took her by complete surprise; she screamed out as Viola yanked it so forcefully that she was left with a handful in her grip. She threw it down in disgust,

"Your rat's tails are filthier than you, *pheasant!* Now hurry up and get inside...I'm sure there's a sink load of dirty pots and pans waiting for your attention...you'll be in your element, *filthy bitch!*"

With tears rolling freely down her face, and her head painfully sore, Lydia realised that since Molly had left, she was without a friend at the gatehouse. Blinded by her tears Lydia failed to notice as Viola stuck out her foot, causing her to come crashing down onto the gravel pathway, only adding to her pain and humiliation.

Relieved that she'd been fed well by the kind Shepherd family, Lydia worked through the night, into the small hours of the morning until her hands were red raw and the kitchen was clean and tidy once more. She had decided that on her next Sunday off, she'd pick a posy of spring flowers to take to Mrs Shepherd since she'd been told how she was feeling under the weather.

CHAPTER SIX

In his anticipation of what was written in the letter from Bruce Brunswick, Silas journeyed the short distance back home with a couple of possibilities racing through his thoughts; an apology from the man was one, with perhaps a small token of compensation, since Bruce would surely realise that Silas would now either have to plough and sow his fields single-handedly or employ a worker, which he couldn't afford without repercussions. The other thought was far more sinister, more in line with Bruce's obnoxious character and one which, for the time being, Silas didn't wish to dwell on.

The cottage was in complete silence when he arrived home, not even the sound of a whimpering baby could be heard. Martha had left a candle lit in the middle of the kitchen table and a small pan of cocoa was simmering gently upon the dwindling stove. Silas took off his muddy boots, hung his jacket up on the back of the door and relished in the first period of peace and quiet he'd had since being woken by Frank that morning, which now seemed like days ago. It had certainly been a long and eventful day and there was still the decision of what they should do with the abandoned baby weighing heavy on his thoughts. As stealthily as he could manage, Silas poured the cocoa into a mug and sat down at the table, preparing to read the correspondence in the dim candlelight before turning in for the night.

There was no payment enclosed and before he'd even begun to read the page of spidery copperplate scrawl, the boldly written words '*hanging*' and '*transported*' leapt out from the page, immediately diminishing any optimism that Silas was feeling about its contents. He took an angry gulp of the strong cocoa, before commencing, wishing he had a bottle of liquor secretly tucked away somewhere, to add to it.

Mr Shepherd,
Disclose this letter to any living soul at your peril and do not take my warning in vain!
If I ever come across any member of your family poaching or trespassing on my land again, you can guarantee that they will not be so fortunate as to walk away alive. Warn your foolhardy son to stay well clear of me and my land if he values his life and if you wish not to witness him hanging from the end of a noose, or transported to the other side of the world for seven years or more. Dare to show this letter to my brother, if you wish to face the consequences and witness your family suffer, one by one. I have greatly admired the beauty of your sweet wife for many years and it has not slipped my attention of how your daughters are mirroring her striking looks as they mature, especially your eldest daughter who I had the greatest pleasure of conversing with a short while ago. You are indeed a most fortunate man, Mr Shepherd.
As a sign of my neighbourly gratitude to your lovely wife, I have left you a gift which you are most likely already in receipt of. No doubt you have discovered the orphan boy in your barn by now. He is yours to keep...I know how you peasants cherish your hoards of children and I was well informed that your pretty wife

is nearing her confinement. If her child fails to survive the birth, I will be left pleased, knowing that I have been able to supply a substitute. If the child does survive, then you can explain to all concerned that she gave birth to twins, call it a bonus. I assure you that you will never be confronted with anyone remotely related to the orphaned boy.
Remember my warning Mr Shepherd. I am not a man to be toyed with or taken lightly.
Bruce Brunswick.

Silas read the letter three times, becoming angrier by every word as they became a blur before his tired eyes in the dim light. This was nothing but an unadulterated threat and blackmail. How could he possibly live the rest of his life on the Squire's land with such a huge secret and how could he trust bloody Squinty Eye not to use this secret to his own advantage whenever the fancy took him, mused Silas angrily. Then there was the issue of Frank, the only reason that he'd jumped the wall was his concern about the distressing screaming which he and Sarah had heard. His thoughts were spinning around inside his head; his tiredness had been replaced by frustration and rage and if it wasn't such a late hour, he'd march straight to the Brunswick Estate and demand to be seen by Reginald Brunswick. For the very first time in his life, Silas had no idea of what he should do and caring for his family by simply working every God sent hour to provide for them was no longer his only worry. This huge threat could very well destroy his family, Bruce Brunswick could make threats whenever he chose to or whenever he required anything which Silas had, mainly his daughters. What was to prevent him in the future from demanding that one of them should work at the gatehouse...the sudden thought that perhaps Joseph Tyler had been forced into allowing Lydia to work there crossed his mind.

The sound of a crying baby broke into his troubled thoughts; he'd barely seen his newborn daughter today and he'd neglected his beloved wife. Never before had she born him a child and he'd not gone into town to purchase her a small gift, but this special day had been marred by the discovery of the baby in the barn. Gulping down the last gritty mouthful of cold cocoa, Silas blew out the flickering candle and headed upstairs, towards the sound of crying.

Sat up in bed, Claire was feeding baby Grace, while George's hungry cries disturbed the tranquil scene. Silas lifted the infant from out of the wooden drawer; his stance was awkward, as he tried to comfort the baby. Jiggling him rhythmically as he paced the few steps around the bed, the baby stared at him, his navy eyes seeming to call out to Silas's very soul. How could he even contemplate sending this innocent young victim to the workhouse he mused? He hoped that Claire was ready and strong enough to face the truth and that together their strength of unity would be a force against the wickedness of Bruce Brunswick.

"He's a tough little fellow, isn't he?" stated Silas, in the brief moment of silence.

"He's also a greedy little fellow too; he's already spent far longer on my breast than our sweet Grace!"

"Is that the attribute of a boy, then? Greedy from the very beginning?"

Claire smiled, "Maybe boys have to build themselves up for their tough, hard-working lives!"

"*No, no*, I can't believe that; you work just as hard as me, if not harder!"

"Well, I'm pleased to hear that my labours have at last been recognised!"

"Ah, Claire, my beautiful Claire, I've admired your strength and determination since we were young uns; when we attended those weekly Sunday school lessons. You were never scared of old Father Greenwood; in fact, I'm sure his nervous twitch always increased when you were confronting him!"

"Oh, Silas, now you're being silly, you *must* be tired."

Swallowing hard, Claire was unable to prevent her tear filled eyes from overflowing,

"Oh, Dear God!" exclaimed, Silas. "Me and my big mouth... "

"It's not your fault, my darling, I'm tired and tearful and the mention of dear Father

Greenwood never fails in reminding me of my poor parents on the best of days, but on days like today, I yearn for them more than ever. Ma would have made the best grandmother!"

"I know my darling, and you must make sure that you never stop telling the children everything about them. I lost my pa too you know, and my only brother! "

"I know that Silas, we are both victims of scarlet fever, maybe that is why we have such a strong family bond...Let's just pray that The Almighty protects us from any forthcoming illnesses and plagues."

Claire gently laid the sleeping baby down by her side before stretching her arms out towards Silas, "Pass me that little mite, it's his turn now, otherwise none of us will get a wink of sleep tonight. Maybe you could get to know your new daughter too; give her a cuddle, Silas...I don't feel that she's had enough of my attention today."

"She certainly has her ma's beauty!" said Silas as his eyes fixed lovingly on baby Grace.

"I'm so sorry, Claire, I've not been able to find time to buy you a gift...you deserve so much, and my hands are empty...but one day, who knows where the Shepherd family might be?"

"One day, my darling we will look back on today and savour the beauty of it!"

Claire's sentiments immediately diverted Silas's thoughts to the letter which was safely in his pocket, his failure to respond to Claire, caused her to take her eyes off the feeding baby.

"What is it, Silas? Did I say something wrong?"

 "No, no, of course not...I'm just a little tongue tied and mesmerized by this precious treasure here."

"Lay her in the crib, Silas, and come to bed...you can tell me what's on your mind in the morning...a new day, when we'll both feel ready to tackle any problem!"

Already sensing that Silas knew something relating to baby George, if she'd not been so exhausted, her disturbing thoughts wouldn't have allowed her to fall asleep the moment her head touched the pillow. Silas, however, lay in thought for a while longer; he would disclose everything to Claire in the morning, she was far stronger than him when it came to such family matters and hopefully, she would know the best way to handle it. The children would have to know too, especially if they were to declare to all that Grace and George were twins.

After eventually falling asleep, horrendous images of Bruce Brunswick's evil and disfigured face crowded his dreams. Distressing scenes where he could only watch in horror as *Squinty Eye* ravished his wife and Martha and took over his entire family, waking him up in a cold sweat.

Martha was up at the break of dawn the following morning, the noisy babies had broken her sleep and she was determined to make the tastiest pot of porridge for her family; still cross about the insults she'd had to listen to from her little sisters...what did they know about cooking, she muttered, annoyingly as she went about lighting the kitchen stove which heated the entire cottage. She was taking pleasure in being the mistress of the kitchen; everyone had thoroughly enjoyed and complimented the stew which she'd made the previous evening and she'd decided on insisting that her ma should spend the next few days in bed. After giving the floor a quick sweep, she carefully measured out three cups of oats into the heavy black porridge pot. It was only when she'd opened the pantry door to retrieve the milk, that it suddenly hit her that in all of yesterday's commotion, she'd completely forgotten to attend to her main chore, which was to milk the cows. Her pa's warning words of how the milk would turn sour and the cows become sick, maybe even die spun around in her head.

"*Oh no!*" she cried out loudly, "*Please, please, please* Dearest God, let the cows be alright...I'll never waste my time daydreaming again...I promise!"

She fled from the cottage, across the yard to the cowshed. All six cows were lowing contentedly and to her delight, the large metal jug was full to the top with milk and had been placed on a high shelf for safekeeping. Breathing a sigh of relief,

Martha carefully carried the jug back home to be instantly confronted by a smug looking Frank, who was sat on the settle, still in his nightgown. "I think I can safely say that you owe me one, little sis!"

Martha glared infuriatingly at her brother; he had changed so much over the past six months and she preferred him in the days when he wasn't so intent on proving to everyone that he was *a man*.

"It slipped my mind, that's all, Frank and I've already paid my debt to you by cooking your supper yesterday!"

"Oh, no you haven't, Martha! But don't worry; I'm sure the day will come when there is something I need your help with!"

"How's your leg today?" enquired Martha, deciding to change the subject before she ended up in a full-blown dispute with her ill-mannered brother.

"You're not my mother, *Martha Shepherd*, so mind your bloody business!" he yelled, aggressively.

"You used to be so nice, Frank. I don't know why that sweet Sarah Tyler walks out with you, I really don't!"

"Be quiet, Martha and leave Sarah out of this...at least she's a real woman!"

"You're mad, Frank Shepherd, as mad as a March hare!" laughed Martha as she turned her back on her brother, unable to hide her amusement.

The family squabble was soon put to an end by the arrival of Jane and Amy, already dressed; they were both over excited about attending school and couldn't wait to announce their intriguing news to their classmates.

"I'll tell them about Frank being shot at by old *Squinty Eye* and you can tell them about baby Grace and since we both sort of found baby George, although I was the one who *actually* discovered him in the barn, we can tell them that together," ordered Jane, in a bossy voice.

"Alright then," agreed Amy.

"Are you trying to make porridge, Martha?" questioned Amy, innocently.

Martha, had her back to everyone as she vigorously stirred the porridge before it turned lumpy or caught on the sides of the pan; she was looking forward to waving her annoying younger sisters off to school,

"I'm not *trying* to make porridge, Amy, it's nearly ready, so you two lazy girls better set the table and Jane, you can come and put some tea into the pot; I daren't leave this porridge for a second!"

"Something smells good!" declared Silas, on arriving into the kitchen."

"Martha's making the porridge!" emphasized Jane.

"Can I go up and see Ma and the babies now, Pa?" begged Amy.

"No my darling; sorry but your ma is still sleeping; it's not easy to take care of two babies all through the night, you know!"

Amy looked downcast, she missed her ma's presence in the kitchen and the special treatment which she always showered her with. Martha had teased her over the past few weeks, telling her that as soon as the new baby arrived, she would have to grow up and stop behaving like a baby herself; she loathed Martha for her cruel words but was now beginning to see that they were probably words of truth.

"Tell you what, Amy; you can take up Ma's breakfast in a little while."

Amy's instant smile lit up her sad face.

"Thank you Pa...I'm going outside to pick some flowers for her tray!" she announced excitedly, not waiting to hear any objections as she raced barefoot towards the kitchen door.

"Make sure you don't bring any more stray orphans back with you!" yelled Frank, a smug grin etched upon his face. His underhand comment immediately put Silas into a prickly mood. He stared coldly at his son; after all, this mess was all his doing, he thought, angrily and yet he had the gall to sit back calmly, issuing his audacious remarks. Claire was right; he was becoming too big for his boots and would have to be reminded of who he was before any more damage was done.

"That was uncalled for, Frank! We're a family,

remember; a family which sticks together through thick and thin and you are as much a part of the Shepherd family as every one of us. The issue of baby George is one which affects all of us!"

Frank glared defiantly at his pa; all of a sudden feeling suffocated by his family; one minute he was treated like a man, the next like a boy...he'd had enough and things *would* change, because he would make them.

"**Frank!** Did you hear me? Are you paying *any* attention to me?"

"Yes Father, of course I am. Why don't we simply take that bastard baby to an orphanage, where he belongs...he's not a Shepherd, after all, ...*or is he?*"

Silas could feel the blood heating up in his veins, he wanted nothing more than to march over to his son and give him the well overdue thrashing which he deserved, but knowing how it would distress Claire, especially when she already had so much to cope with, he gritted his teeth and remained motionless.

"Get out of my sight before I do something that will displease your poor mother!" he shouted angrily.

"*Oh no!*" hollered Martha hysterically. "Now the porridge has burnt to the bottom of the pan; it's ruined! "

"It's your fault, *Frank*!" shouted Jane, as she felt her belly rumbling."We'll have to go to school hungry now!"

"Why do you have to ruin everything *Frank Shepherd*?" cried Martha.

"Oh be quiet, the lot of you!" growled Frank as he hobbled as fast as he could from the kitchen. Silas sat down heavily, resting his head in his hands.

"Look at the flowers I picked!" exclaimed Amy joyfully, with a bunch of wild daffodils in her hand. "Ooh, *what's that horrid smell?*"

"Martha burnt the porridge!" announced Jane, calmly.

"Don't worry, it's still early; I have time to start from scratch and this time Frank *won't be* here to distract me from the pot!"

CHAPTER SEVEN

"You can't simply go marching over to the Estate demanding to be seen by the Squire, Silas!"
"Give me one good reason why not," he yelled angrily. "His bloody fool of a brother has issued us with uncalled for threats and warnings, not to mention blackmail *and* saddling us with the responsibility of an orphan; only God knows from where *he* came from!"
Claire sipped the steaming tea which Silas had brought upstairs to her, she was feeling refreshed after having had a few hours of uninterrupted sleep, she'd read the letter but unlike Silas, whose hot temper had clouded all sense of judgement, she was trying to persuade him that this matter needed careful handling.
"We must keep the girls home from school today, Silas...we can't possibly have them spreading the news of baby George, especially if we have no other choice than to do as the letter requests and raise him as Grace's twin."
Silas leapt up from the edge of the bed; his knuckles white as he clenched his fists in anger; he paced back and forth across the width of the bedroom a couple of times,
"Don't you see, Claire, if we heed to *his* warnings the instructions on this damned letter, Bruce Brunswick will be our jailer and dictator for years to come! He'll be able to use what he

knows to his advantage; *I know his game*; he wants us to become attached and form a strong bond with George; then he will have the upper hand on us forever...*can't you see?"*

"*Silas!* He already *has*; what's to stop Brunswick from having our Frank put on trial for poaching; his brother is the magistrate, for goodness sake and everyone knows how protective he is of his cripple brother."

"I think I could persuade him otherwise, if I go and to see him, Claire, I've always got on well with the Squire...he's a decent sort and with him being a magistrate I doubt he'd condone his brother's threats!"

"Blood is thicker than water, Silas, and the wealthy are renowned for bending the rules to protect their kith and kin. You should never trust them, Silas; my pa drummed that into my head from when I'd barely outgrown my cradle!"

Silas laughed, it was the first time his tension had eased since he'd set eyes on the letter, "You do say the funniest things, my darling! Times have changed you know, it's not like it was when we were children!"

"I don't believe that for one minute *Silas Shepherd*, but I know how stubborn you can be, but please, don't lose your temper; think before you say anything which we all might live to regret. Think of your family, Silas and leave your male pride here in the cottage."

Silas stared lovingly at his pretty wife, his heart swelling with love for her,

"Where would I be without your sensible head at my side, woman? Don't worry, I'm only *doing this* for the sake of my family; it has nothing to do with my male pride, as you put it!"

Silas gently brushed Claire's cheek with a loving kiss,

"Get some rest, my darling; hopefully I'll return with some good news. I love you."

He paused before opening the bedroom door,

"If the question should arise, do you want us to keep the orphan?"

"You mean, *baby George*; don't try and detach yourself from him, Silas, I've seen the way you look at him; your heart is as soft as mine beneath that shield which you insist on holding up!"

"So is that a yes then?" he smiled. "It will mean a lot of extra work you know?"

"Since when have the Shepherd family shied away from hard work? Be on your way now Silas and I love you too!"

"*Oh Pa*, me and Amy want to go to school, don't we Amy?"

"No, I'd rather stay at home with Ma and the babies!"

"Well, regardless of your preferences, there will be *no* school today," confirmed Silas.

"Now I have to go out, so you girls look after your Ma and Martha, I want you to go up and change your brother's dressing."

The look of disgust upon Martha's face quickly had Jane and Amy in fits of giggles which they tried to hide, knowing that they would be sure to pay the consequences later for.

"Ugh, I'm not touching Frank's, stinky leg!" she protested.

"Do as you're told, Martha, he's your brother and his leg needs tending to, he'd do the same for you, I'm sure!"

"I doubt that!"

Not wanting to hear any more complaints, Silas grabbed his jacket and cap, pulled on his boots and rushed out of the cottage without ushering another word.

A continuous drizzle descended as Silas sat tall in the saddle as he headed towards the entrance to the Brunswick Estate. His mind was fully occupied as he went over and over what he intended to say to Reginald Brunswick and how he would manage to phrase it politely. There was, of course, the possibility that a meeting with him would not be convenient and he'd have to make an appointment for another time; he prayed that this would not be the case, wanting to ease the heavy burden which he carried.

On arriving at the Brunswick Estate, to his relief, Silas found the side gate unlocked; after securely tethering his mare to the gate post and patting her muscular neck before parting, he stepped over the boundary line, praying that Bruce wouldn't be somewhere on the grounds brandishing his lethal pistol. The drizzle had now soaked his outer clothes; his face dripped with rainwater as he began to march up the long path towards the stately home.

When he'd been a boy, Silas had been familiar with many of the staff on the Brunswick Estate, the Squire and his wife, Lady Mary had three children who were all quite near his age and now all in their thirties. He had clear memories of the family, all attired in the most exquisite apparel during the special occasions when they attended the local church; the three children, two boys and a girl had always ignored the farmer's children, keeping their heads held high, almost as though shielded by blinkers, they refused to look anywhere apart from straight ahead. In those days, when both his parents were still alive and life held little responsibility for him, everyone seemed to know somebody's older sibling who worked on the Estate. Quite often they would return home with hampers of delicious leftovers after a ball or a grand dinner had need held; the mouth-watering delights would always be shared between every family. These days, Silas knew of nobody who was employed on the Estate, it seemed that all employees were now picked from neighbouring towns.

The impressive sand coloured construction stood amongst a dozen or more lofty evergreens, appearing bright against the oppressive gloomy sky. Silas viewed the thick lush grass; how his cows would benefit from grazing on such pasture, he strangely thought. He diverted towards the back entrance of the grand house and rapped confidently upon the regular looking door. Hearing the noisy clatter of pots and pans emanating from inside, Silas wondered if he'd been heard and just as he was about to knock again, the door flung open to reveal a young tweenie, looking flustered and quite dishevelled. She eyed Silas up and down and stood on tiptoes to peer over his shoulder.

"Don't you have no delivery then, Mister?"

"No, I've come to have a word with the Squire," responded Silas, calmly.

Her eyebrows lifted in surprise, "I best go fetch Mr Langley."

The door was suddenly closed again in his face, leaving Silas in the rain.

Seconds later Mr Langley appeared and invited him in.

"Sorry, to leave you outside on such a morning, Mr..? "

"Mr Shepherd."

"Ah, Mr Shepherd," repeated Mr Langley, causing Silas to wonder if he knew of him, or this was merely his polite way.

The pleasant mix of aromas immediately caused

Silas to salivate; the journey in the cold rain had made him hungry.

Mr Langley directed him to a small recess in the corridor, where a high backed chair and small wooden table were situated.

"Wait here, Mr Shepherd," he requested.

Silas clutched his cap in hand and followed orders. A few minutes later the young tweenie reappeared; she placed a cup of tea and a plate of hot buttered bread down on the table in front of him and handed him a soft white towel.

"You might want to dry your face, Mister."

"Thank you, thank you very much!"

 After drying his face and hands, Silas eagerly bit into the freshly baked bread, allowing it to slip his mind for a brief moment about the nature of his visit.

Mr Langley soon returned, coughing to gain Silas's attention,

"Excuse me Mr Shepherd, but what exactly is the nature of your request to meet with the Squire?"

Silas swallowed the huge lump of bread, wincing as its crust scraped his throat,

"It's a personal and very urgent matter."

Without replying, Mr Langley swiftly headed off along the corridor again leaving Silas to finish his refreshments.

Reginald Brunswick's study was spacious but extremely dark, with the only brightness coming from within the huge burning fireplace. Wooden panelled walls, moss coloured upholstered chairs and heavy brown brocade curtains which shut out most of the light from the windows, adding to its gloominess. The walls were hung with exquisite oil portraits of horses, each with the horses' nameplates beneath them. The Squire appeared cold and unwelcoming and his austere expression was in complete contrast to the friendly face he wore when visiting his tenants. Remaining seated behind his desk as Silas was shown in by Mr Langley; Reginald Brunswick refused to even offer a polite and welcoming hand to him, causing the atmosphere to feel quite hostile.

"Yes Mr Shepherd, how can I help you?"
 Feeling like a timid mouse in front of a menacing feline, Silas seemed to lose every ounce of confidence, as the Squire, waited for a response. He pushed his hand into his pocket, retrieving the crumpled and slightly damp letter and gingerly offered it to the Squire.

It took only a few seconds for him to skim down the page and Silas knew that he'd not bothered to read every line. Annoyingly re-folding the letter he returned it to Silas, sighing heavily as he did so.

"So, *Mr Shepherd*, your son was caught poaching on my land and you presume to be the victim merely because my brother took the action which, by law, was perfectly acceptable! How is your son? Was it a crippling wound worthy of a physician's attention, or, as I suspect, a warning shot which probably inflicted little damage but which, perhaps, taught your wayward son a valuable lesson? You do realise, Mr Shepherd, that as the magistrate, it is well within my power to sentence your son, so if I were in your shoes, I would count my blessings that my brother took no further action."

Silas felt mortified, the Squire's hostile tone already told Silas that Reginald Brunswick was prepared to protect his brother, no matter what he'd done.

"What about the threats which Mr Brunswick has made to my family? He left an orphan boy in our care too...as a gift, he claimed and leaving us no choice but to raise him as our own child. He is blackmailing my entire family!" stressed Silas, his voice becoming loud and angry.

"*What child?* What are you talking about, Mr Shepherd?"

Once again, Silas took out the letter,

"*Please* Mr Brunswick, *I beg of you* to read it *all* this time!"

After snatching the letter, the fuming Squire proceeded to rip it up into shreds,

"Don't you dare to enter my home ever again, making false accusations about one of my family, Mr Shepherd, not if you want to remain living on my land...there is many a family who would jump at the opportunity to rent your farm; I suggest you reflect upon that and go home to your family and I'll be generous enough to forget that this meeting ever took place. I also suggest that you exert a little more discipline where your son is concerned, he might not get off so lightly next time!"

"He wasn't even poaching, Sir," protested Silas. "He's a good, honest lad and was only on the estate because he'd heard the distressing cries of a girl coming from the gatehouse!"

"Then I suggest you teach him that he should mind his own business in future! Mr Shepherd; now I'm a busy man, so kindly take your leave of me!"

Mr Langley, quickly leapt away from the door as Silas left the dismal study feeling quite demoralized.

"I'll show you out, Mr Shepherd" stated Mr Langley, in a superior tone.

Left feeling livid and in a state of shock, Silas squeezed his cap between his hands as he followed the audacious butler.

CHAPTER EIGHT

Reginald Brunswick poured himself a large
whiskey; it was far too early in the day, but he
could think of nothing else which would ease his
troubled mind. Running a hand through his salt
and pepper hair, as the burning liquid trickled
down his throat Reginald stared hard at the
small pile of shredded paper in front of him,
before the impulse to painstakingly reassemble
the letter took a grip of him. It felt as though his
entire life had been marred by his younger
brother; even now at the age of fifty-six, Bruce
continued to be like a spiky thorn in his side and
there was little he could do about it. Reginald
had resigned to the facts that as long as his
brother lived, *he* would spend his days covering
up for his crimes and bailing him out of trouble.
Mr Shepherd was a decent sort who'd always
been most obliging and courteous; it pained him
having to be so harsh in his treatment towards
such a man. He didn't want to see any harm
coming to his family, but if Silas Shepherd
refused to let this matter drop, he knew he'd
have little choice in the matter. Blood was
thicker than water, were his strong beliefs and,
after all, it could easily have been him instead of
Bruce who'd been the injured party and ended
up a cripple. The words of his manipulating
brother leapt out from every shred of evidence

as the correspondence was slowly put back together, his strong suspicions already told him that the orphan boy was yet another illegitimate son sired by his beast of a brother, adding an increased threat to his own sons inheriting the Brunswick Estate after he'd passed on. The mere thought of just how many children Bruce had fathered throughout his life caused Reginald to shudder, it was an absolute disgrace and a habit which must be stopped before he became careless in his tracks and it became public knowledge. Bruce's irresponsible and philandering ways would put the entire family to shame. The reminder that Bruce had recently taken on the Tyler family's simpleton daughter troubled Reginald Brunswick; Bruce was taking risks and becoming far too careless, he mused. The Shepherd's were not ignorant people, Claire Shepherd was an astute young woman as far as he could recollect and it wouldn't take a genius to work out who the so-called abandoned child belonged to. But why, hadn't he merely left the child anonymously on the steps of an orphanage or workhouse; why the need to make threats towards Silas's family? Reginald furiously pushed his chair across the room and marched frustratingly back and forth as his thoughts went over and over in his throbbing head. It dawned on him that his idiotic brother intended to potentially ruin the lives of every member of the Shepherd family and he had to put a stop to it before it caused all manner of repercussions. The three glasses of whiskey so prematurely consumed in the day together with the heat of the intense fire suddenly had an overwhelmingly tiring effect on the Squire, he turned the key in the door, not wanting anyone to see him the worse for drink and threw himself down onto the tiger skin hearthrug. The lifelike oil painting of Didelot, the handsome bay horse with its distinct black mane, tail and ears caught his attention and brought to life the vivid memories of that particular Derby day back in 1796.

The day had begun full of eager anticipation and as usual, on Derby Day, the men attended the races whilst the society women of Epsom and its surrounds preferred the calmer atmosphere of garden parties or inside card games if the weather was unsuitable.

Dorcus Brunswick had received an invitation to Lady Harrington's garden party and with the benefit of her being only a friend of an acquaintance, Dorcus new that word would not circulate when she failed to attend.

"Just look at my three handsome men!" she exclaimed as she stood admiring Reginald and Bruce, whose fine attire mirrored that of her husband, Howard Brunswick; though, in her eyes, her sons were far more handsome than her husband had ever been. Thankfully, she considered, they had inherited their looks from her side of the family.

Embarrassed by their mother's need to stroke
their cheeks and straighten their top hats,
Reginald and Bruce were both eager to leave
with their father and be part of the pageant of
stylish carriages, all heading through the town of
Epsom towards the Downs where the four-
furlong flat race took place every year.
His mother had seemed more animated than
usual; her face was aglow with excitement and
she seemed in a hurry for them to leave.
"Goodness! Is that the time already" she declared
with Reginald's sharp eyes, noticing how she'd
not even glanced at the towering grandfather
clock. "Off you go my darlings and enjoy your
special day at the races...make sure you all
wager on the winner!"
She dutifully brushed her lips upon her
husband's thick whiskers, before planting a kiss
on each of her son's smooth faces.
"Now I must dash and make myself look
presentable for Lady Harrington's grand garden
party in Leatherhead."
With the last word barely out of her mouth,
Dorcus turned about and glided gracefully up
the wide staircase as Howard, Reginald and
Bruce waited for the Brunswick's most superior
and showy carriage to be brought around to the
front of the house.
Dorcus Brunswick sat at her dressing table; she

was pleased with her reflection, unlike many of her friends and associates, she had not lost her beauty or curvy figure after bearing two sons and had less than a dozen grey hairs which blended in unnoticeably with her thick, chestnut brown waves. She winked flirtatiously at her reflection and giggled like the young girl which she still was at heart. Not having felt so excited about anything for as long as she could remember, Dorcus warned herself to put on her normal dreary facade, just in case any of the staff, especially Rosemary, should become suspicious of her enthusiastic mood. She decided to keep her attire and hairstyle simple for this special day, nothing too flamboyant or fussy; she felt wild and reckless; this day's secret liaison had been planned almost four months ago when she'd attended the Christmas ball. She could feel her entire body tingling with excitement as she closed her eyes, remembering the tall and handsome Bartholomew Bagshaw, a rogue amongst the county of Surrey's elite and a man who her husband was so green with envy of that he claimed him to be a fraud, a liar and a man not to be trusted with money or women. Howard's obsessive hatred towards Bartholomew Bagshaw was common knowledge within the Brunswick family which made Dorcus's infatuation with him all the more tantalizing. Howard was a wicked brute of a husband; he showed no respect for women and had practically ignored her existence during the past ten years. Meeting with his sworn enemy gave Dorcus satisfaction in more ways than one. A knock on her bedroom door startled her out of her daydream; it would be her maid Rosemary, no doubt full of ideas on what dress and accessories she should wear for the garden party.

"Come in Rosemary!"

"Good morning Ma'am, I see the young masters have left looking as dashing as their father!"

Dorcus smiled to herself, Rosemary had only recently turned twenty-one but was old fashioned in her ways and phrasings, more so than a woman twice her age.

"Oh my dear, I would consider the young masters to be *far* more dashing and handsome than their father! But keep that to yourself!"

Lost for an appropriate reply, Rosemary quickly changed the subject.

"Have you decided which gown you will be wearing for today's occasion, Ma'am?"

"The ivory, silk with the silver thread embroidery, I think, Rosemary; I want to look like a Roman Goddess today and my fine silver wrap, will also look fetching, don't you think?"

"Oh yes, Ma'am, you will be the envy of every other woman."

"I *do* hope so, Rosemary!" laughed Dorcus.

"How will you be wearing your beautiful hair, Ma'am? May I suggest that I give you some extra height and then leave some pretty ringlets to fall gently on your shoulders?"

Dorcus loved the idea,

"Sounds superb and perhaps you could decorate it with some tiny white buds!"

Half an hour later, Dorcus stood in front of the full-length mirror, twisting and turning to view herself from every possible angle. She loved what she saw; the low cut gown showed off her ample bosom, her hair was lightly pinned up so that with the simple removal of two hairpins, it would tumble down upon her snowy white shoulders. As she slipped her bare feet into the elegant silver slippers, there was just one vital part of her plan which she had yet to address. The staff would view it with extreme suspicion should they not witness her departure from the Brunswick Estate in a carriage but she'd already thought it through and arrived at what she considered a marvellous arrangement.

She pulled hard on the bell cord, bringing Rosemary back, in an instant.

"Rosemary! I have just had the *most brilliant* idea!" she exclaimed jubilantly. "I presume, as is normal on Derby day that Wooten, Barnes and Longworth have already left for the races?"

"Yes Ma'am they left shortly after Mr Brunswick, and the young masters; honestly Ma'am, those men were that excited at the prospect of losing their money! We've heard nothing but horse and winner's talk all week! Was it right for Longworth to go, Ma'am; are you sure that Lady Harrington is sending one of her carriages from Leatherhead for you?"

"Quite certain, Rosemary, I couldn't possibly deny Longworth a day at the races, now could I, which brings me to my idea;"

Rosemary's bright green eyes widened as she listened intently to her mistress.

"I don't see why you and the rest of the female staff should miss out on the fun; there's very little to do here today so I'm suggesting...*no*, not suggesting, *insisting* that you take yourselves into Epsom for the day, the town is simply buzzing at this time of year; there are street shows and delicious delights on sale to savour...*and* as a special token of my appreciation to my dear devoted staff, I'm going to give each one of you a week's wage just to spend on this fun day!"

Rosemary wanted to squeal with joy, already picturing the carnival-like scenes in her mind and becoming excited about showing off her new dress which had taken her most of the winter evenings to sew.

"Thank you, Ma'am, that's so generous, the girls will be thrilled...I'm not too sure about cook though, *she* had it in mind that we'd spend the day cleaning out the scullery and all the kitchen cupboards."

"Then you will have to use your powers of

persuasion, Rosemary!"
"I'll be sure to Ma'am!"

It was approaching midday when Bartholomew
Bagshaw tethered his stallion in the woodland
behind the perimeter wall of the Brunswick
Estate. Climbing onto the saddle he lowered
himself cautiously down the other side of the
wall where the gatehouse was in clear view
before him and the Manor House hidden beyond
the mound of the sloping grounds. Replacing the
thick cape around his muscular body, he hoped
that the position of the key was still where
Dorcus had instructed a few months ago when
the assignation had been prearranged. Staying
close to the wall for a brief moment, he furtively
surveyed the grounds, checking for wandering
staff or garden workers; to his relief, there wasn't
a soul in sight and his clever decision to dress in
shades of moss green and brown proved an
excellent camouflage as he hurried across the
open stretch before reaching the safe seclusion of
the gatehouse. He ran his gloved hand lightly
across the stone lintel smiling wryly as he
retrieved the key. Always the gentleman,
Bartholomew hastily wiped his muddy knee-
length boots on the cast iron boot scraper before
attempting to push the key into the keyhole.
Being larger than most gatehouses and due to it
having stood empty for many months, the
stench of damp immediately filled

Bartholomew's nostrils as he stepped over the threshold. Quickly closing the heavy, squeaky door behind him, he waited motionless in the vestibule, comparing himself to a wild animal as he used every one of his senses to test the safety of his surroundings; the deathly silence convinced him that he was completely alone in the cold and uninviting building. It was not what he'd imagined and knew that if his plan was to be successful, he'd have to at least warm the place up. After inspecting every room, he discovered that the only bed in the house was without bed sheets or blankets and furnished with a scruffy, ripped and mouldy mattress. Every cupboard in the gatehouse was empty and as Bartholomew left the final upstairs bedroom, the pent up excitement which he'd harboured for so many weeks was slowly ebbing away. Deciding that the first room downstairs which he'd entered would be the most suitable, even though the furniture was sparse, he set about kindling a fire. The only good fortune of the day, so far, was that there was an abundance of already chopped firewood, piled up next to the hearth. Kneeling upon the icy stone floor to build up a pile of thin wood splinters, Bartholomew soon had a blazing fire burning, bringing a welcoming warmth to the damp and hostile room.

CHAPTER NINE

The preliminary races had begun in earnest. The crowds of boisterous men stood shoulder to shoulder at the edge of the racecourse, screaming and yelling for their chosen winner to reach the finishing line first and fill their wallets and pockets with some extra money. Wagers were being taken in every available unoccupied spot surrounding the course and as men and boys alike took swigs from their hip flask before every race, it wasn't long before the young and inexperienced drinkers became intoxicated and began picking arguments and brawls with each other. The atmosphere was highly charged and without the presence of a single female, all manners and etiquette were dismissed and young men took to freely swearing obscenities when they lost their bets, blaming each other for coaxing them with false tip-offs. The jubilant winners, however, tossed their top hats into the air, congratulating each other on their skill at picking out a champion.

Bruce and Reginald Brunswick had strayed from their father's circle of associates, they too considered themselves old and wise enough to gamble on a winner; both wanting to prove to Howard Brunswick that he wasn't the only man at Epsom who knew a thing or two about the ability of the fine thoroughbreds. After breaking away from the aristocracy, letting it slip their minds how their fancy attire and distinct accents immediately singled them out, it took little time before a gang of troublemakers from the slums were following them. All four lads had ventured to the yearly races for one reason only; they were quick, nifty and exceptionally light-fingered; all around the same age of fourteen and fifteen and all priding themselves in being able to strip a gentleman of his wallet and pocket watch in a matter of seconds without ever being caught. They were fast-paced runners and could expertly mingle amongst the crowds, appearing wholly innocent to their bystander. Reginald spun around quickly to check on his younger brother who had a habit of becoming sidetracked and lagging behind; he was immediately confronted by two of the rough looking lads as they stood closer than was comfortable to Reginald. Before he'd even had the chance to utter a word of complaint, one of the lads grabbed hold of his throat while the other delved into his pockets, triumphantly robbing Reginald of his monthly allowance. Bruce hurried towards them, his clenched fists ready to strike a blow and rescue his elder brother. Still caught in the clutches of the pickpockets, Reginald was unable to warn Bruce that he too was being ambushed. The other two lads were already close behind him, laughing mockingly at his pathetic stance as he

endeavoured to appear tough and fearless.
Before Bruce had reached his brother the ruffian
had pounced on him from behind, causing Bruce
to fall face-first into the wet and muddy ground.
Like a pack of hyenas, all four jeered as Bruce
struggled to get to his feet. While one of the
scoundrels wedged him down with his boot,
another emptied his pockets.
"Now get lost yer bloody little toff!" they yelled at
Bruce.
He stood up, noticing that they still had hold of
Reginald. He was terrified; his eyes filled up
with tears and he felt nauseous; he wanted his
mother's comfort and love and felt a sudden
hatred for the male-dominated and rowdy
racecourse. As much as he knew he should have
stayed to help his brother, being younger and
smaller in stature than Reginald he was sure that
he'd be of no use. He ran and ran until he was
far from the crowds and alone on the moors.
Reginald watched his brother disappear into the
crowds, sensing that he was not going to rejoin
their father. His concern for Bruce had
temporarily distracted him from the dire
situation which he was in until an uncouth voice
declared,
"You're little brother is a bloody girl! An' you
ain't much better yer toffee-nosed little snob!
You people make me wanna throw up!"
The villain made an animal like sound
accompanied by some odd facial movements

before he proceeded to project the contents of his mouth into Reginald's face.

"Now piss off, toff!"

The rest of the gang all broke into laughter once again, as Reginald was thrust into the crowds, with his face dripping with thick phlegm.

Knowing from experience what it was like to come under the angry fire from his father, especially when there was cause for him to be embarrassed in public, Reginald made the best attempt to straighten out his dishevelled clothes and neaten up his appearance, he wiped his face with his handkerchief, surprisingly the only item on him which had not been stolen; it was discarded immediately, as he cringed at its unpleasant sight. By the time Reginald reached his father, he'd had time to think up what he hoped would be a plausible story.

Howard looked concerned, "Where's Brucie?"

Reginald tried his best to sound relaxed in his tone, "He said that he had a terrible stomach ache, Father and wished to go home...there was no stopping him, he just bolted like a startled mare and I lost all sight of him in the crowds!"

"Confounded boy! Should have left him at home with the women!"

"I'm sure he'll be safe, Father, there are so many people about today; he's bound to get a ride home from someone!"

Howard observed his son for a while, his

expression serious enough to cause Reginald's legs to wobble beneath him as he silently prayed that his father believed him and that Bruce hadn't gone and done anything foolhardy.

The silence was suddenly broken as a new wave of excitement ran through the crowds; it was nearly time for the main race of the day and as the menfolk hurried to place their bets and increase wagers already set, Howard Brunswick's tense face eased.

"Have you backed a horse yet son?"

"I had a spot of bad luck, Father. I'm afraid I don't have your expertise at recognizing a winner and have lost my entire allowance on a mare that came in second to last!"

Howard threw back his head, laughing loudly; he felt proud that his son held him in such high esteem.

"Not to worry, my boy, what say *you* choose the winner for the 1796 Derby?"

"Do you *really* trust me to pick a winner after what I just disclosed, Father?"

"Of course, you're my son; it's in your blood!"

Reginald nervously eyed one of the nearby chalkboards, reading through the names.

"My money's on *Didelot*, Father!" he declared confidently, with his fingers firmly crossed behind his back.

Yet again, Howard Brunswick laughed heartedly finding his son amusing.

"I wouldn't wager on Didelot, Reggi, for the

simple reason that the jockey, John Arnull has won twice before; nobody can be that lucky to win three times!"

"Maybe I'll put my money on *Spread Eagle* then, he appears to be rather popular!"

"Oh no, my boy! Your first choice it must be! Just imagine that by some miracle Didelot wins, you might hold it against me for the rest of my days!" joked Howard.

Blinded by his tears, Bruce kept up a steady pace in the same direction, never once lifting his hanging head. Feeling enraged and humiliated he went over in his mind where he'd gone wrong when trying to save his brother from the ghastly slum boys. He'd waited for this day since Christmas and now it had ended in disaster and what would probably mean another beating later on that evening from his Father. He wondered what Reginald had said, he could usually rely on him to come up with a viable excuse to save his skin. Reginald was the best of brothers and the fact that it had been beyond his capability to put up a fight for him only added to his feelings of failure and mood of gloominess. Desperate to be in the company of his mother, Bruce now regretted ever going to the Derby races and vowed never to revisit such a hostile gathering again.

As time passed by, the sound of carriage wheels upon the dusty track brought him out of his reverie, he looked up for the first time, surprised at how far he'd walked; he was on the edge of Epsom town and hadn't the slightest idea of which direction he should head in, in order to take him back to Bagley village. A carriage suddenly halted alongside him; Bruce looked up, praying that it was perhaps his father who'd come in search of him; he was mistaken and viewed the carriage window which seemed to be full of pretty women all peering out at him; the door swung open but it was an elderly woman who stuck her head out, squinting through her sunken eyes in the sunlight.

"Would you care for a..." she hiccupped loudly and then giggled. A younger woman took over; she was pretty with a pleasant, smiley face.

"What my grandmother was trying to say, little man, was…Oh goodness...what *were* you going to say Grandmamma?"

She too disappeared back into the carriage leaving Bruce stood to listen to, what sounded like a dozen women, all giggling out of control.

"Climb aboard young man, we'll take you to *wherever* you are going!" called out another woman as she waved and gestured for Bruce to ascend into the luxurious carriage.

Feeling embarrassed and slightly wary of accepting their offer, after a brief second of contemplation, Bruce removed his top hat and allowed the women to haul him up into the safety of their carriage. All dressed in the prettiest gowns which Bruce had ever seen, the four attractive and giggly young women began fussing over him as though he were their pet. The older woman continued to laugh and hiccup and occasionally burst into song, which in turn caused the rest of the women to fall about in more bouts of giggles.

"Where are you heading, sweet boy?" asked one of the tipsy women as she patted down his dishevelled hair with the flat of her silky gloved hand.

"Bagley village," he replied instantly, already sensing that his face had turned bright red from embarrassment.

"Ahh! Did you hear that Charlotte, he's almost our neighbour!"

"Such an adorable little man, I do declare!" expressed Charlotte, trying her utmost to speak without slurring her words.

"Do you live in Epsom?" enquired Bruce.

The woman continued to work on Bruce's attire, brushing off the mud and quickly soiling her expensive gloves.

"You're awfully muddy!" she declared. "Did you fall or were you pushed?"

Another round of hysterical giggles began; Bruce failed to see what was so amusing about the woman's question.

"Oh, *Selina*, leave the poor boy alone, he's turned as red as a strawberry!"

"Oh, so he has!" acknowledged Selina, making

way for more chuckles.

Loud snores suddenly sounded over the laughter; the old woman had fallen asleep and was being propped up by the other two, dazed-looking women, who had not spoken a word but only giggled throughout the journey.

"We reside in Leatherhead, dear boy!" stated Selina.

Bruce's face lit up, "That's where my mother has gone today!"

Selina eyes widened, *"I hope she hasn't gone to call on us, because we're not in!"*

Another eruption of giggles followed and as they reached the edge of Bagley village where Bruce was familiar with the surroundings, he felt a huge relief to alight from the stuffy carriage and break free from the drunken women.

CHAPTER TEN

Keeping close to the hedgerows, Bruce scurried through the village, hoping not to meet any of his father's tenants; it was unusually empty; a few women were toiling the land but today was a day when most of the menfolk took time away from their farming to attend the Derby, all hoping to arrive back home a little wealthier. Releasing a huge sigh of relief, Bruce couldn't remember a time when he'd felt so comforted to see the sight of the Manor House before his eyes. He hurried towards the back entrance, in the hope of being able to dodge past the few female staff at home on this day and quickly reach his bedroom where he could change his clothes and wash off the mud from his hands and face. The thrill of reaching home infused him with a burst of energy as he raced up the long pathway, imagining that he was a competing horse, winning from the start, but discovering that all doors were locked and that the entire house appeared empty immediately reclaimed all feelings of jubilation. Bruce couldn't understand it...his home was never locked during the daylight hours. He continued to pummel the door with his fists until they felt numb and painful. He threw gravel up at the windows, but still, nobody answered. His last resort was to wander around to the stables with the smallest hope that one of the stable hands had chosen not to attend the Derby but yet again the place was deserted.

After assuring himself that before long somebody was bound to return home, Bruce made his way to the far side of the grounds where he'd be able to see clearly when someone arrived, without being noticed. Feeling sleepy from his long trek, he nestled down next to the ivy-covered wall. The weak spring sun warmed his mud splashed face as he made a mental list of all the food which he intended to feast upon when somebody eventually showed up. His stomach flipped in hungry somersaults.

Only a few minutes had passed before the smoke wafting out of the gatehouse chimney caught Bruce's attention. It puzzled him, nobody was living in the gatehouse, he knew that for certain because he remembered the terrible fuss his mother had made when Father had suggested to her that they should allow the new gardener and his wife to live there. He clearly remembered her protests that the shabby interior of the gatehouse would reflect badly on her image as Mistress of the Brunswick Estate; she'd suggested that she would arrange for work to be carried out in the springtime. Bruce could still picture his father's annoyed face and remember the way he'd shouted at his mother, "For God's sake, Dorcus, why are you being such a cold-hearted bitch! Cresswell is a damned skilled gardener, one off the best we've had and I don't want to lose him! He wants a bloody roof over his head; his wife is near her confinement! Do you think he gives a damn about a bit of mould and flaky walls, *you ridiculous bloody mare!*"

Bruce felt a tight knot in his empty belly, just from reminiscing about the events of that day; he loathed his father when he was so horrid to his mother; she'd had tears in her eyes but, his father had found a temporary place for Cresswell and his pregnant wife in the village and his mother had been the victor.

Perhaps the gardener and his wife *had* already moved into the gatehouse, he mused and maybe they might invite him in and offer some food, he thought. Bruce dwelled on the matter for less than a few seconds, before racing across the open grounds, feeling the pleasant warm breeze upon his face.

He was soon stood outside the front door of the gatehouse, its old paintwork was badly faded and the handle tarnished and rusty. Feeling on edge as to whether he should be so bold and knock, he gingerly tiptoed towards the window; it was filthy, with only the bright orange flames of the fire visible; everything else was obscure. The muted sound of a woman's voice from inside had an immediately calming effect on Bruce; he hurried back to the door and gently pushed on it. Finding it unlocked, Bruce stepped over the threshold into the tiny tiled vestibule before proceeding into the stifling heat of the parlour. He froze in shock...staring in confusion at the horrendous sight which filled his eyes and paralysed his entire body. *Was that his mother?* Her face and hair looked familiar, but he'd never in his life witnessed so much of her bare flesh. She was completely naked. He watched in horror, his throat becoming so dry that he felt as though he was choking.

Suddenly convinced that the beast of a man was trying to kill her, he forced his voice to project across the room,

"Leave my mother alone!" he yelled, still unable to move his legs.

All movement before his eyes immediately halted; the man peered scornfully over his bare shoulder and his mother hid her face from Bruce's view.

Bruce gasped loudly as the familiar face of his father's sworn enemy, Bartholomew Bagshaw became apparent. His wicked eyes glared angrily as Bruce suddenly hurried towards him, his fists clenched tightly. This time he would fight like a lion he told himself and would not suffer another humiliation like earlier that day. Dorcus Brunswick scurried away as she struggled to cover her modesty with Bartholomew's cloak precariously hanging from her exposed body as she fled up the stone staircase. Bruce continuously plunged his fists into Bartholomew's bare chest; it was almost as though he was striking a marble statue with his punches having little effect on the man's muscular torso. Suddenly grabbing Bruce by the belt of his pantaloons, Bartholomew hoisted him high above his head with one hand as though he'd caught a rodent by its tail. As Bruce kicked and screamed, demanding to be put down immediately, Bartholomew suddenly released his firm hold, causing Bruce to bounce off his elbow and topple headfirst into the leaping flames. The torturous pain was like no other that Bruce had experienced in his twelve years. He surreptitiously took hold of the poker, slamming it down onto Bartholomew's body. The blow just caught his shoulder, causing him to wince from the agony, but at the same time enraging him even more.

"*You bloody little brat!* I'll teach you a lesson on how to respect your elders when they're having fun. *Four bloody months* I've waited to have your *whore of a mother!*"

"*I hate you!*" Bruce hollered. "And my father thinks you're a rotten, cheating scoundrel...and so do I!"

His entire body felt as though it was burning, his tears spilt over but he was determined to inflict a painful punishment on Bartholomew.

Bartholomew stood to his feet, retrieving the poker; he pushed it deep into the centre of the fire before picking Bruce up again.

"You are *never* to mention me to your idiot

father! *Is that clear?*"

"No, it's not," replied Bruce, defiantly.

"Then I will make sure that the entire county and surrounding counties hear what a cheap whore your dear *mother* really is...your father will be as shamed as she will be! Your family will be ruined!"

Yanking the poker from the fire, he ordered Bruce to open his mouth. Terrified, Bruce clamped his lips together firmly. Bartholomew waved the glowing poker in front of his face, a sinister look washing over him like a murky cloud. As he touched the red hot iron bar upon the soft skin of Bruce's cheek, Bruce was unable to contain his screams of sheer agony and his open mouth was an invitation for Bartholomew to push the poker into the cavity. The moment Bruce heard the sizzling sound and smelt his burning flesh, he passed out, bringing Dorcus hurrying back downstairs, looking on aghast.

"What have you done! He's just a boy for goodness sake!"

Bartholomew calmly began to put on his discarded shirt, taking his time as he looked on in disgust at Dorcus's feeble attempts to revive her son.

"Help me, Bartholomew, for the love of God, help me. I fear he will die!" she screamed hysterically.

"Help *yourself* you worthless bitch!"

In her anger, Dorcus picked up the discarded poker and hurled it through the air hoping to inflict some pain onto the heartless man who only half an hour before, she had willingly given herself to. She felt such shame, he was not the compassionate man that she'd mistaken him for; he was a cad and she was no better than a common harlot and was already being severely punished for her sins.

Able to dodge out of the poker's pathway as it hurtled through the air, Bartholomew sniggered wickedly,

"I will always remember this afternoon, Dorcus; it has taught me two most valuable lessons; never to become involved with a woman with young and foolish children again and that paying for my pleasure far outweighs a pathetic desperate whore, like yourself!"

"*Get out! Get out of my sight!*" screeched Dorcus catching her breath between each uncontrollable sob. Clutching her unconscious son in her arms, convinced that his soul had already left his young body, Dorcus rocked back and forth as she cried out in desperation. Bartholomew made no haste in leaving, seeming to enjoy every second of Dorcus's heartbreak. She hung her head over her son and remained in that position until she heard the squeak of the door close behind him.

Darkness began to fall, as the final tiny flickers of the fire dwindled and died. Dorcus hadn't moved and continued to cradle her beloved son in her arms, blinded by her tears and oblivious to anything else that was going on outside the confines of the gatehouse.

Howard and Reginald, along with the staff had returned home and as word soon travelled through the Manor House everyone became concerned about the whereabouts of young Bruce. With there still being no sign of Dorcus's return, it was presumed that Lady Harrington's garden party had been extended to an inside 'game of bridge' evening and not wanting to alarm Dorcus, Howard insisted that they would not send word to her and ruin her evening just yet. As his concerns for Bruce increased with every passing hour, Howard's annoyance that Reginald had chosen the winning horse soon diminished. He continued to question Reginald about Bruce's departure from the racecourse and with his ever-increasing concern that perhaps the gang of slum boys was behind his brother's disappearance, Reginald decided that now was the time to explain exactly what had taken place. Becoming more anxious than he cared to show, the thought that perhaps Bruce had returned home, upset, only to find the house locked up made him ponder on the possibility that he may have made his way to Lady Harrington's home in Leatherhead. Dorcus would be sure to return shortly, Howard considered and until then he would pin all his hope on them returning home together.

CHAPTER ELEVEN

Bruce's pitiful cries brought Dorcus out of her trance.

"Oh my darling, my darling boy, my precious baby! Mother is here at your side my darling, Mamma will make it all better, *I promise*!" Dorcus croaked, deliriously, taken by complete shock to see one of Bruce's eyelids lift and to discover that he was still alive.

Unable to utter a word, Bruce's agony was etched upon his horrendous looking face and rigid body. His once handsome young face was bright red with raw open blisters to the worse affected side; one of his eyes was embedded in the huge and painful swelling and the severely singed remains of his hair fell from his scalp like powder. Dorcus was beside herself, as to what she should do. It was paramount that she should retain her reputation and prevent a scandal no matter what and she knew she must compose herself and put on an act that nothing untoward had happened. But at the same time, she also had to do the best she could to save her son's precious life; she was in a quandary as she tried to take a grip of her emotions.

Suddenly realising that she was still half-naked, Dorcus managed to muster up some inner strength and drag Bruce up onto the worn-out couch. It was small but made an adequate bed for Bruce's stature. His continuous, harrowing cries sounded unlike any sound she'd ever heard before; they were chilling and caused every hair on her skin to stand up. Bruce was in the most dreadful pain and Dorcus knew she had to somehow retrieve a supply of whiskey and laudanum from the Manor House. She vaguely remembered there used to be a water pump to the rear of the property and prayed that unlike most items in the gatehouse, it hadn't become riddled with rust. Taking her silk wrap with her, Dorcus cried tears of relief to find that even though it appeared in disrepair, it was still in working order. She splashed the cooling water upon her face and hands, before soaking her wrap. She found a large glass jug in the pantry, infested with old cobwebs, dead bugs and a layer of grime, but with her frantic efforts, it was soon clean enough to fill with drinking water. For a few seconds, as Dorcus carefully wrapped the length of fine French silk around Bruce's head and face, his crying ceased.

"I'm going to take such good care of you, my precious boy..." The painful swelling in her throat made it impossible to say any more; the look of horror in Bruce's one eye was like that of a sharp dagger piercing her heart. Never before had Dorcus experienced such feelings of guilt and in that instant, she made a solemn vow to herself that if there were no signs of improvement to her beloved son within a week, she would end both of their lives and should he not survive, she would join him in the next life. She gently covered his body with a curtain, pulled down from one of the upstairs rooms and attempted to let him drink the cooling water by allowing droplets to fall from her fingers onto his swollen lips. Covering his hand with kisses, Dorcus felt reluctant to leave his side and return to the house as she wondered what was going on in their absence; had they returned early from the Derby for some reason, or did they presume that Bruce was with her?

The cold night air felt bracing upon her skin as she strolled across the dewy grass towards the house. She was in no hurry to meet with the onslaught of questions which would be asked the moment she stepped over the threshold. How would she keep her composure when the only image which filled her head was that of her badly burnt son, who may not even survive the night. All she wanted was to be left alone but knew that would be impossible, especially when she'd have to put on an act of concern about her son's whereabouts.

The house was quiet and to her relief, none of the staff was anywhere in sight. She took off her slippers and raced up the stairs. Rosemary had left the candles burning in her room and a fire had been kindled. It was the first time she'd taken stock of her dress; it was filthy; soot and bloodstains covered the pretty gown and it reeked of smoke. Quickly undressing and discarding the soiled gown into an empty hatbox, Dorcus put on a pretty floral gown which she considered more suited for a garden party. After brushing and rearranging her hair as best she could she sprayed her favourite perfume liberally, hoping to camouflage the smoky odour which still lingered on her skin and hair. Back downstairs, she took a deep breath before entering the drawing-room where she could hear Howard and Reginald's voices. "Good evening, my dears," she said, casually on entering.

Howard stared at her; she suddenly felt uncomfortable, sensing that she appeared guilty. "We didn't hear the carriage arriving!" stated Howard, sounding more like a detective than a husband pleased to see the return of his wife. "Where's Brucie, has he gone to bed?" she asked, innocently, noticing how Howard's brow creased with worry.

"We thought he was with you, Mamma!" exclaimed Reginald, distraughtly.

"What could you possibly mean? He accompanied *you* to the races!"

Howard and Reginald exchanged nervous eye contact.

"There was an incident...at the races...some young scoundrels set upon our boys and robbed them; Bruce ran off."

Dorcus took a loud gasp, covering her open

mouth with her hand,

"Why didn't you go after him then? Why aren't you out looking for him?"

"Take a grip of yourself, *woman*; we presumed that he'd gone in search of you and that you and he would arrive home together!"

"Oh don't be so ridiculous, Howard; I doubt he even knew where I was...How could you just sit about and do nothing? *He could be anywhere!"*

It wasn't difficult for Dorcus to erupt into a state of delirious sobs; in her mind's eye, she could see only one image, an image which would haunt her for the rest of her days.

Leaping out of his chair, with his hand raised high Reginald was eager to interrupt his parents as a thought had suddenly crossed his mind.

"What is it, Reggi, can't you see how *distressed* your poor mother is!" shouted Howard, belligerently.

"But I've had an idea of where he might have gone, Pappa!"

Both Howard and Dorcus focussed their attention on Reginald, allowing him to voice his theory.

"I think that he probably made his way back here, and when he found the Manor House was shut up and there wasn't a sign of any of the staff, he went to the gatehouse...I bet he fell asleep after the long walk back from Epsom!"

"That's an absurd assumption, Reggi!" declared Dorcus in a concealed state of panic.

"Your mother's quite right, Reggi, besides, the gatehouse has been locked up for months now and…"

"But we went inside it a few weeks ago, we found the key on the ledge above the door."

"Why didn't you tell me that you'd been there, Reginald?" cried Dorcus.

"Calm down, woman, Reginald might just possibly be correct, his suggestion is certainly worth looking into in the first instance!"

"Come along Reggi, we'll both go, no point in waking up the staff now at this late hour," voiced Howard, feeling a glimmer of hope for the first time all evening.

"Well since you insist, while you're there, have a quick look to see if my silk wrap is there, I'm quite sure I left it behind last week when I was assessing the old place for renovation."

Howard shot a mean and suspicious glance at Dorcus, finding it quite difficult to fathom his cold-blooded wife.

"*For God's sake!* Now is not the time to be searching for your damned accessories, Dorcus...*our son is missing!* Reginald, bring the table lantern; let's be on our way!"

Dorcus gulped down three glasses of port; her heart was pounding behind her ribs and the acidic bile had risen into the back of her throat; her hands trembled uncontrollably as she refilled her glass for the fourth time and her mind seemed to have gone completely blank as she tried to think of what she'd say when they returned with the grim news about Bruce. A few long and painful minutes passed, with Dorcus sat staring into space, her mind in a tangle before she decided that the best way would be to act in complete surprise as though she knew nothing; after all, Bruce was unable to talk and when and if he recovered, she would deal with the problem of him disclosing her shame when it arose. She remained calm, in readiness to react accordingly when confronted with the tragedy.

Over the following weeks, Reginald kept a constant vigil by his brother's side, he'd asked the staff to move his bed into Bruce's room to enable him to spend every minute of the night and day close by. Feeling partly responsible for what had happened, even though his parents assured him that it wasn't remotely his fault, Reginald was completely heartbroken by the terrible scene which had confronted him and his father on entering the gatehouse and desperate to have his brother back to the way he used to be; he missed him terribly and when, after a couple of months had passed and he appeared to be improving steadily, he couldn't understand why his mother insisted that he should be sent to a boarding school far away from Surrey. It had disappointed him how distant and unconcerned his mother had appeared to be regarding Bruce, after her initial display of hysterics. There was no reasoning with his parents, his brother was still unable to talk properly and his face was badly disfigured but four months after that dismal Derby day, Reginald hugged his brother goodbye, knowing that they would only spend holidays together from now on.

Even though it has been concluded that Bruce had taken shelter in the gatehouse that day, lit a fire and then accidentally fallen into it, Reginald spent many hours dwelling on the harrowing scenes and there were many things which simply didn't add up. The doctor had also been puzzled as to why there was so much severe burning on the inside of his mouth, Reginald had thought it strange how his brother's head had been carefully wrapped in his mother's shawl and that there was a jug of water by his side. He was also convinced that Bruce would never have bothered to light a fire; it hadn't been a cold day and he'd never lit a fire in his life and probably had no idea on how to kindle one. His mother's entire attitude was another puzzle to him; she had been quite aloof with everyone and had also sacked her maid, Rosemary, claiming that she'd been spreading malicious gossip about the incident amongst the staff. She had spent little time at her son's bedside and had been more concerned as to when he would be able to speak once more. Reginald didn't consider himself to be a detective, but even *he* knew that there was a mystery behind the entire grim business.

Bruce's visits home became fewer and far between over the years, there always seemed to be a friend or teacher who'd invited him home for the holidays and although he continued to correspond with him and his parents, Reginald was quite sure that his mother kept some of these letters to herself; she had also secretly instructed all correspondence from Bruce to be given directly to her.

The Derby day incident had completely changed Bruce's personality, even more as he grew from a boy into a man. He had developed an inner hatred for all women although he thrived on the chase for them, wanting desperately to be loved but having no respect for any woman who should come into his life. His unfortunate appearance had also made a huge impact on his state of mind; he was ugly and he knew that the entire world viewed him as a deformed cripple, which had a poisoning effect upon his character, making him believe that no woman would ever fall in love with him but at the same time, his lowly view of the female race seemed to direct his life along a very crooked path, a path which showed no mercy on any of his female acquaintances.

Unknown to Dorcus, Howard Brunswick continued to pay Bruce a healthy yearly

allowance up until he passed away; Dorcus had had no contact at all with him since he'd reached his thirties and it was only after the death of their father that Bruce wrote a long letter to Reginald explaining exactly everything which had taken place on the day of the Derby in 1796, omitting nothing. The letter shocked Reginald to his core; he found it hard to believe how Bruce had paid so dearly for his mother's infidelity, which had consequently ruined his life.
Bruce had begged that Reginald should not mention this to their mother and that he should continue life as though he knew nothing of the sorry past and the huge secret. During the weeks which followed, Reginald found it impossible to make eye contact with his now aged and frail mother; how could any mother treat her son in such a harsh and wicked way, he continuously mused. The truth had hurt him badly, leaving him feeling like a thief, who'd stolen his brother's share of everything while Bruce's torment had been the cause of his downfall.

It was in the last few weeks of Dorcus's life when Reginald eventually confronted her, asking her to explain to him exactly what had happened on that day so many years ago. Shaken that Reginald should bring up this subject after so many decades had passed by, Dorcus was unable to hide her secret any longer. Already harbouring her suspicions that Reginald had discovered the truth, knowing that Bruce remained in contact with him. She begged Reginald to allow her to go to her grave with a little dignity. Dorcus's only wish was that he would always withhold the truth from his wife and her three grandchildren.

Although feeling a little compassion towards his mother as he listened to her choking as she relived the terrible events of that day, Reginald knew that in his heart he would never quite be able to forgive her. The decisions she'd insisted upon during the months which followed that awful day had only proved what a selfish woman she was, caring only about her reputation and future while disregarding poor Bruce's mental and physical well-being at all costs.

A week later Dorcus Brunswick died in her sleep and her terrible crime remained the secret of her two sons forever. Reginald insisted that Bruce should take his rightful place back at the Brunswick Estate, which he accepted, provided he could live in the gatehouse, a request which Reginald found difficult to believe after all that had taken place there.

CHAPTER TWELVE

Silas Shepherd left the Brunswick Estate, angry and confused as to why the Squire had doubted Frank's innocence; Frank maybe a handful at the moment, but he was certainly no poacher, pondered Silas. Not wishing to arrive home until he'd had enough time to compose himself and come up with a solution to what they should do with baby George, Silas took the horse's reins in hand and dawdled along the dirt track. The earlier drizzle which had now transformed into pelting rain amidst gunmetal skies didn't induce him into increasing his speed or mounting his horse; he was beyond care and so in-depth in his thoughts and unsure as to what course of action he should take for the wellbeing of his family. All of a sudden, his responsibilities felt as heavy as the oppressive skies above him. He prayed that Claire would be able to suggest some ideas which might save them from a life living under the demands of the unsavoury Bruce Brunswick. If only he'd never returned to Bagley village seven years ago, thought Silas, the Squire had been far more amicable and the villagers lived without the fear of what Squinty eye was capable of inflicting on them with his scheming, blackmailing ways.

After giving the horse a rub down and a nose bag of oats, Silas left the barn, determined on displaying a lighter mood in front of his family. Greeted by noisy pandemonium, with everyone eagerly awaiting his arrival with a question or complaint, his more serious problem was temporarily pushed to the back of his mind.

"Frank won't let me dress his leg, Pa; he said he'd sooner lose it than let me touch it!" protested Martha, hiding her inner relief of her brother's negative reaction.

"I don't need my little sister to inflict more damage on me! Thanks all the same!" defended Frank. "I'm capable of dressing my own leg...and I'm not as squeamish as Martha is."

"Martha won't let me go up and see Ma!" cried Amy, her tears streaming down her face as she sat in front of a half-eaten bowl of porridge.

"Ma is busy feeding the babies!" stated Jane, as she assisted Martha with the housework.

Amy hurried to her pa, wrapping her arms around him as she sobbed fervently.

"*Amy!* You're such a silly girl! Can't you see that Pa is wet through and needs to get out of his clothes before he catches a chill?" shrieked Martha, mimicking her mother's commonly used turn of phrase.

Silas prized his clinging daughter from off his soaked through body,

"Now, now Amy, finish your breakfast and then we'll go up and see your ma together."

A gleaming smile instantly overtook her sorrowful face. "Can I tell you a secret, Pa?"

Amy cupped her chubby hands in readiness to whisper into her pa's ear once he'd bent down low enough; Martha and Jane looked on, suspiciously, wondering what tales were about to be told.

"Martha put too much salt in the porridge, it tastes horrible!" she whispered, her eyes straying towards her on looking sisters.

Managing to conceal his smile, Silas rubbed Amy's button nose with his thumb; he felt sorry for all of his children, their world had been turned upside down over the last few days and they were all trying their best to help, with the exception of Frank, who seemed intent to continue proving that he was now a young man, who was no longer in need of his family's love and support. In Silas's opinion, he was going about it in the completely wrong way.

"How about you help Martha prepare a tray of tea and a bite to eat for your Ma and me; I need to have a private talk with her, and then, I promise, you can spend a little time with her." Amy liked her pa's idea.

"I already took up a tray of tea and porridge, Pa!" Martha expressed, annoyingly.

"I'm sure she could quite easily eat another light meal, Martha; it's hungry work feeding two babies you know!" said Silas, feeling sorry for his poor wife having to eat the salty porridge, knowing that she'd not wish to upset Martha's feelings by not emptying the bowl.

There was little sound emanating from upstairs; grateful for the peace, Silas hoped it would mean he could discuss the urgent matter which faced their family and gently inform Claire of the Squire's unexpected reaction to Bruce Brunswick's hostile letter. He prayed with all his heart that Claire would be able to come up with a solution to their imminent problem.

Finding baby Grace sleeping in her mother's arms, while baby George, slept soundly in the drawer, Silas longed to share a private uninterrupted moment with his beloved wife; he missed her so much, and was feeling quite alone. Her warm smile touched his soul; he wished with all his heart that there was a way he could protect his entire family from the evil of the world which had never felt more apparent than during these past few days. He stood motionless for a while in pure admiration of the heartwarming scene, before gently sitting on the edge of the bed.

"I'm planning to come downstairs, this afternoon," she declared in a small voice. "I've had more than enough rest, Silas; I need to put our family in order again!"

"It's too soon, my darling, you must make a full recovery first...don't worry about us, it may sound as though we're in a pickle, but believe me, Claire, everything *is* in order."

"*Chaotic order, no doubt!* Besides, the girls want to go to school and I'm sure there must be some jobs for Frank around the farm, he's quite capable of walking with the aid of a stick...His injury hasn't deterred him from his Sunday walks with Sarah, after all."

As Silas tried to prevent her from leaving her bed, to return baby Grace to her crib, Claire gently pushed his arm away,

"Silas, please don't fuss so, I've given birth, not suffered the plague and I'm still young and healthy my love!"

"Very well then, but we need to talk, Claire."

"By the look on your face, Silas Shepherd, you didn't receive the reaction you were hoping for from the Squire?"

"You were right, Claire, I must be a fool to have even considered that Reginald Brunswick would take my side over his scoundrel of a brother...why in God's name did he ever have to bring him back to reside in this neck of the woods again?"

"Because, my darling, he is the Squire's only brother and as I said, blood *is* thicker than water; none of us knows the truth about Squinty Eye...many of the older folk say that he was a well-liked boy before he went into hiding, after his much 'hushed up' *accident*."

"Well, the past is behind us, and the future doesn't bode well for the Shepherd family with the likes of *Bruce bloody Brunswick* breathing down our necks, making threats left, right and centre!"

Claire was deep in thought as she sipped her tea. Silas looked on pleasingly at the peaceful babies, hoping that they'd remain asleep while Claire was dwelling on their worrying predicament.
"For the time being, Silas, I think we should return our lives to some kind of normality before we have the entire village wondering what's happened to us and all the busybodies emerge from the woodwork!"
Silas couldn't help laughing.
"What's so amusing?"
"You have such a comical way with your phrases!"
"*Silas!* This is a very serious matter you know!"
"I know, I know my darling, but it does feel good to laugh for a change, my lovely wife!"
"Shall I continue to enlighten you with my ideas, or are you simply going to find everything I say hysterical?"
"Please, continue," begged Silas in a stern tone.
Claire took a deep breath, "I, for one, couldn't bear to part with little George...I've held him to my breast and treated him in the same way as Grace; he's like one of my own and I can guarantee that I won't sleep well in my bed knowing that he's in some abysmal orphanage. We must tell the children that he is their new brother and Grace's twin. It is vital that *all* of us keep to the same story; we'll call it our family secret, which must never be disclosed to a living soul."

Silas sat motionlessly, his full attention
absorbed with Claire's suggestion.

"You must take Frank aside," she continued,
"show him the letter from Bruce Brunswick...

"The Squire ripped it up in front of me!"
interrupted, Silas.

"*Oh no!* How typical of a bias magistrate, now
it's just our word against his and we *all know*
who has the upper hand!" Claire's suddenly
amplified voice disturbed both Grace and
George in their slumber.

They reverted to whispers as, thankfully, the
babies resumed their sleep.

"Well, you'll just have to explain in your own
words how his little escapade into the
Brunswick Estate, which was most likely a
heroic show in front of his sweetheart, has
caused irreparable damage to our family!"

Silas released a downhearted sigh, "The way
Frank is these days... I have a strong feeling that
he's not going to believe a word I say!"

"Oh, Silas, you'd hardly invent such a letter;
surely Frank's not pigheaded enough to think
that! "

The bedroom door slowly opened, just enough
for Amy to squeeze her head through the
narrow opening.

"Can I see Ma now?" she pleaded, timidly.

"Of course you can my sweet girl, come here and
let me kiss your pretty face!"

The elated seven-year-old ran to her mother's

side, loving every second as Claire embraced her, kissing her full cheeks.

"I think a family meeting this afternoon, then?" confirmed Claire.

"Are you leaving your sickbed Ma?" questioned Amy in cheerful disbelief.

"Yes, my darling, I'm leaving my sickbed!" laughed Claire, as she planted another kiss on top of Amy's head.

CHAPTER THIRTEEN

It was just after three o'clock when the family
meeting took place. Having fed and changed
both babies, Claire prayed that they'd sleep
contentedly for the next hour or so; she was
looking forward to joining the family hub once
more, it felt much longer than a couple of days
since she'd given birth to Grace. The girls were
over excited; Martha had made a fresh loaf that
morning, a fresh pot of tea was brewing and
Jane and Amy had picked a bunch of pink and
yellow primroses which now adorned the centre
of the table.
Claire's heart blossomed with love as she
witnessed her beloved children all sitting like
angels waiting for her to join them. Silas
had assisted his wobbly wife down the stairs
and into her chair which had been caringly lined
with a folded blanket with another one ready to
be draped over her shoulders, even though the
kitchen felt as warm as a summer's day. A
sudden chorus of joyful greetings erupted with
Amy finding it all too difficult to follow
Martha's strict instructions that she was to stay
in her seat, as she suddenly felt the need to
perform a short on the spot skip and dance.
Martha was being quite the '*mother*' of the house
as she turned over the cups of the Shepherd
family's Sunday best tea set in readiness to pour

the tea. The fresh loaf she'd baked earlier had already been cut into irregular slices and buttered liberally.

"Offer Ma and Pa a shive of bread, Jane!" ordered Martha as she proceeded to pour the tea.

Claire and Silas exchanged a proud glance. Meanwhile, Frank slouched carelessly in his chair, making grunts of annoyance as he watched his sister's efforts to act grown up and sophisticated, ignoring the occasional furtive glares which he received from his father.

"What a lovely spread!" exclaimed Claire, smiling warmly at her girls.

"Does the bread taste fine, Ma?" enquired Martha.

"My darling, your baking skills have surpassed mine!"

"What does that mean?" asked Amy in a small voice, her mouth already full of bread and plum jam.

"*It means that she's better than Ma at baking,*" voiced Frank mockingly, "but we all know that Ma's just being kind!"

Nobody took much notice of Frank's callous remark, especially when they were all too happy to allow anything to ruin the day.

"I helped spread the butter!" declared Amy.

"And you have spread just the right amount my darling. What about you Jane?"

"Oh, I just followed orders from Martha and

washed up every bowl, plate and mug that we have at least ten times! Are you going to come back downstairs every day now Ma?"

Claire sensed an immediate understanding of the pecking order in her absence, feeling sorry for Jane who was not a girl to complain easily and generally went about her chores in a methodical way.

"That's entirely up to your Ma and how she feels; if she wants to spend the next week in bed, then so be it!" interrupted Silas not wanting the children to inflict a guilty pressure upon Claire to return to the running of the house. "When she *does* decide that she's feeling quite up to the task, I want you girls to know that you'll all have to give your ma far more help than you did before the arrival of your new sister and brother!"

"*Brother!*" exclaimed Frank, suddenly bolting up straight in his chair. "That *stray* upstairs, is *no* brother of mine and *never* will be, so don't expect me to treat him like one of this family, because he's not!"

Both Jane and Amy took a sharp intake of breath, wondering how their brother could be so mean to such an adorable baby.

Martha kept quiet, inwardly loathing her brother but at the same time worried that he might disclose how she'd left the cows an entire day without milking them; she knew that he'd take great pleasure in humiliating her, especially while she was receiving so much praise from her parents.

As much as Silas felt like marching Frank outside by the scruff of his neck and giving him a thrashing, as always, he put Claire's feelings first and didn't want to ruin her *special* day. Changing the strained atmosphere, Claire broke into casual chatter with her daughters, ignoring Frank for the time being. The weather, flour supplies and the shipshape appearance of the house were all discussed along with the pretty table flowers before Silas suggested that they should begin their family meeting before one or both of the babies woke up again.

"We have some extremely serious family issues which need discussing!" announced Silas, sternly as he vacated his chair.

"Is it about school Pa?"

"No interrupting please, Amy; listen to what your father has to say."

"Yes, Ma."

Silas took a deep breath, "Now, I'd appreciate it if you'd all pay attention to what I'm going to say; *without interruption*; you can ask questions later. The first and most important issue is that of baby George; your ma and I have decided that we will take him into our family as one of our very own children; we both love him dearly and it would break out hearts to have him put into an orphanage." Silas directed his words at Frank, who had, disrespectfully, turned his face towards the window as though nothing his father had to say concerned him. Silas had intended to have a private word with Frank, but on witnessing his rudeness, first hand, he made a spontaneous decision to keep no secrets from any member of his family.

"It is most important that we tell everyone that George is Grace's twin brother, to protect him, *and* to protect us!"

While Jane and Amy loved the idea, Frank sniggered, mockingly.

Silas continued, "It is a strict and vital order that every one of you stays well clear of Bruce Brunswick. If you see him approaching you at any time, you are to hurry away in the opposite direction as though you have urgent business elsewhere. He is a dangerous man, who is not to be trusted at any cost, and certainly not to be entertained by anyone of you! *Is that clear*?"

"He's *so* dangerous, that he can't even aim his pistol on target!" ridiculed Frank.

"Frank! I haven't finished yet, you can have your say when I'm done, now have the decency to respect my instructions."

"Can I leave, father? I'll go and clean the tools or groom the beasts, anything but listen to this *baby talk*!" Frank attempted to leave his chair.

"*Sit down!*" bellowed Silas, startling the family with his amplified voice.

"I think that *you* should know Frank, along with the rest of the family, the reason *why* George was left in our barn *and* the reason I'm requesting that you all stay clear of Bruce Brunswick is down to your show of *bravado* in front of the *Tyler girl!* It was not due to Brunswick's bad aim that you were merely grazed; he meant it to be that way. I received a letter; remember, the one which Lydia Tyler delivered from her employer, and we all know who that is. The short of it is that Bruce Brunswick has threatened to drag Frank in front of the magistrate for trespassing and poaching if we don't follow his orders. He has made threats to our family, and will surely use his upper hand to blackmail us in the future. It was *him* who left the infant in our barn, but I want you all to know, that your mother and I decided to keep George before we found out about Brunswick's involvement and our love for him remains the same. If you hadn't ventured onto the Brunswick Estate, Frank, we would not even be having this family meeting."

"*I hate that Squinty Eye!*" expressed Amy, crossly.

"Me too, he's as evil as the devil!" added Jane.

"Can't you go and speak to the Squire, Pa?" suggested Martha.

"Your father has already done that, my darling, but it would seem that blood is thicker than water, even when there is an obvious crime being committed."

"*What does that mean?*" quizzed Amy.

"Never you mind now; just listen to what your pa is saying."

"I've got a good mind to pay *Squinty Eye* a visit

and beat the bloody daylights out of that liar with my cricket bat!" yelled Frank, red-faced and angry. "I can't believe that you're going to let him get away with this!"

"*Frank!* If we don't go along with it, he has threatened that you'll either be hung or transported! *We have no other choice!* His brother is the magistrate and clearly on his side, no matter what!"

"Well, what if I leave Bagley village, you'd all be better off then and anyway, it's about time I made my way in life; I'm not a boy any more you know!"

"You're our son! Our firstborn and we all love you Frank!" cried Claire. "Why else would we suffer the consequences? There is a life for you here too, on the land and one day I'm sure you will wed your sweetheart; don't throw all that away!"

"I think enough has been said for the time being!" stated Silas. "You girls can go back to school tomorrow and announce the news that you have a new twin brother and sister, but nothing else...*is that clear?*"

"Yes, Pa!" said Jane and Amy; happy that they could, at last, see their friends again and escape from Martha's orders.

CHAPTER FOURTEEN

With the arrival of summer, it had become common knowledge throughout the small farming community of Bagley village that Claire Shepherd had given birth to twins.
It was inevitable that once Jane and Amy had returned to school, announcing the good news of their endearing twin siblings that the womenfolk would descend upon Claire with their handmade gifts and messages of congratulations. Feeling ill at ease, as she sat around the kitchen table, amongst her neighbours while their broods of children, along with Amy and Jane played in the small meadow adjacent to the cottage; Claire's attention was divided as she strained her ears, listening to the infant's chatter, outside, whilst trying to hold a conversation with her neighbours. Thankfully the women simply presumed that Claire's lack of attention was down to copious sleepless nights and the strain of dealing with two newborns. Knowing how forgetful Amy could be, especially with the excitement and distraction of entertaining her school friends, Claire was overly nervous that she'd accidentally let it slip how she and her sister had found baby George in the barn; the thought caused Claire to feel instantly nauseous, not knowing how she would cope if part of the truth was ever revealed; no

doubt the women would come to a number of conclusion about the lie if it *was* accidentally disclosed, and no doubt their conclusions would bring shame upon the family.

With the babies now a few months old and both filling out, it was becoming clear that there were no similarities between them. George was already twice the size of Grace, who was a delicate looking infant. All of her children had dark brown hair and green eyes, George, however, had blue eyes and his hair was already a few shades lighter than Grace's. It was a worry which seemed to niggle away at Claire constantly, causing her to shy away from any kind of social gatherings, where there might be too much focus on the babies. They were the only twins in the village and were quite the fascination amongst the locals. Even during the sweltering heat of the summer days, Claire would be sure to tightly secure cotton bonnets upon their heads to conceal their differences from the outside world, hoping that people would just accept that Grace had inherited her mother's stature and George, that of his father's. Frank's leg had made a full recovery, but his attitude towards the family seemed to be heading along a downward spiral. He seldom spoke to anyone and kept himself to himself. He continued to walk out with Sarah every Sunday, causing Claire to also worry that he had confided in her; it was obvious that she was the only close person in his life, now that he no longer shared anything with his parents. Claire was deeply hurt by his estrangement; they had once shared a close relationship, which she'd always presumed would last forever. He continued to assist his pa on the farm, although Silas had also expressed his concern about how little he conversed with him these days.

They had to face the sad truth that ever since the day when Frank had ventured over the wall into the Brunswick Estate their happy life had changed considerably. They would spend many an evening discussing a way out of their predicament. Silas could feel his wife's tension and knew it was the cause of her sad face and snappy moods; he knew that if they did nothing to change their lives, the problem would only become worse and their hearts would rust with the anguish. Their financial situation didn't allow them to pack up and leave Bagley village, which Silas knew would be the answer to all their problems. If only they could start a new life somewhere away from the evil Bruce Brunswick who, although, had yet to make any demands upon them, they both knew that he was merely biding his time until he desired something from them. Even the Squire was now viewed upon in a completely different light; no longer the trustworthy man who they could rely upon in times of need and trouble, he had shown his true colours on that day in his study when Silas had sought his help.

Continuing to save every penny he could earn, Frank was even more determined to leave Bagley village and turn his back on his family; he loved Sarah and she had promised to marry him. She was more than enough for him, he considered; one day they would live in a smart townhouse, raise their own family and endure a life far different to that of their parents.

Frank's weekly visits into Epsom had become a far more prosperous means of increasing his savings. It had been many weeks since he'd asked local farmers if he could earn a few pennies from working on their land; he laughed at those days now; how hard he had toiled for next to nothing. His leg injury had been a turning point for him; he was no longer going to be subservient to anyone.

Every Saturday, the market town of Epsom was always bustling with shoppers and town folk simply wishing to take a stroll. Frank had done it before with great ease; stealing was a quick and easy way of striking it rich. He'd moved on from trinkets and ornaments; his new founded technique would be to stand and observe until he caught sight of a wealthy gentleman who was eagerly spending his money. After closely following his victim, carefully studying his every move and taking mental notes as to which pocket the gentleman had put his wallet in; Frank would strike at the exact appropriate time, usually when his victim was fully indulged in conversation with an acquaintance or a costermonger. It was becoming increasingly easy, providing he chose his prey wisely and took every caution before committing the theft. He'd walk the few miles home to Bagley village in a buoyant mood, excited about returning to the privacy of his bedroom to count his booty and with the following day being a Sunday his eagerness to spend time with his beloved Sarah was another anticipation which lifted his spirits. His future was looking increasingly sweet for him and Sarah and maybe after another year, if he continued to filter out the wealthy subjects he'd be one of the richest farmer's sons in the entire village, he boasted to himself.

Although the Squire and his family, excluding Bruce, attended the church services most Sundays, Silas had not spoken to him since the humiliating day when he'd visited the Manor House. The Brunswick family would always be seated to the front of the small church and Silas made sure that he and his family were the last ones to arrive leaving them with no alternative than to occupy the rear pews. They would make a hasty exit as soon as the sermon was over, even though it appeared quite rude to leave without conversing with the vicar, as was customary. Thankfully one of the babies would usually break the peace which gave them the perfect excuse to leave in a hurry. It was, however, during the annual harvest celebrations when Silas came face to face with the Squire again.

With every available pair of working hands in Bagley village having spent ten back-breaking days bringing in the harvest, the celebrations were the pinnacle to the joy which everyone felt as they viewed the healthy bounty of a year's hard work on the land. It had been a generous year and the celebrations which were held upon the village green began early in the morning lasting through to sunset. An occasion for jubilation, relaxation and a well deserved holiday. Every family would contribute a hamper of their women folk's best cooking, the men would set up the tables and chairs and the older siblings would unite in devising games and races for the younger ones with prizes of toffee apples and homemade fudge.

Traditionally, the Squire would always donate a barrel of ale for the farmers, while most of the women were content with drinking tea or lemonade.

"Mr Shepherd!" declared the Squire as he stealthily approached Silas from behind. Silas had no choice but to turn around and give his attention to the man who he'd so obviously avoided for weeks. "Word has it that it's been a bumper crop this harvest!"

"It has indeed, Sir. *Praise the Good Lord!*"

"Yes, quite. How is your family? In the best of health I trust?" enquired the Squire, politely.

"They are thank you, Sir and my twins are soon to be six months old!"

There was an awkward moment as the Squire and Silas held eye contact with each other; Silas waited to see the reaction his words would have, if any, upon the Squire.

"How wonderful," he casually announced as though he knew nothing of how the twins came about. "Please express my regards to your family, Mr Shepherd!"

Silas stood in disbelief, glaring as the Squire walked away to talk to another tenant. He felt his fists clenching as the blue veins in his neck stood out, pulsating angrily. He felt like climbing up onto the table and announcing to the entire village how there precious Squire was a corrupt and deceitful liar, shielding his mad brother from any sin he wished to embark on. He wanted to wipe that smug look from off his face and watch him be belittled and brought to disgrace in front of everyone; but sadly, he knew that he and his family would be sure to come off worse; he would be accused of having consumed too much of the Squire's generous gift of ale and most likely become a spectacle of ridicule. Silas bit his tongue and backed away from the celebrations where he sat alone in quiet contemplation, watching his neighbours as, one by one, they all became like humble servants before the Squire as he did his rounds. He viewed Claire and Martha; they were holding the babies, while Amy and Jane strolled around hand in hand, giggling as they helped themselves to cakes and biscuits. Frank was on the far side of the green, deep in conversation with the Tyler girl and as usual not giving the tiniest attention to his own family. Silas had never before in his life wished for wealth; always content with what the Good Lord felt fit to bless him with, he was grateful for the smallest of blessings and felt rich in comparison to many when he viewed his beautiful, healthy family and the fact that he had a home and land to work on. Today though, he yearned deeply to take his family to pastures new, away from their present life of living with such a terrible lie; away from the Brunswick Estate and its corrupt owners.

His reverie was abruptly broken as he caught sight of none other than Bruce Brunswick, meandering towards the hub of celebrations; he was now walking with the aid of a stick and stopping after every few steps, to catch his breath. He was stooped over slightly and was without a hat, probably because it would be quite impossible for it to sit firmly upon his misshapen head whilst not horizontal. Silas watched, mesmerized by his horrifying appearance. A small group of children, playing in a nearby patch of unkempt grass, suddenly fled as he neared them, some screaming loud enough to cause a wave of silence to ripple across the entire village green. All eyes were suddenly focussed on Squinty Eye; Silas watched with intrigue as the Squire made a hasty beeline towards his brother. The chatter and merry-making continued amongst the villagers, they were used to Bruce Brunswick's grotesque image and not bothered too much by his arrival. There was no brotherly handshake between them as the Squire met with his brother; he appeared quite angry and seemed to be giving Bruce Brunswick a stern talking to. Silas noticed that Lady Mary and the Brunswick's three grown-up children were leaving the harvest celebrations, walking in the opposite direction back towards the Manor House. Silas wondered if their premature departure had anything to do with the arrival of Squinty Eye; had he been told not to show his face, Silas mused. It was when the Squire and his brother proceeded to follow Lady Mary and the rest of the family that Silas felt the sudden urge to confront the pretentious family. Maybe it was the effect of the ale or the effect of simply sitting having observed the Squire's audacious behaviour over the last half hour or so, which had spurred Silas to act this way, but he knew that he couldn't simply watch as though everything in his life was normal.

He hurried to where Claire and Martha were still sat with the babies; Martha was cradling George in her arms as he slept through the noisy celebrations. Glad to see his return, Claire looked up, a warm and welcoming smile springing to her face,

"Silas! I was wondering where you'd got to!"

"Pass me Georgie, Martha!" demanded Silas as he already had both hands stretched out ready to take him from her arms.

Claire's smiling faced changed to a look of horror.

"What are you planning, Silas? What's going on?"

"I just want to have a word with the Squire, that's all my love; trust me!"

"Well if that's all, you don't need to take little Georgie with you! Please Silas, whatever you are intending to do, it will only make matters worse!"

"Don't take him, Pa, he ours now!" pleaded Martha, distraughtly.

"I know he's ours, I merely want to have a word with the Squire and I want George to be in my arms when I do!"

There was no stopping him, Silas left Claire and Martha in tears as he hurried towards the Brunswick family who was now quite far off in the distance.

As they ambled along in the balmy summer's evening, Silas marched like a warrior on a mission, soon catching up. Sensing that someone was following them, one of the Squire's sons turned around and discretely alerted his father. In the fading light, Silas was sure that the Squire had become quite red-faced by his presence.

"*Mr Shepherd!*" he announced, "I trust there is nothing wrong?"

"No, Squire, not at all; I was about to ask the same of you; you're leaving the harvest celebrations rather early, I wondered if there was a problem?"

A trail of dribble dangled from Bruce Brunswick's distorted mouth as he stared hard at Silas, the gentle breeze blew it against his jacket where it adhered.

"How jolly thoughtful, Mr Shepherd! I'm afraid Lady Mary has one of her migraines so we took the decision to call it a day!"

Silas knew he was lying. He'd been watching the Brunswick family and only ten minutes ago she'd been laughing and chatting with some of the village women.

"I'm very sorry to hear that; I do hope you soon feel better, Lady Mary, but anyway, since I'm here now, I thought you might like to feast your eyes upon my lovely son...His *twin sister* is with my wife! "

The entire family was taken by complete shock at Silas's bizarre statement. They all looked at one another, not quite sure how to respond. It was Lady Mary who broke the ice,

"Well Mr Shepherd, he's a bonny looking boy; you and your wife must be overjoyed and so proud!"

"Oh yes, we certainly are; we weren't expecting twins, you know! It was the biggest shock I've ever had in all my life!"

"I'm sure it was," added Lady Mary.

"Well we won't keep you any longer," expressed the Squire, "I'm sure Mrs Shepherd will be wondering where you are!" The Squire laughed nervously, his eyes giving Silas a look of warning.

"Very well, Squire, Lady Mary and Mr Brunswick, I'll bid you goodnight then!"

Silas turned around, marching back along the same pathway that he'd made in the overgrown grass.

"How extraordinary!" exclaimed Lady Mary. "What on earth was that all about?"

"Oh you know these farmers, they can't hold their drink!"

"He was as *drunk* as a sailor!" added Bruce.

"Well. I must say, the man didn't look or sound drunk to me!" insisted Lady Mary.

"It's probably the strain of too many disturbed nights having to put up with screaming babies!" suggested Reginald, relieved that Silas Shepherd had not said more.

CHAPTER FIFTEEN

On the following day, the atmosphere in the Shepherd's cottage was tense; Claire was livid at how Silas had displayed Georgie in front of the Brunswick family, especially Bruce Brunswick. It was a Sunday, she made the excuse of stomach pains to avoid going to church that morning and with her glum face, nobody disbelieved her. "Should I stay at home and nurse Ma?" pleaded Martha, more in the hope of being allowed to forgo the long drawn out service which would no doubt be focused on the bountiful harvest. Silas wanted everything to appear normal; he knew that the Squire's family would be attending the service and after his impulsive behaviour the evening before, he wanted to present an appearance of normality.

"We will *all* be going to church!" he instructed, seriously. "I'm sure your mother will be fine at home with the young uns for an hour."

As expected the service was, as far as Martha could remember, an exact repeat of the previous year's harvest service. She spent the entire hour escaping to her imaginary world; dreaming of her future husband, a man so handsome in every way that every maiden was green with envy because he was so madly in love with Martha; not only was his appearance sublime, but he was wealthy beyond measure, a property and land owner and the most respected man in the entire county. Martha was in the middle of mentally furnishing the interior of her impressive palace when Frank nudged her roughly with his elbow. "Get a move on Martha, we're leaving and *you* are blocking up the exit!"

Turning slightly red-faced, Martha silently proceeded to leave the pew and walk down the aisle to where the vicar stood waiting at the door to exchange a few words with his flock as they politely complimented him on his powerful sermon.

As they emerged from the stuffy church into the bright sunshine, Silas caught sight of the Squire. He appeared to be waiting for someone, as he leaned against the dry stone wall of the churchyard. Silas looked about for the rest of the Brunswick family, but they were nowhere in sight.

After the vicar had proclaimed his blessings upon Silas and his family and enquired after Mrs Shepherd, Silas became convinced that the Squire was waiting by the wall to speak to him.

"Good morning, Mr Shepherd!" he declared with a wide smile aimed at Amy and Jane. Frank and Martha had already begun the walk home, eager to change out of their Sunday best and fill their rumbling stomachs. Silas politely returned the greeting.

"I was wondering, Mr Shepherd, might I have a few words in private with you?" He eyed the youngsters whilst making his request. Silas peered down the lane; he could still see Frank and Martha.

"Girls, run ahead and catch up with Frank and Martha, I'll be along soon!"

They took no persuading and skipped off happily.

"A fine family you have, Mr Shepherd, a great credit to you and Mrs Shepherd!"

Already suspicious of the Squire's sweet talk, Silas was curious to find out what this meeting was really about. The distinctive Brunswick carriage was nowhere in sight and it was now obvious that the Squire's family had already left.

"Shall we walk, Mr Shepherd? The winter months will soon be upon us, and there will be few opportunities to relish in the delights of our beautiful village!"

So far, Silas had said very little to the Squire, but he gladly walked alongside him, still waiting to hear the actual reason why he'd not returned home in the family carriage.

"That day back in April when you came to me, Mr Shepherd, I've been thinking about what you said. It *would* be a great shame if it were, to one day, become disclosed as to how your son was poaching on my land; you see Mr Shepherd, I'm never quite sure of what my dear brother might come out with. He might very well forget the entire incident, but then again, on the other hand, he could quite possibly insist on pressing charges one day. I'd hate to see your son come to an unfortunate end; he's a fine young lad with his future ahead of him. It would be a terrible blow to your dear wife too; sons are always a mother's treasure, I believe."

Silas listened in complete and utter astonishment at what he was hearing, every fibre of his body felt tense and on edge.

"And what about the letter which your *dear* brother left, along with the baby which for all I know could quite possibly be his!"

The squire released a cynical laugh, "Mr Shepherd, I wish that was the case! Why do you think that my brother lives his life as a recluse in the gatehouse? He is man incapable of, shall I say participating in the joys of the *fairer sex!*"

Silas felt his skin turn red, shocked to hear the Squire talk so openly about such a private subject.

"I'm sorry if I've embarrassed you, Shepherd, I trust my words will not be repeated to a soul. Yes, sadly since my brother's very unfortunate accident when he was just a boy, he has been a man in appearance only."

"Well, as much as that saddens me, Squire, it doesn't give him the right to threaten me and my family with blackmail not to mention delivering an abandoned baby to my barn. I assured you a few months ago and I would swear on the good book, today, that my son was not poaching!"

"Once again, Mr Shepherd, as with the contents

of the letter, it's a case of your word against my brother's and I believe that it is only a matter of time before he *will* decide to make you and your dear family's life quite unbearable."

"If you know how unstable your brother's state of mind is, Squire, how can you simply dismiss my side of the story and deny that my problems are all his doing? How can you deny that you didn't read the entire contents of the letter from him and even refuse to admit that there *was* such a letter?" stressed Silas, his voice becoming raised as he was consumed by anger.

"Please, Mr Shepherd, calm yourself. I will deny everything, including this conversation because as you are well aware, blood is thicker than water; I owe it to my disabled brother, to protect him for as long as I'm able to!"

"But you're the magistrate! Surely you took an oath!" cried Silas, in despair.

"Every job or position in life has its perks, Mr Shepherd," he replied, calmly. "Now, hear me out, Shepherd, I have a proposition to put to you and I'd strongly advise that *before* you hastily decline my offer, you allow your wife to have an opinion on whether you choose to accept it or not and I hasten to add, that I *do* believe you would be foolish to decline!"

The two men came to a halt on reaching the junction where they were about to part ways, Silas stared face to face at the Squire for the first time, suddenly realising that the man he'd considered fair and dependable since as long as he could remember, was no better than any of the rest of the richer folk, most of whom seemed to lose their conscience when dealing with the likes of a humble tenant farmer and his family. Greed and Corruption certainly did rule amongst the wealthy, he mused, intrigued as to what Reginald Brunswick was about to propose.

"In the interest of everyone concerned, Mr Shepherd, and to allow you and your family to live without any threat from my brother, I am willing to offer you a small sum plus a couple of fine mares and a sturdy wagon. You could quietly leave Bagley village and travel far enough away to embark on a new and, might I add, a much more prosperous life!"

Silas had nothing to say, he'd listened as though he was in the midst of a dream, all the time sensing that the Squire had more to protect than he cared to disclose. There was not a single thread of trust left for the man he'd held in such high esteem over the years.

"Think about it Mr Shepherd, discuss it with your good wife, and we will meet again next week. Think about the prospect of Christmas celebrations in a new home, new surroundings and with enough money to be able to treat every member of your family to a feast fit for a king!"

With his final words, the Squire hurried off in the direction of the Brunswick Estate, leaving Silas regretting that he'd not been brave enough to voice his honest opinion to the crooked Squire, but as always, the image of Claire and their six children were uppermost in his thoughts; he had a huge responsibility weighing on him and he was not in a position to speak his mind; after all, he considered as he headed towards his cottage, the Squire could quite easily refuse to renew the tenancy which would leave him and his family destitute.

Silas kept his conversation with the Squire to himself throughout Sunday dinner, even though the girls had already excitedly told Claire how their pa was walking home with the Squire. It was an unusual occurrence for the Squire not to return in his carriage and with Silas's subdued mood since returning, Claire sensed he held a heavy weight on his mind.
With Frank in a hurry to gulp down his food and rush out to meet Sarah for their customary Sunday afternoon stroll, Claire instructed Martha, Jane and Amy to venture into the woods to pick the last of the season's blackberries; the cottage was soon empty of listening ears and the twins, although not asleep, were more than content to sit upon Claire and Silas's laps, clumsily playing with a few wooden cubes. "Something's happened, hasn't it Silas!" questioned Claire fervently.
Silas repeated the entire one-sided conversation which had taken place earlier, leaving Claire

feeling completely powerless and shocked as she broke down in tears.

"Bagley village is *our* home, *Silas,* we were *all* born here! It's where we feel safe! How dare he think that he can simply offer us a *sum* of money and the means to pack up and go as though he was herding cattle off his land! That man and his brother are *heartless*!"

Silas had expected his normally strong wife to react differently, he was relying on her to have the answers to the troubles which had plagued his mind throughout dinner, but it seemed that even Claire had her Achilles heel. Claire who usually thought things through with her head rather than her heart was now distraught, and Silas felt like a useless coward as he viewed the tears stream down her face and drip onto Grace's soft hair.

"*This is all Frank's fault!*" bellowed Silas. "That boy should have felt the belt on his behind the moment he went out of line! It never did *me* any harm when I was a lad! You've been far too soft with him, Claire; young lads need discipline!"

"Discipline I agree, but whipping is for beasts!" Claire sobbed. "Don't put all the blame on Frank; he was merely doing what you would have done if you'd been in the same situation!"

"So what are we going to do? You do realise that if we don't accept Brunswick's offer, it is well within his power to terminate our tenancy."

"I *know* that Silas, but I'm convinced that there is

more to this than he is letting on. Why doesn't he do that? Simply refuse to renew our tenancy; he could easily come up with an excuse, after all, he's already proved himself to be a liar. He wants us far away from Bagley village...and there's only one reason for that, and he's sitting on your lap!"

"No, that can't be the reason!" objected Silas. "I feel sure that he wasn't lying about his brother about that issue...It makes sense as to why he's not married and *why* he lives in the gatehouse!"

"It makes sense that he's a strange one, that's all. Maybe George is the Squire's illegitimate son, and they are both in on it together, they do seem to be very protective of one another's crimes!"

"*Heavens above!* That thought *never* crossed my mind; you could be right, Claire, it makes sense; the Squire doesn't want us to suffer any hardship simply because we are caring for his flesh and blood!"

"It's only a possibility, though Silas, we don't know for sure but I *am* convinced that both the Squire *and* his brother know who the real parents of little Georgie are."

"That still leaves us with a big decision to make!" uttered Silas.

"Do I look as though I've been crying, Silas? The girls will be home soon and I don't think I can cope with a string of questions from them."

"You look as beautiful as ever my sweetheart, a little more colour in your cheeks perhaps, but it's a warm afternoon. Let's have some tea; we have a couple of months, at least, before we have to come to a decision and I'm sure I will be able to stall the Squire for a time. It's not an easy task to pack up and leave with a large family. God alone knows where we should go!"

CHAPTER SIXTEEN

Claire looked disheartened at the meagre amount of wool she'd managed to salvage from unpicking the children's old jumpers; barely enough to keep the babies warm during the coming winter months she mused and the majority of it was now coarse after years of wear. Martha was busy trying to cut out re-usable squares of material from old threadbare sheets; they would be sewn together to make nightgowns for Jane and Amy and with the added pretty embroidered flowers which Claire would sew on them, they would turn out as good as new ones.

"Oh, Martha, this will never stretch to knitting enough jumpers to keep us all warm!"

Martha lifted her head, feeling sorry at having to witness the struggle her ma went through in trying to take care of the family, it was yet another reason why she intended to marry for wealth; love didn't keep you in fine clothes and put hearty meals on the table; she was going to live like a princess.

"Why don't I go with Frank into Epsom this Saturday, I'm sure he'll be going as usual; he thinks he's some well to do gent strutting around the town in his best clothes! I wonder if Sarah knows what he gets up to!"

Claire smiled, "I think your brother has even

bigger dreams than you do, Martha, just like most young lads and lasses!"

"Well *my* dreams are going to come true Ma, you just wait and see!"

"There's no harm in dreaming, sometimes, it's what gives us poorer folk hope and keeps us living from one season to another without losing out wits! So anyway, what are you intending to do if you do accompanying your brother to town?"

"There's an old woman who is too old to walk to the market place but she sells lots of odds and ends on her front door," expressed Martha chirpily. "I discovered her the last time I went into town when Frank kept me waiting; I walked around the pond three times before I noticed her, she is quite well concealed down a narrow path, but I'm certain she had a large basket of wool next to her!"

"I suppose it's worth a try, poor old woman...probably unravelling the clothes off her back to feed her belly and to put fuel on the fire! You must take her a small hamper, a poke of tea perhaps and some of the harvest fruit...we have plenty, thank the Lord."

Martha was as thrilled about going to town with Frank as Claire was about the prospect of having a new supply of decent wool to knit with. Frank, however, had a face as long as a condemned man and spent the entire three mile's walk into Epsom issuing Martha with instructions as to where she could and couldn't venture once they'd arrived in the town. Ending in an argument, Martha could find no logic in his requests and felt indignant that her brother should behave as though he had some kind of authority in the town.

"You're not the Mayor of Epsom you know, Frank Shepherd, and I can go to wherever I choose to go!"

"When are you ever going to stop being such a stupid little fool, *Martha*, why do you think that I never ask Sarah to join me on a Saturday? Because the areas I mentioned are not safe; where ruthless criminals skulk around and wouldn't think twice about dragging young maids off into a side street and having their wicked way with them, maybe even giving them a good beating too, or worse!"

"Well Ma said that you *have* to chaperone me, so why don't you just stay with me, then I won't be attacked by one of these so-called monsters who lurk around the shady corners of the busy town!" declared Martha, sarcastically.

"It's not good for my image to be seen on some old biddy's threshold buying thread and ribbons and the likes! I tell you what; you meet me by the edge of the pond after, say...half an hour, you can have a good long chat with the old crow, I'm sure she'll appreciate it!"

"Frank Shepherd, you are turning into the most

appalling brother; you think you're such a man, don't you, but you're nothing but an immature boy and a very nasty one at that! "

"Just be quiet, Martha, it's bad enough that I have to drag my little sister into town with me let alone listen to her trying to sound more like my mother!"

"*Little sister!*" protested Martha. "There is only a year between our ages *brother dear!*"

"Just shut your bloody mouth Martha, before a swarm of bluebottles flies into it!"

The journey continued in silence, with Frank always a couple of steps in front of his sister until they reached the crowded town. He proceeded towards the pond which was situated in front of the lofty watchtower in the town's centre.

"I'll meet you back here in half an hour and if I'm a bit late, don't wander off; *just wait!*"

Martha simply nodded her head, not wishing to speak another word to her brother. She watched him head off in the opposite direction, wondering what he got up to and who he met in Epsom every week. He soon disappeared leaving Martha to go in search of the old woman, praying that she would be on her doorstep today and that she had plenty of wool for sale. Her ma had given her three pennies along with a basket of apples, pears, a small loaf and a poke of tea. Martha was confident that she'd be able to strike a good bargain with the old woman.

Frank was far from happy; being rushed for time, he wasn't able to study his subject for as long as he'd have liked, he had also promised Sarah that he would present her with a gift the following day; she had been talking none stop on their previous day out about a silver moth bracelet which was very fashionable. He could already picture her radiant face when he presented her with such a gift. Not wanting to risk pocketing a wallet in such a limited time, Frank decided to concentrate wholly on Sarah's gift instead. There were two jewellers in the Epsom High street and both were usually fairly busy of a Saturday.

There wasn't a single customer at the old woman's door; she sat alone, half on the pavement and half in her narrow hallway, humming quietly to herself while her hands worked at a speed which Martha had never witnessed before; the crochet needle moved rapidly with the old woman not even having to look at her work. The blanket she was working on already covered her legs as her hands moved speedily causing it to grow faster than the summer wheat.

"How do you do that so quickly, without even looking?" exclaimed Martha as she neared the woman's tiny cottage.

"And a good morning to you too, Miss!" replied the

woman.

"Oh, I do beg your pardon, Misses, I was so fascinated watching you work that I let my manners slip! *Good morning!*"

 The old woman smiled, displaying a mouth full of bare gums, all the while her hands continuing to move swiftly.

"Years and years of practice, girl; I could do this in me sleep!"

Martha surmised that the woman must be at least a hundred years old as she continued watching. The blanket was stunning; she knew how delighted her ma would be to have such a warm cover for the coming winter months. Martha spotted the basket which was piled high with skeins of yarn; she felt a rush of excitement, knowing how pleased her ma would be when she took a good supply home to her.

"My Ma gave me this small hamper; it's for you!" declared Martha, holding up the bundle which was wrapped in an old rag. The old woman appeared suspicious; her hands ceased working for the first time as she squinted at the gift.

"I'm not in a position to pay for anything lass; I just about manage to make ends meet with the bits an' bobs which I sell all year"

"Oh no! We don't want any payment; it's just a handful of fruit from this year's harvest and a few bits from our kitchen."

Slightly hesitant, the woman put down her

handiwork to accept the donation. She untied the knot and licked her lips as she stroked the fruit before taking a huge bite out of an apple. Martha stood in shock, amazed by the way her tough gums cut through the juicy fruit.

"Mmm, just what I needed, lass, they be good apples; tell your ma, thanks, she's made an old woman very happy with her thoughtfulness." She then began chuckling causing bits of chewed up apple to fall from her mouth and on to her blanket.

"*Your face is a picture!* You didn't think it possible for a toothless old woman to bite into an apple, did you? I bet my gums are tougher than your teeth, girl!"

Martha felt embarrassed, "I always thought that when you lost your teeth, you spent the rest of your days eating tea soaked bread and broths!"

"Well there you go, you learn something new every day! Now I'm sure you didn't just come my way to give me this very generous donation; did you wish to buy something, lass?"

"I did!" confirmed Martha. "*Wool!* As much as I can buy with my three pennies, please!"

"For your lovely ma, is it?"

Martha nodded, "She's busy knitting jumpers for my brothers and sisters, ready for the winter."

"And how many is that?"

"Well there are three girls, that's including me and one boy, then there are the twins, a boy and a girl; they are still babies though!"

"Babies still need keeping warm when that fearful North wind brings its ice and snow down our way!"

"Yes, I suppose they do, but they are smaller and won't need so much wool to knit a jumper!"

There was a twinkle in the old woman's washed-out eyes as she stared at the pretty youthful girl before her; it only seemed like yesterday that she had been young and full of optimism for the life ahead of her, love, marriage children, and homemaking they were the joys of every young maiden, always had been and always would be, she pondered.

"You can take this basket!" she declared.

"What? *All of it*, for just three pennies? "

"I've got a wardrobe full of my beloved Jo's old jumpers, waiting to be unravelled; God bless his soul. Come back next week. If you can, lass and I'll have two of these 'ere blankets for your Ma, free of charge!"

Martha couldn't believe what she was hearing; she had sensed that her ma had been troubled of late, probably with the worry of how she was going to manage through the coming months, but this would be sure to put a smile on her face.

"Thank you, thank you so much, my ma will be overjoyed and I know she will love the blankets as much as I do; they are the most divine blankets I've ever seen in my life!"

"You've certainly put a smile on my face today, young lass...What's your name, anyway?"

"Martha, *Martha Shepherd!*" she stated proudly. "I'm Mrs King! Now, Martha Shepherd, don't you go forgetting to come and collect your blankets the next time you're in town and don't forget to thank your lovely ma as well, will you?"

Martha left holding the basket of wool; so elated that she felt like bursting into song. She made her way towards the edge of the pond; there was no sign of Frank, which didn't surprise her, but she was too happy to allow anything to change her mood. She looked through the basket as she waited, the wool was in much better condition than her ma's meagre supply at home; shades of greens, browns and deep red, all very suitable for not showing the dirt she thought. She pondered on the old woman as she waited, wondering if perhaps the old woman's ancestors had been related to royalty, with a name like King; she knew that her family name had come from a long line of shepherds, her pa had told her that when she was young.

There was still no sign of Frank and Martha was becoming impatient; she was thirsty and hungry and beginning to wish that she'd saved one of the apples for herself. She peered through the crowded street, in the hope of catching sight of him. There's were scores of finely dressed women out strolling; Martha felt quite jealous of their expensive attire and matching parasols; she imagined them all to live in the elegant looking townhouses which they'd passed by on the edge of town; rows of neat uniform windows all adorned with brilliant white lace curtains, polished brass door knockers and no sign of any flaky paintwork. She imagined each home was headed by a bona fide gentleman, one of wealth and intelligence who dressed in perfectly tailored suits. There were probably only two or three children to each home, the wealthy always tended to have fewer children for some reason, pondered Martha. Each child would have a well-stocked wardrobe and be proficient in playing the piano...Martha's reverie was suddenly broken with the arrival of Frank. His tense face was puce, the beads of sweat ran freely from his skin and he appeared anxious and in a great hurry to issue his instructions; his eyes were searching everywhere before he caught sight of the basket of wool and proceeded to pull out the silver objects from his pockets,

"Quick Martha hide my shopping for me, some bloody thugs are out to rob me!"

"No, Frank, they'll get me instead and drag me off, like you warned me! *Remember?*"

"You owe me Martha; *hurry up, for God's sake!*"

Martha stared in horror as Frank hurriedly hid the items beneath the wool in her basket; a silver bracelet with an ornamental moth, a matching hair slide and then a large silver tankard, followed by a pair of expensive looking jet, gold-rimmed cufflinks.

"Go home, Martha!" he cried. "I'll meet you somewhere on the road!"

Without giving Martha the chance to say another word he sped off. Already feeling her heart racing out of control, the sight of three affluent gentlemen hurrying along the High street, sent a wave of added fear through Martha's veins. She froze as she viewed everyone step aside for the men. They were, without a doubt, not thugs, concluded Martha, immediately sensing that Frank had committed the most dreadful of sins and stolen the hoard of treasure which she was now holding in her basket. Martha felt sure that her thumping heartbeat could be heard by everyone nearby and then she watched aghast, as the small group of women who'd been deep in conversation since she'd arrived by the pond's edge, stopped the men in their tracks and pointed toward her. It was like a dream, the noise of the High street became completely silent apart from the shrill voices of the women as they declared in unison,

"She's the thief's accomplice; he just hid the stolen property in her basket! We saw it with our own eyes!"

Even if Martha *had* wanted to run, the temporary paralysis of her legs would not have permitted it; she could only stand motionless and wait to be approached by the gentleman.

Already feeling sorry for her parents, knowing that her brother's dreadful crime would break their hearts and ruin the family's good name, Martha was astonished by how the men treated her, instantly presuming that she was working alongside Frank. She let out a loud cry as one of the men grabbed her arm; he was heavy handed and seemed to be gaining pleasure in squeezing her arm so tightly, soon causing it to feel numb. Another of the men emptied her basket on to the street, victoriously pulling out the stolen objects, holding them up high and taking pleasure as the crowds applauded and shouted hurtful insults at Martha. She could feel her face burning but was still unable to speak.

Meanwhile, the third gentleman re-appeared together with a bulky, mean and filthy looking man.

"Is this the little bitch then?"

"She's all yours, Wax! Maybe you can use your charm to find out who she works with."

Martha suddenly realised what a dreadful predicament she was in. The uncouth looking rogue took over from the gentleman who was still holding on tightly to her arm, proving to be even tougher in his firm grip.

"*No, no!*" cried Martha in despair, at last finding her voice. "I'm no thief; it was my brother, he just put those things in my basket...please, you *must* believe me!"

The unpleasant man, who they called Wax, smirked while the gentlemen shook their heads in disgust.

"Alright little lady, that's a new one on me, but don't think you're gonna do yourself any favours by making out it was a *dear wayward brother* you was working with. I wasn't born yesterday you little minx. It's a night beneath the watchtower for you, and up in front of the magistrate tomorrow! I 'ope you ain't squeamish!"

As the crowds dispersed and the three gentlemen left Martha in the hands of Wax, although feeling terrified of what the night had in store for her, Martha felt quite confident that the matter would soon be resolved, just as soon as Frank arrived home and told their parents what had happened.

CHAPTER SEVENTEEN

The watchtower stood on the edge of the pond, an ominous looking building with an elevated wooden lookout tower, beneath which was a dark and foreboding holding cell. Martha could think of nothing else than her cosy bed at home which she shared with Jane and Amy; how could she persuade this awful man that she was a good girl she thought frantically as they neared the place where she was to be abandoned for the night.

"You're making a big mistake, Mr Wax! My father is a friend of the Squire from Brunswick Estate; he's a magistrate, you know and won't be at all happy in the way in which I'm being falsely accused!"

"Now listen 'ere, Miss, if you know what's good for you, you'd best keep the peace and make the best of a night with the friendly vermin of Epsom, with a bit of luck, they might not be too 'ungry tonight! And me name is just *Wax*, not Mr Wax; it's me given nickname cos I've been known to fill the mouths of the noisy criminals, who take to hollering all night long and disturbing me sleep, with a measure of hot candle wax!"

Martha took in a loud gasp of breath, even more terrified of this cumbersome man who appeared not to have an ounce of compassion in his bones.

He laughed out loud; pleased with the fear he'd induced in his young captive. They soon arrived at the wooden door, the front of which displayed a tiny, barred window no bigger than a hand. As Wax pulled open the door, the strong stench seeped out into the fresh air. A pungent mixture of decaying matter, horse dun and stale urine. "Now you might be used to the sweet perfume of roses, but you'll 'ave to put up with me very own fragrant garden tonight, Miss!" he boasted, amused by the look of disgust on Martha's face.

"Do you know Mrs King?" pleaded Martha, in desperation.

Wax looked down at her, "Everyone knows Mrs King! She's the very jewel of Epsom!"

Martha couldn't make out if Wax was being sarcastic but anything was worth a try in hope of preventing a night in the hell hole of Wax's prison.

"Well, she's sort of my friend, and *she'll* be sure to tell you that I'm no thief!"

"I usually give one last request to me prisoners before I bolt the door for the night," Wax sighed. "Most ask for food or water; is that *your* last request Miss, cos you ain't getting another one!"

"Yes!" voiced Martha, adamantly.

"Very well, Mrs King it is then!"

"Can I come with you?"

"*Certainly not!* You might be a threatening influence on the poor old woman! You will remain here and sample a taste of what's in store for the night!"

Martha sensed that the nasty, Wax was quickly running out of patience, as he shoved her into the dark stinking lair, bolting the door behind him. She peered through the tiny window, comforted that he was heading in the direction of Mrs King's cottage.

"What brings the likes of you to my doorstep?" questioned Mrs King, suspiciously.

"I got a little thief in me custody, who reckons she be a friend of yours...She was found with a basket of your wool; did she pay you for it?"

"She did, indeed! Why what's she done?"

"Her partner in crime used the basket of wool to hide stolen property in; he's done a runner, left her to face the consequences, but at least we've retrieved the haul of silver!"

"Why that scheming little so and so; well, she certainly had me fooled and I don't take kindly to being taken advantage of, not at my ripe old age! I haven't lived on this earth for four score years and more to be swindled by a nipper!"

"So do I take it that she's not your friend then?"

Mrs King grabbed the hamper of food, annoyed that she'd accepted it so readily and had trusted the innocent looking girl.

"You can take this, no doubt it's stolen too and I'm not going to risk having my stomach poisoned by stolen victuals!"

"I'll donate it to the workhouse, Mrs King!" lied Wax, already salivating at the prospect of feasting on the hamper later that evening.

Feeling confident that Wax would return to unbolt the door and allow her to walk free, Martha was taken by complete shock when Wax shouted through the window how Mrs King was utterly sickened by how she'd been used as a pawn in such a devious crime.
Not wanting to sit down anywhere in the filthy prison, Martha could do nothing else but stand and cry in despair, trying hard to keep her noise level to a minimum with the fear of hot wax being poured into her mouth.

Whilst Martha and Frank had been in Epsom, Jane and Amy had proudly baked a sponge cake and were eager to show it off to Martha. But it was Frank who burst over the threshold, puffing out of breath and looking dishevelled.
Mother's instinct immediately alerted Claire that something had happened to Martha,
"*Where's your sister?*" she demanded.
 "What? You mean she's not already home?" exclaimed Frank, his face turning ashen.
 All eyes were on Frank
"Jane! Go out and see if you can find your pa, tell him to come in, *urgently!*"
Jane obediently ran out of the cottage in search of Silas, while Amy broke down into tears,
"Where's Martha!" she cried, wringing her

chubby hands, nervously. *"I want my Martha!"*
"Quiet now, Amy, you'll frighten the babies,"
comforted Claire in a soft voice.
"What happened, Frank! Sit down, get your
breath back and tell me!" ordered Claire, as she
tried to stay calm.
In the back of Frank's mind, he knew that his
sister had been caught, there'd been no sight of
her on the road back to Bagley village and he
was a much faster runner than Martha. His mind
was busy trying to think of what he'd say to his
parents; if only they hadn't insisted on him
taking Martha to Epsom, none of this would
have happened.
"There was some trouble in town," blurted out
Frank as he pulled out the chair and rested his
wobbly legs.
"A mob of ruffians were chasing me! Don't ask
why, because for the life of me, I have no idea,
they just came from nowhere, shouting out
'there 'e is! Let's get 'im!' I was running for my
life Ma, I thought they were going to kill me!"
Jane had returned with her Pa, he looked
flustered but ready to take on the entire world to
rescue his daughter, wherever she might be.
"This sounds like the work of bloody Bruce
Brunswick!" he said angrily. "I knew it wouldn't
be long before he set his crooked plans into
action."
"Come and sit down Silas, let's hear what Frank
has to say first, it's no good jumping to

conclusions," affirmed Claire, trying to bring a sense of calmness about the kitchen.

Frank continued, relieved that he was not suspected of being in the wrong.

"I was running for my life, but I went out of my way to pass by Martha, she was waiting by the pond where we'd arranged to meet!"

"Why didn't you stay with your sister in Epsom?" scolded Silas.

"She was going to buy women's stuff, Pa, she didn't want me with her and I certainly didn't want to be seen buying wool and ribbons; *that's women's business!*"

Silas slammed his clenched fist down onto the table,

"You and your damned obsession with being *'the man'* is going to be the ruin of this family! I hope you'll be able to sleep at night knowing that you've broken your ma's heart!"

"*Pa!* Martha didn't want me with her, she insisted that we should meet up after she'd finished her business...I was quite content to have a wander, even though none of my friends were in town today!"

"She can be quite persuasive when she puts her mind to it," uttered Claire, as she viewed Frank, doubtfully, sensing that there was more to this story than he was telling.

"Frank was given the responsibility to take care of his younger sister and once again, he has let the family down because he is so pig-headed and utterly selfish!"

Frank leapt out of his chair and made his way to the door,

"Fine! I'm ready to take the blame as usual!"

"Where d'you think you're going now?" yelled Silas belligerently.

"I'm going out to look for my sister!"

"Can I come with you Frank!" requested Jane, eager to help.

"Over my dead body!" bellowed Silas, causing both Jane and Amy to flinch and little Grace's bottom lip to quiver as she sat in her high chair?"

"While Frank's out looking, I'm going to pay our dear Squire a visit, maybe this time he will take notice of his unruly brother's behaviour and intervene for a change!"

Overcome with a feeling of nausea, Claire struggled with Silas's theory that somehow Bruce Brunswick was behind Martha's disappearance; she knew he was evil, but to arrange for such goings-on in town simply to abduct Martha just didn't seem plausible; Martha would never have gone along with him, not after the strict instructions that Silas had so recently issued and if it was by force, Martha would have been sure to protest loudly; young girls just didn't disappear in the middle of a busy town.

"You go careful, Silas; we're not the Squire's favourite tenants at the moment, remember?"

"Don't you fret my love, I know what I'm doing

and I shall remain calm, for the sake of our dear Martha."

Greeted by one of the maids at the Manor House, Silas felt his heart descend as he listened to her explaining how all the Brunswick family including Bruce Brunswick had gone away to Lord and Lady Shrewsbury's Estate in Bath for the weekend and were not due to return until Tuesday. Finding out that they had left on Friday morning cleared them of any connection with the business in Epsom. Silas left the Estate with a sour taste in his throat as the harrowing thought of his thirteen-year-old daughter being held by a gang of scoundrels clouded his mind. He rode back to the cottage, trying to persuade himself to think more optimistically; Martha could perhaps have twisted her ankle and was sat resting it somewhere along the way, maybe she'd met a friend and had been invited to join her for refreshments; maybe she was even sat at home now, he prayed. Perhaps she'd played a prank on Frank, and hidden from his sight, he wouldn't blame her, what sort of brother abandoned his sister in the heart of a busy town three miles from home?
Changing course, Silas decided to make the journey into town before going home; if Martha hadn't already safely returned he couldn't bear to see the look of anguish upon Claire's face when he had no positive news to tell her. He

might also get a clearer insight into what exactly Frank got up to in town every Saturday; he'd ask around.

Having returned to town, it took little time for Frank to discover that his sister had been accused of his theft and was being held in the bleak jail beneath the watchtower; he'd heard many a tale about the ruthless Wax whose position in Epsom had caused him to become quite tyrannical. It wasn't very often that Frank felt any sympathy for Martha, but the moment he found out where she was, he was overcome with guilt. The light was quickly fading and there was now only a trickle of folk on the High Street, mostly the poorer ones who'd arrived at the end of the day in the hope of a bargain or even a free hand out of provisions which would otherwise perish by Monday morning. Suddenly catching sight of his pa riding towards him, Frank had already prepared what he would say to him.

"*Pa!*" he called out, immediately catching his attention.

Silas hurried towards him.

"I've asked around everywhere Pa and spoken to most of the shopkeepers and costermongers; nobody could tell me anything except a few women folk who were here earlier, they told me that they'd seen Martha leaving town, on her own!"

Silas already had his suspicions that Frank was

lying, the mere fact that he no longer trusted his son weighed heavy on his heart, Frank was hurtling along a downward path to ruin and there was little he could do to save him.

"And how, *please* tell me, did these women folk know your sister? She's hardly a familiar face about town is she?"

"I don't know Pa, maybe she got chatting to them while she was waiting for me?" expressed Frank, shrugging his shoulders, innocently. "I just know for certain that she's not here in town!" Silas looked around despairingly at the deserted town, again praying that Martha had, by now, returned home safely.

"Make your way home Frank, and keep your eyes peeled just in case your sister is injured on the roadside; look into every ditch and secluded area that you pass!"

"Oh Pa, I was hoping you'd let me ride up alongside you; my leg is giving me pain after all the walking and running I've done today!"

"Do as I say, Frank; you're a man aren't you? *Bloody well behave like one then!*"

A part of Frank loathed his father at that instant; he knew that when the truth came out, all blame would be once again piled on him; living under his parent's roof was becoming unbearable, especially since all the business with the baby and Bruce Brunswick had occurred. He could picture it now, Martha would be rescued to become the centre of attention, and he would be branded as the cold callous brother who was selfish enough to abandon his sister to a night in the pits of hell. Frank knew that he had to break away, even if his funds hadn't yet reached the target he was aiming for and even though Sarah would not yet be able to marry him; Frank wondered if she loved him enough, to embark on a journey of adventure with him, smiling to himself at the very idea.

"I don't know what you find so amusing, son, at a time like this!" hollered Silas from the saddle. "Have some respect and be on your way before even the shadows disappear, and remember what I said, search everywhere!"

Frank walked away without even a goodbye to his pa and quickly hid in the recess of a shop's entrance, curious as to where his Pa was going.

CHAPTER EIGHTEEN

From the second Frank witnessed his pa step over the threshold of the *Black Bull*, alehouse, he knew that it would only be a matter of minutes before his pa was told the truth about Martha, and also knew that the proprietor and the customers would not take kindly to drinking alongside the father of a thief, especially one who'd stolen from their town beneath their very noses. Frank knew it was now that he had to make a critical decision on whether to face the wrath of his parents when they discovered the truth, or make his escape; no matter what his decision, he had to arrive home before his father did. He marched along, taking huge strides; the beads of sweat trickled down his face as his tangled thoughts wandered off into a dozen different directions with various scenarios as to what he should do next; staying at home after this would be a nightmare, he concluded, already in the bad books, this would make him even more of an outsider. There was only one issue which would force him into staying and putting up with whatever was thrown at him and that was the fact that his savings had not yet accumulated to a decent amount to set him up properly and from the minute he turned his back on his home, he knew that they would start to diminish.

Silas walked out of the Black Bull, with a cloud of shame hovering over him; the strangers didn't know his daughter and practically laughed in his face when he'd tried to express how there must have been a huge misunderstanding. They likely presumed that he too was in on the theft, a penniless father sending his daughter out to steal. His overwhelming sense that Frank had a lot to do with the goings-on in Epsom that afternoon only increased his current indignity and disgust towards his firstborn. Leaving his horse tethered outside the alehouse, Silas crept towards the watchtower and before reaching the edge of the pond the distinctive sound of Martha's pitiful cries filled his ears and broke his heart. He could just make out the silhouette of her head through the tiny window. He looked up to the top of the lofty tower; a candle burned brightly in the window causing Silas to wonder if perhaps the night watchman had his eyes on him. He moved closer, all the while keeping one eye on the upper window, praying that the candle was merely left there to give the false impression of a well guarded town.

"*Martha!*" he whispered. Her hands clutched the metal bars as she pushed her face up close against them.

"*Pa!*"

"*Shush my darling, keep your voice low!*"

It was near impossible for Martha to speak in a low voice, the state of distress she'd been

suffering since her detention and the sudden
sight of her pa proved too much for her to bear.
She knew in her heart that he would rescue her,
her darling pa; he could always be depended
upon and had the power to make everything
better.

"Have you come to take me home Pa?"
The wave of desperation in her voice only
added to his heartbreak.

"Martha, my darling, you are going to have to be
extra brave for one night; I know I can trust you
to be courageous! There is no magistrate
available at this time of night, so..."

"But I did *nothing* wrong, *Pa*, it was Frank, *he*
filled my basket of wool, which I'd bought for
Ma, with the stolen silver!" her sobs of despair
became louder as Silas stood helplessly unable to
offer any comfort to his suffering daughter. How
could Frank stoop so low, he questioned himself
angrily; he was no son of his and after this day,
he now considered little George to be his only
son; there was no turning back and Frank no
longer had a place in the family.

"*Oh, Pa!* Everyone thinks that *I'm* the thief!"
"Now, listen to me Martha, you are a strong girl
and this nightmare will soon be over, trust me.
Tomorrow will soon arrive and you'll be back
with your ma and sisters again!"

"And little Georgie! He must be missing me Pa; I
always rock him to sleep at night..."
It had slipped Silas's mind of how close a bond

Martha had formed with little Georgie, she was like Claire's pair of spare hands when it came to helping with the babies.

"Everyone will be jumping with joy when you come home tomorrow my darling!"

"But, Pa, it's so horrible in here; it stinks and it's filthy and I think there might be a gang of vicious rats planning on devouring me...I can't even sit down...and that awful Wax fills his prisoner's mouths up with hot candle wax if they make too much noise!"

There was little Silas could do, he had nothing to offer his daughter, and for the first time in his life felt thoroughly useless.

"I'm going to ride home quickly, to put your poor ma's mind at ease and I'll bring you back something to eat and drink!"

"It's alright Pa, you don't have to do that; I couldn't eat or drink in this place anyway; tell Ma I love her..."

"I'll be back at daybreak my brave girl...I'm so proud of you Martha, as much as I'm ashamed of your brother!"

"I love you Pa!" she sobbed in a small voice. Silas was choking; his burning tears pricked the back of his eyes and he didn't want Martha to witness his anguish; lifting his hand in a wave, he rushed to mount his horse and gallop home, leaving Martha once again alone in her dark and gruesome jail.

By the time that Silas arrived at the cottage, Frank had already been and left again. Assuring his ma that he'd only come home to check in case Martha was already there, he'd promptly filled his pockets with his haul of stolen money and silver trinkets, concealed his best jacket beneath the one which was already on his back and with the tiniest strain on his heart, said goodbye to his ma for the last time. His first stop was the Tyler's farm, even though it was too late in the day for social calling to be acceptable. Frank sneaked around their cottage with his eyes and ears alert for the sight and sound of his sweetheart. Mr and Mrs Tyler were sat at the table, deep in conversation as they sipped tea but there was no sign of Sarah. Frank carefully crept to the rear of the small cottage and there she was, in the scullery, engrossed in a stack of dirty plates and pots. He hoped she'd not yell out in alarm as he gently tapped on the window and put his face against the glass. Her initial jolt of surprise was followed by a wide smile at the sight of his familiar face.

"What are you doing here?" she exclaimed in a hushed voice, as she quietly closed the back door behind her. The cold night air caused her entire body to cover with goosebumps as she stood beneath the moonlight, shivering.

"I'm leaving home, Sarah!" he declared, searching her face, for a reaction.

"Why? What's happened, Frank?"

"I can't explain now, I have to hurry. I just wanted you to know that I won't be calling for you tomorrow afternoon; meet me in the woods, by the Brunswick wall; where I climbed over, d'you remember where that was?"
"Of course I do, but..."
"*I love you, Sarah!* You're the only light in my miserable life; I'll explain everything tomorrow, I promise...just don't pay any attention to the gossip in church tomorrow morning!"
With his words spoken, he quickly kissed her rosy lips and disappeared into the darkness, leaving Sarah with a lot to think about until the following day.

Claire paced the wooden floor with Grace in her arms, she wouldn't settle tonight and Claire knew that her baby was sensing her stress. Little Georgie, on the other hand, had cried himself to sleep; he was missing Martha's night time cuddle but crying, even more, when Jane attempted to comfort him. She and Amy were sat at the table in their nightgowns, eagerly awaiting the return of the rest of their family, especially Martha and as Amy burst into tears every ten minutes Jane was trying her utmost to console her young sister, not wanting to add any more burdens to her extremely troubled ma. The sound of the latch lifting on the door caused everyone to freeze, all eyes waiting to see who was about to step over the threshold. His wan face immediately confirmed that he was about to deliver bad news. Claire's hands were sweating all of a sudden; she quickly placed baby Grace into Jane's arms and hurried to Silas, clutching hold of his arm.

"Martha?" her sad eyes pleaded as she stared into her husband's tense face.

"She'll be home with us tomorrow, God willing!" he declared, not wanting Jane and Amy to know the truth.

"But *where* is she Pa! Has she been hurt Pa?" cried out Amy, as she leapt from her chair and ran to embrace her father. Blinking away his watery eyes, Silas pulled Amy's plump body up into his arms, bringing comfort to himself as much as to her.

"She's staying in town to take care of a very kind old lady, who was feeling a little poorly and had nobody to sit with her," lied Silas.

Although Jane was known as the quiet one of the family, she was blessed with an extraordinary sense of empathy for her young age of ten and from her time spent observing most of the family's ordeals; she knew that her pa was protecting them from the truth.

"Come along Amy; let's go to bed before Frank gets home! "

Amy was quick to say goodnight to her parents; she and Jane no longer respected Frank in the same way as they'd done a year ago; it had not slipped their notice how rude and troublesome he'd become and how he was constantly upsetting their ma and pa; he was also horrible to baby George, who they both adored.

"Shall I put Grace in her crib, Ma, she's fast asleep now?"

"God bless you, Jane...she's been such a handful tonight...goodnight girls, sweet dreams," spoke Clair in a low voice. "Don't forget to say your prayers."

"We won't Ma!" they answered in unison. "Goodnight Ma, goodnight Pa!"

"She's being held beneath the watchtower in Epsom...accused of *theft*, would you believe...*our little Martha*, in that terrible place and there is *nothing* I can do to help her!"

Silas broke down as Claire struggled to register his words. It was unbelievable...how could a journey into town to buy wool end in such a tragic state of affairs? They held each other tightly, both silently praying for their sweet daughter before Silas broke away angrily, *"Where's Frank?"* he demanded. "Did he *have* the *bloody gall* to show his lying face under my roof?" Trying to calm him, Claire quickly retold how Frank had explained the events in Epsom and that he was still out searching for his sister but the profound scowl on Silas's face and the way he shook his head in disbelief, soon confirmed to Claire that as usual Frank had been lying through his teeth.

"It is our son who is the thief, Claire!" he yelled at the top of his voice. "After fourteen years of everything we've taught him, Frank Shepherd is nothing but a common thief who would sacrifice his own flesh and blood to save his neck!" Upstairs, Jane quickly placed her hands to make a shield over Amy's ears, as she heard every single word of her pa's bellowing voice.

CHAPTER NINETEEN

It seemed that Amy and the twins were the only members of the Shepherd family to have any sleep that night and as the light of Sunday morning struggled to appear through the thick grey clouds, there was an ill omen about the sudden change in weather.

The pelting, night rain had forced Frank to take shelter in the dense copse surrounding the Brunswick Estate. Sleep was the last thing on his mind, his thoughts fully occupied with making plans for his future; it felt surreal; was he really about to sever all ties with his family? It was the only way, he assured himself, he was a young man now and there was no place for *two* men under the same roof.

Martha had lost all sense of feeling in her feet, and whatever liquid she'd been standing in throughout the night had seeped through the split in the sole of her boots. Her entire body felt icy cold as she waited by the prison door, glad of the arrival of morning and hopeful that her eyes would soon catch sight of her pa's arrival.

Startled by the sudden appearance of Wax as his grubby, grey face confronted her on the other side of the bars, she took a step backwards as the fumes from his fowl breath entered her mouth and added to the rancid stench in the air.

"I hope you got yourself a good night's kip,

Miss!" he teased as his grimy hands shoved a piece of stale bread in between the metal bars." Don't let it be said that Wax doesn't look after his captives!" he chuckled. "Now you'd best put yer prettiest face on and straighten up that sweet bonnet, cos old Cocklestone likes to get his business done before the last crow has sung her morning anthem!"

Martha reluctantly took the bread, even though she'd no intention of consuming a crumb of it. *"Cocklestone? Who is that?"*

"He be our very own magistrate, Miss and since it's Sunday morning with yesterday being a Saturday, no doubt, he's found 'imself detained at the Black Bull for the night...if you catch me drift!" Wax continued to laugh, as he returned back up the stairs of the watchtower.

A foreboding feeling engulfed Martha as she listened to Wax's heavy footsteps fade away into the distance; he was a loathsome being she concluded, who had probably never washed his face in the last ten years, let alone the rest of his body; a repulsive man who seemed to be thrilled as he witnessed her suffering. She could only pray that her pa would somehow be able to arrange for the Squire to enforce his powers in saving her and that help would arrive before the worrisome Cocklestone passed his own sentence.

"What's going to happen to Martha?" Jane

whispered to her ma as she tended to the twins. "I overheard Pa last night...is Frank *really* a thief Ma?"

Claire spoke simultaneously as her tears overflowed, "Please, my darling, just take care of Amy and the twins while we're away...and pray hard that we return home with some good news for a change!"

"I will Ma, don't worry!" assured Jane, feeling suddenly grown up with the new responsibilities falling on her.

Not bothering to eat breakfast, Claire and Silas were soon sat on the horse cart, covered with a wrapping of waxed sacking and heading speedily towards Epsom with the gloomy skies above them showing no sign of lifting. There were few words exchanged as they sped along the lanes, their faces soon soaked and dripping from the relentless downpour. Their arrival to Epsom High Street coincided with the heartbreaking sight of Martha being led through the town by Wax. Claire struggled to breathe and felt her heart sink as she viewed the callous treatment of her daughter; Martha's distressing sobs echoed through the empty market square. "Ma!Pa!" she cried out in despair, the sight of her parents causing her cries to increase; Wax tightened his grip on her arm as he boosted his speed all of a sudden.

"*Please let me talk to my parents!*" Martha pleaded. "They'll be plenty of time for that *when* and *if* old

Cocklestone declares you to be a free woman!"
"I'm not a woman, I'm just a girl!" she protested,
tearfully.

"Well, they're simply words and I don't make it a
habit to believe the words which sprout from the
mouth of a thieving minx!"

Wax held up his hand as a warning signal for
Silas and Claire to keep their distance.

"You may attend the hearing in the Black Bull,
but I must insist that you stay away from the
prisoner, for her own good!"

"She's just a young girl!" cried Claire. "She's done
nothing wrong, she's a good and honest
daughter...please, *I beg of you*, take pity!"

"Keep calm, Claire, there's no point in making a
spectacle of ourselves in broad daylight, justice
will be done; I'm sure," uttered Silas.

"Can't you ask for the hearing to be postponed
until the Squire returns, Silas?"

"I doubt they'll wait another two days my love,
but I'm sure if the need arises the Squire will be
able and more than willing to plead her case
when he's back home; he knows how honest our
Martha is!"

Constructed almost two hundred and fifty years
ago, the Black Bull Inn was one of the oldest
buildings along the High street; its low ceilings
immediately made Claire feel claustrophobic
and the overpowering stench of stale tobacco
smoke, ale and vomit caused her stomach to
contract. Her long skirts brushed through the

thick layer of soiled sawdust as she and Silas were ushered to sit on the antiquated Jacobean settle to the far side of the room. A couple of drunkards remained in the alehouse, their dishevelled bodies flat out upon the floor and the sound of their shallow snuffling, the only indication that they weren't corpses.

The proprietor took hold of their arms, dragging them one by one to the darkest corner of the alehouse, out of sight from the magistrate who'd been given a room upstairs for the night, free of charge; a small price to pay for his discretion surrounding the unlawful acts which went on when the inn closed its door to the public. An aroma of sickly perfume wafted in, most noticeable as its trail of sweetness merged with the existing sour and putrid stench. Claire heard a door slam, it was followed by the sight of two gaudily attired women hurrying past the window; shameful harlots concluded Claire, in disgust.

A loud cacophony suddenly overshadowed the snoring drunks; heavy footsteps upon the wooden staircase and an assortment of deep, masculine voices, laughing and exchanging lewd comments were then followed by the appearance of a short, stocky built man whose elaborate, yellowing judicial wig just reached his hunched shoulders. Claire immediately took a dislike to him, sensing that he was a man without a conscience. Her heart plummeted as she viewed the back of poor Martha, sat in front of her, still being held like a lamb to the slaughter by the awful jailer. On hearing her quiet whimpers she wished with all her heart that she could exchange places with her. Cocklestone and his group of cronies all assembled behind the bar.

"All rise for the Honourable Justice Cocklestone!" announced one of the men. Needlessly, Wax yanked Martha's arm, forcing her to her feet. Sensing that Claire's nervous disposition was causing her legs to tremble, Silas gently eased her up, keeping his arm supportively around her waist. Like a plague of locusts, news of the pretty young thief had spread throughout the town and a handful of curious town folk, hungry for a little Sunday morning excitement before church, appeared in the doorway, eager to witness the outcome.

"Kindly come in and sit down!" the spectators were instruction.

With the modest alehouse now ready to burst and Martha made to stand alongside Wax, a deathly silence soon descended.

Justice Cocklestone sat staring at Martha for a few moments; she felt awkward and on the brink of bursting into tears again. Cocklestone whispered to the man on his left, who then pronounced in a loud voice,

"Does the accused have anyone present in her defence?"

Silas imminently stood up,

"*I am here to defend her!*" he blurted out.

"And you are?" inquired the man.

"I'm Silas Shepherd, Sir; I'm Martha's father!"
The room suddenly burst into a ruckus of
laughter, leaving Silas scarlet faced.

"How quaint; a devoted father, standing in
defence of his daughter!" declared another one
of Cocklestone's cronies, causing another wave
of jeering to reach every corner of the room.

"I think not, Mr Shepherd and I trust that you
don't wish me to elaborate on the reason why?"
uttered Justice Cocklestone, his ample cheeks
wobbling as he shook his head.

Silas remained standing. "Well, could we at least
postpone the hearing until our Squire, Reginald
Brunswick's return to the area?" pleaded Silas.

"*Unthinkable!*" declared Cocklestone. "Now let's
proceed, we have yet to attend the Lord's Holy
house!"

Cocklestone's cold glare focussed on Martha
before he commenced. She was terrified and
even from the back of the room; her shaking
body didn't go unnoticed to Claire and Silas.

"Miss Martha Shepherd, you have committed a
terrible crime...and society has no place for such
immoral and dishonest youngsters who will, by
the law of statistics, only grow up with the need
to feed such an evil desire. When the population
strive hard, day in and day out to earn an honest
living and to fill their bellies with food, and pay

for a shelter in which to abide in, it is wholly unacceptable that *you, Miss Martha Shepherd,* should be left to your own wicked devices. In short, you are nothing more than a common thief; a menace to society and no doubt a shame to your family."

Martha swallowed hard; she had presumed that she'd receive nothing more than a severe reprimand from the Justice Cocklestone, but now she feared the worst and had a dramatic image of her body being strung up in the centre of Epsom for all to see. She felt her legs cave in beneath her and then the pincer-like grip of Wax's sharp and filthy fingernails dug into her soft flesh, bringing her back to her senses.

"I didn't steal anything, Sir!" she cried out, her cracked voice sounding unfamiliar.

"You were an accomplice to a gang of thieves, Miss Shepherd and if you didn't pilfer with your bare hands yesterday, I'm sure you have done on numerous occasions and intended to repeat the crime over and over again. But because it was not, evidently, your hands which lifted the objects from Mr Goldberg's fine establishment, I am prepared to issue a far lenient punishment and you may rest assured that your life will be spared."

As Martha had stood watching the justice Cocklestone's greasy looking lips moving, most of his words had flown over her head; the entire ordeal appeared to her like a nightmare; how could this possibly be happening to her, *Martha Shepherd*; she had to get home and milk the cows and comfort the babies when they cried, she had to help her sisters when they practised their cooking, she had to be at home to help her Ma. It was washing day tomorrow, how would her Ma manage to wring out the bed sheets without her help?

She focused on the three men before her, for the first time taking note of their smart attire; it didn't suit their grim looking faces she concluded as she watched them whispering together in a close huddle. One of them pulled out a small scruffy book from his pocket; he searched through the pages quickly before a look of success beamed on his heavily bearded face. All three seemed to focus intently on one page, all nodding their heads in agreement about what they were reading.

The Justice Cocklestone looked up, his face even more solemn than before as his beady eyes searched Martha's worried face.

"You will be taken from here to Woolwich, where you will be held as a prisoner aboard the convict hulk, HMS Warrior, until the tenth day of December. On that given day you will embark on a voyage from Sheerness, aboard the transportation ship, HMS Duncan, which is destined to arrive on the shores of Van Diemen's Land, in April or thereabouts in the year of 1841. You will serve a minimum sentence of seven years, and let this be a lesson to you Martha Shepherd and to any young delinquent wishing to pursue a life of crime and sin."

As the loud, heartbreaking cries and protests sounded from Claire and Silas, Martha's thoughts were confirming to her that the Lord was punishing her, not for theft, because she knew she was completely innocent, but for all the hours she'd wasted, daydreaming about, palaces, riches and gallant, handsome princes sweeping her off her feet, to wallow in a life of pure indulgence. She was being reprimanded for being such an ungrateful girl. Her only wish now, was for her life to return to how it had been before her cursed journey into town with Frank.

"Be brave Martha!" cried out Silas as he and everyone were hastily ushered out off the back entrance of the Black Bull. "The Squire will be sure to come to your aid just as soon as he hears what a dreadful injustice has been committed!"

"Keep praying my darling, daughter, as we will all pray for you!" exclaimed Claire, trying to hide her heart wrenching sobs of despair.

"Remember, we all love you, dearly!"

For the first time, Wax allowed Martha to turn around without inflicting pain; she watched the rear view of her beloved parents as they stepped out into the morning sunshine, wishing with all her heart that she could accompany them as she wondered if she'd ever see them again.

CHAPTER TWENTY

Silas and Claire waited a long and agonising two days for the return of the Brunswick family, the tension inside their tiny cottage was felt by every member, including the babies who seemed discontented with everyone. They kept the terrible news from Jane and Amy, only telling them that their poor sister would not be released until the Squire had intervened, but never having witnessed both her parents so watery eyed before, Jane sensed that the situation was far worse than they were letting on. Frank had not returned and although Amy continued to ask after him, his absence didn't appear to be such a pressing matter as Martha's imprisonment and as Jane spent more time listening than talking, she detected a definite animosity towards her brother every time his name cropped up, with Silas even refusing to voice his name, referring to Frank as *him*, in a hostile tone.

Relentless, torrential rain had fallen since Sunday bringing a morbid darkness all day long, befitting of the gloomy ambience in the Shepherd's household. Candles flickered all day long as the family went about their daily chores in a mundane manner. Although Claire insisted that they shouldn't forgo church, with the need to pray even more imperative; Silas was adama-

-nt that he'd not show his face in such a gathering until the problem had been resolved. With only a couple of hours passing before the Sunday sermon was to be read, the news had already spread from the town about the dreadful fate of Martha Shepherd. Mr Tyler immediately forbade his daughter to have anything more to do with Frank Shepherd, declaring the entire family to be immoral.

Disobeying her father's instructions, Sarah had to find out from Frank what had truly happened, not believing for one instant that Martha Shepherd was a thief. With Lydia being home for the day, it made her escape a little easier and by late afternoon, Sarah announced that she was walking Lydia back to the Brunswick's gatehouse before the gunmetal clouds made it even more difficult for them to see their way. After leaving Lydia at the entrance to the Brunswick Estate, she hurried through the dense woodlands until she reached the spot where she was to rendezvous with Frank. The intertwined canopy of branches formed a welcome shelter above Sarah's already cold and wet body, she shivered as her heavily saturated clothes adhered to her skin. Sat a third of the way up a beech tree, Frank felt his heart race as he caught sight of Sarah, knowing that at least she had not forsaken him; she was his only hope in life at the moment.

"*Sarah!*" He yelled out, amused as he watched

her searching high and low for him. He leapt out of the tree, landing a few feet in front of her and causing her to scream in alarm. Pulling her into his arms, he hugged her closely undeterred by the wetness of her body.

"I thought you might not show!"

"I'm here clandestinely; Father has forbidden me to see you!" she announced, tearfully.

"*Why*? Why would he do that? I thought your pa liked me!"

"It's not that, Frank, it's because of all this trouble with your sister! He now views your family in a different light!"

"Oh that's nothing," he declared flippantly.

"That will soon all be forgotten, like water under a bridge."

Sarah took a backwards step, leaving Frank's embrace. She looked seriously at him.

"How long have you been out here in the woods, Frank?"

"I spent the night here, everyone at home was trying to blame me for Martha's little escapade in town; I told them it was me who was being chased by a gang of ruffians, but they insisted on chastising me just for leaving Martha alone while she did her shopping!" he chuckled carelessly.

"Then you haven't heard what's happened then?"

The stern look upon Sarah's face changed his carefree mood.

"*Heard what?*"

"Poor Martha was convicted of theft and is to be transported, Frank!"

The bleak news forced him to sit down upon the damp leaves,

"But she's no thief! I was there and I know she never stole anything!"

"Then you must go and clear her name, Frank...it's her only hope...*your poor family*, what must they be going through?"

"I can't do that Sarah, it's not as simple as you imagine!"

Sarah couldn't believe what she was hearing.

"*Frank Shepherd*, either you go and speak out or there is no more *us*. I couldn't possibly continue a relationship with a beau who would stand aside and watch his innocent young sister be accused of a crime which she didn't commit and to be transported because of it."

"It was me, Sarah, I'm the one who took the silver...I did it for you, for us!"

Sarah took a sharp intake of breath, completely shocked by what she was hearing.

"That's why I so desperately wanted to see you today, to discuss our future; come away with me Sarah! *Look!*"

Like an excited dog, about to unearth a buried bone, Frank dashed to the foot of the tree which he'd been resting in and began scraping away the mound of twigs and leaves to uncover his hoard of stolen goods; he then quickly pulled out the wallet from his jacket, flipping it open in a hurry as he held the thick wad of white banknotes in front of Sarah's face. She looked on in shock.

"If I put one foot in Epsom, I will be recognised and hung for my crime, Sarah. There is nothing I can do for my sister, but at least she will not lose her life!"

Left speechless, Sarah bottom jaw dropped; she could do nothing but stare at the small fortune in Frank's hold.

"Please tell me that you didn't steal *all of that!*"

"It's for us my sweet Sarah, for our future together! Didn't I promise you a life of luxury, a life away from the filth of farming and slaving away from sun up to sun down? I must admit, I haven't quite reached my goal yet, but this little lot will set us up nicely for the time being!" In his enthusiasm, Frank had failed to notice Sarah's face crumble and the trickle of tears as they rolled off her freckled face.

"*No! No, Frank, this is all wrong!*" Her outburst immediately wiped the proud expression from Frank's face. "I'd rather work in a ditch with an empty belly than live from such a sinful income! I never imagined that the boy I loved and planned to make my future with would be nothing but a corrupt thief. You are deceitful to your rotten core *Frank Shepherd!* How could you do this to your lovely family? Poor Martha, she might not even survive the journey to the other side of the world, so that will make you no better than a *murderer* too! Do you want to go to your grave with the weight of so many terrible sins on your shoulders? You will *never* be forgiven!"

"First of all, Sarah! I'm not a boy! And you have no right to stand in front of me dictating what my fate will be in the hereafter! One day I will run my own business, I will be a man of great respect and you will be proud of me...this is merely the beginning and the only way in which the likes of us folk can make a break from being land tenants, generation after generation. Trust me, my sweet Sarah, one day you will walk proudly on my arm and be glad of the day when you decided to run away with me, for a new and better life!"

"And what about Martha? What about *your* family and *my* family? I'm already disobeying my pa just by being here and talking to you. What happens when you get caught; because all thieves *do* eventually? You will be swinging by your neck and I will be left to carry your shame for the rest of my life. Unlike you, *Frank Shepherd*, I love and respect my dear parents and there is no way in which I could put them through the pain which you are inflicting on your family!"

"So what do you expect me to do?" voiced Frank, pathetically.

"Leave me alone Frank Shepherd, go and find someone else to support your cause because if you don't attempt to make amends I want nothing more to do with you, *ever!*"

Frank stamped his foot down in protest; he had expected Sarah to be as thrilled as he was about their future together.

"I'm not going to swing for this, just to please you, Sarah...I value my life and intend to live it to the full!"

"What about Martha? What about *all* your family? Their lives changed forever because of you! *Goodbye Frank!*"

With the last of her emotional words, Sarah turned about and fled from the woods, blinded by tears and with a feeling that the sun would never rise in her life again. Her first love had ended in disaster and it would take a long time for her broken heart to heal.

After filling his pockets with the pricey silver trinkets, Frank pulled up his jacket collar, straightened his cap and headed out of the woods. Sensing that Sarah was likely to disclose his whereabouts, he had to hastily get away from the area. Bagley village was about to become a place from his past. He consoled himself with the fact that when he became an established, wealthy businessman, mother's would be delighted to offer their beautiful daughters to him; he would be one of those highly sought after, eligible bachelors who received an invite to every social function in the hope of a perfect match being instigated. One day, Sarah would be just a vague and distant memory, he mused as an uncomfortable lump caught in his throat.

The first glimmer of hope lifted Silas's spirits as he arrived at the Brunswick Estate to find the overloaded Brunswick carriage being relieved of its copious trunks and boxes, the Brunswick family had clearly been on a shopping spree during their time in Bath. He prayed that Reginald Brunswick had returned in the best of moods. Catching a glimpse of the man himself, Silas couldn't refrain from charging towards him. Knowing full well that he shouldn't be seen anywhere near the main entrance of the Manor House, Silas couldn't risk being turned away at the servant's entrance only to be told that the family needed to recover from their travels; his matter was far too pressing.

"Mr Brunswick! Squire!" he called out eagerly. He hadn't noticed that Bruce Brunswick was shadowing the Squire but even old Squinty Eye wouldn't prevent him from his urgent plea.

"Mr Shepherd!" The look of surprise was evident on the Squire's face, but he immediately sensed there was something very wrong; Silas resembled a man who'd not slept in days and his grey ashen face and unkempt appearance caused the Squire to stop in his tracks.

"Can you spare a few minutes of your time, Sir? It's extremely urgent; otherwise, I'd not be bothering you when you likely need to refresh yourself after your travels!"

Although the Squire was weary from the journey, he was intrigued to hear what calamity had struck Silas Shepherd whilst he'd been away in Bath.

"Does it relate to my recent proposal, Shepherd?" he asked discreetly.

The Squire's offer had completely slipped his mind during the disastrous events of the past days. "Oh, no, no Mr Brunswick, this has nothing to do with it!"

The Squire swiftly led him into one of the drawing rooms; the nearest to the front entrance of the Manor House. Bruce Brunswick tagged along too; curious to hear what this troubled man was about to disclose. He sensed that his brother wasn't keen on his presence though, "Do you wish a word in *complete* private Mr Shepherd...I can assure you that anything you say will not go beyond this room!"

Silas viewed Squinty Eye as he stood so innocently alongside his brother; there was a look of malice upon his face, as usual, but as much as Silas detested this obnoxious being, he was desperate to explain the urgency of his visit and on this occasion, it had nothing to do with Bruce Brunswick. Silas could not hold his tongue for a second longer and proceeded to explain everything, including how Sarah Tyler had discovered Frank hiding out in the woods on

Sunday and how she'd told him and Claire that Frank had confessed to stealing the items, but had now fled from the area, afraid of being caught and hung for his crimes.

It was a lot for the Squire to take in and far from what he'd been expecting to hear. But as he listened his mind was already made up that the fewer members of the Shepherd family that lived on his land, the better, and this might even be the catalyst in persuading Silas to accept his offer and leave the area for good along with his brother's illegitimate son.

The Squire faced Silas head-on, deep furrows showing on his forehead,

"This is the most disastrous news, Shepherd; such a strain on your poor family, but I will be totally honest with you and I'm afraid it's not going to please you. In short, Shepherd, there is very little I can do. The Justice Cocklestone is one of the country's most renowned magistrates and I hold no authority to intervene on his territory. What's more Mr Shepherd; you have no new evidence that will likely change the sentence in any way. Your scoundrel of a son has absconded and who is to say that they weren't working their disgraceful scheme together. In fact, Mr Shepherd, your son has done you a favour...He would have been hung no doubt, but at least your daughter will be a free woman after seven years..."

"Please Squire!" interrupted Silas, "there must be

something you can do, or at least try. *I beg of you!* My poor Martha might not even survive the treacherous voyage to Van Diemen's Land...I've heard tales which turn my blood cold about the hardships aboard those terrible transportation ships. She's but a child! Only thirteen years old for God's sake!"

"Never the less, she is old enough to know exactly what she was doing...She could have refused to allow your son to conceal his stolen property in her basket...but she didn't. That in my eyes makes her as guilty, if not more, than your son...It was well within her power to refuse your son's request and I dare say that if I had been the magistrate I would have passed the same sentence. We are a God-fearing nation, Mr Shepherd and the sooner we cleanse our great country of those who seem to think it is permissible to take what is not rightfully theirs the better! I am sorry to hear of your sad and shameful news, Mr Shepherd, but it is entirely out of my hands and I suggest that you get on with your life as best you can. Perhaps now is the ideal time to make that change which we discussed recently!"

Silas couldn't believe what he was hearing; all his hopes had been suddenly drowned leaving him gasping for breath; how was he going to tell Claire, he mused as he felt his spirits diminishing. The Squire had proved to be a huge disappointment and he sensed that he was quite glad of what had happened; ever since the arrival of little George and the issue with Bruce Brunswick's threatening letter, the Squire appeared to be more like a silent enemy than the caring Squire of the land as he'd once viewed him.

"I can't possibly leave Bagley village now, I have to be here for when my children return home!"

CHAPTER TWENTY-ONE

There was nothing that Silas and Claire could do; the law was above them and during the heartbreaking days which followed they were forced to accept that the matter was out of their hands. The thought had even crossed Silas's mind to accept the Squire's offer but use the funds to bribe someone in authority to release Martha before the Duncan set sail in December. Claire assured him that the amount of money that Reginald Brunswick would likely give them wouldn't be a quarter of the amount that would free their beloved daughter and they would be left homeless, penniless and no doubt end up in some appalling workhouse to live out their years. Frank seemed to have completely vanished, and knowing that Sarah had turned her back on him Claire was quite sure that he'd not show his face for a long time to come. He had committed a despicable act, and Silas had no reservations on declaring that he was no longer part of the Shepherd family. Amy cried for her missing siblings, day and night, not quite understanding the seriousness of what had gone on and always hopeful that perhaps, one day, they would step over the threshold, back into her life. A heavier responsibility seemed to be put upon Jane's young shoulders all of a sudden. With her mother in a state of melancholy and her pa's mind continuously preoccupied, Jane tended the twins and cared for Amy as proficiently as any mother would do. She also took the cooking and many more household chores into her hands, remembering all the lessons which Martha had taught her, especially when she'd been in her bossy moods.

The conversation which Bruce Brunswick had listened in on had been uppermost in his mind for many days...it had kept him awake at night, and he'd taken to pacing the grounds of the Brunswick Estate many a night beneath the bright glow of the full moon. His eccentric behaviour had not gone unnoticed by Lady Mary; she'd viewed him on a couple of occasions whilst taking in the beauty of the moonlit evenings from behind her bedroom window. She had alerted Reginald, but he simply dismissed it as 'a new and harmless compulsion' by his disturbed brother.

The subject, however, did come to light, two weeks later whilst Bruce was taking Sunday dinner at the Manor House.

"I'm seriously considering getting rid of my cook and my maid, Reggie!" he declared as the family enjoyed the succulent joint of pink beef.

Although a little shocked, the Squire expressed little objection; Bruce had been known to act quite irrationally in the past, so he simply listened to his declaration.

"How on earth will you manage?" questioned Lady Mary in astonishment.

Bruce refused to answer; he wanted his brother to question him, not his wife, who he looked upon as nothing more than a thief who'd stepped into the place of his mother and was no doubt entertaining a string of lovers behind his brother's back.

"Exactly, Brucie, *how* will you manage...never had you down as a chef before, or a skilled domestic. The gatehouse will become a hovel...you need to keep on the staff, brother dear."

"I'm sure that *your* cook could make a small hamper up for me every day...a selection of cold meats, fruit and bread; not too much. The rest I can easily see to myself."

The Squire and Lady Mary exchanged a furtive glance, while their daughter, who was the only member of the family dining with them, tried to hide her amusement of her bizarre uncle.

"Well, I'm sure we could come to some arrangement, if that's what you insist upon, can't we, my dear?"

"Of course darling," agreed Lady Mary, supportively.

The first part of Bruce Brunswick's plan seemed to have gone smoothly. He smiled to himself, feeling a warm sensation flow through his body.

By the end of that week, Bruce Brunswick had given Mrs Bunting, Viola and Lydia Tyler their marching orders, along with two week's pay and three astounding references; he didn't want any excuse for them turning up on his doorstep in the future. They left happily, apart from Lydia, who feared that nobody else would ever employ her. Mrs Bunting always had reservations about being employed by such an oddly behaved master; there had been many incidents which had gone on in the gatehouse which had troubled her. She was older and wiser to the wicked ways of the world, but with Bruce Brunswick's firm warnings that they would be fired without a reference should they disclose a single revelation outside the confines of the gatehouse, not a single word had ever spilt from their lips. Mrs Bunting was all too aware that her employer had regularly smuggled women of the night into his room, the large quantities of laudanum and whiskey hidden in his bedside cabinet were also no secret to her and there had been many a pretty young parlour maid who'd arrived to work at the gatehouse only to mysteriously disappear with Bruce Brunswick always feigning a display of surprise and shock, as though the young maids had up and left of their own accord in the dark hours of the night. Even more worrying to Mrs Bunting had been the sudden disappearance of young Molly; the Master had arrived home with her one day, declaring that she was to be given her own room upstairs, when the room adjacent to the kitchen had always been the servants quarters; they were told that Molly had come from a royal household but in one of the very few conversations which she'd shared with the pretty young maid, Molly had let slip that she'd been rescued from the workhouse by Bruce Brunswick. She also took offence when he was referred to by his nickname of *Squinty Eye*, protesting that he deserved more respect. Molly had a strange way about her; she was distant and always appeared to have her head in the clouds and neglected most of her duties, which didn't bother the master in the least. She had been another one who'd suddenly disappeared. Molly had become fat and lazy during her time employed at the gatehouse, so it was not a disappointment when Bruce Brunswick declared that Molly had decided to return to London and the so-called royal household.

Bruce allowed a few weeks to pass before putting the next and more tricky part of his plan into motion. The harsh autumn months had arrived in earnest; the semi-bare trees clung onto the last few obstinate leaves which adhered to the branches as though in fear of their demise. A strong northerly wind forced its way through the gaps in the gatehouse windows, singing in a high pitched voice as Bruce lay deep in thought, dwelling over the new era of his life which would soon commence.

As was agreed, one of the maids from the Manor House delivered a modest hamper of food to Bruce's doorstep every morning. He had stressed to Reginald that he wished not to be disturbed by anybody, claiming he'd received some kind of revelation and was about to write a book to better all books ever written. Never taking any of his brother's eccentric ideas and plans seriously, Reginald was just happy that he'd found something to occupy his days with and was more than pleased to co-operate in any way he could.

It was a bright but icy cold morning towards the end of November when Bruce left Bagley village to embark on his 'great journey', a journey he considered to top any he'd ever embarked on in his entire life. He had arranged to have the use of one of the Brunswick's smaller carriages, refusing the use of a driver and footman and informing his brother that he had been invited to stay with an old school friend who he'd not seen for over a decade. Reginald had detected a bracing high spirit about his brother of late; he lived in the hope that perhaps there might be a suitable woman involved in his trip, knowing that Bruce was normally reluctant to accept such invitations.

Bruce had stealthily taken trips into London

over the past weeks mingling with the shoppers in a city where it was unlikely that he'd meet anyone who knew him. Purchasing the finest quality women's ensembles and copious bolts of superior, oriental silk, together with every item a young woman would desire in her wardrobe, he had already set about transforming the main bedroom in the gatehouse to resemble the inside of a boudoir fit for a beautiful princess. He remembered every word which Martha Shepherd had said to him when he'd first been smitten by her youthful beauty and innocence along with her eagerness to dream of living a life in complete contrast to that of her station. He would make her dreams come true, becoming her hero, her very own prince and she would in time, grow to love him.

Locating Martha along the banks of the Thames was easier than Bruce had expected, he hadn't even had to travel as far as Sheerness. His hideous appearance prompted the toughest of drinkers in the alehouses to speak out about what they knew. Drinking dens frequented by the prison guards and where it had become something of a popular subject about the only female convict held in the hulk of the HMS Warrior at Woolwich. Martha had become the stem of many a vulgar comment, the only female destined to sail on the HMS Duncan in December, she was already being viewed as an ill omen and a guaranteed cause of much

disruption amongst the hundreds of male
convicts, making more work for the officers,
who couldn't understand why any magistrate
had not merely sent her to a house of correction;
she was clearly an innocent, God-fearing young
woman who had been raised by respectable
parents.

It was in the 'Thieves Kitchen', a dingy, drinking
hollow along the shores of the River Thames
where Bruce met with a notorious gang claiming
they were able to free any convict for the right
price. He felt every eye boring into his soul as he
entered the vile smelling hovel. A couple of
harlots flaunted themselves, their heaving
bosoms nearly spilling over their grubby low cut
gowns as they circled the groups of men,
collecting their empty tankards and teasingly
brushing against them as they did so. The men,
in turn, groped them, jeering and laughing
loudly as they felt no shame in voicing what
they had in mind for the fallen women.

"What the hell happened to yer face!" yelled one
drunkard.

Bruce ignored the comment, making a beeline
for the group of four men who were sat in a
shady corner of the alehouse. He pulled out the
small mushroom-shaped stool from beneath the
crude table and sat down. The four men glanced
at one another, unnoticed in the poor light by
Bruce's one eye.

"I was told that you could free a convict from the

hulk of the Warrior? Name your price!"
The four looked around nervously. They'd not
seen this man before which led to instant
suspicion; anyone wanting to buy such a favour
rarely came alone. His togs were too fine for a
man wanting to smuggle out a prisoner but
he wasn't the type of person who caused the
gang to sit on edge.
Suddenly aware of someone stood close behind
him, Bruce turned his head slowly; flinching as a
pointed fishing knife was thrust into the table.
The sharp, gleaming blade vibrated close to
Bruce's face as it stood vertical. Bruce knew it
was a warning and for the first time in many
years, felt intimidated. It was he who usually
had that effect on people, but now he was
amongst some of the most unscrupulous and
dangerous villains in London who were not
even slightly fearful of his threatening
appearance. Bruce felt the saliva trickle out from
the corner of his mouth and as he attempted to
retrieve his pocket handkerchief the man behind
him grabbed his arm, yanking it roughly behind
his back until he yelped like a maimed animal.
"Who are yer an' what's yer real business 'ere?"
"Let go of me, *my good man*, and allow me to
explain!" pleaded Bruce as the man retracted the
knife from the wood and held the blade to his
throat.
"One sly move, *Mister*, an' you'll be sleeping at
the bottom ov the Thames ternight, an' yer won't

be bloody snoring, that's fer sure!"

The man was loudly encouraged by his circle of cronies as they all cheered and Bruce sensed that it was the ring leader who had a hold of him.

"I don't intend to make any move at all, just hear me out, if you would."

The knife was lowered and Bruce finally got a glimpse of the man as he sat down at the table. He teasingly rotated the point of his blade in the wood, as he fixed his cold glare on Bruce. Bruce had always thought there couldn't be an uglier man than himself walking the earth, but this man's grotesque appearance surpassed his. Deep, uneven scars covered and distorted every inch of his face, his nose was crooked and almost flattened but the worst sight was the absence of his eyeball. He wore no eye patch to conceal the ugly, blackened void in his face, and Bruce sensed that he was a man who used his battle-worn face to terrorize and that maybe he wasn't as tough on the inside. Nevertheless, Bruce was not about to take anything to chance, he was sat amongst an intimidating group of feral villains, and doubted that anyone would bat an eyelid if they chose to murder him then and there and discard his body into the river.

"I wish to rescue a young girl; she has been wrongly sentenced..."

The instant the word '*girl*' came out of his mouth they all knew who he was talking about.

"What's yer business with that pretty petticoat,

then? Who is she ter you?"

"Martha Shepherd is the daughter of a neighbouring family. She is no thief and has been wrongly accused and harshly sentenced by Cocklestone...have you heard of him at all? He's nothing more than a drunk and a philanderer, who abuses his privileged position as magistrate of Epsom."

"I ain't never 'heard ov no Cocklestone, but 'e wouldn't be the first corrupt magistrate ter pass such a sentence," declared one of the gang. "There ain't a single officer who's 'appy about 'aving a bint amongst the 'undreds of men, down in the 'ulk."

"I heard that she's ter sail on the Duncan, an' there ain't no ovver female convicts destined ter sail on that neither!" uttered another of the men.

The ring leader spoke again, "Reckon, it might not be such a difficult task fer me to 'ave a word wiv one ov the jailors, an' fix something up for yer...if the price is right that is!"

"Why don't *I* just speak with an officer, every man has his price, especially since she is such an unwelcome prisoner!" suggested Bruce.

The knife was swiftly thrust into his chest, piercing through his clothes and perforating his flesh. He pulled back, terrified that this crazed man wouldn't hesitate to end his life.

"*You*, my good man," said the gang leader mockingly, causing the circle of men to cheer and laugh uncontrollably, "yer ain't one ov us, an' would likely be summoned ter the chief officer, interrogated and then sentenced yerself fer interfering with the justice and trying ter bribe an officer...now yer don't want that do yer, Gov? I'm guessing that you 'ave quite some reputation ter look after...am I right?"

Bruce tried in vain to swallow as he heard the sound of his saliva dripping onto the table.

"I would rather not be associated with any unlawful act, that is *indeed* true," admitted Bruce.

"How d'yer come by such an ugly mug?" shouted one of the men, "I always fought that our *Slicer* was the ugliest mug around!"

"Keep yer bleedin' pie 'ole shut, it ain't polite ter insult our guest!" snapped Slicer.

"I was tortured as a young boy!" announced Bruce unexpectedly.

The gang fell quiet for a second, a little shocked by what they'd heard.

"I always fought that you toffs lived a child'ood ov luxury wiv all them fancy governesses!" voiced Slicer. "What sort of mean folk torture young lads?"

Not wanting to discuss his unfortunate childhood any further to the group of drunken villains, Bruce remained quiet.

"Reckon as I can bribe the jailer wiv a few guineas...an' we would, ov course, all need a decent payout for our troubles; we work in a gang an' this is risky business, yer know; one which could easily go wrong an' see us floating off ter Australian soil!" stated Slicer as he repeatedly stabbed the knife in the wood in between his spread-out fingers, enjoying the gasps from his gang as he increased the speed. "Yer got the funds on yer Gov, cos we'd need ter be sure that yer ain't planning on pulling a fast one on us!"

"And how can I be sure that you won't be pulling a fast one on me?" questioned Bruce.

"Yer will just 'ave ter trust us...after all, reckon we're the only coves ready an' willing ter risk our necks, an' rescue yer sweet petticoat!"

Feeling like a fish out of water, Bruce knew that he had to think quickly and make an instant decision...He didn't trust anyone, but he had to take the gamble on the hope that this band of thieves would honour their side of the deal. He felt proud of himself, that he'd had the foresight to conceal his banknotes inside his boot. He'd heard many a tale about the perils which lurked along the banks of the Thames, they didn't employ folk to search for bodies in the murky waters for no just reason; such a gruelling source of income he mused, feeling a cold draught run through his bones.

"Right then! He declared, confidently. "Do we have a deal then?"

"All depends on the price yer prepared ter pay...a wealthy looking cove like yerself surely ain't short of money...Show us just 'ow much yer stashed in yer pockets fer this little escapade an' yer can bloody well quit all the nonsense about this petticoat being a bleedin' neighbour...yer ain't risked yer scrawny neck ter be the local 'ero...She must mean more ter you than yer letting on...we're all hot-blooded men yer know, an' familiar wiv the ways ov the world...don't be finkin' that yer can trick the likes ov us wiv yer fancy bloody ways, now!"

"Name your price and I will make sure you get paid the minute that Martha Shepherd is in my care!"

The gang of men immediately burst into fits of raucous laughter.

"Yer ain't got a bloody clue 'ave yer, Gov?" stressed Slicer. "*Lads,* find 'is stash!"

"Do you honestly think me that foolhardy to parade around this God forsaken pit with my pockets full? Give me some credit, my good man. The money *will* be exchanged when the deal is done."

Once again the knife was removed from the table and pointed directly towards Bruce's face.

"Remove 'is boots!" instructed Slicer, "an' yer best not insult our 'ome again, if yer knows what's good for yer.

As the gang held Bruce's limbs down and Slicer waved the blade precariously in front of his face, his boots were soon forcefully removed to reveal the bundle of banknotes.

"We knows every bleedin' trick in the book, you'd be wise ter remember that!" warned Slicer as he began to furtively count the money under the table.

Knowing that he'd made a terrible mistake, Bruce's fate was now in the hands of this notorious gang and he had little choice other than to play along with them. Slicer had a gleam of victory radiating from his face; he smiled for the first time, his intermittent decaying teeth adding to his unsavoury appearance.

"You an' me both know 'ow easy it would be ter fill yer pockets wiv rocks and chuck yer handsome body in ter the river...but don't yer worry Gov, cos I'm gonna prove ter you that we are decent men and not just a bunch of heartless thieves and murderers! Besides, I feel as though I'm about ter rescue a damsel in distress...an' you, by the sound ov it, 'ave bin dealt a rotten deck ov card in life!"

"That's *most* kind, my good man, but if you wouldn't mind returning a small portion of my money...you see, I have to pay for a room and stable for the night."

"Did yer 'ear that lads? I don't reckon that this 'ere gent knows 'ow we operate!"

The men's throaty laughter echoed around the alehouse.

"We ain't as daft as we look, yer know. You'll be far more comfortable than that poor little petticoat of yours, that's fer sure...we is gonna show yer some genuine East End 'ospitality! You will bunk down wiv us above the glass factory

an' me lads will take good care of yer, won't yer
boys?"

CHAPTER TWENTY-TWO

The simple fact that the prison officers sympathized with the only female convict aboard the hulk of the HMS Warrior was to prove a great advantage to Slicer and two of his motley gang when it came to rescuing Martha. Unlike the male convicts who were heavily shackled and sent out to excavate along the shoreline every day, Martha was allowed to enjoy an hour's fresh air on the river bank before her daily task of cleaning out the filthy hulk of its human waste. Following the inspection of her work, she was then permitted another breath of fresh air, in order to remove the putrid stench from her nostrils, before the rusty fetters were once again secured upon her, already sore and blistered ankles. Slicer had no intention of parting with a single shilling of Bruce's money; he knew how straightforward it would be to cause a disturbance amongst the men while one of them quickly seized Martha Shepherd. He didn't consider it would be much of an effort to rescue her either; he'd heard the talk amongst the naval officers who were to sail on the Duncan; she was considered a needless responsibility to most and it was common talk that she'd been framed and wrongly sentenced.

The perfectly timed thick pea-souper descended

upon the banks of the river the following morning. Thick clouds of dense and putrid smog made visibility extremely poor. Slicer and his men could hear the chants of the prison officers as they tried to induce the reluctant convicts into a synchronized dig along the gravel shores. In the distance, Martha's silhouette was visible as she sat upon a discarded wooden crate. Having the notion that it might be possible to snatch Martha away unnoticed without the need to set up a distraction, as Slicer stealthily approached, the sudden discovery of a hefty warden standing a few feet behind her caused him to freeze in his tracks. Concealed in the thick smog, it was only when Slicer became too close for comfort that the warden spotted him. Sensing an ambush, the warden was instantly ready to blow on his whistle but in a split second, as he placed it to his lips, Slicer made an urgent dash, pulling out his infamous knife as he did so. Throwing himself onto the guard and knocking him off balance, Slicer took hold of the guard's throat as he straddled upon him. His large hand gripped tightly causing the guard's eyes to bulge and his face to become scarlet, as he feared for his life, knowing, just by the copious scars on his face, that this must be the infamous Slicer who he'd heard so many stories about. Slicer's men were soon at the scene, and between the three of them, they filled the guard's mouth up with gravel, gagged him and tightly bound his ankles and hands together. Catching his breath back, Slicer turned to Martha who'd viewed the entire incident, barley taking in a breath of air as she did so. Already convinced that she was to be snatched away by this gang of ruthless pirates, Martha viewed it as a far better alternative to another night spent in the overcrowded, rat-infested hulk of the HMS Warrior with the feral convicts, where she feared for her life every single night.

"Come along sweet maiden! We 'ave bin sent to yer rescue! Keep quiet an' keep low as we escort yer off these muddy shores!"

As Slicer became visible, Martha displayed no reaction to his gruesome appearance; Bruce Brunswick had been a face in her life for many years and she was more intrigued by the stories behind how men came about having such maimed and scared faces, knowing that they had once upon a time been handsome young boys.

"*Where is your ship?*" she whispered, expecting to embark on a high seas voyage, with the gang of pirates.

"Yer is *Martha Shepherd*, ain't yer?"

"*You know my name*!" she declared in astonishment.

"We've bin commissioned ter save yer pretty neck, *Princess*, so you'd best get a move on an' save yer questions fer later when we've reached safety."

The room above the glass factory was hot and stuffy. Bruce had not slept a wink for fear of his life but the tiny glimmer of hope which occupied his thoughts were that since the gang had already taken all his money, there was no reason why they should keep him alive a second longer if that was their intention.

The noisy clamber upon the wooden stairs broke into his reverie. Slicer shoved the door open and stood victoriously with Martha at his side.

"*Mr Brunswick!*" she exclaimed in amazement. "I didn't expect to see *you* here!"

Bruce Brunswick's distorted smile was a sight which Martha never thought she'd be glad to see.

" 'ave I proved me point, Mr Brunswick?" laughed Slicer, noticing the look of shock on his face. "Folk like us *can* be trusted yer know, we ain't all a bunch ov fraudsters!"

Slicer took out some loose change from his pocket and handed it to Bruce.

"Take this, you'll need ter pay the stables for yer 'orse, no doubt; the quicker yer get away the better, an' ter prevent any suspicion, *little Martha* should become *little Mathew* until yer pass through London's gates."

Dressed in a threadbare jacket and heavily stained trousers, both of which were too small and reeked of stale bodily odour, Martha looked like a pauper rescued from the workhouse and that was to be the story which Bruce insisted they tell, should anyone stop and ask; he would say that he required a stable lad and rescuing a workhouse orphan was his charitable duty. Insisting that Martha drank the potion of rum and laudanum from his hip flask, it only took a few minutes before Martha was curled up on the softly padded seats of the Brunswick's carriage and in a deep sleep. Left penniless, Bruce was forced to change his plans and instead of waiting for nightfall to arrive, he now had little choice but to return directly to Bagley village and simply pray that nobody was watching when he smuggled Martha into the gatehouse.

Bruce Left the carriage outside the perimeter wall of the Brunswick Estate, not wishing to alert the family of his return; there was a short distance between the entrance gate and the gatehouse of which only the first few yards were visible to anyone who might be watching from the Manor House. Martha had barely eaten enough food to keep her alive over the past weeks; she was half the girl she'd been on that morning of her unforgettable journey into Epsom with Frank; her curvy figure had diminished leaving her looking more like the thirteen-year-old girl she was. Her lightweight, however, did make it an easier task for Bruce to bundle her up into his arms and make a hasty dash for the gatehouse before returning the carriage to the stables and announcing his arrival to the family.

Reginald Brunswick viewed his brother curiously as Bruce marched through the drawing-room doors. Lady Mary choked on her mouthful of coffee, as she gasped in shock by her brother in law's unkempt appearance.

"*Good God, Bruce*...are you alright? Have you been set upon?" Reginald expressed urgently, aware that many ignorant folk might view his brother to be some kind of threatening monster and take it into their hands to issue him with a physical warning.

"Come and sit down, Bruce, you look dreadful!" cried out Lady Mary as she patted the couch next to where she sat.

In the traumatic events of the last twenty-four hours, Bruce had been so relieved to escape alive from the banks of the River Thames, that he'd failed to notice how dreadful he must look after his time spent in the filthy squalor of Slicer's lodgings above the glass factory. It was only as he stood embarrassingly in the prestigious drawing-room that he got a whiff of his unwashed body.

"Please don't fuss; I'm perfectly well, just in need of soap, water and a long sleep! I assisted an unfortunate family on my return journey, who's carriage had lost a wheel and had run off the road into a bog, that's all...apart from that my journey was most enjoyable. I would appreciate a hamper though Reggie, travelling has given me a healthy appetite!"

"Why on earth you don't take on some staff at the gatehouse again, is a mystery to me Bruce...you're obviously not managing without!" remarked Reginald.

"Please brother dear, we've had this conversation before and I'm too tired to repeat myself today!"

Reginald let out a long frustrated sigh.

"I'll go and have a word with cook," announced Lady Mary, eager to leave the room, "I'm sure she will be able to rustle up a generous hamper in no time at all. Would you like one of the staff to bring it across to the gatehouse, Bruce?"

"That's very kind Mary, but I will wait for it outside in the fresh air if you don't mind...wouldn't want to fill the entire house with my awful stench!"

"There's no need Bruce, you're being bloody petty as usual!" objected Reginald.

Having lost his handkerchief, Bruce wiped his trail of saliva onto the back of his sleeve; the look of disgust from Reginald and his wife did not miss his eye.

"I'll bid you farewell and wait outside!" he stated sternly before making a speedy exit.

Still in her drug-induced sleep, Martha had not moved an inch from where Bruce had, so tenderly, laid her on the couch. He stood gazing down at her for a while, a shadow of her former self, mused Bruce with sorrow in his heart. He would nurture her back to health and make her dreams come true. He had rescued her and in Bruce's mind, he was now her guardian. He placed the selection of food upon plates and displayed them as elegantly as he knew how upon the low table hoping that their pleasant aroma would awaken Martha.

On his return from the small back garden where he'd filled the jug with fresh water from the pump, Martha was becoming agitated in her sleep and was making small whimpering noises. Bruce sat opposite her, waiting and watching her closely as her eyelids twitched. She had thick, long dark eyelashes, observed Bruce and even though her face was drawn and dirty, her underlying beauty was still radiant. She opened her eyes and studied her unfamiliar surroundings. A huge wave of relief washed over her; she was in a pleasant room with the sweet smell of food wafting through her nostrils, a far cry from the atmosphere of the ship's hulk. She stared at Bruce for a while, unlike most young girls she had never been scared by his hideous appearance but remembering her pa's recent warning, all of a sudden, caused a sudden coldness to run through her frail body.

"*Mr Brunswick!*" she exclaimed, her words struggling to make any sound. "*You rescued me!*"

Bruce handed her a damp cloth,

"Wipe your face and hands Martha Shepherd and eat, then we will talk!"

The reddish skin on Bruce's face was taut as he smiled at Martha, she lowered her gaze, embarrassed for him as he dribbled uncontrollably. The rumblings in her belly were loud and she giggled nervously.

"*Eat Martha!*" he instructed.

Not remembering when food had ever tasted so delicious, she filled her belly and gulped down the sweet-tasting, clean water while Bruce set about lighting the fire in the icy cold gatehouse.

"There's some colour in your cheeks now," he stated when Martha had consumed all she was able to. Her stomach had shrunk over the weeks in captivity where stale bread and murky looking water had become her staple diet.

"That was delicious, thank you, Mr Brunswick," she replied politely."I've never before tasted such succulent beef!"

"That's because it is venison!"

Not wanting to appear even more ignorant, Martha simply said, "Of course, I should have known!" as she sat curiously wondering what a venison looked like.

"Could I take a tiny slice home to my ma? I doubt she's ever tasted venison before."

Dabbing his chin with a damp handkerchief, Bruce wondered how Martha was going to react to what he was about to show her and inform her.

"Are you feeling strong enough to walk up the stairs, Martha, there is something I wish for you to see."

"Yes, of course I am!"

Martha instantly conjured up the notion that Bruce Brunswick had arranged for her entire family to be secretly waiting upstairs ready to greet her, maybe this was his way of making amends for all the problems he'd given her family over the months. Keeping her speculations to herself, not wanting to ruin the surprise; infused with excitement, she followed Bruce as he led her through the hallway and up the stone staircase. At the end of the landing, they approached what was the largest bedroom in the house and what, until a month ago, had been Bruce's room. He pushed open the double doors and stood proudly in admiration of his very own artistic handiwork.

Every wall in the ample room was swathed with the finest lengths of silk; draped from corner to corner and from ceiling to floor, the pastel shades of rose pink, soft sage and faintest lemons gave the room a calming but regal atmosphere. The sumptuous four-poster bed was draped with copious richly coloured and elaborately embroidered velvet coverlets and cushions and upon the dressing-table stood an assortment of French perfumes and a selection of beautiful gem-studded hair slides and lengths of beaded necklaces. Bruce walked across the luxurious deep pile floor rug and pulled open the doors of the huge, highly polished mahogany wardrobe, to reveal a row of the finest and most attractive gowns and day dresses in every shade.

"Once you have settled, my dearest Martha, you will find an array of delights tucked away in the remaining drawers and cupboards. This is your very own palace, the one you spoke of during our conversation in the barn. Your dreams have come true, Martha Shepherd and you will now live a life of comfort and luxury...a life fit for the beautiful princess that you are."

Left in a complete state of shock, Martha didn't know how to react. What could he possibly mean, she mused, fearfully; had she been rescued from one prison only to begin a bizarre new sentence as Bruce Brunswick's prisoner?

"When will I be able to see my family?"

"Martha! Don't you like the palace I've made for you...is it not to the taste of Princess Martha?"

Lacking in her usual confidence as she stood, still dressed in the shabby boy's clothes and weakened from her ordeal, Martha swallowed hard feeling awkward in her strange surroundings.

"It looks lovely, but I didn't really mean it when I told you of my dreams; they were only childish fantasies and since that day, I have learnt that family is far more important than any riches. *Please take me home, Mr Brunswick!*"

"Don't be such a little fool!" he declared irately, his face turning scarlet. "You may be free from the abysmal hulk of the HMS Warrior, but in the eyes of the law, you are nothing more than an escaped convict...your home will be the first place to be searched...and what do you suppose the authorities will do with you once they catch you? Transportation will be out of the question! You will hang in the middle of town for all to view. What do you think *that* will do to your poor suffering family, *Martha Shepherd?* If you care so much about your family, you would be wise to forget about them and leave them to get on with their lives in the belief that you are still alive somewhere in the world. Surely this is a far better way to spend your life than as a convict on the other side of the world, that providing that you would have even survived the voyage. A pretty, young girl amid so many lustful men, with not another female in sight…think about the fate which I have rescued you from Martha Shepherd and be grateful. You will want for nothing and in time might view me in a different light, even grow to love me. I know I am far from being handsome, but my heart harbours a true and sincere attachment to you, I am a man of patience and would never do anything to harm you, Martha. Please think of me as your humble knight, your protector! Not a living soul must know of your whereabouts, Martha and you would be wise to always remember that!"

His words spun around inside Martha's head; she wanted to cry but for some odd reason there were no tears; too much had taken place over the past weeks, her mind was confused; weakened in both body and mind, the only consolation was that she was miles away from the dreadful nightmare of the convict hulk and now close to her beloved family even if they were out of her reach. Overcome by tiredness all of a sudden, she cordially asked if she could take her rest upon the alluring bed. Wanting nothing more than a long sleep himself following the tense experience of the rescue, after warning Martha not to attempt anything foolish before he left her boudoir, Bruce secured the front and back entrances to the gatehouse before retiring to his bedroom.

CHAPTER TWENTY-THREE

December arrived; bringing with it the first flakes of snow, fluttering down peacefully from the vast expanse of white skies, but there was very little peace to be found in any of the Shepherd family's hearts. When normally Amy and Jane would be eagerly awaiting the first snowfall to run outside and play, the miserable atmosphere within their home had left them in the most melancholy of moods. They weren't even looking forward to Christmas and by now, had both realised the enormity of the tragedy which has befallen their family. All smiles and laughter within the cottage had been replaced by tears and moments of haunting despair. Claire was wasting away, unable to eat more than enough to barely give her the energy to cope with each day, she felt constantly nauseous. The tenth of December was fast approaching, the day when her darling Martha would sail away to a savage land and be lost to her forevermore. She had never heard of anyone returning to home soil once they'd been transported, it simply didn't happen. But as Silas had repeatedly said when he tried to console her, where there was life there was always hope to cling on to and they should at least be grateful that Cocklestone hadn't placed the ominous black cloth upon his head when passing sentence.

In the silence of the many nights, when sleep refused to ease their suffering, Claire and Silas had discussed the Squire's offer and were united in the decision that it would be for the best to start a new life far away from Bagley village where they were now looked upon by their lifelong neighbours as a broken and shameful family and a family not to be trusted or associated with. For the sake of Amy and Jane and the young twins, they felt forced to abandon their home. They now also both harboured a huge feeling of animosity towards the Brunswick family knowing that if Reginald Brunswick *had* wanted to, he could have intervened and perhaps saved Martha from such an unjust sentence. They would take his money and anything else he was offering and be glad to see the back of their corrupt magistrate and his crooked blackmailing cripple of a brother.

Now lodging in a dreary room above a pie shop in Leatherhead, Frank's dream of wealth and a better life had suddenly lost its attraction. He missed the delicious smell and taste of his ma's baking, the sound of his sister's excited chatter and little Amy's constant, amusing questions. He missed Sarah too; who he knew now viewed him with shame and disrespect and most likely wished she'd never walked out with him. He had lost everything and been the cause of a colossal tragedy, ruining the lives of his family forever. He knew his poor ma would never be happy again; she adored every one of her children with such a loving affection and a tenderness which he had so cruelly thrown back in her face over the past months, she endured far more than she deserved and never once complained. She'd made countless sacrifices throughout her life, seldom grumbling and always appearing cheerful and content for the sake of her family. Frank now realised how wrong he'd been to presume that wealth was the most important aspect of life. Here he was with a stash of banknotes, a hoard of treasure, but he couldn't buy what he was yearning for.

Living above the pie shop had also been an eye-opener as to how devious the wealthy folk could behave and how the poor were often treated as though their lives were of little importance and were void of any emotions; simply living to survive and serve the better folk before returning to their Maker. Frank had pretended to be a destitute orphan, newly released from the orphanage and looking for work, it was the only idea he could think of at the time which would save him from wasting away all his savings on living costs. The pie shop had been advertising for a lad to help in the kitchen; sweeping the floor, washing up and occasionally chopping up the meat and offal. With free lodgings and a meagre weekly pay packet, Frank accepted knowing that it would enable him to become invisible to the outside world while he planned his next move.

Mr and Mrs Bergman were both in their forties; they'd married young but had not been blessed with children. After establishing themselves in the East End of London, where they'd made their initial fortune selling pies, they moved out of the poverty stricken area to Leatherhead. Living above the shop, to begin with, they soon became one of the most popular pie shops in the area and were able to purchase a small but modern townhouse on the pleasant outskirts of the town. Frank watched their faces gleam with delight at the close of business every day, as they counted their takings; Mr Bergman would carry the money home, concealed in a large metal milk jug, leaving local folk to presume they were off to purchase milk from the dairy. They lived for money and worshipped it, it was the core of their existence, but having no family had caused them to become cold-hearted and uncharitable. One evening Frank was unable to fall asleep, a rancid stench seemed to seep through the floorboards from the kitchen below and fill his tiny room with the unbearable odour. He left his bed to investigate and found a huge pan of cooked steak and kidney. The overbearing stink of the fermenting pie filling choked him and turned his stomach as he held his breath and hauled the heavyweight out of the kitchen and into the back yard; he covered the vessel with a lid to deter the invasion a plague of rats. The following morning Mrs Bergman erupted into a state of rage, appalled that Frank could be so wasteful and discard what she considered perfectly good food.

"You best pray that the rats ain't bin 'aving a bloomin' midnight feast!" she yelled, the veins in her scrawny neck standing out like a map's waterways.

Mr Bergman shook his head, clandestinely sympathizing with anyone who'd caused his temperamental wife to lose her composure.

"If I were you, lad, I'd keep busy 'til she's calmed down a bit," advised Mr Bergman, "Don't give 'er any reason ter give yer the sack!"

"I *did* cover the pot, Mr Bergman; I'm not stupid you know, but that pie filling reeked so bad it kept me awake!"

Mr Bergman winked and spoke in a low voice, "She'll 'ave a way will Mrs Bergman, you just wait an' see lad, cunning as a vixen is my wife!"

Frank did wait and see and was horrified when he witnessed Mrs Bergman rinsing the rotting meat and offal before adding it to some freshly made, extra thick gravy.

"There we go!" she announced triumphantly, to Mr Bergman, her hands resting on her bony hips. "By the time we've re-cooked that in a wrapping of pastry, nobody will taste the difference, but make sure yer only sells 'em ter the poorer folk...make 'em 'alf price...after all, it will be 'alf the crime if *they* gets sick an' pops their worn-out clogs!" Her wicked laugh echoed around the kitchen; it was a lesson for Frank and an eye-opener as to how unfairly poor folk, just like his family, were treated. In those few minutes, the attraction of becoming a wealthy man quickly diminished.

With the departure date for the HMS Duncan fast approaching along with the threat of imminent heavy snowfall, Claire felt a huge urgency to leave Bagley village and make a start on their new life as soon as possible. Feeling like a stranger himself amongst his neighbours, Silas was in complete agreement with his wife but knew it would have to be an instant move before they became snowed under for the entire winter months. The news was a welcome relief to Jane and Amy who had silently put up with being mocked and jeered at by the village school children. Parents had warned their children to have nothing to do with the Shepherd girls, whose shameful sister had caused an embarrassing scandal; enough to tarnish the entire village. The children had taken their parents instructions one step further and took to verbally bullying Jane and Amy, causing Amy to spend her days in floods of tears. Claire had sensed what was going on in the schoolroom and admired her girl's resilience, knowing that they were bearing the burden upon their young shoulders in order to shield her from any more grief. A new start in a new place would be the only way of retaining any kind of happiness within her family, concluded Claire and would take them away from all the sad memories of when the family was whole and their life had not been marred by recent events.

In his urgency in attempting to put right all that he'd sabotaged in recent months, Frank had decided to journey in search of the place where his sister was being held prisoner and attempt to bribe anyone, who might have access, to set her free. Convinced that his small fortune would be enough to tempt most prison wardens, for the first time in many months he felt his spirits lifting as a surge of optimism engulfed his heart; he could just picture the expression of delight on his ma's face when he returned to the cottage with Martha at his side, she would be sure to forgive him his past shortcomings and take him into her loving embrace once more. Time was not on his side; he knew it was only a matter of days before the convict ship was scheduled to sail to another world, taking his sister with it; he had even begun to miss Martha, which until recently he'd not thought possible. He missed hearing about her farfetched dreams and prayed that her vivid imagination would keep her sane whilst she was held in one of the notoriously nightmarish convict hulks.

Telling Mr Bergman, who would be less likely to ask questions, that he needed to make an urgent dash to London for personal reasons, Frank set off from the pie shop just before daybreak. The overnight temperature had plummeted, leaving the world sparkling from the hard frost which had left its deposit upon everything it touched. The air was fresh, causing a cloudy plume to emanate from Frank's breath as he hurried to reach the main highway to London. Copious wagons were already rattling along the main thoroughfare, heading towards the London docklands, making it easy for Frank to cadge a lift on the back of one. He sat in deep thought, praying that after this day if he successfully rescued Martha, his life would soon return to normal, he would willingly work on the farm, helping his pa and maybe even be able to win back the heart of his sweet Sarah, before she fell into the arms of another; yes, he mused, he would abolish all ambitions of wealth and of gaining a higher position in society and settle for a future with the love of a devoted wife, the love and respect of his family and a life following in his pa's footsteps, farming the land. His selfish dreams of becoming one of the richer folk would be put behind him forever, he now knew that *his* folk were richer than any King or Queen in the world; they understood the value of family love and were united in the hardships of life.

The freezing temperatures had kept the usual

foul stench of the Thames at bay and on such a crisp morning, there was no sign of the infamous London smog. The City's bustling streets were already full; traders and costermongers dragged their noisy barrows across the cobblestones as they bawled out to one another, in preparation of a day's trading. The weak winter's sun had already begun to melt away the layers of frost making the streets less hazardous beneath Frank's boots. He marched along the river bank towards the Woolwich docks where he'd been informed by a costermonger of the handful of decommissioned ships now used as floating prisons for convicts awaiting transportation. The mere thought that Martha must be so close by increased his pace and before long he was stood at the edge of the shore overshadowed by the colossal ship's masts.

CHAPTER TWENTY-FOUR

To protect and avoid losing their jobs, the gang of wardens responsible for the convicts aboard the HMS Warrior had collaborated on a feasible story regarding Martha Shepherd. The next female body to be hauled out of the river by the body searchers was to be wrongly identified by them as her, who, in the dense river smog had unwittingly or perhaps suicidally, ended up in the murky waters and drowned. No questions were asked and to the naval officers of the convict ship, HMS Duncan, the news was somewhat of a welcome relief. It was unheard of to have a single and juvenile female prisoner amongst hundreds of hardened male convicts. Frank made his way along the steep embankment, drawn by the repetitious sound of metal spades upon the shingles. The long line of heavily fettered convicts all wearing the same soiled, grey overalls soon came into view, a stocky built warden yelled at them every few seconds and another one stood tall, and marched alongside them, issuing the occasional aggressive dig with his iron rod to any prisoner who dared to slack. There was no sign of Martha, these were all men and as Frank felt his heart sink, another warden who he'd not noticed was suddenly crunching his way speedily across the gravel in his direction.

"This is no place to hang out lad!" he shouted, belligerently as he came within earshot of Frank. *"Go on! Clear off;* these are dangerous men and I ain't in the mood for any disturbances this mornin'!"

"I'm looking for someone!" stressed Frank, puffing out his chest in the hope of appearing a lot older and braver than he actually felt.

The warden stared coldly at him, before raising his voice even louder,

"Well, cum on then lad, speak up fer God's sake, I ain't got all bleedin' mornin' yer know...A name! What's the bloody convict's name?"

"M...M...Martha Shepherd, S...Sir!" It was the first time in his life that Frank had found himself stuttering; his words were caught like barbed wire in his throat and he knew he'd have to do a lot better if he was to negotiate some kind of bribe with this ominous man of steel who towered above him.

"Martha Shepherd," he repeated in a quiet drawl. "Be yer sweetheart, no doubt?"

Frank laughed nervously, "No, she's my sister!"

"Oh dear, son, looks like you've 'ad a wasted journey..."

"Is she here? I just wanted to see her before she leaves England, that's all!" interrupted Frank, deciding that he might find another of the wardens more approachable.

"I'm sure word 'as bin sent ter the magistrate where she received 'er sentence an' I'm sure

word will soon reach 'er family, but since yer 'ere lad, there ain't no easy way of telling yer that yer sister drowned...Don't mean ter sound callous, but it were probably fer the best, she didn't stand a chance in 'ell afloat a ship where she was ter be the only female! Sorry lad!"
He turned and walked away, promptly, leaving the sound of his footsteps echoing in Frank's ears.
Frank felt numb, his watery eyes suddenly overflowed as he fell onto the ground in a heap, unfeeling of the sharp rocks and pebbles as they dug into his body. No news could be worse than what he'd just heard and he knew that he would never gain his parent's forgiveness. This was entirely his fault and now it was impossible to put right.
More than an hour had passed before the biting icy wind blowing in from off the Thames forced Frank to rise to his feet and leave the dismal river bank. Froze to his marrow, and numb from being huddled in the same position for so long, Frank stumbled up the steep incline and reached the pavement. Walking blindly, the devastating news had yet to fully sink in; the thought of never seeing Martha again was inconceivable; death was a new experience in his world and he felt unable to come to terms with it. Now he knew how his poor ma must have felt when she'd lost her babies. His ma and pa were always capable of fixing every problem, but this

was so final and would make him even more of an outcast.

The day of the HMS Duncan's departure arrived and although Claire and Silas were far busier than usual, packing up everything in the only home they'd ever known, Martha was at the forefront of their minds and tears were never far from their eyes. Intermittent embraces of support and affection kept them going throughout the day, as they meticulously wrapped everything and loaded what they could onto the large wagon, purchased for them by the Squire as part of the deal. The following day would see them setting off for a new beginning. It was ironic that they were to take over the lease of an Oxfordshire ironmonger's shop whilst the owners had emigrated to Australia to begin a new life of farming. The short days of winter had persuaded them to set off at first light the following morning, with a journey of fifty miles ahead of them, it would take all day before they arrived in Oxford with their loaded wagon and as Silas viewed the white skies, he prayed hard that the threatening snow would hold off until they'd arrived at their new home.

Frank had spent three restless nights since returning to Leatherhead, consumed with the painful news which rested heavily on his broken heart, the thought that perhaps his pa might journey to Sheerness to view the departure of the Duncan in a show of love and support to Martha played gravely on his mind. Suppose his family had not yet been informed of Martha's fate, he considered, he couldn't allow his pa to endure the long trip only to discover that Martha had drowned. Promising a displeased Mrs Bergman that he'd work extra hard on his return, Frank left Leatherhead behind him and headed off to Bagley village, whereupon arrival, from a distance, he caught sight of his pa busily loading up the new wagon. While part of him felt relieved that his pa hadn't ventured to Sheerness, he felt his heart plummet, knowing that the roots to his existence were about to be severed forever; he was to be abandoned in the world and all of a sudden he no longer felt like the man he'd been so determined to prove he was but like a small, helpless boy. He choked on his tears as childhood memories engulfed his thoughts; images of summer days on the land, playing with his sisters, helping his pa and feeling so grown up and proud when he'd declared what a clever lad he was. He reminisced on the long country walks with his ma; his small hand in hers as she taught him the names of flowers and trees along with so many more valuable lessons in life.

Knowing that it wouldn't be long before someone spotted him hidden amongst the hedgerows, he also knew that if his parents did know of Martha's terrible drowning, he would sense it from the moment he confronted them. Thinking that he'd bolted the cottage door for the last ever time, Silas sat down with his family as they prepared to eat their final supper before they turned in early, in readiness for the long journey ahead of them. Having packed away all of the plates and bowls, they all had a spoon and ate directly from the saucepan in the centre of the table. The atmosphere was strained; it was no secret that by now, Martha would be sailing across the rough seas, gone forever from their lives. They said a special prayer for her safety and for her safe return to them one day. Claire knew that her dream of Martha returning would be the only means of allowing her to cope. Thankfully the babies were sound asleep and the mood was lightened slightly as Amy, in her struggle to reach the saucepan and receive her fair share of food decided to leave her chair and clamber across the table. Her desperate action was, on this occasion, permitted especially as it brought about a smile on everyone's solemn faces.

The sudden rap on the door interrupted the meal.

"Who could be calling at this time of night?" questioned Silas as he left his seat.

"Maybe someone has come to bid us farewell and wish us luck!" stated Claire, sarcastically.

Silas sniggered, "I very much doubt it!"

The instant he pulled open the door, Frank fell down at his feet, sobbing hysterically.

"Forgive me Pa! Please forgive me! I beg you!" Claire rushed to his aid, wrapping her arms around his shaking body.

"Frank's come home!" exclaimed Amy, joyfully at the top of her voice.

"He's freezing!" cried Claire, tearfully.

Jane was quick to pull the blanket from the settle and hand it to her ma.

"Come and sit near the stove son and warm yourself!" insisted Silas as he assisted him across the room.

*"I'm sorry, I'm sorry, please forgive me...*I'm a terrible son...*please forgive me Mother!"* he continued to plead. "It's *all* my fault...I'm so sorry, Ma...can you ever forgive me? Pa, please...*I beg of you!"*

As Silas and Claire exchanged furtive glances, Frank continued with his hysterical ranting; his parents had never seen him so distressed before.

"Would you like some stew, Frank? Amy invited. "You have to eat from the pot though, 'cos Ma has packed away *all* our dishes!"

"Shush, Amy, I don't think Frank wants to eat just yet," voiced Jane in a motherly tone.

Claire added some extra sugar to her cup of tea, insisting that Frank should drink it; he was likely suffering from a breakdown she considered.

Holding the mug to his lips, Claire rubbed his back in a soothing motion as he sipped the hot sweet drink. Frank had a strong inclination that his parents had not yet received word and were quite unaware of Martha's tragic accident. He felt his stomach contract, knowing that he had to enlighten them about the heartbreaking news but sensed that when his words were heard, their concern for him would turn stone cold. "We're leaving Bagley village forever at first light, son," announced Silas. "Things have changed for the worse after all what's happened so we're making a fresh start where nobody knows us. We will keep the family's shameful secret close to our chests and nobody will be suspicious of little Georgie either...and in time when Martha, God willing, returns to us, we will simply pretend that she's your ma's niece who's come to stay for one reason or another...anyway, that's a long way off into the future; from now on we will be taking one day at a time and praying that our broken hearts might slowly ease.

"Can I come with you Pa? I've come to realise now that I've still got a lot of growing up to do before I can consider myself to be a man...I'll work alongside you on the new farm and promise never to grumble about a single thing..."

"We're not going to be farmers anymore!" blurted out Amy, as she listened carefully to her brother's words. "Pa is going to be an inronmon-

-ger in a shop! Can Frank come with us, Pa...*please!* "

Once again Jane had to quieten her sister, sensing that this was a family matter for her parents only.

A sudden and devious thought sprung into Frank's mind; if his parents hadn't heard the news, why should *he* be the one to cause them even more suffering? By the time the news reached them, if it ever did, he could have once again established himself into the bosom of his family; why give them even more grief when it made little difference, at this moment in time, whether Martha was dead or sailing across the ocean. He was quickly decided that he'd not mention a word of what he knew or that he'd even travelled to London.

"Please Pa, I'll be your right hand man...or should I say, boy! You won't regret it, Pa, I promise!"

"Please Pa, let Frank come with us too!" begged Amy, unable to hold her tongue for a second longer.

A sharp nudge from Jane and an angry glare quickly silenced her again as she let out a frustrated sigh.

"You have the makings of a fine young man, Frank, but your impatience and unrealistic ambitions have sadly been your downfall and the consequences of your actions have caused a terrible blow to our family; we are being forced to leave our home and live with the knowledge that your poor sister will spend the next seven years suffering more than any of us could ever imagine!"

The sound of Claire's sobs filled the kitchen. "Your poor mother will *never* get over this, Frank, and one day you might come to understand fully, the strong bond between mother and child. However, I will be civil enough to welcome you back into the family, I can see that you regret your dreadful deeds, *but* I will leave the ultimate decision entirely up to your mother."

Claire's heart melted, how could she possibly turn her back on her firstborn, her genuine son; how could she leave Bagley village in the morning knowing that she'd abandoned him, he deserved a second chance, even if it would take a while before she opened her heart fully to him again. Losing one child was bad enough, but to lose two was unthinkable and he *had* shown up at the cottage full of remorse and begging for forgiveness; he had returned home and she knew that it was her maternal bond willing her to forgive him.

The long silence was once again broken by Amy's now timid voice, she'd run to the arms of her Ma,

"Please Ma, we can't leave Frank all by himself in the cold, he's our brother Ma!"

Claire couldn't allow the family to become even

more dismantled; she knew how much Amy adored him and couldn't break her young heart even more. Leaving Frank behind could also lead him down the road to a life on the wrong side of the law and she wasn't about to have that on her conscience too. Amy's soulful pleading eyes promoted her response.

"You may join your family again Frank; families are united by strong bonds and by an unwavering love, they stick together through the rough and the calm of every storm and share the ups and the downs...don't disappoint us again Frank...my heart is already broken...we have lost are darling Martha and the sun will fail to brighten our lives properly until she is with us again. I'm putting *all* my trust in you to become a decent, loving and active member of the Shepherd family; now bring your chair to the table and eat some stew before it goes cold and tomorrow we will all begin our new life."

CHAPTER TWENTY-FIVE

"Just imagine how ghastly it would have been for you my sweet princess if I'd not have rescued you; you would be in the middle of the rough ocean, being hurled from port to starboard, covered in bruises and no doubt suffering from seasickness and God alone knows what you'd be enduring at the mercy of those villainous convicts, not to mention the officers!"

Bruce Brunswick never let a day pass without failing to remind Martha of how fortunate she was; he took all credit for her well being and by the time that the long winter months came to an end, Martha had been slowly persuaded that she owed her life to this eccentric deformed man. She had become used to his hideous appearance and his continues habit of dribbling like a young child and it no longer bothered her. She'd been expecting Bruce to make inappropriate advances towards her and believed that to be his sole reason for rescuing her, but he'd pleasantly surprised her and appeared to relish in her companionship. He insisted that she dressed for dinner every evening, in one of the many lavish gowns which packed her wardrobe, even though the dinner was always a selection of cold meats and cheeses from the hamper which was left on the doorstep every morning.

Up until the beginning of February, Bruce seemed to find pleasure in bragging about how everyone who knew or was related to Martha, presumed her to be halfway on her long voyage to Van Diemen's Land by now, but during the first week of February, when Bruce had been partaking in the customary Sunday dinner at the Manor House, Reginald had sadly informed Bruce of the letter he'd received from the Epsom magistrate, informing him that the daughter of one of his tenants had drowned in the Thames a few days before she was due to be transported. Bruce had no idea that the Shepherd family had left the village, he made a point of never asking about the family, fearing his brother might become suspicious of any interest he showed, especially after the business of the letter he'd written to Silas Shepherd.

It came as a huge shock to hear such a revelation. Bruce immediately realised that the story of Martha drowning had been concocted to save the necks of the wardens; it was somewhat of a relief, however, to know that Martha's family were now miles away, it would put an end to any temptation which she might have to make a sudden escape or try to secretly contact them; he would break the news to her gently.

It was presumed that the Squire would inform Silas and Claire Shepherd about the sad loss of their daughter, but reluctant to send such heartbreaking news, coldly inked from his pen, preferring to break the news to them face to face, he decided to wait a while.

But no matter how strongly Bruce voiced his opinion that it would be kinder to inform the Shepherd family sooner rather than later about the sad news and not let them continue to live in hope of seeing their daughter again,

Reginald was adamant that he'd wait until the treacherous seasonal weather eased a little before embarking on the journey to Oxford.

During the first few Sundays, when Bruce had left to attend the weekly family gathering at the Manor House, Martha had spent the time searching through every room of the gatehouse; she discovered nothing of any interest or that would disclose any hidden secrets about the strange man who had saved her from one prison only to engage her into another life of captivity. He kept no diary or correspondence, that she could find, but she had discovered a safe, concealed behind an oil painting of the Manor House and could only presume that anything he didn't want her prying eyes to see was safely locked away. Every window to the gatehouse was either securely bolted or jammed due to the old wooden frames swelling over the years. Bruce made sure that the front door was always locked, and the key with him at all times. The only outside access was through the kitchen into the small back garden which was surrounded by a thick privet hedge, in front of a towering wall.

Knowing that her family were only a short distance away, on the other side of the wall and that she might even catch a glimpse of her pa on one of his visits to the Squire, was a great comfort to Martha and seemed to make her odd new life more bearable; at least she was no longer imprisoned in the horrendous convict hulk or embarking on a journey across the high seas to commence a seven-year sentence in a strange and inhospitable land. Bruce Brunswick treated her well and she was quite happy to play along and pretend to be a 'princess' although, deep inside she was sure that his make-believe game would eventually fizzle out and there might even come a time when he expected more from her. Bruce truly believed that this was what she wanted, ever since she'd made the foolish mistake of informing him about her dreams for the future; he considered himself to be the heroic knight in shining armour, freeing her and making all her dreams come true.

"Come and sit with me Martha, there is something I have to tell you!" instructed Bruce when he returned one Sunday.

Cautiously adding another log to the glowing fire, he patted the space next to him on the old, threadbare couch. Always reluctant to sit so close to him, Martha perched timidly on the edge, noticing how anxious Bruce appeared.

"Don't fear me, my princess. Have I not been good to you over the months that you've been here?"

"I don't fear you, Mr Brunswick..."

"Bruce...Bruce...how many times must I tell you!" he insisted, in a raised voice.

"I'm sorry...Bruce...it's not my fault; my parents raised me to respect my elders and my superiors."

"There is no such thing as superiors...elders yes, but we are family now and I insist that you call me Bruce...no more of this Mr Brunswick nonsense; is that understood?"

Martha nodded, warily, it was the first time he'd ever raised his voice to her and shown his angry side; she felt uncomfortable in his presence and wished he'd not asked to share company with her.

A pause of awkward silence prevailed before he eventually spoke again. Martha took out one of the many handkerchiefs she now always kept in her skirt pockets; over time, she'd learnt that if Bruce became anxious or excited he lost the ability to swallow. She also knew that he had no sense of taste and ate for the sole purpose of satisfying his hunger.

"That fire was aglow and burning as fiercely on the day of my accident...I think I was left on this very couch to die, you know!"

His odd declaration shocked Martha. Is that what he had intended to tell her so urgently, she wondered. She couldn't think of the right words to say, so remained silent, fiddling nervously with her fingers in her lap.

"My mother's lover threw me headfirst into the fire...before forcing the red hot poker into my mouth! My mother was no better than a cold hearted whore; cheating on my father with a philandering scoundrel who was a sworn enemy to my family. She fled naked, leaving me in his cruel and merciless hands...I was but a boy and that is when my childhood and my entire world came to an abrupt end."

Martha took in a loud gasp, her hand spontaneously shooting up to cover her mouth; taken by complete shock by Bruce's revelation.

"*Shocking isn't it?* My mother turned her back on me on that day, probably wishing that I hadn't survived. There have been many a time when I wished I'd breathed my last breath on that day and more times than I can remember that I've seriously contemplated taking my own life."

Martha sat in complete silence, her breathing shallow as she listened to Bruce's revelation.

"You see, Martha on that dreadful day, in this very room, inside I was still the same boy, still yearning for the love and attention of my family and yet unable to talk or explain or understand. It was a cruel blow which changed my life forever and caused me to rebel and do some very wicked and evil acts throughout my life; acts which I now feel thoroughly ashamed of. That day, in the barn, when we chatted...do you remember, my sweet princess?"

Martha nodded, "I do remember."

"I knew then, in those brief few moments, that you were special...I knew that you would be the one to ease my suffering. I'm not sure if that is what's known as love at first sight, or maybe you and I were once kindred souls floating around in another dimension of time, but from that day forth, I felt the strongest connection towards you and to begin with, I was prepared to do anything to ensure you would one day be mine. Families don't always appreciate and cherish each other as they should, Martha, they can be quick to dismiss members who perhaps don't conform to normality...families can be ruthless in the way in which they single out and wickedly bully the *odd one out!*"

"Why are you telling me all of this?" questioned Martha, confused by Bruce's confession and wondering where it was leading.

"I'm trying to tell you, Martha, that *your* life is destined to be very similar to mine!"

"I hope you don't intend to push me into that fire too!" she exclaimed, nervously. She noticed a tear trickle from his eye as he stared into the bright leaping flames and for the first time, ever, she felt sorry for Bruce Brunswick; he was not the terrifying monster but a tragic victim of cruelty, a lonely, unloved creature, trapped inside his hideous body, and she now knew that he'd endured most of his life, even his childhood in misunderstood torment. He turned to face her

taking her hand in his; she didn't flinch as she normally would have done but allowed him to take comfort in the smallest of physical contacts.
"I wouldn't dream of harming you, Martha, I rescued you because I need you...I love you but wish nothing from you but your company. I have found such comfort in your presence, my sweet princess, my life has changed and for the first time in my life, I feel at peace with myself; those mean and evil thoughts have simply evaporated from my head...I am a new man, Martha. I intended to tell you some news concerning *your* family, but have strangely told you so much more."
Martha immediately straightened her posture, her eyes wide open,
"*My family?* Please tell me, Bruce, *please!*"
Bruce dabbed his chin, with the damp handkerchief,
"There is no easy way of telling you this Martha...I discovered today that your family left Bagley village, before Christmas...they have travelled north to begin a new life. Another revelation which I heard today was that it has been officially declared that you drowned in the Thames, before even embarking on your voyage to Van Diemen's Land!"
Martha gasped loudly, before bursting into tears; cupping her face in the palms of her hands, she sobbed brokenheartedly, now knowing that she was doomed to be a prisoner of the gatehouse

for a long time to come. To her family and the world, she was dead. In those few moments, the image of every member of her family besieged her head; how would she ever cope? Was this what Bruce had meant when he'd said that her life was destined to be similar to his? Her words caught like shards of glass in the back of her painful throat; she was unable to speak.

"I'm so sorry, Martha, I know it's probably the worst news you've ever heard, but you must try to be brave, look on the bright side, you're safe and well and I intend to take the very best care of you."

"But I want to see my family again...and now I don't even know where they've gone...I will just fade from their memory...I'm dead after all...I no longer exist! I actually wish that I *was* really *dead* you know!"

"In time, you will come to terms with what has happened, my sweet princess...you just need a little grieving time first."

"How can you say that...I will never come to terms with this terrible nightmare! And I'm *not* a Princess! I'm going to find my family, and put my poor parents out of their misery!"

"Take a grip of yourself, Martha Shepherd...and remember that if you take one step into the outside world, you will eventually find yourself swinging by the neck; you are an escaped convict, with a seven years sentence on your head...together with the concocted story of your death, it will look as though you bribed your way out of the HMS Warrior! How do you think you might have paid those hefty prison wardens for such a favour? You will cause even more shame upon your dear family and force them to elope for a second time! And when all is said and done Martha Shepherd, you will hang in disgrace and be forgotten forever by all concerned. I don't mean to sound heartless, but the truth has to be told. Just as *I've* had to throughout my entire life, *you* will have to make the best out of your situation and never forget what a grim life you would have endured if I'd not have come to your rescue!"

"But at least I would have still been alive...and given my parents a dream to hang onto!"

"*Martha!* Why do you think that your family left Bagley village? You have bought shame on them and made them outcasts in their home...if you *really* love them forget about them...it's the kindest gift that you can offer them."

Bruce's disfigurement hid his feelings of sadness and rejection; his attempt to comfort Martha was instantly rebuffed as Martha leapt from off the couch, pushing his arm away.

She fled upstairs to her room leaving Bruce to deal with the haunting flashbacks which clouded his mind; flashbacks of when his mother had abandoned him when he'd needed her love and protection more than ever in his life. He knew what it was like to be alone in the world; he would allow Martha a period of solitude, in which to grieve her loss, convinced that with no one else to turn to, before long, her feelings for him would strengthen and an everlasting bond would be formed.

Martha's river of tears soon soaked the silk pillowcases as she lay face down on her bed; The crippling hurt she felt was like no other feeling she'd ever had to face in her life; happiness was now an emotion in a faraway place, locked away and out of her reach. Yet again, she arrived at the devastating theory that she was being punished for the many years she'd spent wishing and dreaming that she'd been born into a wealthy family; her strong desires to be one of the wealthy folk had caused her to lose sight of how precious her own family was and to ignore the pure love on which she'd been nurtured over the years. Being part of her family was akin to being continuously shielded, cherished and loved within a huge protective embrace and now, God had taken it all away from her for being an ungrateful, selfish girl and for living in a world of dreams, like a fool.

CHAPTER TWENTY-SIX
1845

The glowing spring sun in its blue surround was a welcoming sight for Emma and Jake Bird; winters were exceptionally cold out in the countryside but it was a small price to pay for a life away from the smog and diseased streets of London's East End, where they'd lived for their entire working life. Now both in their mid-fifties, Emma and Jake were in no doubt that in the six years they'd been away from London, they had never felt healthier and younger. In 1839, they'd come to a sudden and completely unplanned decision to give up their hardworking life, where Jake toiled all day as a blacksmith and Emma endured a back-breaking life in the stifling atmosphere of the washroom, scraping her hands until they were red raw from taking in folk's washing. It was the year in which they'd both turned fifty.

With their pitiful life's savings, Jake had managed to purchase a small plot of wasteland in Surrey and for three months, they lived beneath a rudimentary constructed shelter while Jake worked relentlessly on the construction of their new abode. A small wooden dwelling, all on one level but divided into four rooms; it was like a palace to Emma compared to the dingy, East End rooms in the rat infested tenement building; her very own palace in which she had the rest of her life to transform it to perfection. Their joint determination soon found their new home completed. They praised each other's skills, Jake's clever handiwork at crafting fine-looking pieces of furniture and Emma's advanced needlework skills. Overgrown with nettles and thorny brambles, the surrounding garden which wrapped around the new wooden house was soon transformed. Neatly aligned rows of vegetables and soft fruit now grew all year round and during the spring and summer months, the borders became a kaleidoscope of colour with blooms filling the garden with their heady scented aroma. Emma and Jake delighted in their time spent, simply, sitting for hours in their little piece of paradise and listening to the harmonious chirping of birdsong; it was a far cry from the rowdy and pungent thoroughfares of the East End.

Emma and Jake's new life had been considerably changed when they'd stumbled across an unfortunate, young woman who'd been abandoned and left for dead in the middle of the dense woodlands. It had been a chilly April morning, in 1840, Emma and Jake had spent the first winter in their new home and were out early, collecting firewood and fresh mushrooms to cook for breakfast. When Emma caught sight of the trail of fresh, bright red blood, she simply presumed it was that of an injured animal; she followed the trail in the hope of it being edible, planning to put the creature out of its misery with the help of her sharp blade; she and Jake would have a well-deserved feast. But as the trickles of blood changed to small pools, Emma sensed that whatever she was about to find was much larger than a small injured woodland creature. She stood in complete and utter shock when the sight of a blood-covered female filled her vision. Curled up in a huddle, wearing only a heavily bloodstained nightgown a deathly silence surrounded the poor young woman. In the distance, Emma could hear the sound of Jake's axe cutting through the logs; she froze momentarily, her words also freezing on her lips...and then she hollered at the top of her voice,

"*Jake, Jake, come quickly, hurry...Jake...Jake...*" she continued shouting, enabling Jake to follow her cries, leading him quickly to her side.

"Oh Gawd blimey...she's in a bad way Em, is she alive, d'yer reckon?" Jake's face drained of all colour, the sight of blood always made him light-headed. He swallowed hard, tasting the acidic bile in the back of his throat.

"Let's carry her inside, Jake, if there *is* any life left in the poor lass, it'll be sure ter leave 'er frail body out 'ere in the cold!"

"D'yer reckon some kind of wolf attacked 'er?" asked Jake as between them they lifted her body from off the ground.

"Don't be so bloomin' daft, *Jake Bird*, it's as obvious as the grass is green that she's bin in the family way...I thought I'd seen the end ov this gruesome business the day we left Whitechapel! She's either come out 'ere ter the woods in order ter shed 'er load or bin ter some bloody butcher ter get shot ov 'er shame! Once we've got er safely inside, I want yer to come back ter this area an' search fer a babby!"

Jake moaned under his breath; he'd been looking forward to a plate of fried mushrooms since early morning, his stomach was empty and he didn't relish the thought of searching amongst the blood-splattered undergrowth, not knowing what he'd find.

"Surely yer don't think there's a little un out in the woods? I never 'eard nothing!"

"Don't mean ter say that there ain't a little babby somewhere; it might not 'ave survived the ordeal..."

"Bloody young gals! Why can't they just keep their bloomin' legs crossed fer 'eaven's sake...makes me glad that we was never blessed wiv any daughters..."

"Don't yer go jumping her conclusions Jake Bird! We know nothing 'bout the lass, an' it ain't fair ter lay all the blame on 'er now is it...that's a wicked thing ter say an' all, I would 'ave loved a daughter yer know...."

Emma's words trailed off.

"I'm sorry Em, I didn't mean ter remind yer, not ter day of all days, not after this gloomy discovery." They eased the body down onto a spare palliasse which was placed on the floor in the back room, next to the scullery; it was where they spent most of their time, especially during the long winter months when they kept the fire burning gently, keeping a pleasant temperature maintained in the room.

"Yer sure you'll be alright Em, I didn't mean ter remind yer... I'm right sorry, my queen!"
Emma gritted her teeth, sometimes she wondered if her husband had lost his wits, he acted quite peculiar on many occasions.
"*Jake*! There ain't no need ter keep apologizing...a day doesn't pass by when I don't remember our three lads; *our angels*...their little faces, looking at me...pleading wiv me ter make their pain disappear...It breaks me heart, every time! An' if there's an ounce ov life left in this poor young lass, then I'm begging the Good Lord ter let it be me who nurtures 'er back ter the land ov the living."
"Steady on, Em, reckon yer getting' a bit above yer station!"
Jake left the neat wooden house in the hope of not discovering anything out in the woods.

Emma Bird looked down sadly at the young ashen-faced lass. The bloody, oversized nightgown she wore swamped her petite frame and Emma wondered why she was not wearing day clothes, it didn't figure in her mind, making her plight even more mysterious. After feeling a faint pulse on the girl's neck, Emma raised the gown above her waist; she had to know what she was dealing with and was not unfamiliar with the tell-tell signs associated with the female anatomy; during her years in Whitechapel, she'd helped many a new life into the world and also witnessed the disastrous results when young, innocent girls had endeavoured to get rid of their unborn babies. It soon became apparent, just as Emma had suspected that the young lass *had* recently given birth; she presented all the proof of a hurried delivery and had probably delivered a healthy sized baby, leaving her painfully lacerated and severely weakened from haemorrhaging. Where was her baby now, mused Emma as she began to wash the pitiful blood-stained girl...she was so young, thought Emma, not more than sixteen, she doubted, barely a child herself. There was little else she could do for her except wash her, keep her warm and comfortable and pray that she might soon come around.

Apart from a few more mushrooms, Jake had found nothing during his hour-long search, leaving Emma now convinced that the girl had left her baby outside the gates of an orphanage or a workhouse, perhaps intending to return to her family as though nothing had happened. The pungent aroma of the wild mushrooms as they sizzled in the pan must have triggered the girl's senses, she opened her eyes for the first time; looking around, cautiously, she felt a huge sense of relief to discover that she was no longer in the gatehouse; it was even more of a comfort to see the kind, smiling face of Emma Bird. Having feared that she would never have survived out in the cold woods and that her body would never feel warm again, a heavenly feeling of security engulfed her as she viewed the friendly-faced elderly couple who displayed such manifest concern for her well being.

Over the following couple of weeks, the girl made a steady recovery and trusted Emma enough to disclose a little of how she'd come to be in the woods. It was often difficult for her to allow her words to flow with ease and Emma sensed that she was holding something back, but in those early days, she merely listened with sorrow and shock as Molly Wright gradually, over time, explained as much of her story as she felt able to and now, five years on from that dreadful day when Emma had feared for young Molly's life more times than she cared to remember, Molly had become like a daughter to them and was forever grateful of the home she'd been allowed to share with the doting Emma and Jake Bird.

Although Emma felt sure that Molly was now a happy and relatively contented young woman she sensed that her past experience had ruined her life and any future plans to marry and raise her own family, which she might have once harboured. There was a hidden sadness about Molly which she usually managed to conceal deep within her heart. Emma would often recollect the day when Molly had unburdened herself of her heartbreaking story; the image of her distraught face and the hopelessness of her state of mind on that chilling day could bring a tear to the toughest of souls.

Emma had to know if there was a living baby abandoned somewhere and was willing to move the sky and earth to reunite Molly with that infant, should it be the case, so as soon as she felt that Molly had recovered enough, she put the question as gently as possible to her.

"What happened to yer babby, sweetheart?" she handed Molly a soothing mug of warm cocoa along with her question.

Initially, Molly appeared shocked, causing Emma to sense that the girl had even hoped to hide the truth from her.

"I know yer suffered the pains ov childbirth, lass, I ain't no ignorant countrywoman who's lived in the middle of nowhere all me life...me an' Jake lived our younger days in London's East End an' there ain't much I ain't witnessed when it comes ter the likes ov young gals finding themselves in the family way an' the risks they're prepared ter take in puttin' things right again ter hide their shame from their families."

Clearly surprised, Molly's sky blue eyes widened,

"We were sort of neighbours then, Mrs Bird...because I spent most of *my* days in the Whitechapel workhouse!"

"Well, *stone the bloomin' crows*...it certainly is a small world...wait 'till I tell my Jake, he'll be dumbstruck! How did yer com ter be in such a dismal place, Molly? I must say, yer don't much sound like an Eastender...yer speak more like one of the better folk!"

"That was on account of the woman who was in charge of me and the rest of the girls my age, she taught us how to talk properly, saying that we would stand a better chance of being offered a position in a stately home if we improved our ways. She had contacts in high places you see, and when we girls became young women, there would quite often be a position waiting to be filled."

Emma already had a crystal clear picture of what was going on,

"Yeah, I bet there were! That woman, will 'ave a lot ter explain when she gets ter meet 'er Maker...I've met the likes of scheming bitches like 'er before...nothing but bad news...an' I bet she found a pretty young girl like you a right respectable 'ome ter work in didn't she...an' no doubt lined her purse along with the deal!"

The thought had never crossed Molly's mind, she had always trusted that the guardians of the workhouse wanted the best for the girls and had released them to a far better life away from the daily tasks that were to be had in the workhouse. The more she thought about it the more it dawned on her that it *was* only a certain type of girl who was offered positions in grand houses up and down the country. The pretty girls; girls who'd been in the workhouse since childhood, and more to the point the girls guaranteed to be virgins.

She took a sharp intake of breath, "I've never really thought about it, but you're right, Mrs Bird...how many more girls have suffered at the hands of a lustful Lord of the Manor and had to endure a similar fate to mine?"

"So tell me Molly, who were you '*sold off*' to?"

Molly came close to spilling her cocoa as she shuddered; the vivid images filling her mind, images which she feared would never leave her.

"In yer own time now, me darlin', we ain't in any 'urry ter go nowhere, but in me own experience, talkin' over life's bad patches of'en works as good as any tonic for yer peace ov mind...me an' my Jake, we lost our three young angels when the typhoid arrived in London thirty years ago an' swept through like a raging fire, not leaving a single family wiv out inflicting its evil curse upon it. I watched me lads suffer...there weren't nothing I could do but pray...if they'd 'ave been animals the kindest thing would 'ave bin ter put 'em out ov their misery!" Tears rolled off Emma's strained face... "Oh just 'ark at me, I'm the one s'posed ter be listening ter your confessions, take no notice ov an old woman an' 'er tendency ter slip back inter the past...my Jake never ceases in tellin' me ter leave the past be'ind me...but I'm a mother, an' a mother never forgets the babbies which she brings inter this miserable world."

"Oh, Mrs Bird, I'm so sorry...that's such a tragedy...my baby boy died...I heard him take his first and only breath, but that was followed by a long silence and then my master was telling me that he wasn't meant for this world."

"An' who exactly was yer so-called *master*, sweetheart?"

Molly gulped down the, now tepid, cocoa as she sat up straight on her palliasse, resting her back against the wall; her eyes had a distant look about them and Emma sensed that she was about to open up her heart.

"I'd just turned fourteen when Miss Wainright called me to one side of the sewing room; she was the woman I mentioned, the one who insisted that we girls all worked on improving our speech and manners. She told me that a wealthy gent was particularly interested in a companion to assist him...He was a cripple she told me, she also told me that I had nothing to fear from such a man as his disability ensured that he would pose no threat and wouldn't expect anything from me... if you know what I mean?"

Emma nodded her head, urging Molly to continue.

"She told me that in time, I would likely meet a male worker on the estate, one who I might fall in love with and live a good and fulfilling life with. I was so grateful to Miss Wainright, I could have kissed her, but of course, I didn't. It was the first time since my parents had died from the fever when I was only five that I truly felt that someone cared about my future happiness. She secretly sewed me a pretty new dress, it fitted like a glove and made me look like a real woman; she also gave me my very first corset...I no longer felt like a scruffy workhouse lass and couldn't wait to start my new life. On the day that I left the workhouse, I saw my new master handing over a thick pile of banknotes to Miss Wainright but I took little notice, I just presumed he was making a charitable donation to the workhouse. He had a fancy coach, its paintwork gleamed in the sunshine, but *his* appearance was a huge shock to me...I knew it was sinful to think such mean thoughts, but I'd never seen such a hideously ugly, deformed face before. I could barely bring myself to look at him as he sat opposite me in that luxurious coach. He only had one eye and his skin appeared to be forcibly stretched across one side of his face, causing all of his features to be distorted; he dribbled profusely, like a slobbering hound dog which turned my stomach. He also appeared to have difficulty in walking normally...and from the first moment I met him, I became a nervous wreck, terrified of having to take care of such a creature."

"But surely you weren't to be left alone with him once you'd arrived at his grand estate?" quizzed Emma, eager for Molly to continue her story.

"Well, that was another shock...It soon became apparent that he wasn't Lord of the Manor House at all, merely the brother of the Squire and it seemed that for some reason or other, my new master had been banished from his family and forced to live in the gatehouse!"

"*The gatehouse!*" exclaimed Emma, sounding quite shocked. "But surely that would have been a tiny dwelling in comparison to the main estate house."

"Well, I wouldn't have called it *tiny*, apparently it was one of the larger gatehouses, according to Mrs Bunting, the cook, but to me, not having much knowledge on the likes of the aristocracy, it seemed like a *huge* house."

"But at least you weren't alone with this man...were there any other staff?"

Molly nodded as she reminisced on the strange assortment of staff who also worked at the gatehouse.

"Bruce Brunswick seemed to employ the oddest

of folk...Mrs Bunting was quite elderly and a *terrible* cook who would probably never find work in any other establishments; it was fortunate for her, that Mr Brunswick, or *Squinty Eye*, as was his nickname couldn't taste a thing. He told me once that his mouth had been so severely burnt that he had lost all sense of taste. Then there was Viola, who was completely subservient to Mrs Bunting, she was like her shadow...I barely spoke two words to her for the entire year I spent at the gatehouse. It was young Lydia though, who I felt most sorry for; the village simpleton who was euphoric about her post of what was more akin to slave to Mrs Bunting and Viola. Luckily for her, she was able to visit her folks often, but she seemed ignorant of her harsh treatment, poor girl. But Mrs Bird, I might as well have been alone in the house with Bruce Brunswick, because unlike the rest of the staff who slept in the room by the kitchen, I was given a room of my own which conveniently connected to my new master's bedroom."

Emma shook her head in dismay; she already had a clear picture of the next part of Molly's woeful story and already despised the gruesome-looking Bruce Brunswick.

"Before yer continues, me sweetheart, let me go an' fetch the rest ov that cocoa, reckon Jake's forgotten 'bout 'is share an' it's a cryin' shame ter let it go ter waste!"

Emma stretched her limbs as she left Molly's

side...her bones felt extra old today, sitting in the same position for long these days caused every one of her joints to become stiff and painful, she topped up their mugs and sat down again, poised to listen.

Molly took a mouthful of the tepid cocoa, before continuing.

"When I questioned Mr Brunswick about why I wasn't to sleep downstairs with the rest of the staff, he became angry, saying that I was his personal maid. He said I was like a female butler, which I thought rather odd. I questioned him as to why he simply hadn't employed a proper butler to which he declared that he would soon enlighten me on his reasons. I didn't have to wait long to find out; two days after my arrival, I awoke in the middle of the night to find that awful beast in my room and I knew instantly that Miss Wainright had lied to me. He was a savage beast, showing me no compassion at all but thankfully it was all over very quickly. That brute of a man stole my innocence and humiliated me, Mrs Bird and I never want another man to touch me for the rest of my days!"

Emma rushed to her side engulfing her in a warm embrace, as the tears rolled down Molly's face. "There, there me darlin' it's all over now an' you're as safe as can be wiv me an' Jake; we's gonna take good care ov yer from now on."

"Do you know Mrs Bird? The strangest thing

was that during the day, it was almost as though Bruce Brunswick was overwhelmed with guilt…he was exceptionally kind to me and insisted I spent my days doing whatever pleased me. Every evening, he would insist that We took supper together, there would always be a bottle of wine too and once I'd consumed a glass, he added some of his special medicine to my second glass; he told me that it would make his night time visits more bearable and he was right…some nights, I didn't even notice him in my bed…which was always a blessing."

Emma frowned, and tutted loudly, "That sly, good fer nothin' scoundrel was druggin' yer every night, lass! So what 'appened when yer found yerself carrying 'is child?"

"*I didn't know…* I had no idea, not until one Sunday morning…I'd woken up in the middle of the night…I thought for a second that Bruce was inflicting some terrible pain on me, but I was alone. Over the months, he'd been teasing me about my increased size. He said I was becoming too accustomed to the wealthier ways of life and that my new healthy-looking appearance was all down to my consumption of fine food and wine, plus the long hours which I spent lounging around. I must have been so foolish, not to even think that I'd end up in the family way! I kept thinking that perhaps that's what Miss Wainright had meant when she'd told me that he posed no threat, that at least he was unable to father a child. I screamed so loudly, as I rolled around in agony on that Sunday morning...every time I thought the pain was going, it just came back again, but worse each time...I thought I was going to die, Mrs Bird...and then Bruce came into my room, he was in a terrible rage and tried to shove a stocking in my mouth, he yelled at me to be quiet and then he left the room only to re-appear a few minutes later waving a pistol in his hand and threatening to put me out of my misery if I didn't stop screaming...but it was impossible...I honestly believed that my life was about to end...and then the strangest thing happened; it was as though my entire body had been taken over by the devil himself; I suddenly found myself heaving and bearing down, my screaming changed its tone and I remember thinking to myself that I sounded more like a beast than a human and then it suddenly dawned on me that I was about to deliver a baby...*my baby*. I was pushing with every grain of strength that was left in my body and outside I could hear Bruce yelling and firing his pistol. I was so terrified that he would soon be pointing that pistol at me...and was filled with a spontaneous and overwhelming urgency to protect my unborn child."

"Didn't that Mrs Bunting come to yer aid or anyone ov the staff?"

"It was Sunday, Mrs Bunting and Viola always spent the day away from the gatehouse...they

went on picnics or leisurely walks after church. I think Lydia might have been downstairs, but as I said, she wasn't a very sharp-witted girl. But Bruce returned to my room just as my baby took his first breath, along with his sweet-sounding cry...I will never forget that sound; occasionally, it returns to my ears, convincing me that my darling son is close by, but I know that's just an impossible dream; Bruce was as devastated as me when he broke the news that our son had died shortly after his arrival into the world...we couldn't even give him a proper burial because of the shame of what had happened...Bruce insisted that I took my medicine and slept for the rest of the day and later that evening he returned to tell me that he'd placed our baby in the coffin of a local old woman who was to be buried in the morning. It was a relief to know that my sweet child wouldn't be alone, and I prayed that she was a kindly old woman who he lay beside."
Molly could do nothing in her power to hold back her sobs leaving Emma, once more, to console her.

"*You poor, poor lass!* Sounds ter me that you've 'ad more than yer fare share ov life's trials already...reckon it's about time yer luck changed an' as I said, this is yer new 'ome, an' you'll 'ave nothin' ter worry 'bout as long as me an' Jake are in the land ov the living!"

"Thank you, Mrs Bird...you've been so kind to me!" she cried.

"Oh don't be daft, I'm simply doing what any God-fearing woman would do! Tell me, Molly, 'ow did yer come ter end up 'ere in the woods?" She wiped away the tears with the back of her hand, "I don't remember much. It's still like a vague dream, but I do remember that the following morning, my white bedsheets were bright red, sticky and damp from the blood which was still pouring from me; I was horrified. I remember screaming out but feeling so tired that all I wanted was for the bedding to be changed so I could continue sleeping. After that, I saw Bruce's face a few times, but I'm not sure if that was a dream or reality. It was so, unbearably cold and dark…I recall him carrying me down the stairs of the gatehouse; he put me in the back of a carriage…I couldn't stop shivering but my eyelids felt so heavy. I just wanted to sleep…and then I woke up, *here!* You saved my life, Mrs Bird and I will never be able to thank you enough!"

CHAPTER TWENTY-SEVEN

There was no longer any pretence about Martha
being a princess, now as beautiful as a fresh
young rosebud, at eighteen she had confidently
taken all of the household chores into hand. Still
a prisoner in the gatehouse and unable to leave
its confines, in a strange way, she had formed a
strong attachment to Bruce Brunswick. It had
surprised her that in the five years they'd lived
side by side under the same roof, he'd never
once tried to take advantage of her and had
stayed true to his word in that she was his
companion only. With the desire to escape from
the gatehouse having diminished over time,
Martha now dreaded the thought of venturing
out into the world again, her biggest fear being
that she would be captured and dragged up in
front of a ruthless judge. The haunting image of
Cocklestone had never quite left her over the
years. The combination of knowing that her
family believed her to be dead, together with
Bruce's many warnings that the sudden shock of
seeing her alive could have detrimental effects
on her parents was a strong deterrent in
dampening any desires which Martha might
have, to go in search of her family. Bruce was
convinced that his brother's meeting with
Martha's parents had caused him such an
upheaval that it was the source behind the start

of a spell of bad health which had led to his early death.

It had been during April of 1841 when Reginald Brunswick had decided to travel to Oxford and call in on the Shepherd family, the bleak winter was at last making way for a glorious spring and the weather had been exceptionally warm for April, making way for a pleasant journey. Claire and Silas were finding the transition from being a farming family to living in the town and running a busy ironmongers shop a difficult undertaking. They felt like fish out of water living in the busy town of Oxford and missed the spacious land and the peacefulness which went with it. Jane and Amy attended the local school which was close by in St Aldates. It was ten times larger than the simple schoolhouse in Bagley village and with so many pupils attending Jane and Amy feared they'd never feel at home or be able to remember everyone's name. Adding to their dismay, they had been separated from their very first day; it appeared that in such an overcrowded school pupils were sorted out into classes according to their age. Lunch breaks had been the only opportunity when Jane could comfort her younger sister who she knew was finding the new way of life just as daunting as she was. The children of St Aldates school, considered the new girls to be ignorant country folk, they mimicked their accent and laughed at their washed-out country attire. But as usual, Jane convinced Amy not to let on to their parents that they were anything other than happy at their new school; she would bribe Amy with a farthing's worth of sweets from the confectioners in Oxford's High Street which they passed by every afternoon on their way home. It had been a pleasantly warm afternoon in April, as they dawdled along the High Street, both thoroughly engrossed in the sweet lollipops they'd just purchased when Jane immediately recognized the familiar carriage stood outside of the ironmongers. As they neared it, the elaborate gold-lettered monogram of '*RB*' on the side of the carriage only confirmed Jane's suspicions. She encouraged Amy to walk faster, wondering why anyone from the Brunswick Estate would be calling on them especially after she'd heard her pa voice his anger at the Squire many a time for the terrible way in which he'd done nothing at all to try and have Martha set free; her ma and pa were both of the opinion that he was able but for some spiteful reason, just not willing. To find the Squire himself present at her home was even more of a surprise but the excitement quickly diminished as Jane entered over the threshold to the shop and was confronted by a gloomy and downcast atmosphere, with her ma seated on a stool sobbing her heart out and her pa, clearly distraught as he stood cupping his head in his hands.

The Squire appeared instantly relieved by the arrival of Jane and Amy, he gave them the tiniest of smiles as he asked how they were liking their new life and then told them that he'd had to deliver some sad news to their parents. He said his goodbyes hurriedly and within minutes he was sat in his fancy carriage as the driver sped off along the thoroughfare.

Silas and Claire broke down and held each other as Jane and Amy looked on knowing that the Squire had delivered the most terrible of news to them. Then Frank, who'd been out on a delivery, arrived home and Jane couldn't help but notice the look of anger which her pa viewed Frank with. She could no longer remain silent.

"What's happened Pa?" exclaimed Jane, still holding tight to Amy's small hand.

The words froze on Silas's lips, he just couldn't bring himself to repeat what the Squire had told them; his tears left his eyes and Jane immediately sensed that the only news to have such an effect on her parents had to be news of Martha.

"Is it Martha? Has something happened to her?" pleaded Jane.

Frank stood motionless by the shop door; he knew that his secret was out and he mentally prepared himself to put on a display of shock and sorrow. It had taken four months to win back his parent's affections and trust and he was not about to let that fly out of the window and become the black sheep once more.

"*Ma, Pa*, let's close the shop early and go upstairs!" suggested Frank. "You're obviously not able to face any customers."

"*Martha is dead!*" cried out Claire. "She never even left England all those months ago, but was drowned in the river! All this time I've been thinking of her, praying for her...I should have sensed it I should have known...what sort of mother am I not to have sensed that she was no longer living beneath the same moon and stars as us?" Claire's cracked voice trailed off into more sobs and Silas helped her up the narrow staircase which led to the cosy parlour.

Reginald Brunswick had found himself in a dark place as he sat in his carriage on the return journey; he had always been fond of the Shepherd family and knew that if it hadn't been for his brother's foolhardy behaviour, he could have intervened and saved young Martha. The look on Claire Shepherd's face had broken his heart and the fact that Silas had the look of a broken man about him and for once had nothing to say or object about had left him even more guilt-ridden. The heavyweight on his chest was intensifying as the bumpy road caused him to be tossed about. He pulled out his handkerchief and mopped his sweating brow; his neck scarf seemed to restrict his breathing all of a sudden and as he tried frantically to loosen it, the inside of the carriage spun around and he fell off the leather seat gasping for breath. Discovered by the newly employed footman who was eager to open the carriage door for the Squire, he quickly alerted the household to the horror of what had confronted him; convinced that the Squire had already left the world. Two hours later and heavily sedated, the Doctor explained to Lady Mary that her husband's heart was failing and if he lasted another twenty-four hours it would be somewhat of a miracle. Defying all scientific speculation, the Squire lived for another ten days, slipping in and out of consciousness but still with all his wits about him. He had to do something right by the Shepherd family before he finally went to meet his Maker and so regardless of his Doctor's and his over-concerned family's advice, he insisted that the family solicitor was summoned to the Brunswick Estate.

Edward Chapman was now the sole solicitor of John Chapman & Son; the old and trusty solicitor who'd always taken care of the Brunswick family's legal matters for two generations had passed away two years ago at the age of eighty-five, leaving his sixty-year-old son in sole charge until he found a suitable partner to join his practice. Having heard many shocking stories about the Brunswick family, most of which were strictly guarded by the code of confidentiality, Edward arrived at the Manor

House with an open mind and was consequently not shaken by the Squire's disclosure that a young infant named George Shepherd was, in fact, the illegitimate nephew to Reginald Brunswick. In the privacy of his bedroom, the Squire made a special request that on his death, a substantial sum of money from his personal savings should be equally split; half to be bequeathed to Mr and Mrs Shepherd immediately and the other half secretly held in a trust fund until George Shepherd reached the age of twenty-one. The Squire was strict in his instruction that under any circumstances, no member of his, or the Shepherd family ever be enlightened to the blood connection between Bruce Brunswick and young George Shepherd. The Squire had no qualms about telling his family how he wished to help the Shepherd family since they'd suffered the devastating loss of their daughter in such tragic circumstances. Expecting an initial chorus of objections to be voiced from his greedy family, he was sure that they would soon come to terms with it and be grateful for the rich futures which they were all guaranteed.

Silas was so consumed with a raw hatred for the Squire, that three months after he'd shown his face in Oxford, he was not stirred by any emotional feelings when the news of Reginald Brunswick's passing away reached him along with the news that he'd left him a tidy sum of money in his will. Money was merely the wealthy folk's way of easing their troubled conscience, he believed and no amount of money would lift his spirits or return the youthful smile upon his beloved wife's face or bring his eldest daughter back to them. Claire's only dream which had kept her going since they'd left Bagley village had been sabotaged. She forced herself to rise from bed of a morning for the sake of her family, but the element of joy was now deeply submerged beneath her sorrow. Normally she would have put up a fight in persuading Silas to put the Squires money to good use, she would have swayed his stubborn thoughts, convincing him of the advantages the sum of money would be to their family, but those were the days of old and now she accepted Silas's decision to leave the money in the bank and out of their reach without the slightest objection. The new relationship which Silas and Claire had rebuilt with Frank since they'd moved to Oxford had suddenly buckled. Claire could barely bring herself to look at her son, she was reminded of the day he and Martha had set out to town together; the day when everything was to change forever. Silas viewed Frank as an irresponsible and cold-hearted son who had been the root cause of the huge cracks which had broken his once-happy family.

CHAPTER TWENTY-EIGHT

The early morning July sun was already beating down strongly and becoming trapped in the modest back garden of the gatehouse. Over the years it had become one of Martha's favourite spots; she would spend hours sat sketching the shrubs, wildflowers, visiting birds and butterflies and had Bruce to thank for encouraging her to learn this new skill; he had proved to be the most tolerant of teachers and they had often laughed together at her early sketching attempts. To make the outdoor space more accommodating, Martha had, over the years, positioned some smaller items of furniture into the garden; an old unused settle and a scruffy, worn table which she'd covered with a square of silk were now put to far better use. Always being the first to leave the house to enjoy the outside, Martha would follow Bruce with a tray of tea and freshly baked scones or tea cakes. He had never been happier in his life and as his relationship with Martha deepened with every passing year, Bruce had never once taken advantage of her and Martha remained as pure as the day he'd rescued her from the convict hulk. His impeccable behaviour was far from his initial intentions, but he'd grown to adore Martha more deeply than he could ever have imagined and couldn't risk another tragedy like that of poor Molly's but he lived in hope that when Martha was officially a free woman, she would perhaps harbour similar affections towards him and be willing to become his wife. No longer having anyone else in his life, since his brother's passing, Martha now, more than ever, meant everything to him. He'd refused to set foot over the threshold of the Manor House, having never liked Lady Mary and always sensed that it was only out of duty and respect for Reginald that she'd been civil towards him. He wanted nothing from her or from his spoilt nephews and niece, who he knew had mimicked and ridiculed him behind his back since they were young children. Reginald must also have known these home truths and had been most thoughtful in granting permission for Bruce to reside in the gatehouse for the rest of his life with a clause in his last will and testament stating that should he ever marry, which Reginald had thought most doubtful, his wife would also be granted the same allowances. Reginald had also bequeathed a sufficient sum of money to his brother, allowing Bruce to sever all ties with the family at the Manor House. No longer requiring a hamper of food to be delivered daily, he had since made arrangements for the local grocery to deliver weekly. Martha was more than happy to take over the cooking duties, she'd missed cooking and it would also help to pass the time of day.

Poised with her pencil ready to sketch a solitary jay, perched on an overhanging branch, Martha couldn't help wondering what had happened to Bruce; he was normally the first to be out, enjoying the morning sun. He'd been tired of late and had taken to retiring early of an evening. Martha had also noticed that his breathing had become more laboured causing a wheezing sound to rattle through his chest, but Bruce had assured her that he was fine and merely suffering from a summer cold.

"*Martha!*" His strained voice suddenly broke into her thoughts. She turned to look at him as he struggled out of the back door, his face pale and his body nearly doubled over in agony.

"*Oh My Lord!*" she cried out, dropping her book and pencil as she hurried to his side. "Bruce, you must let me go out and fetch a doctor...you're clearly unwell!"

"*No, no,*" he protested in short laboured breaths. "I can take anything that this miserable life throws at me, my princess, except for losing you!"

"You must rest then, I insist; you won't be comfortable out here, Bruce, let me help you inside."

Martha struggled under the weight of his bulky body as he leaned on her; unable to even attempt climbing the stone stairs, Martha helped him on to the couch in the front parlour; it was the coolest of rooms with the sun's rays not reaching the window until late afternoon. The relief to lie down was apparent in Bruce's face; his brow already appeared more at ease. He splattered and choked as Martha held a glass of cool water to his lips, all the while whispering kind words of comfort to him.

"It's not the first time I've been laid upon this couch to die!" he declared, shocking Martha, who was suddenly overcome with a feeling of nervous nausea as to what would become of her should Bruce pass away. As he closed his only eye, he found it impossible to shake off the vivid flashbacks of his mother from all those years ago, he felt like a schoolboy once more and the searing pain in his body was similar to that which he'd endured decades ago.

"Please don't talk like that Bruce, you'll be fine in a few days...as you said, it's just a cold!"

By the afternoon, Bruce's health had deteriorated significantly, leaving Martha in a huge quandary as to what she should do.

"Please Bruce, let me go and fetch help...I could slip a note through the door of the Manor House later tonight when it's dark, no one will see me...I'll be extra careful, I promise...*please Bruce!*"

Bruce took a firm hold on her arm, shaking his head as Martha knelt by his side; the mere thought of his precious princess leaving the confines of the gatehouse was causing him to become perturbed and beneath her bravado, Martha was dreading the day when she would have to step outside of her well-appointed prison and home. The fear that Bruce could quite easily pass away, even more so, since the Squire had left the world four years ago played heavy on her thoughts...what on earth would she do? How would she manage? Having no idea as to where her parents now lived, her imagination conjured up an outside world packed with mean people just waiting to pounce on her and hand her over to the authorities the moment anyone should recognise *Martha Shepherd*, the girl who had shamed her lovely, God-fearing family, forcing them to elope to endure a life of misery and most likely a life of poverty and hardship far away from their home. A girl, who had then gone on to pretend that she'd drowned; causing even more stress for her poor mother. She couldn't go on, her stomach contracted and her body began to shake nervously. She would spend the entire night praying and begging the Almighty not to take the life of Bruce Brunswick. Throughout the night, Martha nursed Bruce as best she knew how, she mopped his sweating brow and regularly changed the towel which she'd propped beneath his mouth, although as the night progressed, his usual flow of saliva seemed to ebb away and the few words which he forced out with gasps of breath were hoarse. But in his struggle to be heard, he made an extra effort to issue Martha with some strict instructions.

"Under the floorboards, my sweet Martha, if I should leave...look under the floorboards…in my room...Martha...my room..."

"Please rest now, Bruce, you're not going anywhere...and tomorrow we will sit in the sunshine and sketch together." She rested her head against the side of the couch, still with her small hand concealed in Bruce's. The ticking clock and the gentle sound of Bruce's shallow breathing soon caused sleep to overcome her and in that period, Bruce took his final breath and his life which had been thwarted with trials and disasters since his childhood came to a peaceful end. The sudden release of Martha's hand as it flopped down from the couch immediately woke her; one look at Bruce and she knew that he had left the world...A true gentleman who had lived behind his hideous mask all of his life but had caused her no harm at all even if his reputation was one of complete contrast. She took hold of his hand again and cried, Bruce Brunswick had been her entire world for the past five years, he had rescued her from what might have been a life which she preferred never to dwell on and had shown her more benevolence than anyone apart from her parents had done; even throughout those early months when she had been convinced that Bruce would one day desire her body, he had turned out to want nothing other than her companionship; he continuously cared about her happiness and protecting her became his most paramount purpose in life. She had matured from a girl with her head in the clouds to a mature young woman, Bruce had taught her many skills and lessons which would be invaluable to her future, but now she could only sob, her broken heart telling her that life would never be the same again without Bruce Brunswick as part of it. She would greatly miss him and never forget him for the rest of her days.

As the dawn sun slowly began to warm up the new day, the cold facts suddenly hit Martha; she knew she'd have to act quickly in preparing herself for a completely new way of life; she was on her own from now and already feeling frightened and vulnerable without Bruce there to protect her. She straightened Bruce's body, tenderly kissed his forehead and covered him with two large pastel lengths of silk taken from her bedroom. Her heart was like a heavy weight beneath her ribs as her tears rolled liberally down her face. She kept telling herself to be strong, knowing that she'd soon have to face the strange world outside the gatehouse. She'd already decided to spend the rest of the day packing in preparation for her departure and destroying any evidence that she'd been living in the gatehouse, although she was quite certain that no suspicions would be aroused should evidence that a female had spent time with

Bruce be discovered. He was a man, after all, and one, according to the Brunswick family, who had lived an eccentric existence of secrecy over the years. She remembered Bruce's instructions to look under the floorboards and sensed that he'd probably left her well provided for.

She stripped her elaborate bedroom back to its original bareness, folding the copious lengths of expensive silk which had adorned her beautiful room over the years and placing them neatly away in the chest of drawers; Bruce had gone out of his way to bring this sophisticated comfort to her life; her tears fell relentlessly as she remembered the early days when she and Bruce had begun their outlandish relationship; she had always sensed that he'd grown to love and care deeply for her over time, as she had him; it was an odd relationship and she doubted that anyone in the world would understand it or believe it.

There were far too many gowns hanging in the wardrobe for her to carry and most of them quite unsuitable for everyday life, especially if she didn't want to appear conspicuous. The two modest day gowns which she's worn whilst tackling the household chores would be perfect to travel in, even though they were the sort of dresses which her mother would have kept for Sunday best. With a dark shawl draped around her shoulders, Martha hoped to create a more serene appearance to her ensemble which would allow her to blend in with the rest of the womenfolk and avoid any unwanted attention. Finding herself in Bruce's room as she went in search of a modest travelling case, his words suddenly floated into her thoughts *'look under the floorboards'* he had said, *'my room.'* Catching sight of an antiquated case beneath his bed, she instantly began choking on the thick dust as she hastily pulled it out and wiped its surface. It was a little larger than she'd have liked, but it would have to do and it also meant that she'd have enough space to take a selection of her lavish gowns too, plus a selection of winter clothes...She had to look ahead to the future, who knew where she might end up once she'd left the gatehouse. It was a thought she didn't wish to dwell on and was consumed with dread every time she imagined herself stepping out, into the outside world. She meticulously scanned the floorboards, looking for tell-tell signs of one which had been lifted; beneath the bed was a commonplace she thought, but found nothing, she stood up, her eyes still surveying the floor...*The rug!* called out a voice inside her head. She hurried towards the old and faded Persian rug, rolling it back to reveal a loose floorboard which had been intentionally marked by a large black ink stain. Her hands were sweating and the intense beat of her heart drummed against her ribs. The floorboard concealed a long wooden box which she carefully lifted out, gingerly opening the lid. There was nothing fancy or secure about the archaic chest, it was meant to be discovered. A row of wax-sealed envelopes filled the box she flicked through them; each one was addressed to a member of the Brunswick family but the largest and thickest of all of them had her name upon it. Her mind drifted as she held the envelope close to her chest. Bruce had been misunderstood for most of his life and she doubted many people actually knew the kind-hearted and caring Bruce; taunted and cast aside since the terrible incident at the hands of his mother's lover, the nickname, Squinty Eye had stuck with him over the years along with folks wicked need to turn him into some kind of a monster. But she knew the real Bruce Brunswick and was glad of the five years which she'd come to know, and in a strange way, love him.

Leaving the box in Bruce's room, Martha took her envelope into her bedroom and flung herself onto the bed. Afraid, and feeling so desperately lonely, she tried to coax herself into facing reality, *'this is what you've dreamt about all these years'* she encouraged herself, *'Now is your chance to be free and go in search of your family!'*

A thick bundle of banknotes slipped from the envelope, more than she'd ever seen in her entire life, but having expected Bruce to leave her healthily financed, she wasn't surprised and allowed them to remain scattered upon the bed as she took hold of the letter. Feeling the sudden urge to be close to Bruce while she read his words, she fled back downstairs and sat on the floor next to Bruce's body. With shaking hands, Martha took a deep breath before unfolding the letter which had been dated eight months ago,

My Dearest Martha, my princess,
I know that if you find yourself reading this letter that I have most likely passed away, hopefully into a kinder place where I will, at last, be free of my life's trials and turmoil. I hope too that in my resurrection the Creator will bless me with a more presentable and, perhaps, handsome appearance.
First of all Martha Shepherd, I want to apologise to you and pray that you can find it in your chaste and kind heart to forgive me. All those years ago, when I set out to free you from the wretched convict's hulk and in a way make you my own prisoner, my intentions towards you were sinful and selfish and as I sit here writing this letter, thinking of you sleeping close by in your room, I cannot even bear to explain what I had in mind for you, my treasured one. Please forgive me and know in your heart that those wicked intentions disappeared in the very early weeks after your arrival to the gatehouse.
You have enhanced my once miserable existence with your charm and kindness and over the years I have grown to love you in the purest of ways and have sought nothing more than your most valued companionship. You have become as precious to me, Martha, as any princess could be...You have, over the years, changed the hate and revenge in my heart to love and acceptance and I can never thank you enough for bringing about this miraculous

transformation in me and changing the final episode of my life in this world to years of pure gold.

Martha's tear-filled eyes made it impossible to continue, she took hold of Bruce's arm, separated only by the fine layer of silk, "Oh Bruce, of course, I forgive you...You saved me from a life of hell and have shown me nothing but compassion...I will pray for you for the rest of my days." Wiping away her tears, she continued to read,

*I write this letter in the hope that by the time you read it, seven years would have elapsed and you will be a free woman. Not many people would have heard the news that you supposedly drowned and never set sail for Van Diemen's Land, so I'm sure you will be quite safe. Even now, as I write, more than four years have passed and your plight likely to have been forgotten by the locals by now, but I do strongly advise you to leave this area, Martha; I would hate the thought of any harm ever touching you. Find your new life in Oxford...I believe your family are living there...and once more, my beloved, I beg your forgiveness, that I kept this secret from you over the years...you may call it selfish, but know that I **did** intend to tell you when the time was right. That brings me to another huge and sinful burden which lays heavy on my conscience and one which I fear will shock you more than anything I have disclosed to you over the years. Please don't hate me, my princess, remember I was a different man before you filled my life with sunshine and sweetness, a cruel unscrupulous beast in fact.*

Taking a deep breath, as she came to the end of the page, Martha was almost scared to continue to the next one. What on earth could Bruce have done she pondered as she took a glance at his shrouded body upon the couch, "Oh dearest Bruce, I am fearful of continuing!" she gently sobbed.

I am unaware of whether your parents ever disclosed anything to you about a letter which I wrote to them, just before your imprisonment? I would ask that you also beg them to forgive me should you find yourself united with them once again. It was a cruel and evil letter.
My dearest Martha, I have committed the most abominable sin and crime which sadly caused a young maid in my charge to lose her life. Molly Wright gave birth to my son and tragically died shortly after his delivery. In my fear and haste, I embarked on a most unforgivable period in my life, firstly informing poor Molly that her baby hadn't survived and then discarding her dead body in the woods. There is no excuse for this dreadful and callous deed and I don't expect you to forgive me but please try to understand that my soul was tormented inside my disfigured body for so many years that perhaps there was even a period of my life when I was nothing more than a man driven insane due to circumstance. I placed my young son in the barn of your parent's farm...

Martha took a sudden gasp, dropping the letter as she remembered that long-ago day when her sisters had discovered little Georgie...*her darling little Georgie,* who she'd missed so much and had formed such a close bond with.

The only person who knew of my son was my late brother...and now, of course, yourself. I gave your parents little choice as to whether they took my son into their care, unashamedly using blackmail and threats. Perhaps one day they will understand why my brother was forced to treat them so harshly, he did not wish it for one second and of course, was only shielding his dishonourable brother. I beg of you, sweet Martha, to take my son into your loving heart and care, and perhaps one day, if you feel it to be appropriate, tell him a little of me. I pray that I haven't complicated your life to such a degree that you will abandon me from your heart forever. I know that you will make all the right decisions regarding my last revelation. My precious Martha, I pray that you will encounter a long and wholesome life filled with love and adventures...never try to dismiss your vivacious imagination, it is what makes you the adorable and kind soul that you are. Martha Shepherd, it has been a true pleasure knowing and loving you; know that you have given back to me a contented happiness which I feared never to experience again. Be happy my sweet and beautiful princess,

Your adoring companion,
Bruce Brunswick.

CHAPTER TWENTY-NINE

The rest of the day was spent meticulously tidying every room of the gatehouse and searching through Bruce's belongings to make sure nothing that might lead to her existence in the house would be left for someone else to discover. Soon concluding that Bruce must have already taken such steps, there was very little in the way of personal effects or past correspondence to be found. Martha collected all the loose change she came upon in the drawers and inside various pockets in Bruce's wardrobe; it would be essential for her forthcoming travels, allowing her to keep the wad of banknotes safely hidden. Her work was continuously interrupted by bouts of heartache and uncontrollable sobbing; the entire process of closing this bizarre chapter of her life was proving to be extremely emotional. There were times throughout the day when Martha just couldn't believe everything was so final, she half expected Bruce to suddenly appear or to call out for her and couldn't remember ever feeling such loneliness and anxiety since her time of being abandoned in the convict hulk to await her fate.

Her stomach rumbled loudly and even though her appetite had vanished she could hear Bruce's voice inside her head telling her to take care of herself and eat before she embarked on her traumatic journey; even in death he was still guiding her and offering his sound advice she mused with deep sorrow.

As the long drawn out day slowly gave way to evening, Martha sat at Bruce's desk, with pen in hand, not quite knowing how to phrase what she wanted to say. She chewed reluctantly on a plate of bread and cheese, washing it down with cool water. She hadn't even formulated a plan as to where she would head to in the early hours of the following morning. Oxford was her destination but how to arrive there was far beyond her knowledge and she viewed the world outside the gatehouse with feelings of immense trepidation.

Dear Lady Mary Brunswick,

She wrote for the fourth time, telling her herself that whatever she wrote this time would not be scrapped.

You do not know me, and I would prefer to keep it that way, but I have been a very dear friend to Mr Bruce Brunswick over the years. I have been a guest at the gatehouse during the past two days after he contacted me complaining of ill health. I am so terribly sorry to have to inform you that sadly, he has since passed away. Please attend to him as I have urgent business to attend to and cannot delay my departure a moment longer,
Yours sincerely,
A friend.

Martha read the brief letter over and over again, not liking, it but unable to think of any other way of simply doing what had to be done. It sounded cold, she reflected and she didn't come across as a friend, at all; more like a thief in the night. But, she concluded, why should she concern herself so much with those whom Bruce had despised all his life; all that mattered now was for Bruce to be given a decent burial.

She remained fully dressed for most of the night, dozing off on occasion only to wake with a start, fearing she'd slept right through to the morning and finding that the hands of the clock had moved a mere ten minutes. It was to be the longest night but as the first thread of daylight became visible, Martha said her final goodbye to Bruce. Pulling back the silk sheet she tenderly kissed his forehead, dripping tears upon him as she did so;

"Goodbye Mr Brunswick, my brave knight; I will remember you forever. I love you." Leaving the candle burning brightly on the table next to where he laid, Martha quickly put on her bonnet, picked up her case and left the gatehouse for the very last time. Glancing at Bruce's silver pocket watch which she'd taken as a personal keepsake, the alarming thought that the staff at the Manor House would likely be up and preparing to start their day set her into a panic. It was approaching five-thirty. She left her heavy case concealed behind the shrubbery near

the entrance to the Estate, which was close by
the gatehouse and instead of running across the
dewy stretch of grass, in full view to anyone of
the maids who might be drawing back the
curtains, she sneaked around the perimeter wall,
bent almost to half her height. She nervously
pushed the letter which she'd addressed to Lady
Mary Brunswick through the gleaming brass
letterbox and re-traced her tracks, praying that
no one had caught a glimpse of her.
A few minutes later, Martha was hurrying as
fast as her wobbly legs would allow, along the
familiar lanes of Bagley village. Little had
changed over the course of five years, apart from
the lanes now appearing shorter and the hedges
not quite as tall. She arrived at the entrance gate
to her old home, stopping to stare at the cottage
for a brief second; there was no change there too,
everything looked exactly the same. Tears filled
her eyes and for the next few minutes, she
allowed them to fall freely as she sobbed for the
warm and loving family life that once was. The
lanes remained empty throughout her walk to
reach the main highway; a highway which also
rekindled memories of the day she'd last walked
it with her brother as they'd made the journey
into Epsom on that ill-fated day.
With Epsom being the only town where Martha
knew she could travel by stagecoach to London,
and hopefully then on to Oxford, her main
concerns and worries were whether she might

still be recognised in Epsom. Five years was a long time she persuaded herself, people were bound to have forgotten about her by now and she had also grown older and was now dressed elegantly, just like the womenfolk who she'd admired and aspired to when she'd been thirteen years old.

She waited opposite Epsom pond, the place where, according to an overheard conversation between two gentlemen, the stagecoach was scheduled to depart in half an hour. Her heart was beating riotously and her hands sweated copiously as she held the few coins in her gloved hand. Praying that nobody would talk to her and that the loose change in her hand would be enough for the journey, she fidgeted from one foot to another, anxious for the stagecoach to arrive and whisk her far away from home soil. A couple of finely attired ladies strolled along on the opposite side of the street causing Martha to become over conscience that her ensemble was lacking a reticule; the fact that her money was inside her glove made her suddenly feel quite childish. A modest reticule would be an essential purchase once arriving in London, she decided, providing she could muster up enough confidence to make such a transaction and speak to a shopkeeper.

She and the two gentlemen were the only passengers on the stagecoach and much to Martha's relief they spent most of the journey deep in conversation, seeming in complete oblivion to her presence after their initial polite greetings. It was nearly two hours later when they arrived at the coaching inn in London. Martha followed the two gentlemen naively thinking that perhaps they too were travelling to Oxford but soon realised, as they entered a huge building, that their business must be in London. Walking blindly amongst the crowds, Martha hadn't a clue as to where she was or where she was heading. She'd seldom witnessed such crowds apart from the occasion when she'd been to the Epsom races with her family and then she'd always had her ma's hand to clutch hold of. There were so many people all seemingly heading in different directions and all with a look of determination about them. It only took a few minutes for Martha to conclude that she didn't like London. The sight of a young girl standing at the side of what she now knew was Westminster Bridge, at last, gave her some hope; the young girl couldn't have been much older than nine, she thought and was stood alone holding a basket full of dainty flower posies and single buttonholes. The child shied away from Martha as she approached, pulling down the brim of her bonnet over her eyes.

"Hello, there!" greeted Martha in a small voice. The girl looked up, a tiny twitch of a smile upon her drawn face.

"What gorgeous posies! May I buy one?"

Martha suddenly caught sight of an irate looking woman hurrying along the street towards them and although lacking in the girl's angelic characteristics the similarity of their features confirmed that this must be the girl's mother.

"What d'yer want wiv me gal?" she demanded angrily, as she snatched the basket from the girl's hand and stood protectively in front of her.

"I only wanted to buy a flower...I mean no harm."

The woman eyed Martha from head to toe, "The likes ov fancy folk like you ain't usually in'trested in these button 'oles!"

"Please Misses, I'm far from fancy!"

"Yer must 'ave stolen them fancy togs from off some poor corpse in the funeral parlour then, cos they *is fancy* whether yer choose ter deny it or not."

"So may I buy a flower?"

"A penny!" she demanded, holding out her grubby hand.

Martha sighed, wondering if all Londoners were as rude as this one or whether it was just her luck that she'd stumbled upon such an aggressive first encounter. She handed over one of the pennies from inside her glove, smiling warmly at the young child,

"Would you like to pick one out for me?"

The girl took a sneaky glance at Martha and cleverly picked out a posy of pink carnations, a perfect match with the pink pinstripe of

Martha's dress.

"Thank you! That's exactly what I would have chosen myself! How old are you?"

"She don't speak none!" interrupted her mother in a strict tone.

"Oh! What a shame." Martha was suddenly lost for the right words, but seeing as she had nothing to lose; she risked asking the woman if she knew where she could find a coach which would take her to Oxford. The woman appeared shocked by her question.

"Yer ain't travelling all that way on her own are yer?" She seemed to be growing even more suspicious of Martha.

"Where's yer folks, then?"

Martha hesitated, not sure if she should trust this stranger. A sudden flashback of her wrongful arrest as she'd so innocently waited by Epsom pond told her to trust no one and to disclose nothing.

"Oh my folks are waiting in a tea room, my ma had one of her funny turns; it's the travelling and this hot weather I think. We are going to live with my grandparents on their farm in Oxfordshire!" she lied.

"Well, I ain't never left London afore, but I *can* tell yer there's always a stream ov stage coaches leaving the *Bull and Mouth* couch 'ouse; most ov 'em stop in Whitechapel Road an' all. I reckons one ov 'em will take yer there.

Feeling her spirits lift, Martha thanked the

woman and hurried back from the direction she'd come from, in the pretence of rejoining her parents in the tea room.

CHAPTER THIRTY

Much to the annoyance of Grace and Georgie, Claire insisted that Amy should take and collect them from school every day. The twins were inseparable and shared such a close bond that it was impossible to view them as anything other than true blood twins and a fact now forgotten by most members of the Shepherd family.

"We're not babies, Amy!" protested Grace, "and we promise to hold hands until we reach the school gates, don't we Georgie?" she continued as they marched through Oxford's busy thoroughfares.

Amy sighed crossly, "Am I to have to listen to your complaints every single morning of my life Grace! Just button up your lips, otherwise, I won't bring you any sweets for the walk home!"

"Yeah, Grace, Amy is only doing what Ma told her to do otherwise *she'll* be in trouble!" voiced the wise words of little Georgie.

At twelve years old Amy no longer attended the local school, and now helped out in the busy ironmongers, mostly in the back of the shop where she made up the orders which Frank would deliver throughout the day. Being considered as the family's math genius, she now kept the account books in order and was up to the date on every penny leaving and entering the business. Jane, on the other hand, spent most

of her time above the shop in the Shepherd
family's living quarters, where she helped her
ma out with the daily chores and learned the
skills needed to become the perfect wife. She
also spent long hours perfecting her needlework
and while Claire and Silas prayed that she
would soon be walking out with a suitable beau,
Jane was more intent on becoming an exemplary
seamstress with the hope that one day she might
find employment in one of the Oxford High
Street's exclusive ladies' gown shops. At fifteen,
although not having been blessed with a beauty
equivalent to Martha's, she had a certain calm
sophistication about her which was greatly
admired. Unlike many girls of her age, Jane
wasn't flighty or loud which earned her the
reputation of being mature and sensible; a
characteristic which most parents wished for in
their future daughter in law. Jane's refusal to the
abundant requests to walk out with a potential
beau of a Sunday afternoon also left her with the
ever-growing reputation of being pretentious
and before long, much to the disappointment of
Claire, the offers slowly dried up like a summer
brook. Claire would always be the first to object
about her daughter's continuous refusals,
"Why do you turn every young man down, Jane?
Do you want to end up an old maid!" she
questioned as they stepped over the threshold
one Sunday morning after church.
Jane laughed, "Ma, I'm fifteen years old...it's far

too early to be giving me the title of *old maid!* I don't intend to marry until I'm ready. I don't need a man to support me, either; I'm going to be a famous seamstress one day, designing gowns for the wealthy!"

"Don't you start with all that dreaming nonsense my girl, haven't you learned anything from your poor sister's fate; she was a dreamer and look where that got her!"

Jane hung up her bonnet, taking in a deep breath and biting her tongue. She turned and looked Frank directly in the eye; he quickly diverted his gaze,

"Come on Georgie, how about we go fishing for the rest of the morning?"

George's face lit up,

"Can I come too?" begged Grace, sadly.

"Of course not silly, *girls can't fish!*"

"*Well said*, Georgie!" laughed Frank.

"As I was about to say," continued Jane, returning her attention to Claire as Frank led George though the shop to collect their fishing rods from the garden shed. "I wasn't *such* a little girl five years ago, Mother, not to know that it wasn't Martha's imagination which was to blame for her fate, but Frank's ugly desire to become a wealthy man! I *knew* what went on Mother and in my opinion, *if* I'm allowed to voice one, Frank got off too easily!"

"*That's enough!*" declared Silas, crossly. "Take pity on your poor mother, Jane! All she's ever wanted was the best for all of her children and that doesn't mean taking sides. Every human being upon God's earth is entitled to make a mistake in their life, so long as they come to realise it and seek forgiveness and repent!"

"May I be excused Pa; I need to change out of my Sunday best before I prepare the vegetables?" stated Jane in a level headed manner.

Silas nodded his head.

"Come along girls, we've got work to do! Let's leave ma and pa to have some peace and quiet for a change."

"Can I scrape the carrots, Jane?" pleaded Grace as they climbed the stairs.

"I suppose that means I get the muddy old potatoes!" objected Amy.

"*No!*, actually *you* get to clean the cabbage, Amy!"

"*Caterpillars!*" they all cried out in unison.

Claire and Silas listened to their fading giggles.

"Oh, Silas, did we do the right thing in bringing our family to live in the City! Jane wouldn't have all these farfetched ideas if we still lived in Bagley village...she'd be walking out by now and dreaming of her future as a married woman. Living in Oxford has put all kinds of ridiculous notions into her head!

"Don't worry so my love, listen to them, they're all as happy as can be *and* Jane is still young, what's the big hurry to get her married off? Times are changing Claire. We've already lost one daughter! Don't be in such a hurry to lose another!"

Already annoyed with himself that he'd mentioned Martha so unkindly, without thinking, it came as no surprise when Claire suddenly burst into tears.

"Oh My darling, I'm sorry, I didn't think as usual!"

He took Claire in his arms, "Come on, let's go out for a walk!"

"Dinner! I need to help the girls with the Roast!"

"They'll be fine! They are more than capable you know," assured Silas.

"I'll just pop up and tell them then!"

"No you won't, we'll be back before they've had time to pick off all those caterpillars!" joked Silas as he pulled the shop door open.

The midday, July sun was intensive, as they ambled along the High street towards Magdalen Bridge, "It will be a welcome sight when the river comes into view, we can rest in the shade of that huge weeping willow that you so adore!" voiced Silas.

Claire's mind was miles away, "Do *you* think that Jane is right? She's such a sensible girl; I often have to remind myself that she's only fifteen but she's so mature for her age and I *do* trust most of her suggestions and opinions. *Did* we let Frank off too easily? We never really asked about what he got up to during his many trips to Epsom...I doubt that was the first time he'd stolen anything."

"*Claire!* We can't bring that up now, the lad has proved himself worthy of our support time and time again during the last five years. He's a man now and I mean a man; he was merely finding growing up a struggle and he made some mistakes along the way; you have to forget the past, what's done is done and nothing can bring out beloved Martha back but that doesn't mean we have to spend the rest of our lives in misery...Martha wouldn't have wanted that now, would she?"

They left the stifling street and stepped down the flight of heavily worn stone steps where they found themselves in a different world. The river rippled gently as the tips of the willow gently dangled into to water. A pair of graceful swans glided along, their brightness standing out against the background of dense greenery. There was an abundance of shade to be found, causing the air to be refreshingly cool. Claire and Silas rested beneath the century-old willow, sitting in silence for a while as they listened to the chorus of delightful bird song.

"Do you know, Silas, that sometimes I doubt that I will ever truly forgive Frank for what he did...sometimes I have to pinch myself when my mind travels back to that awful period in time. How could I have forgiven him so readily and yes, you are right, it's too late to bring the subject up again but sometimes when I remember our darling Martha and the appalling way in which her last weeks were spent; how alone and terrified she must have been, I feel like cutting all ties with him. *Am I a bad mother?*"

"Oh, Claire, you are the *very* best of mothers, you made a very difficult decision so quickly and easily...only a true mother would be so compassionate. If you presume that I don't give the subject any thought, then you are mistaken, because believe it or not I harbour the very same thoughts and suspicions as you have just mentioned and I too sometimes find myself looking at our son, still unable to fathom what happened. I must admit, all too often, it feels as though I'm still in the midst of a nightmare."

"I do know that you hurt as much as I do, Silas; *my darling Silas*...we must be strong for each other and our girls *and* little Georgie...they deserve the *very best* we can give them."

"I couldn't agree more, let's just try to fill our hearts with forgiveness and give Frank the benefit of the doubt...I'm sure it will only be a few years before he settles down with his own bride and once he's a father himself, he will fully understand the pain that his misadventures have caused us."

"You're right as usual, Silas...thank God I have such an understanding husband."

"Don't get too comfortable now, *Mrs Shepherd*, I don't much fancy burnt or overcooked brisket."

"Oh! And who was it that said the girls were

more than capable!"

"Ahh, yes, my dear, but I've had a worrying thought...*what happens to a ship when the captain is missing?*"

"Come on let's go home to our family, Silas Shepherd!"

In his heart, Frank sensed that he'd never gain his parent's complete forgiveness, he'd noticed how his ma clandestinely stared at him on occasions and wasn't blind to the way she became instantly cold towards him whenever Martha's name was mentioned; then there was Jane, most of the time she was quite aloof and if he cast his mind back to the day he'd shown up in Bagley village, she was the only family member who'd ignored him and was against his parents welcoming him back into the family again. He often wondered if she knew more than she let on; she'd always been the quiet natured one of the family, with a sharp eye and ears that missed nothing.

"Georgie! Quick! I reckon there's a whopper on the end of the line! I'll need your help with this one!"

George's face lit up as he raced back from the water's edge, imagining a gigantic fish on the end of Frank's rod. He found fishing boring but loved spending time alone with Frank; he admired him, thought him funny and clever and he didn't treat him like a baby. Amy would be screaming her head off is she'd seen him so close to the river's edge, on his own, but Frank trusted him; Frank treated him more like a grown-up.

"Ah! George! You weren't fast enough...now that rascal of a trout has escaped our supper plates!" teased Frank. George's look of delight instantly changed to one of dismay.

"Was it really a whopper, Frank, or were you just teasing?"

"Of course it was, how else d'you think it got away...*to strong and clever*...that fish had better things to do than end up on our table tonight!"

George giggled, "You're funny, Frank! I hope you don't ever move away!"

Shocked by his odd statement, Frank asked, "And *why* would I be moving away?"

"When you get married of course!"

" *Who's* been saying that I'm getting wed?"

"Every one! Well, the girls have...and you *are* a man...and everyone gets married...*don't they?*"

Frank stared thoughtfully at him, it was strange to think that everyone except for Grace, knew that he had no blood ties to the Shepherd family...he was an outsider and Frank felt a little sorry that George was going to live his life being fooled by those he loved and trusted so much and annoyed to think that George would probably be treated a lot better than he was when he grew up and his parents would have a closer bond with the *bastard child* than they'd have with him.

"Well you don't *have* to get married you know, Georgie; there's no law that says you must; anyway, I'm not even walking out with a pretty young maid yet, so think it'll be a while 'till you come to *my* wedding breakfast!"

George listened carefully to Frank's words as he sat plucking out the long strands of grass and wrapping them around his small fingers.

"Well, I'm going to get married as soon as I'm a man!" he confessed.

"You'll soon change your mind, Georgie. Who wants a nagging wife, bossing you around all day and forcing you to work from dawn to dusk just to provide for all the mischievous children which go hand in hand with marriage!"

"Ma doesn't do that to Pa, does she?"

Frank laughed out loud, amused by the innocent way in which George viewed the world.

"So who will *you* marry Georgie! Who has captured your heart?"

George looked up at the sky, his fair hair glistening beneath the sun's bright rays; he thought for a while before giving his answer, "Well, there isn't really anyone yet, except for Grace, and I know I couldn't marry her because she's my sister, but if there was another girl just like her, then I would definitely make her my wife!"

"Hmm, that's interesting." Frank had a sudden urge to tell George the truth; he held his tongue wondering if a young lad would be capable of handling such a huge secret, but the temptation proved too great to simply brush it aside.

"Well, Georgie, that's where you are mistaken!" George looked curiously at his older brother, "What do you mean, Frank?"

"Can you keep a secret?"

George nodded eagerly.

"I mean a *real* secret! A grownup's secret?"

"Of course I can!" he answered eagerly.

"How about if I told you that you *will* be able to marry Grace when you're older...that's if you truly love her?"

Georgie looked puzzled, "You're just teasing me again, Frank, just like you're always teasing Grace and Amy!"

"No, I'm not! Ma and Pa, aren't your real parents you know?"

"Be quiet Frank...that's not funny!"

"It's not meant to be! You were discovered in our barn...somebody didn't like the racket you were making so they left you in our barn!"

George got up and stood rigid, his face slowly turning red and his features screwed up as he tried hard not to burst into tears.

"Jane always says that you're like a rotten piece of fish...that's a horrible thing to say...it's not a secret because it's not true! You're bad Frank and I'm gonna tell Ma and Pa what you said!"

Frank grabbed hold of his arm, squeezing it so tightly that George screamed out loud. The riverbank was now deserted; the fishermen had all headed home for their Sunday feast.

"Leave me alone!" He tried with all his might to wriggle free from Frank's hold.

"Listen to me, you stupid idiotic boy! You're not to say a word to Ma and Pa...If you do it will just make Ma upset and you don't want that do you?"

Upset and confused, George wished that he'd never come fishing with Frank and he desperately wanted a cuddle from his Ma.

"You're only saying such horrid things because they love me more than you...it's all your fault that Martha died; everyone knows that!"

"Shut your stupid blabbering mouth, Georgie, what would you know about Martha, you never even knew her, you were just a squalling baby...she wasn't *your* sister...neither is Jane or Amy or your *dear little Grace!*"

In his raging anger, it had slipped his mind that George was only a child; he'd said too much and knew that George was about to ruin everything for him and that he'd go running to confide in the family. Frank had hold of George's arms, he was shaking him like a rag doll and George was now screaming to escape the pain which consumed his small body.

"Let me go!" he cried in despair.

For a split second, Frank released his hold. George took the chance and began to flee up the grassy embankment determined to find his way home and escape from his malicious brother. Frank was quickly behind him, he lunged through the air catching George by his ankles and causing them both to roll back down the slope. George's body flew through the air and with an added kick from Frank, the sound of a splash and the spray of showering river water was a pleasing confirmation to Frank that poor little George had accidentally stumbled into the river; what a terrible shame that both he and George couldn't swim he mused with a sly satisfactory grin upon his face. He didn't stay a second longer but raced towards home planning his distraught speech for when he arrived. The family would be better off without that little Brunswick bastard anyway, he considered; he had done the entire family a favour, even if they wouldn't realise it yet; he would cause nothing but trouble when he grew up and if he'd inherited any of his father's characteristics he'd mature into a vile man and probably be out to destroy everyone and take what was not his from under their noses.

Out of breath and dishevelled, it was only when Frank had reached the pavement of St. Aldates that he ceased running and took his breath. Having lost all sense of what time it was the strong aroma of meat and cabbage which blew through the air indicated that it must be well past midday. He searched every pocket for his silver timepiece, the only stolen item from his past which he'd hung on to; there was no sign of it.

"*Damn!*" he voiced angrily, knowing he'd have to retrace his steps to search for it, already suspecting that the pocket watch had slipped from his pocket during his roll down the river bank.

CHAPTER THIRTY-ONE

Above the ironmongers, in the private rooms of
the Shepherd home, Amy had taken extra care
laying out the dinner table; she took a step back
to admire the artistic touches, which she'd
learned from a recent chat with an old school
friend who'd gone into service.

"Where d'you think this is Amy Shepherd!
Buscot Park?" laughed Silas as he viewed the
vast display of cutlery and the neat row of cone-
shaped serviettes.

"It's just something that Jenny Wilkins taught
me...she works at Kingston Bagpuize House
now!" Amy proudly explained.

Silas glanced at the clock, "Where have those
lads got to? Frank should act more responsibly;
he knows what time we eat Sunday dinner!" He
left the parlour, shaking his head in annoyance;
his stomach was rumbling and the delicious
smell of food which filled with the house was
making him desperate to commence with the
meal. He tried hard to restrain his anger but as
usual, it was Frank who'd disrupted their
schedule. He marched to the kitchen; everything
was cooked and Jane was about to carry the
dishes of hot vegetables to the table while Claire
prepared the carving knife and fork for Silas to
slice up the slightly shrivelled piece of beef.

"Hmm, that smells delicious, girls!" he declared.

"Are Frank and Georgie home yet? Claire enquired.

"They've probably caught a huge fish and are struggling to carry it home as we speak!" suggested Silas in a bid to keep Claire calm. She was not amused,

"We've spent all morning cooking this meal; Frank is well aware of what time we eat Sunday dinner and I'm not going to let good food go to waste because of his selfishness! Come along Silas carve the joint please, we're all famished!" After hearing Claire's earlier confessions Silas knew that inside, Claire was furious with Frank and although he shared her feelings, he kept them to himself, not wanting to add fuel to the already fiercely burning fire.

"I quite agree my love, we're all starving; anyway, I'm sure those scallywags won't be too fussed about eating cold food; let's eat; just wait 'til you see the fancy way Amy has laid the table!"

While the family hungrily tucked into their meal, Claire had suddenly lost her appetite, sensing that something was amiss. She chewed a mouthful of the cheap cut of beef over and over before piling her share into Silas's plate,

"What's wrong?" he asked in surprise. "You need to eat your meat, Claire, it's good for you!"

"That's the last time I buy beef from that butcher in the covered market, it's as tough as old boots!" Grace and Amy giggled at their ma's words,

"Have you ever tasted old boots then Ma?" asked Grace.

"Eat your vegetables!" snapped Claire, with a huge sigh.

"Don't agonize, my darling, they'll be fine...they're probably having such a successful time of it that they've lost all sense of time!"

"Is Georgie going to be in trouble when he gets home?"

Silas issued Grace with a stern warning glare, causing her to lower her head and continue eating her cabbage.

"This is a delicious meal!" declared Silas, "Fit for a king I'd say; I'm pleased your friend gave you some tips on how the better folk have their tables laid, Amy!"

"It *does* look fancy," added Jane, "but I don't know what we're going to do with all of these spare spoons!"

"Those better folk have three dinners and three puddings and soup to start with!" asserted Amy.

"That's why they're all so fat!" laughed Grace.

"There's no need for rudeness, now, Grace," cautioned Silas, trying hard to keep a serious face.

"Maybe that's why they have servants to dress them...they are always so full up that they can barely breathe!" she continued.

"Grace! Enough talking, now finish your food!" scolded Claire.

"Sorry, Ma."

"*Oh, it's no good!*" cried Claire as she pushed back her chair and left the table.

"Come along Silas, *you* know where their fishing spot is don't you, let's go and look for them and woe betide *that Frank* if he's not got a feasible excuse for missing Sunday dinner!"

Quickly popping his last roast potato into his mouth, knowing that there'd be no peace until George and Frank were back home, he reluctantly obeyed his wife.

Within minutes they were heading towards Folly Bridge and the river Isis.

When Frank arrived back at the riverbank, he was confronted by a completely unexpected sight and was shocked to see a middle-aged couple attending George. He felt his heart sink as he viewed his helpless imposter of a brother sitting up, coughing and spluttering, with the man's large jacket draped around his shoulders. Quickly taking a backwards step, Frank cowered behind the heavy summer foliage. His thoughts were in a tangled confusion yet in his mind, he knew that now would be the final parting between him and his family. He cursed under his breath with his eyes not moving from the scene in front of him. He'd worked like a mule over the past years, to regain his parent's trust and love, he mused; to leave empty handed with only the clothes on his back was not about to happen, he decided angrily; he would simply

have to take what he was due. His mind quickly
formulated a plan and with one last glance at
George, he realised that there was
no way in which he could go in search of his
precious pocket watch. The gentleman suddenly
caught sight of Frank as he stood at the summit
of the riverbank, he raised his hand, in an angry
gesture, bellowing,
"There he is, that's the mean scoundrel!"
Frank knew straight away that George had not,
or, perhaps, could not disclose the fact that it
had been his brother who'd treated him so
cruelly; he quickly turned his back on them and
fled.
On reaching the main thoroughfare once again,
he was met by yet another shock; even from a
distance, the angry frown upon his parent's faces
as they hurried towards him was as clear as
daylight. He slowed his pace, frantically forcing
his brain to come up with a viable story to tell
them; it wouldn't be easy, he considered, but he
had to save himself *and* his future.
"*Frank!*" his ma cried out to him on approaching.
She stared firmly at her son already sensing that
something terrible had happened. "Where's your
brother?" she added urgently.
'What brother', he yearned to reply as he
witnessed his ma's tense expression, but he held
his tongue, knowing it wouldn't help his cause.
He felt the intimidating stare of his pa, as he
stood studying him, but strangely on this

occasion, he was silent. Frank felt awkward, wishing his pa *would* speak; he felt his cheeks burning even more.

"There's been an accident!" gasped Frank, trying to appear concerned. *"Poor little Georgie fell in the river!* But don't worry Ma, a sympathetic couple helped me to pull him out...He's going to be alright, but on their instruction, I'm going to fetch a doctor!"

Claire spontaneously raised her hand to cover her gaping mouth, her eyes moist with unshed tears.

"Where are they Frank?" voiced Silas, sternly, not blind to how guilty his son looked and sounded. He was impatient to wait for a response. *"Were you fishing at the usual spot? Is that where we'll find him?"*

"How could you be so irresponsible, Frank! He was in *your* care!" exclaimed Claire distraughtly.

"I'll go and fetch a doctor!" replied Frank, unable to look his ma in the eye and desperate to be on his way.

They hurried off in opposite directions both with completely different thoughts of urgency on their minds.

Frank went straight to the small office at the back of the shop before showing his face in the living quarters upstairs. The weekly takings were locked in a secure box on a shelf. He ran his hand along the underneath of the desk until he located the spare key which dangled out of

sight from a short length of string, tied around a
nail head. He yanked it forcefully and within
seconds had filled his pockets with half of the
week's takings. Dashing up the stairs taking
three at a time, he was soon bombarded by an
onslaught of questions from his sisters.

Grace ran to his side smiling widely only to be
rebuffed as Frank roughly pushed her aside;
there was no time for soppy sentimentality he
warned himself, he had to be in and out of the
house and on his way out of Oxford as quickly
as possible.

"What have you done with George?" demanded
Jane as she hugged her tearful sister.

*"Get out of my bloody way you bunch of pathetic
hens!"*

Amy and Grace were shocked by their brother's
foul words and his brutish manner as he shoved
them out of his way. Jane, however, saw the
nasty streak in her brother that she knew had
been hidden below the surface for many years.
Her memories of him were all bad and she
always knew that the day would come when he
would rock the peaceful Shepherd's boat again.

"You're a disgrace to our family, Frank
Shepherd! You're evil and you'll rot in Hell!"
Frank reached out and grabbed her wrist,
pulling it violently behind her back. She
screamed out loud as Amy and Grace shouted
for him to leave their sister alone.

"You're not my Mother, so shut your pathetic

mouth you stupid little bitch! In fact, you're *all* pathetic, the damned lot of you and I won't be sorry to see the back of you all!" he yelled as he gave Jane a hefty shove, causing her to crash to the floor. He hurried to his room, quickly wrapping his spare set of clothes in a bundle and adding his own savings to his pocket. His pa's silver pocket watch caught his eye as he passed by his parent's bedroom; he must have left in a hurry to have forgotten that, he thought smugly as he snatched the watch and chain from off the dresser. Having to pass through the kitchen once more to gain access to the stairs he coldly ignored the tearful sight of Grace and Amy and the scowling looks from Jane. He said nothing not wanting to delay his departure for a minute longer.

Down by the river's edge, George was too upset and in a state of shock to utter a single word. His young mind couldn't fathom how the brother who he'd always admired and looked up to had turned on him and been so cruel. Maybe he'd imagined it, he thought, as he sat shivering uncontrollably, barely comprehending the words of endearment issued from the strangers who were taking care of him and continuously coaxing him into telling them where he lived. During their secret assignation, the couples romancing had been disturbed by the ruckus; alarmed that their illicit affair had been discovered they'd instantly unlocked from their embrace and peered through the curtains of the weeping willow tree, horrified at what they'd witnessed. The entire area by the river was empty and as the midday sun beat down strongly, George sat ashen-faced, bursting into tears in-between bouts of shaking.

"Who *was* that young man, you were with? Did you know him?" asked the woman in a small voice as she gently combed George's fair curls with her slender fingers.

"He's in shock, darling, as will we be if someone happens to walk by and recognise us!"

"Don't worry my love; the Oxfordian folk are all too busy consuming their Sunday roasts!"

Silas and Claire suddenly appeared over the top of the embankment, hurrying down towards them; George took one glance at his parents and burst into tears again.

"He seems fine!" voiced the man, noticing the tension upon their faces.

Claire was at George's side within seconds, "my darling boy, Oh you poor love..." she choked, hugging his small body close to hers.

"I can't thank you enough for taking care of our boy!" expressed Silas.

"Oh don't even mention it, just thankful that we were here and able to drag him out of the river in time! That evil being who did this fled, but your brave son put up a good fight; you should be proud of him; I'm sure he'll be back fishing in a day or two!"

Silas felt his insides convulsing, *'that evil being'* was his son, his own flesh and blood, but he'd never felt more ashamed of being his father.

"Come along, my dear, we should be making tracks ourselves," reminded the woman, cordially.

Silas gratefully returned the man's jacket from George's shoulders, replacing it with his own.

"Thank you, thank you so much!" exclaimed Claire, feeling more assured that little Georgie was going to make a full recovery from his harrowing ordeal.

The woman smiled, "Goodbye young man, I hope you soon feel much better!" she stroked his hair one last time and returned to the man's side.

"Goodbye," they said in unison, before hurrying off.

"You should have asked their name!" stressed Claire as she stole a glance at the couple in the distance.

"How are you feeling son?" Silas whispered in George's ear as he scooped him up into his arms.

"I want to go home," he replied, in a sad voice.

There was so much that Silas and Claire wanted to discuss as they made the return journey, but were both all too aware that the subject in question was not one for George's ears. They walked in silence, both deep in contemplation and both thoroughly hurt by the actions of their firstborn.

CHAPTER THIRTY-TWO

It was no surprise to Silas and Claire to discover that in their absence, Frank had returned home thrown his weight around, taken his belongings and left again. They were deeply hurt that he'd robbed them. Amy and Grace were still shocked by their brother's violent behaviour, with Grace left tearful by the terrifying transformation of her brother which had shaken her to her core. The entire Shepherd family had been witness to the wicked and evil side of Frank and, in a way, quite relieved that he'd left home. Claire, once again, found herself questioning the decision she'd made five years ago when they'd left Bagley village; had she been foolish to forgive her son and allow him back into their lives she mused; what if the couple hadn't been by the river, it didn't bear thinking about what might have happened. It was quite obvious to her and Silas that Frank had intended George to drown and that he'd claim it to be a dreadful accident. Frank had always been jealous of George and had never accepted him into the family as the rest of them had.

Treated like a young prince, George spent the following two days in bed, recovering from his accident. His sisters doted on him and when the news had spread locally, neighbours, friends and customers gifted him generously with bags of sweets and chocolates and delicious seasonal fruit. As much as Claire wanted to get to the bottom of what had happened, she sensed it was an episode which George wanted to subconsciously block out of his mind. A couple of times he'd nervously inquired when Frank would be coming home, but she knew it was out of fear, not because he was missing his older brother. Then the following week, just when Claire felt hopeful that George had put the ordeal behind him, as they sat together in the kitchen, he shocked her with his unexpected question, "So *can I* get married to Grace when I'm a man, Ma?"

Claire looked at him, confused and completely thrown by his bizarre question. Her initial thoughts were that, perhaps, he hadn't fully recovered and his mind was muddled.

"Nobody can marry their sister, Georgie...it wouldn't be right."

He blinked rapidly, appearing deep in thought. "What made you asked such a question, my sweetheart?"

"Frank told me that I could marry her; he told me that she wasn't my sister and that you and Pa aren't my real parents."

His quiet voice was edged with sorrow and Claire was instantly heartbroken by his words which swam around inside her head. At that moment she despised Frank with all her soul.

She patted her lap,

"Come and sit here, my sweet boy there's something I have to tell you."

George's cheeks flushed, it had been a while since he'd sat upon his ma's lap, he felt shy and far too grown up, but at least his sisters weren't nearby to tease him, so he gingerly climbed onto Claire's lap. She kissed his soft cheeks and ruffled his unruly hair.

"Now, young man, you listen to me; Frank is a very bad boy, and has done some cruel and wicked things to our family throughout his life. He has gone now and I doubt we will see him again. He told you a terrible lie because he likes to hurt people especially those who love him. You must forget those silly things he told you because they are simply *not true!* We are your parents and Jane, Amy and Grace are your sisters."

"What about Martha?" he quickly added.

"Yes, and our darling Martha, who used to rock you to sleep when you were a tiny baby, God rest her precious soul; she was, *without a doubt,* your sister too."

Not a single word was ever spoken on the subject again, George miraculously returned to his old happy self as though a heavyweight had been lifted from his young heart and Claire prayed hard that he would never hear the real truth from anyone else, at least not until he was a young and hopefully level headed man, should the need ever arise.

Martha gingerly eased herself down onto the grubby bed in the dingy lodging room which she'd just paid an extortionate sixpence for. It was a far cry from the luxury of her boudoir in the gatehouse. The stench of mildew had adhered to her nostrils, leaving a foul taste upon her tongue. The walls of the room were streaked with black mould; it could be worse, thought Martha, glad that at least it was the hot summer months; A dozen or more flies circled the room, buzzing loudly past her ears every now and again before making their flight towards the stinking chamber pot, which looked as though it hadn't been rinsed for months. The room wasn't worth a farthing considered Martha as she rested her tired head carefully onto her folded arm, not wanting it to come in contact with the stained and colourless coverlet. Her fancy clothing had once again given the wrong impression, causing her to be ripped off by the scavengers of Whitechapel. She laughed to herself, knowing how out of touch with the world she'd become; and how her daily work dress was considered fancy...what if she'd have worn the silk taffeta trimmed with fine French lace? She mused, consoling herself that it was only for one night and then she would be departing on the early morning stagecoach to Oxford. The very reminder that within a day or two she might be united with her family immediately snatched away her sleepiness, exchanging it for a nervous excitement. She pondered over what Bruce had once told her about how shock could sometimes cause older folk to suffer irreversible health problems; how awful would it be to cause such an effect on her parents after all the suffering and heartache she'd already inflicted upon them. She had no idea of the state of their health, five years was a long time; they might have become old and frail, possibly having endured the toughest of lives in order to earn their living in Oxford. What if one or even both of them now had a weakened heart? She bolted upright, her mind worrying about the days to come and now realising that when she did finally locate her family, her plan to give them the surprise of their life was now much removed from being a good idea. She would have to plan a way which would break the shock gently and kindly to them. Wringing her clammy hands, Martha felt suddenly overwhelmed by the stuffiness of the airless room, her entire body felt overheated. She felt the perspiration trickle down her back as she caught a whiff of her own unpleasant body odour and longed to be soaking in the pristine bathtub of the gatehouse with the copious amounts of sweet-scented rosewater she'd always add to it. What was she doing in such a hovel? She questioned herself; Bruce would be so cross with her if he could see where she was; he had left her well provided for; enough for her to be relaxing in one of the better folk's grand hotels, but although not lacking in funds, she was lacking in confidence and was still convinced that every pair of eyes in the outside world might recognize her as a liar and an escaped convict. It would be different in Oxford she told herself, as her tears tumbled off her face, she *would* change her ways, for the sake of dear Bruce. She missed him terribly and had never thought it possible to have such feelings of grief for him; but without him, she felt desolate, vulnerable and scared of her own shadow. Knowing that she was in for a prolonged and uncomfortable night, the words of the aged landlord, who lived in a downstairs room, came to mind. He'd given her permission to make use of the scullery which now prompted Martha to investigate if there were the facilities to brew a much needed pot of tea.

With the thick bundle of banknotes, tucked firmly beneath her stocking and held in place by a lace garter, Martha placed her travelling case inside the wardrobe, put on her bonnet and left her room, making sure to lock it firmly before proceeding down the rickety old staircase. She followed the strong aroma of cooking along the dark and narrow passageway on the ground floor to the rear of the house and the scullery.

"Look Ma! It's that fancy lady!"

Martha stood dumbfounded as she witnessed the flower seller strike the child with the back of her hand, causing her to fall to the ground, screaming.

"*Yer stupid little cow!*" the mother yelled, before turning on Martha.

"I thought she was mute!" expressed Martha, impulsively.

"*So*, you're the fancy new lodger, eh? What d'yer do wiv yer poor old folks then?" she sniggered wickedly before roughly grabbing her daughter's arm and yanking her back on to her feet. "Get up yer *silly cow*! Yer dress will be filthy an' I ain't gonna rinse it 'til next week!"

She turned her focus back to Martha, "Looks as though I ain't the only bloody liar standin' in this scullery!" she announced smugly.

Infuriated by how this obnoxious woman was comparing herself with her, Martha took an instant dislike to her.

"Well, *my* white lie is a mere way of protecting myself since I have been forced to travel without a chaperone, *you*, on the other hand, have enforced a terrible disability upon your poor child!" expressed Martha, bravely.

"What der the like's ov you know 'bout surviving an' scratchin' a livin' just ter put 'alf a plate ov boiled spuds an' the odd cabbage leaf on the supper table. Bet yer ain't never gone ter bed starvin' not knowin' when the next crumb is gonna touch yer dry lips!"

"Can I 'ave me supper, Ma, I'm right 'ungry," whispered the young girl, timidly.

The girl's mother proceeded to dish out the boiled vegetables, she glanced at Martha, "Come an' join us if yer like, we may be poor folk, but if there's enough victuals fer two, it can always be stretched ter feed three an' there's a brew of Rosie Lee an' all; who knows, maybe yer could do me a favour in return!"

Reluctant to leave the lodging house now that evening was approaching and with the aroma of boiled potatoes causing her stomach to rumble, Martha accepted the offer and followed them into their room. Expecting to be confronted by a more inviting and homely surrounding, she was surprised that there was little difference from her room upstairs; it was grubby and sparse with the added vile smell of rotting flowers which overwhelmed the few fragrant blooms. An old pinewood table was cluttered with bottles and jars of every shape and size; filled with flowers, some of which were dead, their stalks fermenting in the pond like water. A few bunches of dried posies hung down from the ceiling on lengths of string, attracting swarms of huge blue bottles which buzzed loudly as they landed briefly, flitting from one bunch to another. Martha swallowed hard, wondering how she would eat in such a polluted room.

"Is it alright if I speak now Ma?"

"Gawd 'elp us all! Course yer can yer silly little

cow! Ain't no bleedin' secret now, *is it!* "

The girl smiled sheepishly at Martha, "We 'ave ter sit on the floor ter eat!" she announced shyly. "Me ma likes ter keep the bed nice...just in case."

"Sweep them bleedin' mouse droppings away, Lucy!"

"Sorry Ma, I fergot!"

Lucy grabbed a sheet of newspaper from a pile in the corner of the room and expertly folded it into four before using it like a brush to sweep the floor, moving all the debris to the edges of the room.

"That's one of my favourite names, Lucy, it's a very pretty name and did you know that it means light!"

Lucy looked intrigued; nobody ever spoke to her in such a kindly way and she was immediately taken to Martha.

"How d'yer know!"

"Stop yer bloody chin-wagging an' eat...she don't wanna 'ear all yer stupid nonsense!"

"We'll have a lovely chat after supper, Lucy, if that's alright with your ma," Martha said in a small voice, feeling sorry for the waif-like girl.

The meal was eaten hurriedly, with Lucy cramming as much food as she could fit into her mouth; the girl was starving and seemed to lose all traits of shyness as she bolted down the mixture of boiled potatoes, cabbage, and carrots. Martha only ate a couple of potatoes, insisting that Lucy had her share as she confessed to being thirsty more than hungry and in need for a cup of tea.

When the humble meal was finished, Lucy dutifully took the plate and the three forks to the scullery, leaving her ma alone with Martha, "Pour the Rosie Lee, Lucy and sniff the milk afore yer pour it...don't wanna be givin' our fancy guest no lumps ov sour cheese in 'er cuppa!" she yelled out, chuckling as Martha unwittingly screwed up her nose.

Martha licked her parched lips, wishing that she'd dared to ask for black tea but instead, she said a quick and silent prayer beneath her breath.

"I'm called Dolly. What's your name then?"

"Martha."

"Well now that's out of the way per'aps yer might repay me wiv a small favour?"

Unnerved by Dolly's sudden directness, Martha hoped she wasn't about to ask too much from her. Lucy soon returned, struggling with the tray which carried three badly chipped and stained cups. The tea splashed out of them with every step she took, prompting Martha to rush to her side and rescue what was left of the tepid and weak looking tea.

"*Clumsy lass!* Waste of good Rosie Lee!" bellowed Dolly. Lucy took little notice of her mother's continuous insults and nagging and Martha drew on the conclusion that the poor child knew no other way of being spoken to.

The tasteless tea was nearly cold but at least it wet the throat and persuaded Martha that when morning arrived she would take breakfast at the finest restaurant she could find before her long journey to Oxford.

"What *is* the favour anyway, Dolly?"

Dolly turned her nose up at the tea, leaving Lucy to gulp down her second cup.

"Ooh sorry, Misses, did you wants ter drink it?"

"No, Lucy, *you have it*, but thank you for asking and my name is Martha, by the way."

"That's a right pretty name an' all, ain't it Ma?"

"Shut yer bleedin' pie 'ole fer Gawd's sake!" screamed Dolly as she stood up straight and unashamedly began removing her clothes until she was left wearing only her corset and stockings. Martha took a furtive glance at the skinny woman before lowering her gaze, feeling her cheeks burning with embarrassment.

"I want yer ter look after Lucy fer the night...let 'er kip up in your room...don't worry none, she's used ter kipping on the floor so yer won't 'ave ter give up yer bed!"

An expression of excitement glowed on Lucy's face, "Yeah, I always kip under the table...just like a little kitten!"

Martha's heart went out to the poor child who seemed to be enduring such a harsh childhood, thoughts of Amy and Jane darted through her mind; how she had missed them over the years; they'd be so grown up now and the twins would now be five years old. She quickly blinked away her watery eyes.

"How old are you Lucy?"

"Eight!" she proudly announced, with her eyes fixed cautiously on her mother. Martha thought how she looked much younger than an eight-year-old; she'd clearly had a harsh start in life which would probably only become tougher as she grew up thought Martha sadly.

"So is that all right wiv yer then? Only I can make more dough in one night wiv out that little brat snoring under the table than I would in a week an' what's more, I can entertain one ov the toffs...they always like ter be discrete yer see an' they pay decently an' all!"

Martha sat in shock as Dolly's frankness suddenly registered with her as to what type of woman she was. She was sat in the same room and had shared supper with a common harlot, she mused indignantly, trying to mask her feelings of revulsion.

Dolly was now dressed in a gaudy scarlet dress, its bodice cut so low that her bosoms seemed to balance precariously on its gold ribbon border. Martha was quite sure that should Dolly cough or sneeze, the dress would no longer contain her dignity. She felt embarrassed for her, wondering how any woman could feel so at eased when displaying their treasures so openly. In the next minute, Dolly took hold of a small tin and began to smear her lips and cheeks with its crimson shaded contents, making her look even more hideous. She then dabbed her neck with some cheap and overpowering perfume.

"That's my ma's best French perfume," whispered Lucy as she snuggled up close to Martha. "Don't she look beautiful!" she declared, gazing wistfully up at her ma. "Prettier than when she's selling posies!"

"Yes, Lucy, your ma is very attractive!" Martha humoured.

CHAPTER THIRTY-THREE

Excited by the fact that she was to spend the
entire night with the lovely Martha, Lucy
suppressed her yawns insisting that she wasn't
at all sleepy. Martha didn't mind; already having
succumbed to the fact that she'd not get a winks
sleep, she'd rather listen to the effervescent
chatter of an eight-year-old than sit in solitary
silence. Lucy was the sweetest of girls, roughly
spoken and lacking in manners at the fault of her
mother's careless upbringing but she had a heart
of gold and forgave her ma for every beating
she'd received and made excuses for her
whenever she found herself on the receiving end
of her ma's vicious tongue, being cruelly
ridiculed, which would have caused many
youngsters to hide away inside their own shell.
Lucy's tough upbringing had moulded her
character into that of a little fighter and Martha
sensed that the young skinny girl had far more
confidence than she had, especially in the
devious part of London which she found herself
in.
"Why d'yer 'ave ter leave ter morrow?" Lucy
asked for the third time since she'd been in
Martha's room. "Yer should stay 'ere; Yer'd be
like me big sister an' Ma would fix yer up wiv a
job...She knows lots ov nice folk yer know!"
The mere thought of Dolly finding work for her

made Martha shudder, she dreaded to think what was going on downstairs and had already heard the voices of at least three different men and the front door busily opening and closing all evening and it wasn't even midnight.

"I have my own Ma to return to Lucy and I've not seen her for a few years!"

"I know," voiced Lucy, glumly, "Yer already told me that yer bin away working in a toff's 'ouse, but couldn't yer just stay fer a few days, or weeks then Ma might become rich, so we wouldn't 'ave ter sell flowers all day long an' I could talk as much as I like!"

"Why *does* your ma insist that you don't talk when you're selling flowers?"

"Don't really know...'appen it's cos I give 'er an 'eadache! And she gets tired of telling me ter shut me pie 'ole!" replied Lucy with a cheeky giggle. "Ooh, should I sit on the floor now, Martha, just in case I makes yer bed dirty!"

"Oh Lucy, you couldn't make this bed dirty if you tried!"

Lucy looked curiously at Martha, still not believing how kind she was to her.

"Ma says that little uns are no better than flea-ridden dogs an' should always kip on the floor!"

"Do you *always* sleep on the floor Lucy!"

"Course I do! I got a bed of newspaper under the table...it's right cosy 'specially when Ma 'angs the big blanket over it...makes it like a secret cave, an' if I stays as quiet as a mouse so as me uncles don't even know that I'm there me ma gives me an extra bowl of porridge in the morning! Some nights though, them misbe'aved mice make more noise than me!"

Martha was getting a clear picture of what was going on and her heart went out to the poor innocent girl who held her ma in such high regard and loved her dearly. Martha also had a dark feeling that when Lucy became a young woman she would be forced by Dolly to earn a living in the same degrading way.

"Well tonight, Lucy you will sleep, in true princess fashion, on my bed for the entire night!"

"Ta Martha, but can we keep it secret from me ma, else she might give me a walloping if she thinks I ain't bin good."

"Consider it our very own secret, sweet Lucy, now you'd best shut those beautiful hazel eyes of yours and get your beauty sleep before we hear the chiming of the midnight hour!"

Lucy's tired face lit up, as she wished for this special night to never end.

"You're me best friend, Martha...is that alright?" she asked, unable to stifle any more tired yawns.

"And you are *my* dearest friend Lucy, now, nestle down beneath the covers and dream of what tomorrow might bring!"

Within minutes Lucy was sound asleep and apart from Lucy's gentle breathing, the dreary room fell into silence once again. Martha's state of overtiredness increased her sad emotions; she'd been putting on a brave face since her departure from the gatehouse and now, as though an icy blizzard had swept through her body, she felt cold and alone. Thoughts of Bruce were still uppermost in her mind and cutting deep into her heart, she wondered who had read her note and if he'd yet been laid to rest. Burning tears trickled down her face. Life was so strange, she deliberated; if anyone had told her, years ago, that one day she'd be crying over the death of Bruce Brunswick, she'd have laughed in their faces. She loved him in her own special way, a way which only she could understand and she knew it would be a long while until she'd fully recover from his sad departing. Her thoughts drifted to little Georgie; the reality that he was Bruce's son still hadn't quite sunk in. She wondered how he looked after five years, along with her dear sisters. Jane would be a young woman by now and then there was Frank, who had instigated her ruin all those years ago...where was *he* now and how much of the truth did her poor parents know? As Lucy turned in her sleep and curled up into a small ball, Martha reached out to stroke her curly hair, it felt coarse and gritty and on closer inspection, Martha noticed a dark band of grime around the girl's neck. How she'd love to scrub her clean and clothe her in a pretty new dress, she found herself thinking. It shattered her heart to witness any child so pitifully undernourished and forced to endure such a harsh life; she spontaneously prayed, thanking The Lord that she had been born into a farming family and had enjoyed a wholesome upbringing far away from the hardships of the East End of London or any other similar location. The sound of a distant clock chimed out that it was three O'clock then four O'clock; that was the last of the hourly distractions which Martha heard before she was overtaken by sheer exhaustion and fell into a deep sleep alongside Lucy.

A stream of bright sunshine filtered through the filthy window, temporarily transforming the depressing room and infusing it with a more hopeful feeling at the start of the new day. Lucy smiled at Martha as she opened her eyes and waved her arms playfully through the copious dust motes, attempting to catch the dust.

"I weren't dreamin' then!" she declared. "I really did kip in a proper bed an' this room is full ov magical fairy dust an' all!"

Martha laughed, as she gave Lucy a gentle hug. "Did you sleep well, Lucy?"

"I slept like a log! 'Ow 'bout you, did yer sleep alright...I 'ope I never snored none!"

"No," laughed Martha, "You were as quiet as the night sky! Do you think that your ma will be awake by now, Lucy, only I have to leave London quite early this morning?"

Lucy's smile instantly vanished.

"Can't yer stay a bit longer...Ma will be sure ter make some porridge...an' it ain't lumpy...I promise!"

"Oh, sweet Lucy, I'd love to taste your ma's delicious porridge, but if I miss this morning's stagecoach to Oxford, I could be stuck in London for another couple of days and I really *must* go home!"

"Oh....please stay fer just one more day!"

"I'm sorry, sweetheart, but I promise to write to you, and tell you all of my news...how does that sound?"

"It don't sound good, cos I can't even read, nor can me ma," she admitted miserably. "I'm gonna go an' see if Ma is awake, an' ask 'er ter make the porridge early, then!"

Jumping out of bed, Lucy disappeared through the door before Martha could object, but no sooner had Martha had a chance to stretch her weary body, she came running back in again.

"*My goodness*, you're a proper little Jack in the box! Is your Ma still asleep?"

"Fast asleep, she didn't even wake up when I accidentally knocked one ov the bottles off the table...don't reckon there'll be any breakfast fer hours! But at least I won't 'ave ter stand wiv me mouth shut selling stupid flowers all day!"

"Oh dear, did the bottle smash?"

Lucy nodded, gravely "But it weren't *my* fault...it were right on the edge ov the table!"

"Why don't you help me tidy the bed and then

I'll pop down into your room before I leave and we'll sweep up the broken glass...I wouldn't want you or your ma cutting your bare feet on the shards."

Lucy smiled cheerfully, happy with the sound of Martha's suggestion.

The bed was swiftly made and while Martha set about tightening her bootlaces, Lucy made another quick dash down to her room in the hope that her ma might have woken.

Yet again she returned disappointed,

"I don't fink she's gonna wake up 'till supper time...she looks a bit funny too…well not funny really, just different...she's gone a strange colour; sort ov like…blue...but I guess it's cos she were cold in the night, cos she's wrapped 'er stockings 'round 'er neck, like a scarf!"

Having not been paying full attention to Lucy's chatter, Martha immediately stopped fiddling around with her laces and looked up in horror as her words formed a sinister image in her mind.

"What's wrong, Martha? Why yer so cross, 'ave I done something wrong?"

Martha could hear the strong pulsating of her heart as though it had leapt up into her head...Lucy's words repeated in her terrifying thoughts and she harboured an awful feeling that poor Dolly had been strangled by one of Lucy's so-called 'uncles'.

"I'll go an' tickle 'er feet," Lucy suddenly proposed, "that always wakes 'er up; just puts 'er in a mood fer 'alf the mornin'...I'll tell 'er that yer wanted ter say goodbye!"

"*No! No Lucy*...you stay here and I'll go and wake her, at least that way she won't be cross with you!"

Lucy happily agreed.

Before she'd reached the last stair, Martha froze as she suddenly remembered how she was still a wanted, escaped prisoner who'd yet to serve her full sentence. What if she was once again wrongly accused? What if Dolly *had* been strangled to death and she became the prime suspect? The landlord's door suddenly flung open, he glared curiously at Martha,

"Me ears don't usually deceive me! Thought I 'eard footsteps, I did!"

"I was just about to knock on your door, Mr...I'm sorry, I don't know your name!"

"Folks just call me Billy...so what did yer want wiv me...want the room fer another night do yer?"

Martha licked her dry lips, nervously, "Actually, Billy, I've got little Lucy in my room and I'm a bit worried about her mother...she tells me that she won't wake up. Perhaps you, being the landlord, might take a look; she tells me that her ma has gone a shade of blue!"

Billy screwed up his bulbous nose as a look of distaste washed over him.

"*Huh, Mother!* That bleedin' woman is nothing more than a cheap whore, not satisfied wiv the takings she gets from selling 'er flowers, *no*, that ain't enough ter buy the bottles of gin she drowns herself in every day!" Billy kept up his continuous one-sided conversation as he made his way down the passage. "She ain't fit her be called a mother, that sweet Lucy would be far better off wiv out 'er...forces the poor little un ter keep silent all day long...don't ask me why." He knocked hard on the door before opening it and marching in.

"*Looks like a goner ter me...*"

Martha remained outside in the hallway, not wishing to witness the ghastly scene.

"Dead ter the world...an' I ain't shocked...didn't get a wink ov sleep last night on account ov that bleedin' trollop...in and out of 'er room all night long...heavy-footed menfolk, wiv no bloody sense between their ears!" He spoke as though he'd discovered a dead rat, there was not the tiniest trait of sympathy in his tone for his fellow human...London was a tough and cold place, mused Martha as she felt faint and light-headed. " Said the girl was up in your room, didn't yer? Well, she might need these," he handed Martha a pair of old and worn-out boots.

"I'll fetch a peeler, but I doubt they'll even bat an eyelid...she were well known 'round these parts...it were only a matter ov time...I'll see that the lass is taken down the work'ouse an' all!" Martha's head was spinning, she'd barely eaten since Bruce's death and together with the lack of sleep and her raw emotional state, it suddenly became too much; she felt her legs give way beneath her as she slid down the wall.

Having waited long enough, Lucy had left the upstairs room; she screamed at the sight of Martha lying on the floor.

"Martha! Martha!"

"Don't fret, now, she's just swooned that's all...unlike yer ma who's as cold as a stone slab in a morgue!"

Lucy collapsed on to the floor next to Martha.

"Me Ma's dead! Me Ma's dead..." she continued to cry out until Martha opened her eyes and remembered what had happened.

"Please don't let Billy put me in the work'ouse, Martha, *please!* Let me come wiv you...I'll be right good, I promise!"

"Let's just go back upstairs, for the time being, sweetheart..."

Ten minutes later, Billy knocked on the door; he was carrying a tray laden with two mugs of tea and a plate of toasted bread.

"Don't fink that I treat all me lodgers like this Miss, but I know you've 'ad a nasty shock an' yer ain't no Londoner who's used ter the wicked ways of life!"

Martha was so grateful, of his thoughtful gesture.

"I'm going out ter get things sorted, Miss...No landlord like a corpse on 'is property!"

He was right, thought Martha, she certainly

wasn't accustomed to the atrocities which went on in London and the sooner she left the better.

CHAPTER THIRTY-FOUR

"Claire, my love, as difficult as it might seem right now, we're better off without Frank in our lives." It was Silas's new mission in life; trying to persuade Claire that it was no fault of hers that Frank had turned out to be such a disappointment to them. "You'll soon realise that I'm right…at least we can rest easy in our beds knowing that he's not up to no good!"
"Well that might be the case for you Silas Shepherd, but I, for one, will never sleep soundly again!"
A customer came into the ironmongers putting an end to their conversation. Silas had not mentioned to Claire that Frank had stolen his pocket watch, she was struggling in coming to terms with the truth of what had taken place and to rub more salt into her painful wounds would be cruel.
"Where's your young man this morning?" inquired the gentleman as he browsed through the slim catalogue. "He *is* your son, I'm right in presuming? Such a polite young chap, a credit to his parents. Now, I need to purchase rather a hefty load, which needs to be delivered."
"I can assure you, Sir, that all deliveries will continue as normal. Our son has left to spend some time with family in Surrey."
The gentleman picked out the style of wrought

iron gates he required, giving Silas the exact measurements; he also selected some garden seats and an elaborate bird feeder before leaving. Claire's brow knitted together as she stared coldly at Silas, "*More secrets and lies!* Where will it all end Silas? I loathe having to think so hard before I can speak...lies always get found out you know! I wish we'd never left Bagley village, our neighbours would have come around eventually and stopped treating us like lepers...at least we wouldn't have to keep up this facade...*they* knew the truth and so what? I'm sure that everyone in the world has at least *one* skeleton in the cupboard!"

"What did you expect me to say to a complete stranger then!" voiced Silas, sharply. "That our eldest son tried to drown our youngest son who is the bastard son of God knows who in Surrey's aristocratic society! Then perhaps I could have gone on to tell him the story of our Martha! *For the love of God*, Claire, it pains *me* just as much as it does you to live this way, but it's the best option and we must make the best of what the Good Lord has given us!"

"Please lower your voice, Silas, Jane and Amy are upstairs...and *don't ever* refer to our darling little Georgie in that abusive manner again! He's far too sweet and adorable to be associated with that ugly word!" cried Claire.

"I'm sorry, my love, I didn't mean it; you know that don't you? That wasn't me speaking, I don't know what possessed me but I promise never to speak along those same despicable lines again...The very *mention* of Frank never fails in bringing out the worst in me, even after he's left!"

"Oh Silas, please hold me, I feel so very fragile and downhearted!"

For a few precious moments, they cherished a silent embrace. Silas enveloped his strong arms supportively around his sad wife as she allowed her watery eyes to spill over onto his warm chest.

"What's happened to my fighting wife who always takes the bull by the horns and puts me to shame whenever I wallow in hopelessness?" he whispered jokingly into her ear.

"I've lost control, Silas; it's as simple as that. Life's burdens have suddenly become too much to bear and I feel so weighed down these days."

"Then we will all have to work harder to get you back into the fighting ring again, won't we?" Silas tilted Claire's tearful face up towards his and planted a tender kiss upon her soft lips.

"You're beautiful, Claire, as beautiful as the day we wed!"

"Then *you* must have lost half of your eyesight over the years Silas Shepherd!" she laughed.

"We'll be alright, my love, trust me...one day we'll look back on these trying times and wonder why we allowed them to infuse such grief into us!"

"Do you mean to tell me that life will only get worse?"

"No no, my sweet lamb, life can only improve...I'm certain of it!"

"Well, I've heard that before!"

"We must count our blessings, my darling, we have four healthy, good and honest children, a business and a roof over our heads, food on the table and the biggest blessing of all is that we have each other!"

The bell above the door jingled as another customer stepped over the threshold, Claire and Silas quickly took a step away from each other, and Silas greeted his customer as though it were just another ordinary day.

A vast assembly of birds had gathered on branches, chirping passionately like an orchestra putting on its grand finale. There wasn't the hint of a cloud in the rich cerulean sky and the scorching sun suggested penny licks, toe-dipping in the river, straw bonnets and all things fun and summery, but yet here they were stood hand in hand in the pauper's graveyard. Lucy sobbed for her mother, a woman who had on all accounts not shown her a happy day throughout her entire life and as Martha's tears rolled down her cheeks, her thoughts were solely with Bruce; she was mourning him properly, as though it was his body being lowered into the depth of the earth. There wasn't another soul attending the burial; Billy had declared that it would be an insult to his beloved wife, who'd departed five years ago if he attended the ceremony of such a fallen woman. Lucy had spent the previous evening making a huge posy for her mother's grave using every flower she could lay her hands on, be it fresh or dried, knowing that her days of being a mute, selling them on the streets were now over. She had temporarily moved into Martha's room who had postponed her journey, in the hope of relocating Lucy to a safe place before she said her goodbyes. There were few options for her though; at eight years old she was even too young to work as a tweeny in one of the grander properties on the other side of London. Billy had mentioned a dozen or more times that the Whitechapel workhouse was the only option, but in Martha's eyes it seemed such a daunting place to leave a vulnerable, heartbroken, young child whose mother had so recently been strangled to death; she could imagine poor Lucy being bullied and living a cruel and lonely life in such a place.

She led her out of the small graveyard and back into the noisy thoroughfare of Whitechapel. Lucy had ceased her sobbing but was exceptionally quiet and hadn't uttered a word in a long while.

"Shall we go and find a chophouse and have breakfast, Lucy?" suggested Martha.

Lucy smiled for the first time in days.

"I'm right starvin', Martha...I could eat ten bowls of porridge!"

"You won't be eating porridge in the chophouse sweetheart; you will fill your belly with sausages, bacon and eggs and anything else you fancy!"

Lucy squeezed Martha's hand as they strolled along the pavement, "I wish yer didn't 'ave ter leave," she said somberly. "Can I really 'ave all them victuals, just fer me?"

"Of course...I wouldn't have said it otherwise!"

It was even hotter inside the chophouse with swarms of irritating bluebottles, buzzing noisily as they circled above every table, but the sweet aroma of meat, fish and fresh bread worked like a magnet guiding Martha and Lucy to the nearest vacant table. Although they'd gone in for breakfast It was already luncheon time; the chophouse was bursting at the seams with hungry customers, making for a pleasant atmosphere and with everybody so engrossed in eating and conversing, Martha didn't feel as though all eyes were on her; she felt safer with Lucy at her side, knowing that folk wouldn't be suspicious of her.

Martha studied the faded menu which was roughly scribbled upon a chalkboard.

"What on earth is a gravestone!" she exclaimed. "Two for half a penny?"

Lucy giggled at the look of alarm on Martha's

face.

"Yer don't know much 'bout the East End do yer? Gravestones are slices ov bread...they looks like small gravestones!"

"Well, I think it's highly inappropriate, especially in light of where we've just come from!"

Two plates of sausages, mash along with four gravestones and a huge jug of thick gravy and a jug of water were shortly placed in front of them. Martha had barely eaten since leaving the gatehouse and had already noticed the extra room in her dress. She was famished, as was Lucy, who had never eaten so much food in one sitting in her entire life. They devoured the food with little conversation and as much as Martha was tempted to issue Lucy with some well-needed table manners, she turned a blind eye, knowing that they came from different worlds and as Martha viewed the other diners, she thought it more likely that Lucy was embarrassed by the reserved way in which she tackled her plate of food.

"That's the best victuals I ever tasted!" expressed Lucy when she'd moped up the last of the gravy, leaving a clean and empty plate in front of her." Ma would 'ave loved that!" she added sadly.

"Have you got room in your belly for some apple pie and custard, Lucy?"

She nodded enthusiastically, "reckons I got 'ollow legs...that's what me ma used ter say!"

"Well, I will wash that delicious meal down with

a mug of tea or Rosie Lee as you call it here, and
you can have pie, then we must be on our way,
providing we can still manage to walk after all
this food."

"I'm glad yer came ter London, Martha, an' that
yer moved inter the same 'ouse where I
live."

"So am I Lucy, so am I!" replied Martha, as she
pondered on the fact that she would have been
in Oxford by now if she'd not purchased the
penny posy from Lucy's mother.

"I'd like you to take me to see the workhouse, on
our way back home...if you know where it is."

A wave of sorrow clouded Lucy's face, "Course I
know where it is, me ma used ter swear 'er
mouth off every time we passed by it...I could
'ardly ferget *that* place!"

"Don't you have *any* relatives Lucy, who might
take you into their lives and care for you?"

"Gotta lot of uncles, some ov 'em is nice, they
bought me sweets an' stuff, but I don't know
where they live," she replied innocently.

"What about your pa, Lucy!"

She gazed up at the circle of flies for a moment,
her thoughtful eyes open wide.

"My Pa 'as got more money than Queen Victoria!
That's what me ma used ter say, an' then she'd
say that 'e was as filthy as the fleas on the back
of a sewer rat an' older than the East End...then
she'd usually spit on ter the ground and tell me
'ow the thought ov 'im filled 'er mouth with

poisonous bile...She'd say that every single time I asked 'er 'bout 'im, so I stopped in the end; I knew it only upset 'er."

"What about aunties or cousins or grandparents, didn't your ma have her own Ma and Pa?"

The arrival of the dish containing a large slice of apple pie together with the jug of steaming custard distracted Lucy from what she was about to say, she licked her lips as she picked up a spoon. "Careful Lucy that looks too hot to eat just yet and there's nothing worse than a burnt tongue!"

She replaced her spoon and began blowing hard on the desert, causing Martha to giggle at her childish impatience.

"They're all dead, I fink...Ma came from the work'ouse, same place where yer gonna take me. But she said they sent 'er ter some posh 'ouse in the country...that's where she was treated badly by the rich, old Lord!"

"The old Lord?" quizzed Martha, becoming absorbed in Lucy's story.

"The cove I told yer 'bout...that old rich one who attacked me ma an' left 'er wiv *me* in 'er belly! Can I eat me pie now?"

"Oh yes, of course, you can, Lucy...just one more question though before you start...how did your ma end up back in the East End if she was sent to work in the country?"

"She ran away afore they could give 'er the sack...She wasn't gonna stay where that old bastard could attack 'er every night, so she nicked some silver an' came back 'ere! "

"*Lucy!* You shouldn't say that word...it's not nice you know...it's a horrible grownup's word!"

"What word?"

Martha looked nervously over her shoulder, "*bastard*," she whispered.

Lucy laughed, "Ah that ain't no bad word Martha, everyone says it, *all the time!*"

Martha sipped on her mug of tea as Lucy crammed her mouth full of pie and custard. She was beginning to get a vivid picture in her head of how Dolly had become so destitute and was forced to sell her body so that she and Lucy would survive.

"There is *one* really bad word that me ma hated, though; shall I tell yer?" stated Lucy as she swallowed her last mouthful of pie.

Martha became nervous, "I don't think you should be saying rude words in the chophouse, Lucy, people might be offended!"

The familiar puzzled look reappeared on her face, "I don't know what that means, but the word ain't gonna 'urt no one's ears, it's *Wright*! It's me name too. Lucy Wright. My ma was given that name when she went ter the work'ouse...She said it was cos she were one ov old Wainright's gals. She 'ated it an' she 'ated 'er an' all, said she were a greedy, good fer nothing bitch who deserved ter be dangling from a rope cos of all the lives she'd ruined!"

Lucy had certainly given Martha a lot to think about, the name, Wright sounded familiar somehow but it wasn't until they were back outside on the sunny pavements of Whitechapel Street that she remembered having read the name in Bruce's letter...It was that poor girl Molly's name if she was correct. She wondered if they had perhaps been related, but on the other hand, she mused, perhaps it was a common London name.

Since Lucy was complaining of a stomach ache and Martha was feeling too full up and sleepy to visit the workhouse, she decided that it could wait until the following day. After reconsidering, Martha felt it to be quite inappropriate to take Lucy to such a place on the same day as her mother had been buried *and* in view of everything Lucy had told her throughout the long day.

CHAPTER THIRTY-FIVE

"Come along now Jake, we ain't got time fer dilly-dallying, 'e 'ad a good innings did yer brother an' I know it's a sin ter speak ill ov the dead 'specially when they ain't even 'ad time ter go cold, but 'e never 'ad the time ov day fer us when 'e were alive; fought 'e were a bit above us if yer ask me. Doubt he'd 'ave taken trouble ter leave Whitechapel an' see you off if it were t'other way 'round…"

"All right, Em! Yer made yer bloomin' point...I'm 'ere cos me dear old ma would 'ave wanted it. Don't fink I've forgot 'bout all them times that 'e turned 'is back on us...."

"He never even came ter pay 'is respects when our poor little lambs were laid ter rest...too bleedin' scared he'd catch som'it!"

"It's done now Em, an' me dear old ma, Gawd rest 'er soul will be lookin' down wiv a smile on 'er face, pleased that I didn't abandon 'er first son!"

"That's a laugh if ever I 'eard one; 'e ain't bin abandoned, Jake, *yer old fool*... just look at all 'is cronies, they *all* reckons they're cut from a different piece ov cloth, but when all's said an' done, the bleedin' lot ov us is just common *East enders!*"

Emma Bird turned her back on the foreboding six-foot hole, walking briskly in between the copious headstones as she made her way to the black wrought iron gates. Jake said his final goodbye to a brother who'd had little to do with him since they were young lads. The rest of the mourners were all strangers to Jake, his nieces and nephews were not even familiar to him and nobody had bothered to greet Jake and Emma nor attempt to make them feel welcome. He caught up with Emma, blinking rapidly to rid himself of his tears which threatened to tumble down his wrinkled skin; he knew Em would scold him for wasting precious tears on his cold-hearted brother, but in truth, he was saddened by life and at the speed in which it had flown past him. Childhood memories of his beloved parents, his two brothers and one sister seemed as clear as daylight in his mind. He was the last to remain. Life was fraught with sorrow and he felt as though he'd stood at a graveside far too many a time. His heart now harboured more sorrow than joy and he secretly prayed that this would be the last funeral he attended as a mourner, knowing that he'd never cope if he had to say farewell to his darling Emma.

"You alright me darlin'?" inquired Emma as she felt Jake arrive at her side.

"Life's a funny old bag ov chestnuts ain't it, Em?"

"Come on yer sentimental old fool, let's go an' get a cup ov Rosie Lee...that'll put a smile on yer droopy face!"

"Then we'd best get going, don't like ter leave

Molly all by 'erself fer too long; that lass is still as nervous as a kitten, even after all these years!"
"Ah, she's tougher than yer gives 'er credit for *Jake Bird*; yer just turnin' inter an old softy in yer twilight years! She'll be fine...anyway, there's someone I gotta pay a visit to since we're in Whitechapel...an' give a piece ov me mind to, an' all!"
"*Who?* We barely know anyone 'round 'ere anymore!"
Emma laughed at the inquisitive look on Jake's face "You'll soon find out, Jake Bird I'll tell yer over a cuppa!"
Shaking his head, Jake always became a little nervous when his wife said she had to give someone a piece of her mind, it usually meant trouble and she was too long in the tooth to be brawling in the streets, he considered.

Half an hour later Emma and Jake entered through the lofty iron gates into the dismal world of the Whitechapel workhouse, with Emma's stern expression a clear indication that she meant business.
"*Em!* It's all in the past now and thank the Lord that Molly survived! Yer don't know what yer getting involved in!"
"I'm surprised at yer Jake Bird, there's bin a terrible injustice done an' 'ow many uvver young scared lasses 'ave 'ad ter be put through the same ordeal...'ow many weren't as lucky as our

Molly ter survive? *No, that bloody Mrs Wainright* is gonna get 'er comeuppance else when the time comes I won't rest easy in me grave!"

It was no use, Jake knew she had a bee in her bonnet and wouldn't return home until she'd said what she had to say. She had that determined stubborn look about her which although he'd always admired; he also knew how it had got her into many battles throughout her life.

"She might not even work 'ere no more!"

"Well, at least I'll know that I tried!"

Martha held on tightly to Lucy's petite, sweaty hand as they walked across the grey courtyard of the workhouse... Martha was grateful for the summer sunshine which lifted the depressing building by a minute degree. A huge and intimidating brick building with rows of grime-covered tiny windows stood in front of them.

"I don't like it 'ere, Martha...please don't make me live 'ere...*I'll run away!*"

Martha didn't answer, she couldn't; the lump in her throat was making swallowing too painful. Whilst Lucy had been fast asleep during the previous night, Martha had read through Bruce's letter again, it confirmed that George's mother *had* been called Molly Wright and she intended to try and find out if she was related to Dolly. She knocked on the small wooden door, still not letting go of Lucy's hand; she intended to inquire about Dolly first before even mentioning that she'd come to deliver Lucy and had already decided that if the workhouse turned out to be as bad as it was reputed, she'd not part with her. A wizened old woman gingerly opened the door, welcoming them with a broad toothless smile. "Come in! Come in!" she sang, "the party ain't begun yet, but yer can wait in me parlour...we'll be using me best dinner service...the one given ter me by the old King, Gawd Bless 'im!"

Lucy's giggles were short-lived, as they stepped over the threshold and were instantly assaulted by the stench of human waste and gruel.

"I fink I'm gonna spew me guts!" she whispered, pinching her nose tightly.

"Hold this beneath your nose, I had my suspicions that it wouldn't smell too good in here!" Martha pulled out a pouch of dried lavender and rose petals, from her skirt pocket; used for keeping her clothes smelling fresh, they were the perfect aid when in such a foul-smelling area.

Lucy breathed in the sweet perfume, "Ta Martha, that's a lot better...don't know why me ma didn't fink ter make these, they'd 'ave sold like hot cakes 'round 'ere, 'specially when the Thames is clogged up!"

An austere woman marched noisily into the workhouse waiting area, her face red and angry as she confronted the woman who'd let them in.

"Get back to your room this instant, Sally! I'll deal with *you* later. You know the rules! You are *not* allowed to unlock that door and you certainly shouldn't be anywhere near it in the first place!"

"Are yer comin' ter me party? Matron *dearie*?"

"*Certainly not!* Now do as you've been instructed or you'll face the consequences!"

Martha wondered what those consequences might be as she witnessed the encounter. The poor old woman was clearly batty, she thought, wondering if it was the result of a lifetime in the workhouse.

As Sally shuffled off, the matron completely ignored Martha and Lucy, turning her attention to the old couple who were sat in the waiting area.

"Mrs Bird? Did you especially want to see Mrs Wainright, only she's rather busy at the moment?"

Emma pursed her lips, "*That's fine*, we can wait."

The matron turned to Martha, "*Yes*, what did you want?" she uttered rudely.

"I'm looking for a relative of mine...her surname is Wright!"

The matron raised her eyebrows, "Well you've most likely had a wasted journey...I hope you didn't travel far!"

"So is there or *has* there been anyone of that name here? Is there another workhouse in

Whitechapel?" stressed Martha, shocking herself
by her unusual confidence.

Emma Bird left her chair and was soon at
Martha's side.

"Don't fink me prying lass, but did me lug 'oles
'ear yer say the name, *Wright?*"

"That's correct!" asserted Martha, glad of a
friendly face.

"Do you know how many young girls get given
that name when they turn up on our doorstep?"
the matron butted in.

Martha was puzzled, "Why do they all get given
the same name?"

"*Not all!*" she voiced aggressively, "but Mrs
Wainright likes to give her *special girls* that
name, she has a knack of seeing the potential in a
handful of the poor destitute young girls, does
our Mrs Wainright and over the years she's done
a remarkable job in training them to be
employed in service in some of the finest Stately
Homes up and down the country which has
proved to be beneficial to all concerned. Their
new employees are always so appreciative to
have these well trained and well spoken girls
that they inevitably contribute generous sums of
charity enabling the Whitechapel workhouse to
provide its inmates with all they deserve and
that's why, *Mrs Bird*, Mrs Wainright is so
extremely busy!" she added, looking down her
nose at her as she spoke.

Emma Bird stamped her foot hard on the stone

floor; her face was scarlet with rage,
"*Special gals!*" she yelled out, allowing her
temper its freedom.

"Oh I've seen an 'eard it all now...an' I s'pose yer
got nuffing ter do wiv this filthy racket ov
turning poor orphan lasses inter cheap
mistresses fer the bleedin' toffs an' wealthy
perverts ov this world, 'ave yer, Miss bleedin'
high an' mighty matron!"

"If you don't escort your highly-strung wife
from off these premises Mr Bird, I will send for
the constable. She has no business here...you *both*
have no business here!"

"Me an' me old man found one ov yer so-called
special gals; left fer dead she were an' would
surely 'ave departed from this sorry world if it
wasn't by the Grace ov The Almighty bringing
the life back into our poor Molly's ravaged
body!"

"*Molly Wright!*" gasped Martha, breaking into the
crossfire of raised and angry voices. There was
an instant silence apart from Lucy who was
concerned that Martha had suddenly muddled
her ma's name, "She were *Dolly Wright*, Martha,
not *Molly!*" she repeated twice before Martha
acknowledged her.

"If yer ain't got nuffing ter do wiv this Mrs
Wainright's so-called *special gals*, I suggest yer
look inter it afore yer finds yerself swinging
from the gallows fer murder!" warned Emma.
"Come along Jake, we ain't stayin' in this foul

place a second longer!"

"*I don't wanna live 'ere!*" bawled Lucy as she rubbed her knuckles into her tear filled eyes.

"Don't worry my sweetheart, I wouldn't dream of leaving you here, in fact, we are leaving now!" assured Martha as she hurried after Jake and Emma Bird.

"Mrs Bird!" Martha called out as she hurried to catch up, pulling Lucy along behind her.

"Mrs Bird, could I have a word?"

Overtaken with a fuming rage Emma was marching out of the workhouse yard with a string of abuse accumulating in her head which she now regretted not firing at the haughty matron. She was also livid that she'd not been allowed to meet face to face with the Wainright woman; she would have found a few choice words to throw at that evil woman she mused as she barely heard Jake shouting at her,

"Em! Fer Gawd's sake! That young woman wants a word wiv yer by the look ov it...'old her bleedin' 'orses!"

Emma came to a halt, sighing heavily as Martha caught up with her. Out of breath, she could only stand staring as Marta spoke.

"I hope you don't think me rude, but I couldn't help overhearing you mention Molly Wright...I know there are probably quite a few women with that name, but I happen to know of a Molly Wright and wondered if it could be the same one?"

Looking a little suspicious, Emma's deep-set eyes seemed to dance from Martha and Lucy. *"Martha!"* Lucy cried out, "I need the piss pot! I can't wait...that stinkin' work'ouse 'as turned me guts ter jelly!"

As Jake chuckled at Lucy's declaration, Emma Bird became suspicious. She warned herself to tread cautiously, thinking that this well-spoken and expensively togged out, young woman was one of Wainright's spies. She'd mentioned how she knew Molly...had that awful Brunswick man got wind that Molly was still alive she mused...perhaps he wanted what he believed was rightfully his. She had to protect poor Molly; she'd been through enough and suffered more than most for a girl in her early twenties.

"Can't you hold on for a few more minutes, sweetheart?"

Lucy shook her head as the tears rolled down her face, "Please Martha, let's go 'ome, I ain't fibbin'!"

"I know that, you poor little love; you've had a horrid few days, enough to give any grown up a jelly belly; you're a brave little soul, *Lucy!"*

"Would you like to come with us?" asked Martha politely, crossing her fingers and praying that Mr and Mrs Bird would accept. "You could have a cup of t...

"Rosie Lee!" Lucy butted in as she hopped from one foot to the other.

"That would be right kind, wouldn't it Em?"

expressed Jake Bird, licking his dry lips.

"Well I suppose it can't do no 'arm," echoed Emma who was now eager to find out the connection between the skinny young lass who looked like a street urchin and the well-spoken young woman who, Emma estimated, didn't look much older than Molly.

The sparse and grubby upstairs room in the Whitechapel Street, lodging-house was not at all what Emma and Jake had been expecting when Martha had issues her invite. Billy had wasted no time and had already swept out Dolly and Lucy's old room and collected a week's rent from the new lodger, a quiet elderly gentleman who Billy hoped wouldn't disturb him as Lucy and her mother had over the years.

By the time Martha had brewed the tea and returned to her room, Lucy had disclosed quite a lot to the elderly couple who appeared to have taken a shine to little Lucy. Mrs Bird also seemed more cordial towards Martha on her return.

"That's very kind, what yer done fer poor Lucy! She's a lovely little gal an' if you 'adn't ov bin passing through London on yer way 'ome, reckon she would 'ave bin thrown inter that awful work'ouse by now! We've bin finking ain't we Jake?"

"We 'ave?" he questioned, confusingly.

"Reckon we could take little Lucy 'ome wiv us, we got plenty ov room an' Molly would love a youngster 'round the place...reckon she gets fed up wiv us oldies sometimes!"

Sensing that Emma had already made up her mind, Jake knew better than to do anything other than go along merrily with his wife's suggestion.

It *did* seem like a good solution considered Martha as she sipped her mug of tea, thinking how she might, at last, soon be on her way to Oxford and her family. The Birds seemed like a lovely, caring couple, but she still had to inquire about Molly, could she be the same Molly who'd resided at the gatehouse...was *she* little Georgie's mother...if she was she deserved to be united with her son, but that would rip painfully through her family and break her mother's heart. Could she really turn up after all these years only to cause her ma more heartache and suffering? Suddenly the journey to Oxford had lost its magic. She had enough money to purchase a modest cottage and start a completely new life where she wasn't known to a living soul...She could change her name and invent a lie about her past even; perhaps that was the answer and solution to the entire situation. ..

"What do you fink?" voiced Emma, breaking into Martha's reverie.

"That's very charitable of you, Mrs Bird," was all Martha could think to reply.

"She'll be treated like one ov our own, won't she Jake?"

Martha felt as though she was sitting on the top of a high wall, looking down at these three strangers who had suddenly arrived from nowhere into her life...her days in the gatehouse now seemed like a lifetime away. She desperately needed her family, needed her identity because at this present time she had no clue as to who she was and felt like a lost soul. She viewed Lucy, her thin pale face looking happier than she'd ever witnessed as she chatted excitedly with the elderly couple who had already captured her young heart. Lucy was desperate for love and attention and Mr and Mrs Bird seemed like the perfect guardians for her.

CHAPTER THIRTY-SIX

Following a long night of poignant discussions, the parting between Martha and Mr and Mrs Bird evolved into yet another emotional roller coaster for Martha.

While Lucy had slept soundly upon Martha's bed, it had been decided that she should return with the Birds in the morning. Emma Bird harboured a strong yearning to nurture her as though she were her own daughter; encouraged by the placid and agreeable Jake, who doted on his wife and unreservedly trusted her judgement. The sad loss of their sons many years ago had left a gaping void in Emma's life and with an abundance of energy and eagerness to mother young Lucy together with Lucy's instantly formed fondness for Mr and Mrs Bird, Martha was convinced that it would be the perfect solution.

During their night-long talks, although Martha felt confident that they would fully understand, she could hear Bruce's voice, warning her not to disclose a thing about her past so she stuck with the same story as she'd told Lucy. Now certain that the Molly Wright who Emma had spoken about was the same Molly who'd been so cruelly treated by Bruce, Martha kept quiet about the connection, making the excuse that in light of the recent findings from the workhouse, there were likely to be dozens of '*Wright*' girls in service. She was glad of not mentioning young George too and even though touched by a niggling feeling of guilt, for keeping apart a mother from her child, she knew the devastating effects it would have on every member of her family should little Georgie be wrenched away from them. The secrets of the gatehouse weighed heavy on Martha, leaving her to struggle with so many dilemmas, including disclosing the fact that Bruce Brunswick was George's father. Although her heart was soft towards him, and she'd shared the final years of his life; years when he'd undoubtedly become a kinder and more compassionate man, there were too many folk who he'd caused the ruin of and no matter what picture she tried to paint of him when all was said and done, his enemies far outweighed his allies. Folk would never understand her relationship with him, neither, for when the facts were laid down, she had been his prisoner and some might consider his slave and it was only at the mercy of his death that she was set free. Maybe, she pondered deeply, she should simply bury the past and all that went with it; she was only eighteen, with her life ahead of her and with, hopefully, many happy years to be spent in the bosom of her family once again; why should she risk upsetting the apple cart when everything was so neatly balanced. Molly was also a young woman who, albeit had been severely traumatized by the tragic events in her life, was now, according to Mrs Bird coming on in leaps and bounds and she also believed that Molly would become like a mother to Lucy, leaving her and Jake to take the more appropriate roles of grandparents. The more Martha mulled over the entire situation, the more she was convinced that sometimes secrets were best kept undisclosed. Perhaps one day in the future there might be a call for some truths; when they might cause less of an upheaval, but for the time being, considered Martha, everyone involved around the secrets she held seemed content, so without further ado, her final decision was to lock them securely in her heart and find a safe hiding place for Bruce's letter.

Jake left the womenfolk to their tears and emotional farewells, while he went to collect his horse and cart from the nearby stables. Unable to face any more outbursts, he longed to return to the peace and tranquillity of his countryside home. Feeling relieved that he no longer lived in Whitechapel, he wondered how, in past years, he'd ever been happy surrounded in such squalor and deprivation.

"Ta, fer lookin' out fer me, Martha, I'm really gonna miss yer!"

"Now, now Lucy, she ain't going ter t'uther side ov the world, 'appen she could even come an' visit one day in the future!"

Lucy's face immediately cheered up, "Could yer, Martha...yer could bring yer 'ole family an' all...couldn't she Mrs Bird?"

Martha and Emma shared a warm exchange, "You must write to me once you've been to school and mastered your letters, Lucy! I will write to you with my address just as soon as I have located my family in Oxford!"

A sad look shadowed her face once again, "Oh Martha, what if yer never find 'em!"

"Don't be silly, Lucy, *course* she'll find 'em," Mrs Bird butted in, "Everyone in Oxf'rd will know where Martha's folk live!"

Having no other option, when Jake had asked Martha for her address in Oxford she'd falsely told him that her family had recently moved house and that she'd mislaid their new address.

"Mrs Bird is right, Lucy, you mustn't worry about me...Mr Bird told me your address, so if I have any problem, I'll simply turn up on your doorstep!"

"Gawd Bless yer, Martha, it don't bear finkin' 'bout what would 'ave 'appened ter poor young Lucy if yer 'adn't showed up when yer did!" declared Emma, her eyes moist with unshed tears.

"Lucy is a fortunate girl, to be going home with you, Mrs Bird!"

Lucy suddenly let go of Emma's hand and wrapped her arms around Martha, "I fink I love yer, Martha...can I be like yer little sister? I know yer already got free an' two bruvvers, but I won't be no trouble, I promise, an' when I learns me letters an' writes yer me news, I could pretend ter be yer sister!"

"Oh, dear, sweet Lucy, I couldn't think of anything more delightful than to have you as an extra sister! You'll be my special sister!"

Jake soon pulled up alongside them, eager to commence on the homeward journey. Their farewells were said and Martha stood on Whitechapel Street waving until they'd disappeared from her view. After sharing every single emotion with Lucy during the few days which they'd spent together, Martha felt as though she'd known the likeable girl for a lifetime and was now, once more, left feeling quite alone in the world. The sooner she left, the better she mused, hopeful that there would be an Oxford bound coach, later that day, so she'd not have to spend a lonely night in her miserable lodgings.

From the very moment that she arrived in Oxford, Martha was engulfed with a sense of security in the pleasant and welcoming City. Gone were the harrowing scenes she'd witnessed in the East End, of begging, flea-infested infants, dressed in their filthy rags as they ran through the streets causing havoc. There were fewer signs of poverty in this grand looking city; the inhabitants of Oxford walked proudly and were clothed in clean and well-tailored outfits cut from the finest of cloth, making Martha feel less conspicuous. Making her way directly to Cornmarket Street, she'd taken some information from a fellow passenger aboard the stagecoach as to where she could find a respectable place to stay and was told that the Claredon Hotel was one of the most, if not *the* finest hotel in the City. Pretending that she was to rendezvous with her aunt who was travelling down from the north, Martha took a deep breath and marched proudly into the Claredon Hotel with her head held high as though it were common practice in her life. She explained to the smartly attired man who stood behind the desk in the stylish foyer, that she wished to book a shared room for herself and her aunt, who would be joining her as soon as she arrived in Oxford; without a second thought, she gave her name as Miss Brunswick, not wishing to cause any unwarranted scandal for her family.

The spacious room on the first floor was luxurious in comparison to the dingy lodgings in Whitechapel and more in line with what she was accustomed to in the gatehouse. With a view from the window looking out on to the bustling Cornmarket Street, Martha studied every female in sight hoping that by a small miracle she might spot her ma or one of her family. The mere thought that only a short distance now separated her from them infused her with a comforting warmth and eased her sense of loneliness. It was late in the afternoon and the shopkeepers were just beginning to close for the day, she wondered if any member of her family had visited the City that day, feeling sure that they were living somewhere in the beautiful Oxfordshire countryside on one of the many farms which she'd passed by on her journey. A torrent of thoughts rushed through her head as she pondered where to start in her search for them and for how long she would have to keep up the pretence that her aunt had been delayed before she would be united with her family, leaving her to foot the bill for a room, far too big and expensive for her own needs. Thank God for Bruce's generosity towards her she mused, as she felt her rolling tears tickle her face. Her reverie was broken by the loud rumbling of her stomach but feeling reluctant to join the other guests in the hotel's dining room, she decided to have a quick wash, change her clothes and go for a stroll around the city before it became late and on her return, she would ask the gentleman at the desk if a light meal might be brought to her room.

Reluctant to venture too far from the hotel, Martha took a stroll in the nearby Cornmarket Street and Broad Street. Although the traders were all closing up for the day, the streets remained busy; Martha was mesmerized by the uniformed scholars who marched in groups with their flimsy black gowns seeming to take flight in the gentle breeze; engrossed in conversations, they trod their path as though sleepwalking and were oblivious to anything taking place on the streets. A similar group of young boys of varied heights glided two by two through the city streets, resembling a flock of angels in their voluminous white gowns which caused a swishing sound as they passed by before disappearing through the arched doorway of a nearby church. The terrifying and somewhat hideous faces of the gargoyles on the odd-looking circular building of the Radcliffe Camera was where Martha decided to take an about-turn and make her way back to the hotel; she already had a premonition that those faces would all feature in her dreams later that night.

The pleasant young gentleman at the hotel reception had been replaced by a much older, plumper and sterner looking, man. He studied Martha with narrowed eyes as she stepped over the threshold, causing her earlier confidence to immediately vanish. She could feel his glare upon her as she hovered nervously. The delicious mixed aroma of all her favourite foods mingled into one, reminding Martha of how starving she was but before she had time to make any decision as to whether or not she should approach the formidable-looking receptionist with the request to be served food in her room, an amiable waiter hurried through the double, glass-paned doors to greet her.

"Miss Brunswick! I have your table ready for you...Is there still no sign of your aunt?" Completely taken by shock, Martha had not expected her business to be so well broadcast. Before she had time to answer, the smartly dressed waiter continued,

"My colleague, Mr Ward, mentioned that you had gone out for a breath of early evening air and would soon be returning, he made a special request that I should look after you. So, Miss Brunswick, I have reserved a table for two by the window for you and your aunt."

Still aware of the receptionist's glare burning through her, Martha hurried into the dining room, closely shadowed by the pleasant waiter.

"Thank you," she finally managed to utter as he pulled out the chair for her and handed her a menu. She wondered if the staff had seen through her lie about her elusive aunt.

"Have there been any messages for me or a telegram perhaps?" she enquired, a look of concern on her face. "I'm beginning to feel quite worried about my aunt's whereabouts!"

"I don't think so Miss Brunswick, but I will certainly check with Mr Roach on reception." The waiter who appeared to be in a continuous hurry rushed out through the double doors leaving Martha amused by the receptionist's name; *cockroach* would have been a more apt title for the sour-faced man, she thought.

There was, of course, no news from Martha's aunt, and after a delicious wholesome meal, she retired to her room, leaving instruction with Mr Roach that she should be woken at any hour if there was a message for her. Exhausted, and full, it took less than the time in which she marvelled at the luxurious clean and soft cotton sheets against her skin and the comfortable bed before Martha was in a deep sleep.

CHAPTER THIRTY-SEVEN

Mr Ward was once again manning the reception and as Martha arrived downstairs, now feeling confident enough to waltz into the hotel's restaurant for breakfast, he called out to her as she passed by,

"Excuse me, Miss Brunswick!"

Martha immediately turned to face him, and after having a decent night's sleep, the smartly attired receptionist appeared even more pleasant on the eye than on the previous day. Martha smiled coyly as she warmed to his equally inviting smile.

"Mr Roach asked me to inform you that there were no messages during the night, Miss Brunswick and he suggested that the Hotel would gladly pay the cost should you wish to send an urgent telegram to your aunt. Perhaps you would write down an address?"

His unexpected offer didn't fail in bringing a scarlet glow to Martha's cheeks, she could feel them heating up as the dashing Mr Ward waited for her reply. She busied herself, adjusting her lace glove as she frantically searched for an answer.

"I hope you haven't found the manager's offer offensive, Miss Brunswick."

"Not at all, Mr Ward," Martha expressed hoping she sounded confident in her response. "It was an extremely kind gesture by Mr Roach, but alas, it's not the first time my dear ageing aunt has kept me waiting...She has the habit of becoming easily sidetracked and has most likely remembered an old friend during her journey and taken a detour, so a telegram would fail to reach her hands, you see."

Mr Ward lifted his thickset eyebrows as he listened to Martha's explanation. Both he and Mr Roach were suspicious of the latest guest at the Claredon Hotel; it was highly unusual for a young, unaccompanied woman to book into the hotel and even more bizarre for her to book a double room; why had she not just waited until her aunt had shown up; they were not short of rooms in the hotel at present. Mr Roach detested anything untoward going on in his hotel; it had a fine reputation and people from every corner of England stayed there when visiting Oxford. He had a strong suspicion that Miss Brunswick was up to no good and he could smell a definite rat beneath his waxed moustache.

Martha continued to the dining room and sat at the same table as on the previous evening. A little shocked to discover that Mr Roach was the hotel manager, she quietly warned herself that she should tread carefully. Having had no experience of staying in hotels throughout her entire life, her limited knowledge sprung from Bruce's life stories involving him staying in various hotels. Little snippets of information she'd recalled had now made her think that it was an unusual suggestion by the manager to send a telegram, unless in an emergency. With her sudden loss of appetite, Martha's original plan to consume a hearty breakfast before setting off on her search had now been cancelled; she ordered a pot of tea and buttered toast and jam instead, in the hope of appearing calm and unaffected by her worries.

Deciding to take a wander around the city, making inquiries with shopkeepers as to whether they knew of a Mr and Mrs Shepherd, Martha had already concocted a story, should anyone ask what business she had with them. She would pretend that her late grandmother was a friend to the Shepherd family before they moved to Oxford and that she had bequeathed a silver brooch to Mrs Shepherd, who had always been kind and caring towards her and since Martha was visiting Oxford regarding another matter, she thought to bring the brooch with her and fulfil her dear grandmother's request.

Martha had also decided that purchasing a reticule was paramount on her shopping trip, her ensemble was not complete without one and it appeared extremely odd for any decent young woman to keep her loose change inside of her glove.

Relieved that there had been no sighting of the severe faced Mr Roach, Martha quickly gulped down her tea and toast as quick as she could without appearing ill-mannered, hoping to leave before there was a risk of bumping into him. A smile spread across her face as she remembered how Lucy devoured her food; imagine the glaring looks of disgust she'd receive if she imitated her, mused Martha amusingly. She prayed that Lucy was happy with Mr and Mrs Bird and that she and Molly had also taken to each other.

"Could I bring you some more toast, Miss Brunswick?" The waiter's voice broke her reverie.

"No thank you," she replied abruptly, sending him on his way to the next table.

Gracefully dabbing her mouth with the serviette she left the dining room, stealing a quick furtive glance towards the reception area as she made her way to the front entrance. Pleased that there was still no sign of Mr Roach, she breathed a sigh of relief and stepped out onto the Street.

A steady mixture of working horse carts and prominent carriages trotted up and down Cornmarket Street. The shops were all open for business and various costermongers eager to sell their wares were spaced along the thoroughfare. The yeasty aroma of freshly baked bread lingered in the air and as Martha passed by two young chimney sweeps, already blackened from head to toe, she wondered how much soot they'd consume in a week, as they bit into the grubby loaf they were sharing. The gunmetal sky threatened rain but the temperature was such that there was an oppressive muggy feel about the morning. Martha peered into the window of a ladies dress shop, there was little in the way of fashion to see; one solitary gown hanging from a pole and copious unravelled bolts of fabric forming waves like a stormy ocean upon the wide window ledge; there were, however, a few pretty embroidered reticules amongst the display. She stood for a while, searching for a glimpse of the shopkeeper; the curly hair, piled neatly on top of the heads of two women soon came into view; they were sat behind a cluttered workbench, thoroughly engrossed as their hands busily stitched the fabric they were working on while they chatted away without diverting their eyes from their needlework. Once again, Martha's nerves set in as she went over in her head what to say after she'd summoned up enough confidence to step over the threshold. Her own words were becoming entangled with Bruce's words...'*Folk can't be trusted my sweet Martha, they are not always what they seem, the world outside can be a tricky place...*' Why wouldn't his words leave her alone and allow her to make her own judgments, she thought angrily; he was always there, advising her, warning her, just as he'd done all the while she was captive in the gatehouse. She sighed heavily, trying to block out his voice as she entered the small shop. The jingle of the doorbell immediately gained the attention of the two women; they cast aside their needlework appearing to be mesmerized by Martha's presence, she wondered if perhaps the shop was not yet open to customers as her confidence quickly abandoned her.

"Can I help you?" asked one of the women.

"I wish to buy the peacock blue reticule, the one with the drawstring and the powder blue and gold embroidery."

"Are you local?" asked the second woman whilst her colleague fetched the said reticule from the window display. Disliking such personal questions, Martha immediately felt uneasy.

"No, I'm staying at the Claredon Hotel with my aunt."

The women exchanged a peculiar glance.

"That will be half a crown, please, would you like it wrapped?"

Martha took the coin from out of her glove, "No thank you, as you can see I am in urgent need of its use!"

"So you don't have any relatives here in Oxford then?" pried the woman as she took Martha's money.

Feeling her legs weaken beneath her, instead of replying, Martha declared her gratitude and hurried out of the shop almost running along the street before she turned the corner where, in a state of panic, she struggled to breathe as she leant against the wall. She had been stupid she scolded herself and missed a golden opportunity to bring up the Shepherd family in conversation. But uppermost in her thoughts were that she'd been recognized as the thief and escaped convict who'd gone on to feign her death. Was she overreacting, she mused as her breathing slowly returned to normal and her hands stopped shaking.

Inside the dress shop, Marigold and Edwina were unanimous in their suspicions that this girl was related to the Shepherd family, there was an uncanny resemblance to Jane Shepherd who was a regular customer. Their passion to gossip brought them to the conclusion that the nervous young woman was Mr Shepherd's secret love child. It would explain why they'd suddenly arrived in Oxford five years ago with no experience of town life, they concluded. An original farming family running away to start afresh before the truth came to light and before local folk recognized the similarities between father and daughter.

"I do hope Jane Shepherd has reason to call on us today!" expressed Marigold. "Be sure to save three slices of the strawberry sponge cake, Edwina, we'll sweet-talk her into the truth about her family's past! Maybe bribe her with a couple of remnants if need be!"

"You are positively wicked, Marigold! But if your theory is correct, I doubt very much that any of the 'Shepherd' children are aware of the truth!"

"Oh, Edwina, don't be so naive! There's nothing like the wagging ears of children to take note of what goes on between their parents! Just leave it to me, but pray that Jane calls in on us before that young woman leaves the Claredon!"

With her plans for the day suddenly thrown into chaos, Martha decided to return to her room, and rethink how she would go about searching for her family. The summer sun had failed to put in her appearance and as the first large drops of rain began to descend heavily Martha increased her speed to reach the hotel before the heavens opened and gave her a soaking. Mr Ward, who was manning his usual place behind the reception desk was red-faced and being reprimanded by an elderly man, who was stooped over and leaning heavily on to his walking cane. Edging her way slowly towards them in order to collect her key, the old man lifted his head, appearing to delight in Martha's arrival.

"Ah! *My dear young lady!*" he bellowed, "I wonder if you would be so kind as to oblige in taking part in a trivial but *most important* experiment!"

As Mr Ward's complexion took on a more pronounced shade of scarlet, Martha was curious as to what the experiment entailed.

Without giving her a chance to accept or refuse, the old man requested that she ring the reception desk bell.

"As forcefully as you can, I might add, Miss..."

"Miss Brunswick." Mr Ward hurriedly informed him.

"What's that boy? Speak up won't you, for heaven's sake! Oh, fiddlesticks, just ring the bell please, I've yet to give that oaf, *Roach* a piece of my mind too and I promised to make up a foursome for a game of bridge at my club and I do hate to keep the chaps waiting!"

Taking a step closer to the desk, Martha raised her hand and allowed it to fall heavily on to the bell, causing it to ring out sharply.

"Ah! *Do you see?* I was right all along; the damn thing is broken, can barely hear a sound!" stated the cantankerous old man. "I don't pay your wages for the sheer pleasure of throwing my money away Mr Ward, I expect you and Roach to use a bit of initiative."

By now, Martha had deduced that the deaf gentleman was, in fact, the owner of the Claredon Hotel. She sympathized with Mr Ward as he glanced sheepishly at her, his face still red. "Could I have my key?" she requested in a small voice, eager to retreat to her room. The hotel owner took out a huge white handkerchief from his pocket and wiped the beads of sweat from his brow. Mr Ward lifted the key from its hook and passed it to Martha, quite relieved that she wouldn't witness any more of his embarrassment.

"I'll man the station lad; you go and see if Silas Shepherd has a new reception bell in stock!"

Martha came to an abrupt halt, freezing on hearing mention of her pa's name.

"Excuse me, did you say *Silas Shepherd?*"

"He runs the local ironmongers," confirmed Mr Ward, knowing that his deaf employer had not heard Miss Brunswick's soft voice.

"Is it nearby then?" she asked, rather foolishly.

"It's in the High street, just around the corner."

"Thank you, Mr Ward."

"Hurry up lad, I've not got all day you know...Bridge to play, you know...and where has that confounded Mr Roach got to, *for heaven's sake!*"

Martha practically danced up the flight of stairs, she hadn't felt such joy in a long while, the thought that she was so close to her beloved family filled her heart with a kaleidoscope of fluttering butterflies and presented a wide smile upon her face. She arrived eagerly at her door, only to turn cold as she noticed that the door was ajar. Quickly reassuring herself that it was likely to be the hotel maids cleaning her room, she pushed open the door and stared in alarm as the back view of Mr Roach came into focus; he was completely immersed in searching through her wardrobe.

"What do you think you're doing! How dare you search through my personal belongings..." she screamed out, hysterically. Mr Roach turned to face her, his stern look unwavering.

"I have the right to know *who* and *what* goes on under my roof, Miss Brunswick and it would appear to me by the huge sum of money that I have discovered that you are not the person you pretend to be and it is my opinion that you have recently left service after robbing your employer of her clothes *and* money...you are, by all accounts, Miss Brunswick, *an imposter* and a *common thief!*"

Horrendous flashbacks of her days aboard the convict hulk clouded her thoughts, she could feel her heartbeat pounding and knew that she must escape the dire situation before she was once again falsely accused and left to face the consequences.

"Everything you see before you is rightfully mine, Mr Roach, I was left them by a very dear and close companion!"

"Take a good look at me Miss Brunswick; do I look as though I've recently climbed out of my cradle?"

His smarmy self-righteous grin turned Martha's stomach, she was lost for words and up against a man whose shell was as tough as rock. She thought of Bruce and wondered what he would do in such a situation, and instantly knew that he would fight his way out. At least she now knew that her family were living somewhere in the High Street and would be easy to locate even if she hadn't planned to ascend on them so suddenly and without warning. Her eyes search the room for anything to temporarily put Mr Roach out of action. As he approached her Martha quickly jumped onto the bed and ran across it,

"So, Miss Brunswick, you wish to play cat and mouse do you?"

With Mr Roach now stood in the doorway, Martha kept her eyes on him as she frantically stuffed the dresses into her travelling case, along with the bundle of banknotes which were on the side table. Mr Roach laughed out loud. "And how exactly do you propose to escape past me, Miss Brunswick?"

"If you don't let me pass Mr Roach, I will scream at the top of my voice and claim to the entire City of Oxford that you have attacked me and ruined my virtue! Now step aside and allow me to pass!"

"Who in their right mind will believe a scheming juvenile thief over *me*, a respectable hotel manager in my prime!"

"I am not who you think I am Mr Roach and *you* will end up regretting your hastily drawn up conclusions if you're not careful! "

"Am I being warned by a common thief?"
Clutching the case against her body, Martha suddenly began to scream; A high pitched howl

which immediately wiped the smug look from off Mr Roach's face. She ran towards him and without stopping, collided into him, knocking him off his balance and sending him toppling over. She didn't wait to see if he was getting up to pursue her but hurried down the stairs and out through the main hotel entrance.

CHAPTER THIRTY-EIGHT

Outside the heavy rain was falling like stair rods. Cornmarket Street was now at its busiest as it approached mid-morning with people rushing about in a bid to keep dry. After a prolonged dry spell, the sudden torrent of rain had caused the pavement to become hazardous underfoot. In her panicked state of mind and with the fear that Mr Roach was chasing after her Martha fled from the hotel with only one purpose in mind, which was to head towards the High Street and her family. Without stopping she dashed across the street, blinded by her tears and letting it slip her mind that she was in the heart of a busy city, the last image she could remember was a latticework of horse's legs as her body slid across the slippery street without stopping and her entire world blacked out. The cacophony of high pitched neighing horses, men's angry, raised voices and the clatter of carriage wheels prompted shopkeepers to brave the elements and pour out on to the street. The pedestrians in Cornmarket Street froze in horror, gasping at the sight of Martha's dishevelled and blood-stained body. Whispers of doom passed over lips as folk formed little hope of anyone surviving such an accident. Mr Ward was also out on the street; he'd witnessed Martha hurrying from the hotel, without stopping to deposit her key and sensed there was something wrong, with a sneaky feeling that Mr Roach was somehow behind it. He'd been behaving strangely all morning and had appeared far too interested in the comings and goings of Miss Brunswick.

"Oh Dear God!" he cried out, catching sight of Martha. He hurried across the street to where she lay and where half a dozen womenfolk surrounded her.

"It's Miss Brunswick!" he announced, suddenly feeling faint at the sight of her blood as it mixed with the rainwater to create murky, blood-red puddles. In all the commotion his presence was ignored but he had been heard and as the women folk chanted in unison, *"Miss Brunswick, Miss Brunswick,"* a doctor who was also a patron at the Claredon Hotel, arrived on the scene and began to calmly and meticulously examine her. Ten minutes later Martha was gently placed onto the back of an open cart, covered with a blanket from the hotel and a waxed sack to keep her dry and rushed off to the Radcliffe Infirmary. Mr Roach stood annoyed and crimson faced with one foot on the street and one still inside the hotel lobby,

"Stupid, stupid!" he muttered under his breath. "Where's that young Mr Ward gone! That rude boy turned his back on me and fled the hotel you know Mr Roach!"

"Mr Spencer!" exclaimed Mr Roach, "I had no

idea that you were on the premises; I trust Mr
Ward has been taking good care of you! I'm
afraid there's been a terrible accident involving
one of our guests!"

"Damned reception bell doesn't work Roach, that
won't do; that won't do at all and to top it all, I'm
late for my club meeting...when's this ghastly
rain going to let up?"

"Don't you worry about a thing Mr Spencer; I'll
see to the reception bell and hail a Hanson cab to
take you to your club!" voiced Mr Roach loudly,
familiar with his employer's eccentric ways and
his deteriorating hearing.

"Good show Roach! Good show; I know I can
always depend on you old boy! Make sure that
young chappie buys a new bell for the reception
now, won't you, Roach!"

"Very good Mr Spencer, I'll send him to the
ironmongers in the first instance!"

"Now where's that cab! Hate to keep the men
waiting; they rely on me to come up trumps you
know!" boasted Mr Spencer, proudly, completely
ignoring the fact that a guest had been seriously
injured, under his very nose.

It was with great relief that Mr Roach aided the
frail old Mr Spencer into the cab and sent him on
his way, to the Wig and Feather Gentleman's
Club in George Street. Mr Ward was dutifully
back behind the reception, with an ashen
complexion and his clothes dripping wet. He
was unable to shift the image of the pretty Miss

Brunswick from his mind as his hands trembled uncontrollably.

"Go to my office, Mr Ward," ordered Mr Roach. "I have a spare uniform in my cupboard. Take your lunch break early and be sure to be on good form again by this afternoon. Rest assured I will man the reception in your absence."

"Thank you, Mr Roach...do you think Miss Brunswick will pull through?"

"Come now, Mr Ward, you don't want to be wasting your time over a flighty Miss like her...I have my suspicions that she is an imposter and I intend to take the matter up with the local constabulary in due course!"

No longer sharing the same suspicions as Mr Roach, Mr Ward decided to ignore his stuffy, old fashioned superior; he liked Miss Brunswick and felt sorry for her, she appeared timid and nervous and that was likely the reason why Mr Roach harboured his uncertainties surrounding her.

"What about the new bell?"

Mr Roach waved his hand flippantly through the air, "Oh that can wait, Ward, fetch it in your own time and ask Mr Shepherd to send the bill of payment to the Claredon Hotel."

Having lost his appetite and with the relentless rain, at last, coming to an end, Simon Ward left the Claredon deciding to use his early lunch break to meander along the High Street and call in at the ironmongers. With the vivid images of poor Miss Brunswick still flashing before him, he wondered if it would seem improper to inquire after her when he'd finished work for the day; she appeared to be a very lonely, young woman and with her aunt still failing to show up, Simon couldn't help but feel sorry for her and if he was totally honest with himself, he knew that he'd fallen for the mysterious Miss Brunswick. As he hurried down the High Street his thoughts turned to Frank Shepherd, he'd always got on well with him, when he used to make deliveries to the hotel; he'd not seen him in a while though and it would be a good opportunity to chat with him and take his mind off the awful morning he'd had.

Greeted by Frank's father, Simon gingerly inquired as to Frank's whereabouts and immediately got the feeling that Mr Shepherd didn't wish to discuss his son.

"He's gone away for a while...What can I do for you today Mr Ward?"

"Just a new brass reception bell if you've one in stock, please, Mr Shepherd."

Claire emerged from the back office and cordially greeted Simon,

"Good Day Simon, how are you?"

"I'm well thank you, Mrs Shepherd, and yourself, I trust you are in good health?"

"Thank you, yes. What a dreadful accident outside the hotel earlier! Did *you* witness it? A few customers came into the shop quite overcome by the trauma of it all; A young woman apparently? Staying at your hotel too I believe?"

"The gentleman has come to purchase a bell, my dearest! He's not the town crier!" Silas joked. "Excuse my wife, Mr Ward, she has an *inquiring* mind!"

"Oh, Simon doesn't mind do you?" Claire persisted.

Eager to share his worries about Miss Brunswick, Simon was glad to ease the burden from his mind, "It was quite awful, Mrs Shepherd, she was dragged across the street beneath the traffic! Covered in blood and with barely a sign of life left in her; she looked more like a discarded child's rag doll upon the street! I doubt I'll ever be able to rid my mind of that haunting image of poor Miss Brunswick!"

Silas and Claire's eyes met,

"*Miss Brunswick?*" repeated Claire, her voice having a distinctive urgency about it.

Simon sensed the sudden change in the atmosphere "Do you know Miss Brunswick?" he blurted out.

"We used to know of *a* Miss Brunswick," admitted Silas, "but there are probably hundreds of folk with that name; I wouldn't have thought it was the same person!"

"Do you know her home address, Simon, perhaps someone could inform her family of what's happened?" Claire advised.

Simon shook his head, "That's just it, Mrs Shepherd, she seems to be quite alone in the world; Mr Roach thinks there is something quite suspicious about her and is already speaking of informing the police!"

Claire and Silas became even more intrigued.

"*Suspicious? Why?*" questioned Silas.

Simon shrugged his shoulders, "Oh, he thinks she's too rich and fancy and doesn't believe that she's waiting for the arrival of her aunt, as she claims to be; he reckons she's an imposter!"

"What's your opinion of her, Simon?" prompted Claire.

"She's lovely and kind but I get the feeling that she's scared of something or someone, but she doesn't appear in the least bit harmful or malicious as Mr Roach seems to think; I don't think she'd harm a fly! And now she's in the infirmary, fighting for her life!"

"Oh dear, what a sorry state of affairs! Do you know how old she is Simon?"

"She's young and *very* pretty Mrs Shepherd and she's not married either, well, as far as I can make out."

With his thoughts thoroughly distracted, Silas wrapped the shiny, brass reception bell in a sheet of brown paper and handed it to Simon, "We must all pray for her, Mr Ward and hope the poor young woman makes a swift recovery! I'll send the invoice along later."

The second Simon Ward stepped out on to the street, Claire turned the 'open' sign on the door around.

"Let's take an early lunch break, Silas," insisted Claire.

Amy emerged from the office, she'd heard every word that Simon had said, "Do you think she's come from Bagley village?"

"I very much doubt it, Amy, it's just pure coincidence; maybe she's a very distant relative to the Brunswick family at Bagley village."

Unconcerned, Amy made for the stairs, "I'll go and get luncheon started, I doubt Jane's lifted her head from that fancy gown she's been working on all morning...probably has no idea of the time."

Claire waited for Amy to be out of earshot before continuing.

"What if she's the late Squires daughter, Silas...What if she is George's mother and she's come to claim him back!"

"That's dangerous talk, my love. Calm yourself, you're letting your imagination run wild...why would she be in a hotel if that were the case?"

"Well, we know that *one* member of the Brunswick family has either fathered or given birth to our George! Perhaps his mother is simply using that name...maybe she is a poor soul who has suffered as much as us from the unscrupulous behaviour of the Brunswick men!"

Even though Silas harboured a niggling feeling after listening to Simon Ward's news, he knew he'd have to persuade Claire otherwise until he'd had an opportunity to investigate further into exactly who this young woman was and if there was a connection between her and young George.

"I suggest we put this entire matter out of our minds, for the time being, my love, and go upstairs to enjoy luncheon in the company of our daughters."

CHAPTER THIRTY-NINE

Claire and Jane sat at the kitchen table both engrossed in their needlework, thankfully Jane was working silently, with every ounce of her concentration being instilled into the outstandingly beautiful gown she was embroidering to present to the ladies in Oxford's finest dressmakers, where she hoped to impress them enough to be offered permanent work as a seamstress. Claire, on the other hand, was working on everyday clothing for the twins, who were constantly outgrowing their clothes or ruining them on the school playground.

No matter how much Claire had tried to preoccupy her mind throughout the afternoon, the mere thought that Miss Brunswick had been in Oxford alone and casting enough suspicions to persuade Mr Roach, the hotel manager to doubt her intentions wouldn't leave her mind. She didn't know Mr Roach but had heard him mentioned in many a conversation and by all accounts, he was an upright steadfast character with a serious disposition; surely he wouldn't have been mistaken in his judgement, mused Claire. With Miss Brunswick in hospital though, it at least gave them some breathing space and although she knew her thoughts were positively sinful, Claire was relieved that this woman was temporarily out of harm's way but did wish her a full recovery, if not, perhaps, a slow one. A sudden thought sprung to mind, causing her to drop the half-finished dress and rush downstairs to find Silas. Her timing was perfect; Amy was adjusting her straw bonnet in front of the looking glass, ready to fetch the twins from school.

"Take them to the confectioners Amy; take some change from the office!"

"I can't do that Ma, I spent all day writing up the books and if I withdraw any funds, they will no longer be accurate!"

Sensing Claire's anxious temperament, Silas delved into his pocket, "Here Amy, do as your ma says!" he ordered sternly, placing the silver thrupence into her hand.

"Fine Pa!" she sighed, avoiding eye contact with Claire.

"You'd think she was the owner of this establishment sometimes!" complained Claire.

"Ah she's just at that age when she likes to feel important!" consoled Silas. "I can tell that this whole Miss Brunswick business is eating you up; isn't it my darling? What did I tell you? You're not to worry...it's something of nothing...merely a coincidence!"

"I'm sorry, Silas but I don't share your casual attitude...there must be a connection and I'm not going to sit around sewing and cooking as though everything in the garden is rosy while that woman is on our doorstep waiting to waltz in here and take little Georgie from under our noses!"

"Don't be so dramatic, Claire, this isn't one of those *'penny dreadful'* stories coming to life, you know..."

"I've had an idea," stated Claire, adamantly. "The twins finish school for the summer at the end of this week; we could close the shop for a month..."

"*A month!*" yelled Silas, totally shocked by his wife's foolhardy idea.

"Please, hear me out, Silas. We could use some of the money that the Squire left us and go away until this has all blown over!"

"*All what has blown over!* Can you hear yourself, Claire? Have you taken leave of your senses? A woman with the coincidental name of Brunswick has turned up in Oxford and you suddenly want to sabotage our business and send us scurrying away, to God knows where like guilty villains! If the accident hadn't taken place we would be none the wiser about her...perhaps there have been handfuls of guests staying in hotels in Oxford over the years with that very same surname. Believe me Claire; if she *is* after retrieving her son, which I can safely bet my last shilling that she *isn't*, she'd have called on us by now!"

"Perhaps she doesn't know where we live, just that we are in Oxford."

Silas reached out to his tearful wife, he was

worried about her state of mind; she was not thinking at all rationally; taking her in his arms he held her tight and whispered reassuring sentiments in her ears in a bid to calm her. "Maybe we could all go to the seaside for a day during the school holidays? The twins would love that, wouldn't they?"

"Don't treat me like some kind of half-wit, Silas, I'm a mother and it's my powerful sense of motherly intuition which is sending these clear messages to me...*I know I'm right, Silas, I can sense it!*"

Still thinking that Claire was simply behaving like a typical over-emotional woman, he had little choice other than to admit that perhaps there could be an element of truth in what she was saying. "Would it make you feel better if I went and had a word with Mr Roach tomorrow, I can personally deliver his invoice to him and ask a few questions...maybe find out where she comes from or what business she has in Oxford. How does that sound?

Claire nodded tearfully, "Thank you, Silas, I just pray that what he has to say will put my mind at rest, but on the other hand, if she *is* intent on reclaiming her son she has probably lied about who she is and where she comes from."

"Ah! *There!* You said it yourself!" Silas exclaimed jubilantly. "If she *is* who you think she is, then surely she would have given herself a false name too!"

That was a point which Claire had overlooked, Silas was right, she mused, suddenly feeling a little less threatened.

No matter how convincing Silas's words had been, deep down inside Claire knew that she was correct. Troubled by feelings of doubt, she'd spent the entire night trying to enforce sleep upon her exhausted body but to no avail and at four o'clock in the morning found herself sipping tea in the kitchen as she waited for the first light of the long-awaited new day to arrive. Her thoughts were constantly diverted to the poor young woman who appeared to be completely alone in the city and without any nearby family. Now she lay in solitude probably fighting for her life. By the time the patter of Georgie's bare feet sounded upon the kitchen floor, Claire had already decided to visit the unfortunate woman, with no other reason than to show that someone cared for her well-being.

"Morning Ma!" announced George, rubbing his eyes and yawning.

"*Georgie*, my *sweet* boy, why are you up so early this morning?" Claire held her arms out and without hesitation, George ran to her, snuggling up close against the warmth of her body.

"My belly was rumbling and it woke me up!"

"You're a growing boy, that's why my darling; I think you will be the tallest in the family one day!"

"Hmm, you smell of tea, Ma...can I have a cup..."

Cupping his round face in her hands Claire kissed his cheeks, "You, my boy can have tea *and* a slice of fruit cake, but not a word to your sisters that you had cake *before* breakfast...it will be our little secret!"

"I won't Ma!" he said excitedly.

George was already half a head taller than Grace, and year after year his appearance was becoming distinctly different from his siblings. Claire often found herself clandestinely studying him, just to see if she could catch a glimpse of any similarities to anyone in Bagley village. She prayed that as he grew older his differences would go unnoticed to him.

"May I have a big slice of fruit cake, just like Pa does, because I'm *really* starving...*Please Ma?*"

Claire laughed out loud, "I suppose so!" George's face beamed with delight.

The early morning peace was shortly outlived and the kitchen full with noisy chatter as the rest of the family, one by one, arrived for breakfast. As usual, a large pan of creamy oats was already simmering on the stove and Jane, Amy and Grace wasted no time in laying the table. Silas was the last to arrive and appeared exceptionally smart in readiness for an important meeting with the ground manager of a renowned local Stately home with the opportunity of sealing a large commission. Dressed in his Sunday best Silas had neatly trimmed his moustache and tidied his bushy sideburns.

"Doesn't your Pa look like the most handsome gentleman in Oxford this morning, children!" expressed Claire. Silas smiled, his cheeks taking on a distinct pink hue as all eyes were suddenly cast upon him.

"He's wearing his Sunday best!" Grace exclaimed.

"Your pa has an important meeting this morning," confirmed Claire, proudly.

"Can I wear my best dress too, Ma?" pleaded Grace.

"Don't be silly, Grace!" scolded Jane. "You're only going to school."

"And praise the Lord that this is the last week I'll have to take you and George there and back every day!" Amy declared.

"Amy! Don't use the Good Lord's name in vain!"

"I didn't Ma; I am truly grateful, I'm sick of the sight of that school building!"

"Can we go to school on our own after the holiday, Ma? I'll take good care of Grace and we *are* both nearly six now!"

"Eat your breakfast, George, and stop troubling your ma, otherwise we'll all be late!" ordered Silas as he pulled out a chair.

"I have some errands to run in town this morning, Silas; would it help if I dropped the invoice into the Claredon Hotel?"

There was a pause of thought before he replied, "That *would* be a help, Claire but no questions or prying please, it doesn't look professional and I don't want my wife discussing any of our business with *Mr Roach*!"

"Honestly Silas, what do you take me for!" scolded Claire.

"What questions?" quizzed Amy, intrigued.

"Never you mind!" snapped Silas, annoyingly. *"For heaven's sake!* I believe a man would get more peace at the breakfast table if he was to sit with a brood of clucking hens!"

Claire dutifully obeyed her husband and handed in the sealed invoice to Mr Roach before her quick diversion to the florists where she was confronted by an abundance of sweet-scented and vibrant summer blooms, to choose from. She purchased a small and inexpensive bouquet of pastel pink rose buds which were set against a spray of delicate green fern. It was a good ten minutes walk to St. Giles Road West, where the Radcliffe Infirmary was situated. Claire had already contrived a story which would hopefully persuade the staff to allow her a quick visit to Miss Brunswick's bedside and as she marched briskly before her nerves convinced her to abort her mission, she couldn't remember a time when she'd felt so nervous.

It took little time after describing to the porter the accident of the previous day for him to register the incident and he immediately directed Claire to the women's ward where Miss

Brunswick had been admitted to.

Guarded by an austere and inhospitable looking nurse who was dragging a filthy mop over the hospital floor, Claire immediately sensed that it would be a difficult task to gain entry into her domain. The nurse stood upright, rubbing her back as she heard Claire's footsteps upon the stone floor. She moved her body, blocking access into the ward as she issued Claire with an intimidating glare.

"The visiting hour is from two o'clock until three o'clock, madam, and mind you don't slip up on the wet floor!"

"I'm here on behalf of the shopkeepers of Cornmarket Street, we were witness to Miss Brunswick's terrible accident and since she has no nearby relatives, we simply wanted her to take comfort in knowing that she is being thought of and prayed for!" voiced Claire, sheepishly.

"I don't care if you're here on behalf of the Lord Mayor of Oxford! This is a hospital and rules are rules and the doctors are about to do their rounds and they don't take kindly to seeing anyone on the ward, getting under their feet, apart from myself and the sick patients!"

Sensing that it would be pointless to try and negotiate with this stubborn headed nurse, Claire resigned to simply asking after Miss Brunswick's condition, only to come up against another brick wall.

"I take it you're *not* related to Miss Brunswick?"
"Well, actually, that's another reason why I'm anxious to visit her; I believe she might be related to a family to whom my own family used to live close by to, in fact, we were tenant farmers on their land!"
"It's not my place to discuss the patients with any Tom, Dick or Harry, it's more than my job's worth, but I will tell you that as far as I know, she's off the critical list and although covered from head to toe in cuts and bruises, she *will* by all accounts make a full recovery."
Returning to her pail of murky water, the self-righteous nurse continued to mop, turning her back on Claire.
"So, do you have *any* idea when she will be well enough to leave the hospital?" continued Claire.
"You just don't give up, do you! Mrs... "
"Mrs Shepherd...I don't mean to be a nuisance, but *I am* genuinely concerned for Miss Brunswick's well being."
"Tell you what, I'll do for you, *Mrs Shepherd*, I'll ask Miss Brunswick if she would mind you visiting her and if she agrees, then I will permit you through my doors this afternoon during the appropriate hour! *That's the best I can do!* "
Thanking the nurse, Claire left the hospital, quietly praying that Miss Brunswick would agree to the arrangement and allow her to finally put her mind at ease.

CHAPTER FORTY

Two o'clock couldn't arrive fast enough, Claire had returned home, baked a sponge cake and prepared an offal pie for the family's supper trying her utmost to remain calm so as not to arouse suspicion in anyone, especially Silas who seemed to be monitoring her emotions and moods like a hawk ever since the business with Miss Brunswick. Jane was another sharp-eyed and sensitive member of the family, who could always pick up on her mother's mood, so when Silas reported that she'd gone out to purchase a reel of thread it came as a relief to Claire. On her return, however, Jane's conversation caused an entirely new wave of anxiety to flood Claire's thoughts.

She placed the dainty paper bag onto the corner of the flour-covered table as she removed her bonnet; she was quieter than normal and appeared quite preoccupied. Claire took little notice and was glad that she'd not issued a barrage of questions as to where she'd been all morning; Jane was somewhat of a master at detecting lies.

"That was so odd!" she suddenly declared in a distraught voice.

Claire took her eyes from the pastry, tilting her head as she waited for Jane to continue.

"Those two old spinsters were behaving in a

most peculiar way, Ma. They befriended me as though I was their long lost cousin, insisting that I joined them for tea and cake!"

Claire smiled, "They have most likely come to realise what an expert seamstress you are and that you have great potential. Perhaps they are worried that another establishment will snap you up! Did they offer you a position with them?"

"Not at all, they didn't seem one tiny bit interested in my work, even though I took a sample of my embroidery, hoping to tempt them...Oh, They praised it briefly, but I got the distinct feeling that their overwhelming hospitality was for the sole purpose of fishing for information about the, now famous, Miss Brunswick!"

Intrigued by what Jane was saying, Claire wiped her messy hands on her apron and sat down.

"Why is everyone suddenly so interested in this woman?" protested Jane, clearly annoyed that Marigold and Edwina had not given her needlework the attention it deserved. "Where did she come from for God's sake? I for one will be *delighted* when she returns and I hope it's very soon!"

"Come now Jane, that poor woman suffered a horrendous accident by all accounts, and she's in hospital nursing her wounds and by the sound of what folk are saying, she is without any family close by to care for her."

"Well perhaps, Ma, when I tell you what those two *foolish* women believe, you might feel the same as I do!"

"What do you mean?"

Jane pulled out a chair and sat opposite her ma, she was flustered and Claire knew that it must be serious to have affected Jane so intensely.

"After they plied me with tea and a huge slice of sickly, strawberry, cream cake, they began asking me questions; questions about our past, about why we came to Oxford and whether I'd noticed a rift between you and Pa? Then they went on to ask me if any other members of our family remained in the place where we used to live."

"Did they mean Frank d'you think?" stressed Claire, as she felt her blood heating up in anger.

"Oh no, Ma, those interfering two busybodies know *all* about Frank, they must have their spies on every street corner of Oxford, it seems they don't miss a thing that goes on!"

"Do you think they might have found out about our dear Martha, God rest her soul?"

"That was exactly what I thought at first, but then it dawned on me by what they were saying that they believe there to be a connection between *that* Miss Brunswick and *our* family. They also told me that she'd been in to their shop and purchased a reticule...apparently the very one she was holding during her accident! They had said it in such a proud way, it quite

445

turned my stomach."

"Did they mention anything of what she'd said to them whilst in their shop?"

"*No Ma*, they simply advised me that no man, no matter how decent he might appear, should ever be trusted and how they rejoiced in the fact that they were spinsters!"

Completely lost for words as she sat in shock mulling over Jane's report, Claire arrived back at her original theory that Miss Brunswick was, in fact, George's mother. She suddenly felt unsure as to whether or not she should still visit her as planned and realised that she'd played right into her hands by telling the nurse her name.

"*Oh, yes!*" Jane suddenly exclaimed, "I forgot to mention what Miss Marigold said to me, just as I was about to leave; she laughed in a strange and cynical sort of way and declared that she doubted there was a single man on God's earth who hadn't sired a love child!"

Claire shook her head, astounded by the recklessness of Marigold and Edwina.

"What do you think she meant, Ma? She was speaking in a cryptic sense. Was she talking about Pa? Do they think *he* has a love child?"

"I've got a good mind to give those thoughtless gossips a piece of my mind; spreading malicious tittle-tattle...it's downright criminal!"

"*Was* she talking about Pa?" Jane continued to question.

"Of course she wasn't, Jane! Your Pa is a decent

and honest man and don't you ever forget that! It's bad enough that folk are allowed to spread such slander but even worse when their lies are so quickly believed! Please don't mention a word of this to your pa, Jane...at least not until I've got to the bottom of it! "

"What are you going to do ma?"

"I'm going to solve a mystery and *that* is all I'm saying for now!"

Hurriedly placing the pastry lid on to the pie and wiping down the table, it was approaching the time for Claire to make her journey back to the hospital. Informing the rest of the family that she was going shopping and meeting a friend for afternoon tea, Jane already knew that her ma was fibbing and believed her to be calling on Marigold and Edwina, who she had now lost all faith in and had already decided that she wouldn't work for them even if they went on bended knees, begging.

Infused with anger, it took Claire far less time than anticipated to arrive at the Radcliffe Infirmary, she had marched without pausing like a soldier heading into battle and as she stopped to catch her breath before entering the huge hospital building, she could hear every beat of her heart and feel the droplets of sweat trickling from every pore of her body. It had turned out to be a sweltering afternoon and she'd arrived ten minutes too early; thankfully, the kindly porter, who instantly recognised

Claire from her earlier visit, permitted her to wait in the entrance hall. The flagstone floor and lack of sunlight penetrating through the tiny windows created a welcoming coolness in the hospital. Claire rested on the ladder back chair, slowly gaining her composure and cooling off as she rehearsed in her head how she would steer her conversation around to disclose how her adopted son had so tragically died a few years ago. It was the only plan she could think of which would convince Miss Brunswick to terminate the search for her son. Riddled with guilt at the very thought of the lie she was about to declare, Claire prayed that her sentiments would not tempt fate, especially in light of how George had so recently come close to what could have been a tragedy. She would go directly to church on leaving the hospital, she fervently decided, and pray for forgiveness.

As the clock's hands approached the hour of two, a few more visitors had assembled in the waiting area which was now heavily scented with the aroma of seasonal blooms. Claire realised that in her hurry, she'd left her own modest bouquet at home. The chiming of the clock echoed loudly and was needlessly followed by the porter promptly ringing his handbell and signalling that the doors were finally accessible to the assembly of visitors. Claire was suddenly aware of how dry her mouth had become; she regretted not asking the porter for a glass of water before the other visitors had shown up; she licked her dehydrated lips as she trod the corridor towards Miss Brunswick's ward.

Met by the same nurse who had at last finished mopping the floor, she appeared to be wearing a far amiable face and greeted Claire and the other two female visitors with a pleasant smile, as she explained how she would find suitable vases for the bouquets. She reached out to touch Claire's arm in passing,

"Mrs Shepherd! You decided to come back then?"

Claire had no reply for this rhetorical question and simply nodded her head.

"Well, you'll be pleased to know, that it would appear that Miss Brunswick is as eager as you are for this meeting to go ahead and welcomes your visit! So I *will* allow you through these doors!"

Already having established a firm dislike for this conceited nurse, Claire found it difficult to show her any gratitude; the fact that Miss Brunswick was enthusiastic to meet her was a clear indication that proved her theory to be even more correct, causing Claire's heart to plummet.

"You'll find her in the last bed on the right-hand side and I'd appreciate it if you wouldn't excite or exhaust *or* upset her in any way since *I* will be on duty all night and *will not* appreciate any extra work from a patient who's likely to disturb the rest of the ward"

Claire walked slowly through the ward wondering if the nurse issued the same warnings to all the visitors or this was a tailor-made one just for her. She sensed they shared a mutual dislike for one another.

Martha had prayed and longed for this moment since the day she'd been dragged from the makeshift courtroom in Epsom; she had never anticipated being in a hospital bed swathed in bandages from head to toe though. Through the narrow eye slits in her bandages, she studied her ma as she walked gingerly towards her and was immediately overwhelmed by a sense of safety and comfort which swept through her battered body. She hadn't changed at all, a little slimmer perhaps but her face was as beautiful as she remembered. She did, however, appear very straight-faced, even angry. Martha knew that her ma presumed her to be one of the Brunswick family and concluded that to be the reason for her austere facade. Feeling her bandages become soaked by her tears, Martha knew her ma would never recognize her behind them and was glad of the chance to break the news by slow degrees, protecting her from an instant shock.

Claire sat down slowly on the hard chair alongside Martha, her anger melting slightly at the sorry state of the poor young woman, whoever she might be.

"Thank you for allowing me to visit you," she

stated dryly. "I hope you're not in too much pain."

"Nothing is actually broken, Thank God!"

Claire immediately warmed to the sound of her voice, she sounded younger than she'd expected her to be. It wasn't the voice of a woman out to harm, she mused, but at the same time, warned herself that this was a lonely female in a vulnerable state, seeking sympathy and assistance.

Martha lowered her glance, just in case her ma recognized her eyes between the bandages.

"Do you not have any family who I could get in touch with, Miss Brunswick?"

Martha's gentle nod of the head only alerted Claire that she could mean George since she'd not admitted to having family to anyone else.

"Well, I dare say it will be a while before you are healthy enough to leave here!"

Again, Martha nodded, as she held her tongue which was so desperate to announce herself. Claire couldn't bring herself to stick to her original plan of claiming that George had tragically died.

"I don't mean to sound cruel, Miss Brunswick, but my family is a happy and contented one, and if you have any intentions of disturbing that happiness in any way, you will live to regret it. George is loved and well cared for and adores his family; he knows nothing else and I know it would break his heart should you even think of taking him away from us. I'm not in the habit of issuing stark warnings, Miss Brunswick, but sometimes, it's better, for all concerned, to keep things as they are; perhaps not how they should be, but this is a young boy's happiness which lies in the balance and I'm sure if you truly love and care for him, you'll see fit to do what's best!" Martha was taken aback by her ma's words, it was not at all what she'd been expecting and hadn't realised that by calling herself Miss Brunswick, her ma would assume she was connected to little Georgie. It was now evident that her poor ma viewed her as a threat. Martha knew she would have to ease her ma's anxieties as soon as possible and not wait until she'd made a full recovery before springing the surprise of who she was onto her.

"How is dear little Georgie?" Martha enquired. Claire pursed her lips and held her head high, "I can see that you've done your research then!" she snapped, "I suppose it was the Squire or his loathsome brother who kept you informed about him! I might have guessed they'd have a part in all this. He *wasn't* your son five years ago and he's certainly *not* your son now! You have nothing to prove it either!"

Claire couldn't take much more, she was on the verge of bursting into tears and wished she'd never come to the hospital; she should have listened to her instincts and taken George far away from Oxford while this Miss Brunswick was at large. The chair scraped noisily across the stone floor as she stood up to leave, causing a few heads to turn and be momentarily distracted from their conversations.

"Please don't leave!" stressed Martha, wincing from the pain as she urgently sat upright in her bed. "I'm not who you think I am...You're right, I *do* love little Georgie, and I love you too, Ma!" Before she had even said the word '*Ma*', Martha's familiar voice had Claire gasping for air. How could it be possible, were the thoughts spinning around in her mind...her darling Martha had drowned!"

"Ma, please, come and sit down...let me explain." Claire wanted to take her precious girl in her arms; she wanted to hold her close against her own body and make up for so many lost years. This was a miracle...*Martha was alive*; she would no longer have to spend the rest of her life mourning her first daughter, and tormenting herself year after year about what her daughter might be doing and what she would have looked like or how she would have developed into a fine and beautiful young woman if she'd not been taken.

"My darling, my precious daughter," choked Claire. "Please forgive me, I can't find the right words to express how I am feeling right now!"

"Me too, Ma!" cried Martha, her heart bursting with joy.

"Can I hold you in my arms? Would it be too

painful? "

"Hold me gently Ma, I've missed your embrace so much and never thought to feel it again! I've missed you so much Ma...I love you Ma!"

"And I love you too Martha Shepherd, with all my heart and soul!"

Against all hospital etiquette, Claire abandoned her bedside chair and sided up close to Martha upon the crisp white sheets, slowly and gently wrapping her arms around her. The close bond between mother and daughter was united once more as they sobbed for joy in each other's arms.

"Mrs Shepherd! I must insist you vacate Miss Brunswick's bed *and* these premises forthwith ...you have completely disobeyed my instructions and I can see that your presence has caused poor Miss Brunswick to become distressed and quite hysterical!"

The cross faced nurse seemed to pounce on them from nowhere, disturbing the beautiful reunion.

"*Nurse!*" implored Claire. "This is *not* Miss Brunswick, but Miss Shepherd, *my daughter* who has been presumed dead to me and our family for five long and agonising years!"

"It's the truth, nurse!" added Martha, in defence of her mother under the wrath of the glaring nurse. "*This is my dear mother!*"

Without one word passing the nurses lips, she marched off, only to return a few moments later accompanied by a doctor.

In the first instance, the grave faced Doctor didn't acknowledge Claire as she still remained semi perched on the bed. He slowly began to remove the bandages on Martha's head whilst speaking,

"I trust you realise that it is an extremely serious offence to give a false name, and a dangerous one when admitted to hospital suffering from head injuries. I hope I haven't overlooked an underlying problem, Miss...What do you believe *is* your correct name?"

"I'm Martha Shepherd, Doctor, and I've never been anyone else. I simply gave myself an alias name to avoid inflicting any harm on my mother! You see, Doctor, we haven't seen each other for five years *and* my family believed me to have drowned all those years ago!"

The Doctor didn't show the slightest reaction to Martha's declaration but continued to unravel her bandages while the nurse stood cross faced her lips pursed and her brow tightly knitted together.

For the first time, the Doctor diverted his eyes to Claire, "Do you suffer from a weak disposition, Mrs Shepherd?"

"I was worried that seeing me alive might cause her heart to stop beating!" Martha blurted out. "I'm not crazy Doctor; my story is the truth!"

As her bruised and swollen face was revealed Claire felt the strongest urge to embrace her daughter once more, it really was Martha and apart from her obvious injuries, the only noticeable change in her over the five years was that she had blossomed into a beautiful young woman, mused Claire as she shuddered at the sight of the blood-encrusted row of stitches which stretched across her forehead.

"Martha!" she cried out, unable to conceal her emotions for a second longer. "My precious, beautiful girl, I never believed I'd see you in this life! It is indeed a miracle! Can I take her home Doctor, where she belongs?"

By now, the extraordinary goings-on during visiting hour and the drama of it all had attracted an audience. The rest of the visitors, together with the able patients had become enthralled by the miraculous reunion between mother and daughter. As the Doctor completed his examination of Martha's eyes and head and proceeded to give his consent for her to be discharged, the entire hospital erupted into a tidal wave of euphoria, applauding and cheering with delight.

"I hope you realise how difficult a task it will be for me to induce calm into all these over-excited patience when visiting time ends!" scolded the nurse. "It's going to be a long and tiresome night for me, I can sense it already; and as if I didn't have enough on my plate trying to keep this ward ticking over like a finely oiled clock! ...*never* in all my days have I witnessed such pandemonium on the hospital ward...anyone would think we were at a punch and Judy show in the town square!"

"Nurse!" expressed the Doctor belligerently, "Would you stop your tedious complaining for one minute and prepare Miss Shepherd for discharge, which includes arranging a carriage to transport her *and* her mother home *and* bring Mrs Shepherd a cup of extra sweet tea! That's an order! "

As Claire held on to Martha's hand, they exchanged a smile which spoke a thousand words. This special moment would remain alive in their hearts forever; they had so much to catch up on and years ahead in which to do so. Through watery eyes, Claire gazed proudly at her beloved daughter, knowing that she'd grown up to become a caring and sensible young woman and was no longer the child who dreamed her days away.

EPILOGUE

When Claire had announced to her family that they had an extra special guest staying with them, Silas had been the first to voice his objections, presuming his soft-hearted wife to be taking on more responsibilities and extra work, not to mention another mouth to feed. That extraordinary day would always remain a day talked about at every Shepherd family gathering and event for many years to come. They still laughed when remembering the shocked expression upon Silas's face, he had expected to see the late Squire's daughter or one of the Brunswick's relatives and couldn't for the life of him understand why his wife had brought her into their home when she posed such a threat to George. As he'd stood and watched the young injured woman aided by his wife, walk into the kitchen at supper time, he was speechless; believing his mind was playing tricks on his vision. It was only when Martha had spoken her first words to him in over five years that he realised he was not in the midst of a dream. "I'm home at long last Pa!" Martha had casually said before the tears and outburst of elation from the entire family were proof of the joy they all felt. Even Grace and George who had been babies and couldn't remember Martha were in tears; they'd heard so many stories about their older sister during the five years that their love for her was as strongly felt like any other family member. It had been a momentous day marred only by the absence of Frank Shepherd.

It had only taken a short period of time before Martha's homecoming felt as though she'd never been away. Surrounded by the love and support of her family once more, Martha soon recovered from her accident and already had plans to transform her family's lives.

Claire and Silas had listened in shock and disbelief, with Claire continuously breaking down into tears, as Martha explained how she'd been rescued by Bruce Brunswick and had been so well cared for by him. She had been constantly forced to calm her parents every time they became angry at what had taken place, reminding them of how fortunate she was to have been saved from transportation. It didn't take long for Claire and Silas to sense the extraordinary bond which had developed between their daughter and the unpopular and eccentric Bruce Brunswick. He had claimed a large portion of Martha's heart and as much as they were grateful to him for taking care of Martha, they found it impossible to trust his motives and between themselves, quite certain that if it hadn't been for his passing away, Martha would never have returned to them. Sensing how suspicious and upset her parents became whenever she spoke of Bruce,

Martha did not disclose the fact that he was George's father but decided it would be one of the secrets of the gatehouse she would take with her to her grave.

During the first year after Martha's homecoming, she spent every moment with her family, making up for lost time and getting to know Grace and George. Every cuddle and kiss she shared with George was done with Bruce in mind and would often bring tears to Martha's eyes. She couldn't abide how her family spoke so cruelly about him and knew in her heart that they would never understand her odd but undeniable love for him.

Martha had been persuaded by her ma to walk out with the handsome Simon Ward. He and Mr Roach had turned up on the doorstep after hearing the news about the Shepherd family's long lost daughter. They arrived with enormous bouquets in their arms and an apology. Silas had already concocted a cover story for Martha, which they had all agreed upon, hoping it would not arouse anymore suspicions from anyone; as much as they had believed that their daughter was no longer alive, Martha had been on a trip to London with neighbours when she'd fallen into the river, having taken a blow to her head she'd later been found downstream by a member of a wealthy London family; she had no recollection of who she was but the family had nursed her back to health and having developed a fondness for her, Martha became the paid companion to the lonely Mistress of the Brunswick family. For five years Martha had no idea of her roots and it was only when the mistress passed away leaving Martha in a traumatic state of mind that part of her memory began to slowly return and she'd embarked on her search for her real family. Silas was sure that nobody would delve deeper into this story and that the truth of her conviction and sentence for transportation would never surface.

Martha, however, felt she'd never feel free from worry until she'd convinced her family to move away and start a new life.

"It wouldn't be running away, Pa!" she had stressed one day as they sat together in the ironmongers. "It will be a completely new way of life...you won't be renting the business and the roof over our heads, but will own it. I have enough money Pa and I want it to go to good use, not sit in the bank while we all struggle. Bruce Brunswick loved me as though I was his own daughter Pa, and he worried about my future when he would not be around anymore. I know you might find that hard to believe, as did I during my first months in the gatehouse, but it *is* true, you must try and believe that, Pa!"

"Perhaps he did a better job than me then," muttered Silas, the hurt and jealousy clearly visible.

"Oh Pa! You are the *best* pa in the world!

Nobody could ever fill your boots. A day never passed by when I didn't think of you and Ma and the family and longed with all my heart to be with you all. I don't understand why you still feel the need to hold a grudge against Mr Brunswick ...he rescued me from that dreadful convict hulk, where I was the only female amongst hundreds of convicted male criminals! In my opinion, he not only saved my life but my virtue too!"

Deep in thought, Silas circled the modest shop floor, "Do you know Martha, sometimes I do believe that you have gained more wisdom than any of us during your time away. I'm so proud of you my darling, you have grown into a fine and compassionate young woman; it's just a little difficult for your ma and me to accept that a huge portion of the lovely person you've grown into is down to someone who we've despised for most of our lives! Can you understand that? "

"All I'm asking is that we put the past where it belongs and move on. I know you and Ma would much prefer a life in the country, away from the noisy, dirty city. We could buy a small farm, just outside of Oxford, so it wouldn't be such a wrench for Amy and Jane...and one day perhaps Frank will return to us and hopefully be a better person, maybe even with his own family in tow. There would be enough space for him to build a cottage on our land too!"

Silas did like the sound of Martha's idea; he'd never taken to city life and knew how much Claire pined after the old ways. The countryside was a far safer place to grow up a family in and Grace and George were still young. The thought of Frank undergoing a character change, however, didn't infuse him with an ounce of optimism; he'd hurt him too much for that.
"It's a grand and generous idea Martha!" he eventually expressed. "I suddenly have a good feeling about our future! Now, which one of us is going to tell your ma?"
"Why don't we find a place first Pa, then we could take the family on a picnic one Sunday afternoon to show them...it would be such a surprise...I can just picture Ma's face now!"

It took another six months before Martha and Silas found the perfect new home but it *was* perfect and after they'd made many clandestine excursions which had caused Claire to become quite suspicious the huge surprise was at last revealed to her.
Sweet pea Farm was only four miles outside of Oxford but seemed like a hundred miles away in its complete contrast. A modest six acres of land, one of which was a mature fruit orchard, surrounded the modern farmhouse. It was idyllic and every member of the Shepherd family immediately fell in love with it and was overjoyed about the prospect of starting a new

life.

In 1849 the family celebrated their first of many harvests to come and in that same year, they also celebrated the wedding between Martha and Simon Ward. From his first-ever meeting with Martha, Simon had set his heart on her and knew that she was the only girl for him, likewise, Martha, who had initially admired his handsome appearance, discovered, during their months of walking out together, that he was a sweet and kind natured man; she fell in love with him in an instant and when Simon proposed to her, she felt like the happiest woman in the world. The first extra cottage was constructed upon the farmland and under Silas's guidance, Simon began to learn the many skills of farming.

During the early spring of 1850, Silas received a letter from Frank. It was the first time he'd been in touch since the dreadful episode with young George at the river and the letter which had taken a while to eventually be delivered was back dated from New Year's Day. Frank was in London's notorious Newgate Prison, sentenced for two years for petty larceny. Silas kept the dismal news to himself, his family had suffered enough and he wasn't going to subject his wife to anymore heart ache. He secretly wrote back to Frank, advising him to use the time of his sentence to plan a decent future, to change his ways and to pray for forgiveness for the many sinful acts he'd committed. Silas made it quite clear that he wouldn't be welcomed into the family until there was genuine evidence that he had amended his ways and was a reformed character to be trusted once more.

The second harvest at Sweet Pea Farm became a double celebration; the fine weather of that year had produced a bumper harvest and Martha gave birth to her first child, a beautiful daughter, who she named Joy. Claire and Silas were grandparents and they cried tears of sheer delight, never quite overcoming the trauma they'd suffered during the shadowy years when they believed their own firstborn daughter had been lost to them forever.

"I'm sure I don't need to tell you how precious daughters are, Martha," whispered Claire, as she cradled the tiny newborn. "Never let her out of your sight, my darling!"

"Don't worry, Ma," assured Martha as she lay recovering from her confinement "she will be the most guarded daughter in the county! I couldn't bear for anything to happen to her...love is a kind of pleasant torture, don't you think, Ma?"

"I never really thought of love in that way before, but there could be a lot of truth in your sentiments, my darling!" agreed Claire.

Jane had also been mesmerized by young love and had fallen for a local blacksmith; A strong, fine-looking man, who was totally devoted to Jane and although she had given up on her dream of becoming a professional seamstress since the family had left Oxford, Amos Barnet had encouraged and persuaded Jane to keep hold of her vision and when she began her six months initial trial period at '*The Spires Exclusive Ladies Fashion*' shop, which was far superior to Marigold and Edwina's store, Amos took the trouble in taking and bringing her home again every day. Soon establishing herself as an indispensable seamstress, Jane was offered a permanent position and went on to become one of Oxford's finest needlewomen, creating gowns for the social elite. She also designed and created a sensational wedding gown for her own wedding which took place two years later. Baby Joy had developed into a mischievous toddler and Martha announced that she was with child again.7

With so many joyful occasions taking place, Silas had managed to sustain a happy facade covering his heartbreak. In the morning of Jane's wedding, he'd received devastating news; Frank had been taken ill with cholera and subsequently lost his brave fight. He had died along with Silas's dream to one day witness his firstborn become a changed and loyal son; he'd imagined that one day Frank might even come to live on the land with his own wife and children, working alongside the rest of them. It was a dream never to come true but this sad news would be for his heart only to bear, as far as everyone else was concerned, Frank was out there somewhere in the world and quite possibly doing well for himself.

Although Martha had often wondered about Lucy Wright and how she was getting along with Mr and Mrs Bird and Molly Wright there had never been any correspondence between them; Martha had not found the time especially after her accident, and when she marvelled at the strong and loving bond between George and the rest of the family especially her ma, she didn't want to risk the truth surfacing. She was convinced that Bruce would approve of her decision and would be completely satisfied that his son was truly loved and cared for and was not missing out on anything in his childhood. It was also a huge comfort to Martha that a part of Bruce was still with her and she could hug and kiss him clandestinely on behalf of his father. Nobody would ever understand the relationship she'd shared with Bruce; she owed so much to him and he would remain in a safely tucked away part of her heart for the rest of her life. Perhaps one day in the future when all the children had matured into adults, there would be a reunion, perhaps one day all the truth and the secrets of the gatehouse would be exposed, but for the time being life was sailing along on a gentle breeze quite satisfyingly and there was no reason to invite a storm.

Printed in Great Britain
by Amazon

47832803R00271